Charmed Log Cabin

Enchanted Life Series

Robert S. Baker

Charmed Log Cabin: Encanted Life Series

Robert S Baker

Paperback Edition First Published in the United Kingdon in 2016 by aSys Publishing

eBook Edition First Published in the United Kingdon in 2016 by aSys Publishing

Copyright © Robert S Baker

Robert S Baker has asserted his rights under 'the Copyright Designs and Patents Act 1988' to be identified as the author of this work.

All rights reserved.

No part of this book may be reproduced or transmitted in any form or by any means, electronic, mechanical, photocopying, recording, or otherwise, without prior written permission of the Author.

Disclaimer

This is a work of fiction. Names, characters, businesses, places, events and incidents are either the products of the author's imagination or used in a fictitious manner. Any resemblance to actual persons, living or dead, or actual events is purely coincidental.

ISBN: 978-1530137961

aSys Publishing
http://www.asys-publishing.co.uk

Contents

Charmed Log Cabin 1

Charmed Log Cabin and White Witches 77

Charmed Log Cabin and the Realm 173

CHARMED LOG CABIN

ROBERT BAKER

Charmed Log Cabin

It's funny how life kicks you in the butt when you least expect it. I thought I had a good marriage. Obviously, Jenny didn't after announcing that she was moving in with her boss, a bank manager. I should have been surprised and in the back of my mind I should have realised something wasn't right. Jenny had elevated from a PA to financial adviser and of late there have been many overnight business trips in London. Jenny is very petite and likes the best in clothes cars and lifestyle. She would spend a fortune on cosmetics she really didn't require. I thought at the outset I've married above my class. We have two children, Katie, 18 and Johnny 16. Katie looked exactly like her mother with her blonde cascading hair and great bone structure. Johnny on the other hand, was much more like me a bit of a slob, didn't mind getting his hands dirty and enjoyed country pursuits. I worked on a farm just outside London owned by my grandfather, 500-acre spread growing mainly cereals 100 acres of the farm is woodland which had mainly conifers standing although in the centre is a very old oak tree. No one knew the exact age of the tree. But it was estimated to be well over 500 years old. Johnny and I had spent many hours walking through the woodland shooting rabbits, stalking wildlife and generally having a good time. The trouble we would get into for preparing rabbits on the kitchen table ready for the pot. Jenny thought we were barbaric and preferred her Sunday joint to come from the butcher or better still in a bloody packet from Tesco's. Katie was similar to her mother in attitude all food products should come in a plastic bag ready to cook. We lived approximately 10 miles from the M25 in a small village in quite a large detached house with six bedrooms. The house was approximately a hundred years old and in places showed its age.

Of course it was me who had to rectify any defects when they occurred. At least I am good at something. The property extended to about half an acre in total with lawns and fruit trees. Jenny's parents resided in South Africa, trading in gold in the financial sector. Her grandmother passed away just after we were married and left the property to Jenny, along with a few thousand pounds, which was a stroke of luck for us. Although her parents wanted to shoot me at dawn and told Jenny she was absolutely stupid for getting involved with me. Perhaps I should have seen the writing on the wall, at the time, nothing mattered. I was madly in love with a beautiful girl. Jenny's announcement she was leaving, she rose from her chair, resting her palms on the table turned to Johnny saying. "You're coming with me." Katie, who was still in shock sat there very silent with her head slightly bowed. Jenny continued firmly. "Katie, you'll be leaving in a couple of days for University. I'll give you my contact number until my solicitor sorts the situation out." I'd just gone cold and numb. Johnny stood up saying. "Like hell I'm not coming with you mother." He stormed off out of the room. Jenny followed him. Katie on the other hand just looked across the table at me and proclaimed. "You know she's been having an affair for a long time dad?" Had I really known? Or just put to the back of my mind, refusing to face something wasn't right. Katie continued, "what are you going to do? You will have to find yourself a solicitor otherwise she's going to take you to the cleaners. She's a bitch, how could she do this to you?" Katie confessed "I knew she was having an affair, but I hoped it would end and everything would return to normal." Katie then stood up and left the room crying.

I heard a commotion. Arguing continuing upstairs I felt betrayed my whole world was crashing around my feet. Having an affair, would never have crossed my mind. I was happy in my own surroundings. Obviously she wasn't and from what Katie had said it's been like this for some time. Someone had taken my heart, beating it with a sledgehammer. Should I find the man and shoot him? What should I do? I didn't see much point while Jenny was in that frame of mind trying to discuss matters further. Besides, I didn't want her back. She had betrayed my trust and the children. God how they must be feeling. I sat for a while listening to the muffled arguing upstairs, then rose to my feet, heading for the door. Grabbed my keys and drove off in my old tatty Land Rover parked by her new Porsche. I hope she'd be gone by the time I got back. I noticed my shotgun laying across the back seat. Should I go and blow my brains out? Considering suicide, that would make her life so much easier if I'd disappeared. I wandered across into the woodland and lent my back against the old oak tree, clutching my shot gun in one hand and wiping my tears with the other. What had I done to deserve her betrayal? It was late August and the nights were drawing in. I stayed there for almost 3 hours with a confused mind that wouldn't function properly, trying to think clearly and make a decision. I slid my back up the tree to stand on my feet, walking slowly through the woodland back to my Land Rover which had somehow acquired a puncture. I looked up into the clouds for some sort of reason. Perhaps I'm being punished? I will really have to get my act together, although I was in no mood for confrontation. I changed the wheel on my Land Rover and proceeded back across the fields towards home. On the way I bumped into my grandfather, who was walking down the muddy lane shrouded in trees. I stop and before I could open my mouth, grandfather with his tired eyes. "I know son. Johnny's phoned me. Be strong, if you need any money for legal expenses, just let me know." I smiled and said "Thanks Gramps." He turned and took the footpath across the field. He didn't look well. He hobbled along with his walking stick for support after an accident on the farm many years ago, injuring his hips. I parked on the drive way. Jenny's gold coloured Porsche had gone. Katie and Johnny ran out from the front door and gave me a reassuring hug as I stepped out of the Land Rover. "I'm so sorry dad." Katie voiced. Continuing to say pulling me by the arm. "Come and have something to eat." Johnny in the meantime, removed my shot gun from the Land Rover putting it back in its case and returned to the house. I sat at the kitchen table, resting my elbows on the edge and holding my head in my hands. "I'm not really hungry. Katie" I voiced. "You must eat something dad." She insisted. This was a whole new side to Katie I'd never seen. She was actually caring. Or perhaps she just felt sorry for me. She'd be gone in the next couple of days. She placed a plate of potatoes and meat in front of me. She'd obviously cooked herself because the potatoes weren't quite cooked and the meat had been cremated, full marks for trying. Johnny returned after locking the gun away in the cabinet. He sat down opposite saying. "I'm not going to live with her dad and her new man." I smiled and reached across the table and squeezed his hand. "Thanks son I don't think there's anything to stay for. "I should imagine she will sell the house. We'll have nowhere to live." "You're entitled to half of everything dad." Katie spun round remarking, spilling my cup of tea she had just made. "I won't return to university; somebody must look after you." "We can manage." Johnny shouted, "you're just like mother.". I continued on I insisted don't start arguing and throwing insults at each other. It won't improve the situation. "She is just like her dad." Johnny claimed. "I'm not!" Katie shouted back running off upstairs. The whole family was at each other's throat. Not just me and Jenny. Johnny suggested. "We can manage we don't need anybody." "Not as simple as you think son, your mother has influential friends to help her fight for what she wants." "I'll run away!" Johnny shouted. I stood up annoyed. "Will you please stop it? I have enough on my mind without you starting." Katie came running down the stairs and stood with her arms folded. "You're being stupid Johnny."

Johnny said "I'm not leaving." He reinforced by banging his fist on the table. "Let's get one or two things straight." I said firmly looking at them both. "Katie, you're going to university you need a good education. I don't want you to end up like me. Johnny your 16 I think the courts would let you decide who you'd want to live with, providing I could provide you with a home and fund your schooling." Johnny's smile broadened. Katie rubbed my shoulders. "That's it dad fight!" She said. Was this really Katie saying those words an absolute new side to her I'd never seen. Perhaps she wasn't like her mother as I first thought. Once the children had gone to bed, I crouched in front of the open fire listening to the wood crackle and spit staring into the flickering flames for a solution. I phoned the bank to check my bank account going through the usual rigmarole of numbers pressing keys to select the right combination. I finally got through to the joint savings account. The £30,000 that was originally there had now shrunk to £5000. She had obviously planned everything far in advance leaving me nothing to fight with. My current account had just a thousand pounds remaining. I'd used £1000 the previous week on repairs to the house. Oh, I could kick myself I should have been more observant and realise what was going on. Katie had cottoned on to her mother long ago. There was always grandfather he would come to the rescue I'm sure. I slumped back in my armchair by the fire, regretting I had not tried harder at school, but suffering from dyslexia. Learning didn't come easy and I barely scraped through secondary modern. If it wasn't for the job on grandfather's farm, I'd probably be collecting unemployment benefit. The next morning, I awoke to Katie making the breakfast scrambled eggs on toast. The toast was that hard you could kill someone at 200 yards the scrambled egg was still runny. Johnny came stumbling down the stairs as he usually did running his fingers through his black hair which really needed cutting. The phone rang It was grandfather. He told me not to come in today hoping I would start and sort my problems out. I thanked him very much and return to my breakfast. "Must I go to school today?" Johnny enquired. "I'm afraid so son stopping at home with me will not make a blind bit of difference to the situation." He grunted, finished his breakfast and prepared himself to catch the school bus. I didn't tell the kids the state of my finance. I thought I'll keep it to myself for the time being. Katie's mobile phone rang. She moved to the other side of the room and answered. I could tell from the conversation it was her mother, I heard Katie say. "I don't want it, leave me alone!" and she switched off her mobile, placing her hands on her hips, turned to face me. "That was mother. She just bought me a brand-new mini she thinks she can buy me, She's in for a shock." I responded quickly. "You'll need transport for University you should have accepted the car." "Not on your life dad. She's not buying me like she does everyone else." Half an hour later there was a knock at the door. I opened to see a very smart man holding a set of keys. He enquired "Is Miss Katie Jones available please. I have her new car here." Katie came storming to the door. She grabbed the keys from the chap's hand and through them across the drive; "I don't bloody want it, take it away." I felt sorry for the salesman; he stumbled back from the steps jumped into the awaiting car and disappeared down the drive. He had thrust some paperwork in to my hand stating the car was insured for Katie to drive only, obviously top of the range mini Cooper. Her mother had really lashed out or her boyfriend obviously trying to win Katie over. I think they failed miserably. "What am I going to do dad?" she screamed. To be quite honest by this time I was laughing. I'd never seen Katie so angry for being given a brand-new car. "Use it Katie; take her for everything you can. I know that sounds horrible thing to say, you might as well love." Katie snatched the keys from the gravel stormed past me muttering. A little while later, she had calmed down and Katie decided to take her new car for a spin. Perhaps I should phone a solicitor I usually left that decision to Jenny. She was the brains at sorting out problems not me. I drifted off to sleep in the armchair.

I was startled by the sound of the front door opening and in walked Jenny as casual as you like as if there was nothing wrong in the world. "I need to talk to you" She said abruptly. I sat up in the armchair. "I'm listening I said frostily." "I don't know where to start, she said quietly", flicking her hair over her shoulder sitting down in the opposite armchair. "Well I suppose I better come straight out with it" she remarked. "You're not Katie's father." "What!" I shouted in disbelief. "You're not I'm with her real father now. In fact, I met him before you; we've been with each other ever since you and I were married." "Why didn't you bloody marry him then?" I replied. "It's complicated he was already married and if he had a divorce it would have ruined his prospects. He had just made bank manager. Now he's moving on to bigger things. His wife was diagnosed with cancer some months back and has since died. He didn't love her at all." She proclaimed standing up. I said "You're taking the piss." "No I'm not." "Why are you bothering to tell me now just trying to twist the knife a little more?" I could feel the outrage running through my body. "I've been conned all the way along. What about Johnny?" I shouted. "He's yours definitely can't you tell? Katie has blond hair like me Johnny has black hair just like yours. He even looks like you more's the pity. I should have had him aborted." I sprung to my feet in a flash and slapped her across the face saying "You cold bitch." She staggered backwards held her face in shock. I continued, "What is your point bringing this into the open now?" Jenny continued "I had lunch with Katie and explained everything to her. She stormed off in a rage telling me to fuck off, she'll come round when she short of money. I thought you should know the truth." "So you were never in love with me? The whole marriage was nothing but a charade?" "I really don't know. At times I thought I loved you." I flopped back down into the chair, exhaling as my life deflated in front of me. She was a hard bitch. Katie came bursting in through the front door ran straight over to the gun cabinet, which was thankfully locked. She shook the doors in frustration trying to break in. "I'll shoot you, you cow you have ruined my life." Jenny didn't move just looked on. I ran over to Katie holding her by the shoulders and turning her gently into my chest. "It's alright love you will always be my daughter." She sobbed unreservedly. "Let me kill her dad. She's evil!" Katie sobbed, "She's evil!" Jenny turned and headed for the door quietly closing behind her. I think she'd finally got the message the way Katie felt about the situation. Thank goodness Johnny had locked the gun cabinet. I dread to think the outcome if Katie could have reached one of the guns in her state of mind. I guided her to my armchair sitting her down. I sat opposite saying nothing, giving her chance to calm down before I approach the delicate subject which was like a knife cutting into our hearts. I threw some more logs on the fire. Katie continued to sob. Johnny had returned from school walking into the room. He looked at Katie then glanced to me with a bewildered expression. He perched on the arm of my chair in a low voice. "What's going on dad?" he whispered. Katie looked up, came over, and hugged him? "What's up?" He asked, placing his arms around her waist, which is something he'd never done in the past and gave her a hug. It was obvious to Johnny. Something was really wrong. I stood up and joined in the group hug. Don't worry kids, nothing has changed I said. Katie pulled back. "It will never be the same. Now we know the truth." Johnny looked very confused. "What's happened?" I said calmly "Let's all sit down." "Dad what's wrong?" Johnny expressed earnestly. I explained to Johnny what we'd been told. Katie dried her tears. Johnny said "Well, you're still my half-sister" he voiced brightly. Katie smiled and hugged him once again. "Hey Sissy," he laughed, "less of that." She smiled and sat back down, looking a little relieved. I tried to put a brave face on everything. Yet my insides were feeling like I'm in a cement mixer and I couldn't switch it off. Katie and Johnny went off into another room to talk. I was trying to recover from an 18 year lie, my relationship with Jenny had been just that from start to finish, which left a feeling of emptiness. The upside was the children and their continued support. The next morning, everyone was up early. Katie was leaving for University,

Although I don't think she really wanted to go under the circumstances. We loaded her cases into the car. Embraced said goodbye and she drove off. Johnny was running late for school as usual and ran off down the drive with his bag in one hand and a piece of toast in the other. I went back inside to finish my cup of tea when there was a very loud knock at the door.

Dave brought bad news from grandfather's farm, he was flustered standing at the door. He said, trying to catch his breath. "It's your grandfather, it your grandfather. He's had an accident." "Is he alright," I enquired quickly. "It looks bad Rob. He was getting out of the tractor slipped and banged his head on the wall. He's on the way to hospital." We both jumped in my old Land Rover and tore off down the drive. The nearest hospital was 20 miles away. When we approached his two son's Don and Fred were standing in the doorway, smoking a cigarette. By the expression on their faces this was not going to be good news, before I could ask. "He didn't make it Rob. He didn't make it." Fred glanced up from his handkerchief. "You have your own problems Rob, there's nothing you can do here, go home and we'll be in touch." On that comment, I returned home after dropping Dave off back at the farm and returned to an empty home. Where my life had been just a lie. When Johnny come home from school, I broke the news to him. My grandfather and Johnny had been quite close at times, having spent many hours going round the farm. Johnny said nothing and just went upstairs to his room. I decided to leave him alone with his thoughts until he wanted to discuss further. I phoned Katie and explained the situation to her. She was not overly concerned, her and grandfather had never been close. I wasn't going to phone Jenny; she was no longer part of the family. All she was ever interested in was money and the last thing I wanted was to give her any opportunity to rock the boat further. An hour later Johnny returned to the living room, you could tell by his eyes he had shed a few tears. "When is the funeral dad?" He continued "I want to come he was very good to me." "Of course Johnny." I expressed placing reassuring hand on his shoulder. "It won't be for a few days; arrangements have to be made." Johnny ran back upstairs, I returned to the fireside, leaning on the mantelpiece staring into the flames of hopelessness. It suddenly occurred to me I may be out of a job? That would really put a cat among the pigeons. How could I survive without an income who will take over the farm? I don't think Don or Fred have any interest? How many more problems were going to land on my door step? The last few days have been a nightmare. Surely it can't get any worse? I looked out of the window into the twilight sky searching for answers. I'd done absolutely nothing to protect my own interests or that of the children. I've just allowed myself to be dragged along with the flow of events. Sooner or later I would have to make a stand. My mind is so full of grief with the onslaught of events. I didn't know where to start or gain control of the situation. I saw a set of headlights flash across the sitting room window. I went across, looked out a black range Rover had pulled up. Who was that? I wondered. I went to the front door and opened much to my surprise it was Sam from Goldings stables situated at the other end of the village. "Hi Rob," she said, "is there anything I can do to help you I know it's none of my business, but it's all round the village." I invited her in. She sat in the armchair still in her riding gear she'd obviously just come straight from the stables. "Can I get you anything to drink Sam?" "No, I'm fine thanks Rob." Sam was a tall girl she had very long red hair and almost a porcelain complexion a figure most women would die for. I'd never noticed her before how attractive she is. Johnny came into the room. Sam rose to her feet, placing her arms around him. "Keep your chin up" Sam remarked softly. Johnny replied with a glint of a smile. "I'm okay as long as I stay with dad I'll be fine." Sam returned to her armchair. Johnny remarked, "Dad, we will have to do some shopping we are out of milk." Okay I replied with a hint of frustration in my voice.

"Sam . . . typical man!" She grabbed my hand, "come with me." "Where are we going," I enquired? "You will see," taking me to the range Rover opening the tailgate, inside were boxes of groceries. "I didn't know quite what you'd need. So I bought everything I could think of." "Sam you shouldn't" I remarked flabbergasted. Sam shouted "Johnny, give us a hand." Johnny ran out to join us and started removing the groceries. "You must let me pay you Sam. It's so kind of you to even think about us." "No, you won't pay me Rob. It's a present. Now shut up and carry the boxes." After we'd taken everything to the kitchen and restocked the shelves. Johnny went upstairs to carry on with his homework after making coffee for all. Sam and I went to the living room and sat by the fire. "Sam you shouldn't have it's not your problem." "To be quite honest Rob a lot of us feel guilty in the village for not enlightening you to what was going on with Jenny and her bank manager boyfriend in London. Everyone hoped it was just as stupid fling, obviously not. I should have probably realised long ago, just didn't want to face the facts." Sam stared into her empty coffee cup. "You know what one of my father's businesses is?" she enquired calmly. "No, not really. I know you own stables." "That's not all." She interrupted. "My father owns a large firm of solicitors in London. That's what keeps the stables going she chuckled. Listen she exhaled. Jenny has been in touch with father's firm to represent her against you." "Oh great, that's all I need you're just fattening the calf before the slaughter." "No!" Sam replied in a firm voice. "That's not the case, father turned Jenny away." I breathed a sigh of relief a reprieve for the moment. She placed her hand on my knee. "My father said to tell you, she said, looking me straight in the eyes. He will represent you without you incurring any costs." I collapsed back into my armchair in shock. "You are joking Sam." "No I'm serious. Why would he do that for me, he doesn't even know me?" "Everybody in the village has great respect for you. You've helped numerous people out over the years with repairs to their house. In the high winds a few years back you worked day and night round the village, making trees safe on resident properties to prevent damage. It's about time we showed you how much you are appreciated by everyone. We know your grandfather has just passed away. Another man who was greatly respected in the village like you would never turn away someone who needed help. If the farm is sold there is employment waiting for you at the stables. We could do with a good handyman." Sam rose to her feet, saying. "I must go, one last thing Rob. You need a bath you smell like a polecat and a shave wouldn't go amiss, smarten up. Don't let Jenny beat you into the ground. Excuse me for saying" she voiced smiling, heading towards the door. I followed closely behind open the door for her. She turned, kissed me on the cheek. Bye for now, she expressed. I watched Sam get into the range Rover and drive off. Three hours ago my life was doom and gloom I could see no light at the end of the tunnel, now I could feel a smile coming to my face. Unbeknown to me, Johnny had been standing in the stairway listening. He came into the room with a smile. "Dad, that's great he proclaimed." "Don't get too excited son, there's still a long way to go before the battle is won." I headed for the bathroom for a shave and shower which made me feel more relaxed. I retired early to bed and for the first time I actually slept. The following morning, I awoke to the phone ringing beside the bed, I answered, grandfather's funeral would be held on Wednesday at St Michael's Church, situated in the middle of the village. Fred informed me. He then went on to say. "The farm will be sold at auction. "I'm sorry Rob just doesn't make sense for Don or me to continue in the farming industry." "I sighed, sorry you feel that way Fred. I do understand we will see you at the funeral." I searched for a black suit which was not a thing I usually possessed. My main dress code was a raincoat jeans and shirt. Going to any type of function was a very rare occasion, at no time with Jenny. I can't remember ever going to a restaurant, usually the local pub for a meal, the dress code there was my boots and work clothes. Finally, I found a very dark blue suit, how long it had been there I don't know? The suit just about fitted which is the story of my life. I felt like a trussed up chicken, not my sort of gear at all. Johnny wore his school uniform with a black tie. The first time I'd seen him look really smart for a long time. I suppose the situation will change when he goes to university.

We scrambled to make ourselves presentable, making our way to the church. The church was packed. The whole village was attending I situated myself right at the back. It reminded me of school where I would try and hide myself from view. Sam attended along with her father Mr Goldings. They situated their selves on opposite side of the church. Sam looked up and gazed around until her eyes caught my location. She then whispered something to her father, who looked across and smiled. I nodded back in acknowledgement and peered down into my hymnbook trying to work out the words. A lot of them were a jumbled mess because of my dyslexia. I pretended to sing trying to fit in as best I could. This was a feeling I knew very well. I'd suffered all my life in education and work. When the service was finished and they laid grandfather to rest and a gathering was held in the village hall, I decided to go home. I really wasn't in a sociable frame of mind. We had not long arrived home and made ourselves a sandwich before there was a knock at the door. Johnny ran upstairs to continue playing on his PlayStation while I answered the door. There standing in the doorway, was the postman with a registered letter for me. My heart sank as I signed for it. I thanked the postman and closed the door running upstairs to my computer, open the letter and scanned. Transferring the information to the computer. Whereupon the computer could read the letter to me. I listened carefully. Jenny was demanding custody of Johnny and the sale of the house. Unbeknown to me the house was actually owned by her father. I originally thought it had been left to Jenny in her grandmothers will. That's another bloody lie she's told me. I'd been given three months to vacate the premises or be evicted. I heard someone knocking at the front door. I peered out of the bedroom window and could see Sam's range Rover. I grabbed the letter from the scanner proceeded downstairs. Johnny had already beaten me to the door receiving a hug from Sam as she entered. "I didn't see you at the village hall Rob, why didn't you come?" she questioned. "Johnny and I didn't feel like socialising" I replied. "Johnny could you leave Sam and I for a moment, we need to talk." Sam looked concerned. Johnny ran upstairs. "What's happened Rob?" Sam expressed with concern. I showed her the letter she read it quickly sitting down on the settee. "Oh!" she exclaimed with a sigh, "so you can't fight for the house because it doesn't belong to Jenny. We all presumed it belonged to you and Jenny. Can I take the letter to father?" "Yes!" I agreed with some eagerness in my voice "I may need to take you up on your offer of a job. Fred told me they're selling the farm." Oh dear you poor thing," she said embracing me. "I'm going to catch father before he leaves for London and show him the letter. He'll be in touch I'm sure." On that note, she left quickly. I stood in the doorway and waved watching her range Rover, leave the end of the drive. Johnny came running downstairs. "What was all that about dad?" "Only legal stuff I have received a letter from your mother's solicitors." Johnny expressed. "Come on, come on dad, you can tell me." "Not at the moment son. Sam's taken the letter for Mr Goldings to read and assess the situation. There's No point in upsetting you or anybody at the moment until we know our legal position." 3 days later I received a phone call from Fred. "They're reading my father's will. The solicitor will be here at 10.30 AM tomorrow morning. Your presence is requested." "Why?" "Obviously my father has left you something." "Oh, okay, I'll see you tomorrow. Thanks Fred." That was an absolute surprise. Perhaps grandfather has left me the old tractor I liked? We used to take it on the trailer to the vintage shows those were the good old days before my life was turned upside down. The next morning, I drove to the farm. The farm I'd spent so many years working with my grandfather.

The reading of grandfather's will at the farm: I was let in by Fred, Don sat at the kitchen table, holding his balding head, staring into a glass of whiskey. The solicitor turned up shortly after. He sat at the kitchen table, opened his briefcase and pulled out grandfather's will. The farm was to be sold at auction, excluding the hundred-acre woodland the old forestry tractor, saw bench, chainsaws, which were to be left to Robert Jones, along with a sum of £10,000. Fred and Don jumped to their feet in a rage. "He's not entitled to that give him the bloody old tractor." "That's enough!" they protested. "Gentlemen, please!" the solicitor insisted, "your father was in sound mind and judgement when he altered the will a month ago. You have both been well provided for in the will, not only the sale of the farm alone will net a considerable sum. I think you would find it difficult to find any court to consider a dispute relating to the will." The solicitor looked across to me and said. "Deeds of ownership and all documentation relating to your grandfather's request will be sent to you shortly." I shook the solicitors hand, turned to Fred and Don. They just turn their backs on me and said. "Get out!" Without further delay I left not wishing to inflame the situation any more. I'd never smiled so much in all my life. One minute I had nothing with my whole world falling around me and now I had everything and more than I had ever wished for. A chance to start a new life. I couldn't understand why Fred and Don were so upset they already owned other businesses, but I suppose it's the old greed factor setting in. That is their problem not mine I didn't want to fall out with anybody. I've known Fred and Don all my life and was quite surprised by their attitude. After all, we were related. I couldn't wait to tell Johnny the news, when he returned from school. He was absolutely ecstatic hearing the news. Although it was nearly dusk we drove down to the wood land just to survey what we now owned, it was 8 o'clock in the evening before we returned to the house, as we drove up the drive Sam was sat in her range Rover waiting. She jumped out to greet us. We all went inside I stoke the fire and sat down. Johnny just could not contain his excitement. "Dad owns the wood land grandfather left it to him." Sam smiled, "That's great news for you both at least you could sell the land and gain some capital." "Not on your life" I expressed. She looked across at me confused. "Why, it's no use, it only has trees and most of the land is boggy." "We are going to live there. I'm going to build myself a log cabin." "That's not going to be straightforward. Sam remarked, you will need planning permission and you won't get that on greenbelt land. The most value on there is the timber, cut the trees down and sell" Sam suggested. She then changed the subject. "My father's been in touch he's read the letter you gave me, I'm afraid it's not very good news. He's done some investigating and apparently. Jenny's parents have always owned this property they purchased it for her grandmother to live in. If you don't find suitable accommodation prove to the courts that you can look after Johnny. You will lose that battle too," Sam expressed with concern. Johnny said with some urgency. "My dad can build a cabin he can do anything he puts his mind to." "I wish I had your confidence Johnny" Sam remarked. "He hasn't much time." "I have three months before we are evicted if I can't complete in that time, I could always buy a static home as a temporary solution." "I can't believe my ears. Sam exhaled, shaking her head." "Oh well" She continued giving me a hug. "By the way, we have a job waiting for you at the stables as soon as you feel ready." "Thanks Sam" I expressed. "I do appreciate everything you have done for us." Sam left. Johnny turned to me. "Dad can you really build a cabin in three months?" "I don't know son, but I'm going to try." The next morning, I made breakfast. Johnny prepared himself for school. "Johnny" I said "I'm going to start work in the woodland today in preparation to build a cabin." "Can't I have time off school dad and help?" he expressed with enthusiasm. "No your education is very important to me." We finished our breakfast and went our separate ways. I jumped in the old Land Rover and drove to the farm, expecting a frosty reception. Don was still there and saw me pull up outside the shed where the chainsaws were kept. "He came across Rob I'm sorry, we shouldn't have said the things we did." He patted me on the shoulder, saying, "take what you need." He then walked off across the yard a very broken man deep in sorrow for his loss.

    I loaded the chainsaw and tools I could carry. I looked in the old tractor shed and lifted the tarp of the old standard Fordson tractor she was made in

1945 and ran on petrol and TVO. She had a logging winch fitted which would help me move the trees. She had a pulley fitted to drive the saw bench. I just hope the old girl could stand up to the workload. She spluttered into life with a sense of urgency. Once she'd warmed for a few minutes I turned the fuel tap over onto TVO, which is tractor vaporising oil a cheaper fuel to run her on. I drove out of the shed, coupling it to the saw bench and drove the 2 miles to the woodland. I struggled for some time to find a way through the thick covering of trees until I reached the oak tree in the centre of the wood. This is where I'm going to build my log cabin. I switched her off and started walking back towards the farm to collect my Land Rover. Don came across. "I've just had a phone call. It's all round the village you're going to build a cabin in the wood?" "I'm going to try" I expressed with some trepidation. "Just make sure it isn't a permanent fixture" Don suggested "you'll never get planning permission for a permanent fixture." "I know" I sighed. Sam had obviously said something to somebody and now it was common knowledge "I could have done without the publicity." Don remarked. "I don't know whether you'll get away with it lad. The excavator is in the barn and you might as well have the old generator. We don't have any use for it now." I smiled with gratitude. "Thanks Don I'm going to need all the help I can get and a few prayers on top of that." I backed up to the old generator and towed it to the wood struggled again to fight through the undergrowth, finally arrived at the oak tree. The first thing I had to do was put in a service track to the build. I searched for various suitable routes to the road and discovered an old track which had been covered over in undergrowth, along with the odd conifer growing in the middle. I started without any delay clearing away and cutting any trees down that were in the way. I towed the good timber back to the oak tree where it could be put to good use at a later date. The next morning, I drove to the farm and collected the JCB digger. From the roadside I started cutting my way through discovering, there'd been an old kart track here for many years just 6 inches below the topped soil. I carefully graded my way through to the oak tree taking most of the day. Just before nightfall I started clearing an area ready to sit my new cabin on. Much to my surprise, there used to be an old barn by the oak tree. Large flag stones were still there, just buried 1 ft. beneath the ground. I couldn't believe my luck. I carried on clearing the area until it was too dark to continue. I drove home almost falling asleep at the wheel. I flopped down in my armchair by the fire. Johnny had attempted to make something to eat God bless him, beef burger, sandwiches. They did taste good after a hard day. "How's it going dad," Johnny enquired eagerly. "I'm going as quickly as I can son, you can help the weekend if you want to?" "I'm coming, I'm coming," he said eagerly. I started work early the next morning, uncovering the remaining flag stones. I quickly realised if I was going to achieve my goal. I would have to hurry up winter was advancing. I excavated large holes at each corner where the main supports for the cabin would be. Then equally spaced further holes to support the building around the perimeter of the flag stones. Towards lunchtime. I sat on an old log with a flask of tea and a cheese sandwich in my other hand. I saw a horse approaching. Sam gazed around what appeared to be a bombsite and dismounted from her horse walked across sitting beside me on the log. "You're crazy Rob you know that," she implied. "Everybody says you're wasting your time you will never complete the building in time. At least I will have tried Sam." "I will prove you all wrong. I have two months left before we are evicted." Who did you tell about my project?" "I didn't," she protested, standing to her feet. "Someone must have heard me talking to father on my mobile." "I brought you some food. I thought you'd be hungry? It looks like you catered for yourself." "I can eat it later Sam thank you. It's going to be another long day." She looked at my hands, which were rather bloody. "You should wear gloves" Sam suggested. "I should really I remarked. I just haven't got round to buying any yet." "Right then," she said, removing a bag from her saddle and hooking it on the mudguard of the tractor. "There's some food and what else do you need? If you're going to be so foolhardy and stubborn I might as well help" Sam confessed mounting her horse. "I haven't any money with me Rob explained." "You can pay me back later. Now what do you need She said impatiently." I don't need anything Sam I should be going to the wholesalers tomorrow to pick up one or two items." "Okay, she replied. I did offer." and trotted off. Two months quickly past. The building had gone very well. A single-storey cabin all I required was the plumbing and water supply.

A miracle! I'd managed to achieve so much. Even the weather had been reasonable most of the time I had used many trees, far more than I wanted to and promised myself I would replant when I was financially able. Money was becoming a concern, buying window frames and glass had eaten into my savings. At least the place was now watertight. Johnny had been a great help on weekends, keeping the site tidy. The next expense I was facing having a borehole drilled to supply the cabin with fresh water. It took me just one day to dig a trench to the road and lay the electric cable ready for connecting, another extremely expensive operation. Within a week the plumbing had been finished. I had fitted a wood burner for a source of heating and an Aga to cook on hoping to use the resources around me to provide the fuel. I was quite surprised. I'd heard nothing from Jenny and her solicitor. Perhaps they were convinced I was down and out and had no chance in court in a custody battle for Johnny. I finally felt a man and I had achieved something worthwhile. I had heard nothing from Sam for a while either. Like they say, speak of the devil. Sam appeared on a horse trotting through the woodland. She dismounted her Appaloosa horse in amazement. "I don't believe it. I just don't believe it" she gasped. "Can I have a look around?" She enquired, without waiting for a reply she walked in. I had created a three bedroomed log cabin from my own blood, sweat and tears and determination. I was almost broke, I didn't care. "It's absolutely beautiful Rob I didn't think you'd do it. I really didn't." I had two old deckchairs I'd taken out of the garage from home it's all we had to sit on for the time being. Sam sat down in one and I sat in the other by the wood burner I had fitted radiators which were working quite well, but would do better when I had a pump fitted. "I think this cries out for a celebration," Sam concluded. "Let me treat you to a meal at the Ploughman's inn," I started to shake my head. "I won't take no for an answer," she insisted gripping my hand. "They will only laugh at me and take the mickey." "No, they won't you've achieved a miracle." "It's a miracle I would like to keep quiet for now. The less people realise what I've done, the better." "Okay, then, we'll go somewhere else." "You don't have to Sam." "I want to, please?" Before I could argue any more. She jumped to her feet kissed me on the cheek, saying. "I will pick you up at 8 o'clock." Ran out of the door and jumped onto her horse and rode off. Tomorrow was a big day for me. The borehole was being drilled and the electricity connected at the end of the track. I really didn't want to go out because I was knackered, not because I didn't want to be with Sam. I didn't think I'd be really good company at all in the circumstances. I finished early that night and drove home slowly thinking to myself, Grandad must've known and that is why he changed his will to help me. If only I could thank him. When I arrived home I explained to Johnny. Sam was taking me out. "Great dad I'll be okay here on my own don't worry I can play on my computer games after I've finished my homework of course," he smiled. I patted him on the head and dashed upstairs to wash and change into my usual attire Jeans T-shirt and trainers.

At eight o'clock on the dot Sam arrived. I looked in my wallet quickly. I had my credit cards with me and only a fiver in cash. I grabbed my brown leather jacket and went out to meet her sliding onto the range Rover seat. "I thought I would have to drag you out the house." Sam said, laughing. "Where are we going?" I enquired. "It's a surprise wait-and-see." Sam was wearing a black miniskirt, white blouse, and denim jacket. She looked absolutely stunning and here I was dressed in my casual gear as usual. We appeared to drive for some miles, way out of the area I knew. Then she pulled over into a car park at a secluded inn. She grabbed her purse from the dashboard as we got out. We entered the public house. Everyone glanced from the bar as we entered. We continued walking through to the snug. Sam said sit down I'll get the drinks. I didn't argue I was broke and struggling to keep my eyes open. My hands were sore with bad calluses from the continual onslaught to complete the cabin. Sam had ordered me a Bacardi and coke double and she had a large glass of orange juice with a nip of gin I was confused. We had never been out for a drink before. Yet she knew my tipple? I had to ask. "How do you know what I drink?" She looked at me with a pleasing smile her beautiful eyes pierced my soul, casting a spell on my every thought. "I asked Johnny, you have a suspicious mind Rob, placing her hand on my leg and giving a gentle squeeze." The Barman entered the room, placing two menus on the table. I couldn't stop yawning Sam rubbed my arm. "Come on, wake up, you make me think I'm bad company." "I'm sorry Sam; I'm just so tired, you look beautiful." We ordered two Ploughmen's which went down a treat. It had been a long time since I've been out. I was beginning to become attracted to Sam. Which I knew would only end in tragedy if I pursued, I tried to play it cool. She didn't help matters. She was almost encouraging me to take the initiative. I'd already experienced the pitfall of becoming involved with a woman that outclassed me in wealth and intelligence. I was not going to be stung again or become someone's plaything. We finished eating and Sam drove me home. I was asleep by the time we arrived there. "Hey sleepy" Sam said, patting my face. "Sorry Sam, I'm just so tired" "I know," she replied, "you'd better go to bed." "We'll do this again sometime" I said, jumping out of the vehicle. I watched Sam drive off and went indoors and straight to bed. Morning came too quickly and by the time I'd reached the cabin. The firm I had hired into drill the borehole were already working. By the end of the day they had not only discovered freshwater they had fitted the pump. It was just a matter of me connecting to the cabin and the power supply. I looked across to my old tractor shrouded in its old tarp. I wondered if grandfather was looking down. It was all thanks to him and his generosity that made this possible. By Friday afternoon the electricity was on and the water pump working. I looked up into the canopy of the oak tree that shaded the cabin, and decided I hadn't finished, I uncovered my old tractor started the saw bench running, cutting more timber. I made a staircase up into the top of the oak tree then created a platform that went from limb to limb around the whole tree with a guard rail to stop anyone falling off. There was two weeks left before Johnny and I were going to be evicted. I sat on the porch of my creation and sobbed. I never dreamt I would manage to complete. I only needed to finish off and whatever is left to do I can do at my leisure. I phoned the bank only to discover I was overdrawn and my savings were all gone. I still hadn't received the £10,000 grandfather had left me in his will, I could really do with that money now, I thought. I dried my eyes replacing the tarp back over my old tractor. Without that old machine I'd have never done it. I drained the water out of the tractor's engine to avoid frost damage. The weather was changing, it held off till now. The snow had started to fall and the air was decidedly colder. Almost like the story in the Bible of Noah building the Ark the rains held off just until he'd finished loading the animals. I wasn't going to take any furniture from Jenny's house. Giving them the opportunity to accuse me of theft. We moved into the house, fully furnished, so that's how I was going to leave it, they could get stuffed. I didn't need them anymore, what I did need was money. I drove slowly home in the snow.

One more miracle God? Johnny opened the door to greet me. "Have you finished?" "Good enough to live in. Once I find some furniture from somewhere" "There's a letter on the table for you, dad," Johnny said, handing to me. I opened it. The deeds to my land and a cheque for £10,000. The cheque wouldn't clear for a few days. That didn't matter. I'm sure the bank would help me now. I hadn't spoken to Katie for some time I decided to give her a call. She was pleased to hear from me. She explained her mother had been sending her cheques for support. She realised she needed the money university was very expensive and I didn't have the money to support her. She had met her real father and didn't like him she said. I can't see what mother sees in him. I'm pleased you're getting on okay Katie. I didn't mention the cabin I had built I thought it was best not to give too much information away. If she was finally speaking to her mother. Johnny had a few words with Katie and didn't mention the cabin either. They said their goodbyes and Johnny and I sat down to eat the sandwiches he had made. He was becoming quite good at cooking and making sandwiches. He'd had plenty of practice while I was on the build. Christmas is approaching but I couldn't think of anything to celebrate other than the new home I'd built. I went in to see the bank manager first thing Monday morning to present the cheque from my grandfather's estate. I explained to him I needed some money to furnish my new property. I also showed him the deeds. He smiled pleasantly "Of course, Mr Jones, I didn't realise you had property or you were a businessman." I smiled "I'm not. I just own land covered in trees and accommodation. I shall construct a saw-mill in due course." He increased my overdraft by £5000; while the cheque cleared. Furniture shopping had never been my strong point I strolled along the footpath peering into shop windows wondering what to buy. I knew £5000 wouldn't go far. So whatever I purchased would have to be cheap for now. I suddenly had a brainwave. IKEA everything is flat packed and cheap. I wondered where the nearest store was situated. I returned to my Land Rover and drove to Goldings stables, hoping Sam would know. Plus, I would need to borrow her horsebox to transport the furniture home. I parked up just outside her house, or should I say mansion to be more accurate, her property made mine look like a chicken shed. I rang the doorbell. Mrs Goldings came to the door, looked me up and down remarked. "You the new handyman?" I replied. "Not at the moment, I'm trying to find Sam." Mrs Goldings replied quickly. "You mean Samantha and what is your business with her?" I thought to myself. She's a right old battle axe. "I just need" ... Sam came to my rescue, pushing past her mother grabbing me by the arm Instructing. "Come with me Rob." She marched me around to the stable block. Sam remarked "I see you've met mother." "Oh yes" I smiled. Sam continued "I'm flattered you've come to see me. How can I help?" "First I need to know where the nearest IKEA is situated and the second I need to borrow a horsebox to transport furniture please." Sam lent with her back against the timbered stable wall in thought, looking extremely sexy in her riding outfit. "To answer your first question, she voiced there is a large IKEA store about 20 miles from here and your second question, no, you can't borrow the horsebox, you're not insured to drive Rob. Then smiled but I am! Why are you purchasing flat packed furniture for your cabin?" She enquired. "A means to an end it's all I can afford at the moment. As long as I can furnish the cabin with essentials for the time being, that will have to do." Caroline, one of the young stable girls walks past smiling. "Caroline." Sam asked "The horsebox? Is it clean?" "Yes," she replied. Sam continued "I will be away for a while if there's any dramas my mobile is on. Okay?" Caroline continued walking carrying a halter on her shoulder and with her other hand, covering the snigger on her face. We climbed aboard the old Bedford horsebox and off we went. There was still a light covering of snow on the ground. The roads had been salted but there was always a danger black ice. I felt more comfortable once we'd reached the main roads. Sam drove the horsebox very steadily. "I'm sorry to be such a pain Sam." She glanced across to me and smiled. "You owe me a meal that should cover the cost." "That's a deal" I grinned. "Better still, I'll cook you a meal in the cabin." "I like the sound of that" She said, turning into the car park.

Sam took over in IKEA. Sam came into her own, she took charge immediately and within an hour she had managed to spend £4000 of my money. We went and had a coffee while the store staff loaded the horsebox with my purchases. "I must confess" Sam said, sipping her coffee. "I enjoyed myself I haven't been shopping for ages. I just seem to be surrounded by horses and miserable owners." Sam's mobile started ringing. "I'm not a child I'm helping a friend out she said firmly, I don't quite see as it's any of your business." Sam switched her phone off with an expression of thunder creeping across her face. She continued "I suppose you realise she is my stepmother. Why father married her I don't know." "I must confess," I replied calmly, "she does come across as a bit of a dragon." Sam laughed, spilling her coffee, remarking. "Come on you let's go home. They must have loaded the horsebox by now." We started our journey home on the M25 it was nose to tail with traffic, on the other carriageway. There'd been a serious accident, a car had been crushed between Lorries I didn't think anybody would survive that accident. We decided we couldn't take the horsebox down the narrow dirt track to the cabin. I fetched the JCB and transported everything from the horsebox to the cabin and stacked inside ready for assembly. After Sam struggling to turn the horsebox round in the narrow lane, we headed back for the stables. The snow was falling quite heavily and we were becoming concerned, we would get stuck. A mile or so from the stables, a car had gone off the road, slid down the embankment. Sam hit the brakes shouting that's my Father's Jag. I scrambled out of the truck slid down the embankment. The engine was on fire. Mr Goldings slumped over the steering wheel with his face in the airbag. He'd obviously collided with a tree by a side of the road, causing the car to slide down here. I shouted to Sam ring for an ambulance. Sam fumbled with the keys on a phone in a state of panic. I tried to open the car door but it was locked. I banged on the window. No response from Mr Goldings. I looked around for something to smash the window. In the end I kicked the window till it cracked and then my fist, finally breaking through. The pain was excruciating I had to get him out. The flames were getting worse I could feel the heat. I unlock the door from the inside removed his seatbelt. He came to in a daze. We stumbled our way up to the side of the road. I instructed Sam. Open the back of the horsebox we can shield ourselves from the weather and keep your father warm until the ambulance arrives. Sam did exactly what I'd instructed, then ran to the horsebox cab and retrieved the first-aid box and a horse blanket returning to us. Mr Goldings was just dazed but physically unhurt and sat on a bail of straw with his back against the wall. Blood dripped from my left hand. Sam embraced her father asking with some urgency. "Are you hurt anywhere?" He held his head and. Said, "no," quietly. Sam placed the blanket around him. Then came across to me and started to bandage my hand the car was totally a blaze. We were lucky we come along at the right time and able to help. The ambulance and the fire brigade arrived, along with the police. Mr Goldings had lost control in the adverse conditions. No one else was involved. The fire brigade soon had the fire out, the car was virtually unrecognisable. The ambulance crew helped Mr Goldings into the ambulance. Then examined my hand, apart from losing a lot of skin I appear to have got off really light. I hadn't broken any bones although it felt like it. The ambulance crew wanted me to go to hospital. I refused, however did agree to come along later just to have my hand x-rayed. I said to Sam "You can go with your father. I'll take the horsebox back." "No," she replied "father's okay I'll fetch the range Rover to collect him from the hospital once he's been examined." The police finished taking statements from us all.

Sam burst into tears in shock. I held her in my arms trying to comfort. She looked up from my chest searching with her beautiful hazel eyes, saying softly. "Do you realise what you've done, you have saved my father's life!" Without further word being spoken she pressed her lips tenderly against mine and I couldn't stop myself from responding We continued to embrace for a few minutes Then finally managed to struggle through the snow back to the stables. Sam wanted to take me to the hospital. I said "no. I'll go in my own Land Rover Sam." "You can go straight home with your father in yours from the hospital." She kissed me again on the cheek and sped off to the house. I jumped to my Land Rover selected four-wheel-drive and made my way back to the cabin. I immediately stoked the wood burner. The weather was turning extremely cold I didn't want burst water pipes I looked at the pile of flat-pack furniture I had to assemble. With a heavy sigh I opened my toolbox and spent the rest of the day assembling furniture. Johnny phoned. "Dad Where are you?" He questioned, "you realise it's nearly midnight?" I looked at my wristwatch he was right I'd spent nearly 6 hours assembling furniture, but I'd finished and that's what matters. "Okay, son. I'm on my way home. Just give me a few minutes." My phone rang again it was Sam, her father was being kept in hospital overnight and he sent his thanks. "Have you been to the hospital she queried?" No not yet I've been too busy assembling furniture." "Sod the furniture," she scolded. "Have your hand checked it could be fractured." "Tomorrow if I have time I replied," continuing "I will see you soon, bye." I struggled home the snow had become quite deep I walked indoors. Johnny pounced on noticing my hand I explained to him what had happened while eating a fish finger sandwich and a packet of crisps. I said "Johnny to bed with you you've school in the morning. No arguing and thank you for the sandwich good night son." During the night the snowploughs must have been out clearing the roads. Johnny managed to catch the school bus. I returned to the cabin to continue organising the furniture. I hadn't purchased any carpets I rather like the flagstone floor seeing the glistening affect at night. Barely 9:30 AM in the morning and I heard the sound of a vehicle approaching. Sam had driven her smart range Rover down the muddy track through the wood to the cabin. I open the door she was carrying an armful of groceries. "Mind," she remarked pushing past me heading straight for the kitchen. She returned and started looking around. I said sarcastically. "Does it meet your specification your ladyship!" She carried on going from room to room. "Nice and cosy," she commented on returning to me, placing her arms gently around my neck. Before I could say another word she had placed her lips against mine, tenderly. I moved my hands to her waist and eased her away. "What are you doing Sam?" She looked at me rather puzzled. I held her hand guiding her to the settee. "Sam" I explained with concern. "You don't want to become involved with me. I'm 36 years old. I have nothing to offer you, your circle of friends are way over my head. I'm dyslexic and not well educated. What could I possibly offer you, I'm still married." Sam placed her hand over my mouth, saying. Shush. We sat on the edge of the settee, gazing into each other's eyes. "Haven't you ever heard the phrase, you can't buy love?" She said softly. "Don't throw away this special moment." My mind was running wild I wanted her and feared the consequences. Sam gently held my hand and led me into the bedroom. I was about to speak. She placed her finger on my lips. She then started slowly to removed her clothes unbuttoned her blouse. My heart was pounding with anticipation. She released her bra. Her beautiful formed breasts, unblemished skin. She stepped out, of her jeans and pants lying on the bed, inviting me to join her, she watched me remove my garments quickly, almost falling over myself in the process. We kissed caressing, finally penetrating her beautiful warm body. We were still there at 2 o'clock afternoon holding each other. "I don't want to but I will have to go Rob." We dressed quickly, I kissed Sam goodbye and watched her leave slowly down the track. What have I done? I questioned myself? History is repeating itself. The uncertainty of her true intentions worried me considerably. Yes, I could love her forever, could she love me back in the same way. Was I just a conquest? So many unanswered questions. I suppose only time would reveal the truth. I went into the kitchen and look through the groceries she had purchased a bottle of wine, fruit and vegetables, which I put away for another day.

    Reality returned in a phone call. Jenny crying on the phone her lover had been killed in a road accident on the M25. My mind immediately flashed back forming a picture of the Lorries and the mangled wreckage of a car. She pleaded; "I want to come home Rob. I want to be with you. Katie is coming home for the Christmas holidays. I want to see Johnny I miss him so much" she proclaimed. I responded in a cold calculated manner. "It's your family's property not mine. We are due for eviction any day. I have somewhere else to live now so moving out a few days earlier will not make any difference to me. You are welcome to live there if you wish." "Don't be like that Rob please everyone makes mistakes." "An 18 year mistake I responded in anger. After what you've done to the children you can go to hell." I switched the phone off gritting my teeth. I drove home for the last time to that bloody brick monstrosity. I couldn't wait to leave I packed my clothes and was loading them into the Land Rover, when Johnny came up the drive. I explained the situation to him and gave him the option of coming with me or waiting for his mother to arrive. "I'm not stopping here." He packed his suitcase while I loaded the computers and games in the back of the Land Rover. Johnny jumped in as keen as mustard. I asked, have you got everything. He nodded. We returned to the log cabin. Johnny soon made his self at home it felt as if we'd always lived there. I started preparing food. Johnny came into the kitchen. So you're taking over my job then dad, he laughed. No, I replied. Let me do it he insisted your hand needs a rest dad. I stepped aside and un-wrapped the bandage from my hand. It had scabbed over quite nicely and was slowly mending although still extremely painful at times. I had little money left in the bank and I wasn't going to start borrowing now I had to find employment. I should try working at the stables, they'd offered me employment I had my P45 returned to me. I decided to contact Sam in the morning to see if the position was still available? Johnny came back into the front room. "What are we going to call the place?" He said deep in thought continuing. "We must have a name and postcode." To be quite honest, the thought had never crossed my mind. "We could call it treehouse dad he suggested." I sat for a moment. "I suppose that's a good description as any and almost accurate" I remarked. "I will have to make a post box and fit it at the end of the track. No post man will want to bring his van down here, until I renovate the track and grounds." Next morning, I went to the post office to diverted all my mail to the new address, I couldn't give them a postcode because I didn't have one. The postmaster smiled. We know where you are Rob and what you've achieved. You should be very proud of yourself. I was absolutely shocked by his comment I didn't think anybody cared. I left with a broad smile, a sense of really achieving something. I hurried back to the log cabin and constructed my post box and erected at the end of the track. Once I'd dealt with that problem. I drove over to Goldings stables to see if employment was still available. I avoided the house because I didn't want to bump into the Dragon, Mrs Goldings.

I found Sam in the tack room. She smiled saying "hello you." I explained to Sam the phone call from Jenny and I'd moved Johnny and myself out of the premises to the log cabin. She looked rather concerned. "She's not trying to repair the marriage surely?" "She can try all she likes, that's not going to happen." I assured Sam firmly, "not after all she's put me through." Sam breathed a sigh of relief. "I've come about a job." When do you want to start? "Tomorrow if that's okay?" "I'm sure father will agree you'll be on a six-month trial," she sniggered. Then adding "you've certainly passed my trial." Lifting her eyebrows, smiling, Sam said "I'll go and speak to father you have a wander round and prioritise what needs repairing urgently." Sam returned with her father accompanying her. He held his hand out for me to shake. I responded likewise. "We finally meet you Rob." "Yes Sir!" I replied nervously. "Don't call me Sir; call me Rupert" he continued "I don't know how to thank you for saving me." He patted me on the shoulder in a friendly manner. "Samantha has kept me appraised on events. For you to build yourself accommodation in a matter of three months is unbelievable. I must pop down and see your achievement." "You're very welcome Rupert" I replied cautiously. "To business Rob I will pay you £10 an hour. Repair whatever is necessary; we have an account at the local builders I will insure you to drive the pickup and horsebox to transport materials. Just keep Samantha informed of expenditure." He shook my hand again and return to the house. That was an improvement on my last salary. At least it would keep Johnny and me for the time being I turned to Sam. "Thank you. The work is greatly appreciated." Sam responded "he's not paying you enough." "I didn't want to start an argument in front of you, but we will be having words later she said firmly." "Sam" I expressed "don't rock the boat a little money is better than no money at the moment. It will keep the wolf away from the door. Just remember who your speaking to Rob, she said. I am your employer and I say what you get paid." Her expression broke out into a smile holding my hand pulling me inside an empty stable, gently placing her arms around my waist easing her lips on mine. She then pulled away and said "Go away your distracting me. I will see you in the morning." I started for the cabin just before I entered the track. I saw a mini parked on the side of the road. Katie. I couldn't see her anywhere I continued down the track, only to discover she was sat in a chair on the porch, huddled in a coat and wellies. On spotting the Land Rover, she rose to her feet and greeted me with a big hug. "I'm freezing" Katie announced. I unlocked the door and we went inside the wood burner had really worked well. Katie looked around, and sat down on the settee. I went into the kitchen and made us both a drink and returned a few minutes later. "There you are Katie" I said, passing her the mug. "You built this dad on your own" she enquired. "Yes, with Johnny's help on weekends." "It's beautiful. Why, three bedrooms, dad There are two of you?" "What about you Katie? You're part of the family" I reassured. "Mother wants Johnny for Christmas Day." "You didn't come to see me?" "Yes, don't be silly." Katie quickly answered. "I'm the sort of go-between here I don't like it." "If Johnny wants to go to see his mother Christmas Day, I don't have a problem it's entirely up to him." "She also wants you to come." "You must be joking Katie." "I guessed that's what you'd say I told her it was waste of time asking you. I think mothers realised what she lost, won't you give her another chance?" "Well it's too late now, how would you feel if you found out your husband had been sleeping with a girl all of your marriage?" Katie started to cry I placed my arm around her shoulder. "It's not your fault Katie I will never ever go back to your mother." "Oh what a bloody mess. How could she have been so stupid?" Katie professed. "We both, have to make new lives I am sure your mother will soon find somebody else." "I suppose you're right dad. Have you found somebody else?" "No not interested after my experience with your mother that's enough for me. The only good to come out of the marriage is you and Johnny. You are still my daughter as far as I'm concerned." Katie hugged me again; I heard the sound of a vehicle approaching.

I broke out into a cold sweat. I hoped it wasn't Sam, because that would really put the cat among the pigeons. Katie would immediately put two and two together. I looked out of the window. It was Sam and Johnny. She'd obviously bumped into him down the road and offered to give him a lift. Johnny entered closely followed by Sam I saw the expression on Katie's face. "Hi Katie, meet my dad's new boss Samantha Goldings". Katie and Samantha greeted each other warmly. I don't think Johnny realised how he had defused a situation that could have become a disaster. Katie then turned to Johnny. "Mother wants you to come for Christmas dinner." Johnny looked at me, then back to Katie. "No thanks I'm staying here where I belong." Katie continued, "mother has brought you a wonderful present I think it's a quad bike." Johnny didn't hesitate in replying. "Give it to charity I'm sure they'd find a use for it." Sam was becoming uncomfortable and announced she was going home, turning to face me, "I'll see you in the morning Rob. Don't be late." I heard her vehicle drive off. Katie stood up, "You're being unreasonable Johnny." "I'm not!" he replied. "She is your bloody mother not mine. She's dead, as far as I'm concerned." Ouch I thought the conversation is becoming nasty I must bring it to a stop before matters go too far. "I'm sorry Katie. You asked Johnny yourself and heard his reply." "It's because you wouldn't come dad." "Hey stop throwing the blame around the room. Johnny and I didn't create the problem so just calm down both of you." Katie put her coat back on. I said I would run her to where she parked her car. It was dark outside and treacherous to walk along the track in these conditions. I dropped her off by her mini on the side of the road. "Dad would you not reconsider please for my sake it's going to be a miserable Christmas without you and Johnny." I sighed, "I'm sorry Katie I just couldn't stand being in the same room as her. You on the other hand, are always welcome to come to us in the cabin." "I can't leave her on own," Katie explained, "although she's done an awful lot of harm to everyone I just can't be that cruel." "It's your choice Katie." She started her car and drove off, I returned to the cabin. Johnny had already started cooking. He was somewhat concerned with the situation and his decision. "You could have had Christmas with your mother if you wanted Johnny." "No I'm happy here, I'll stay with you. I'd have liked the quad bike Johnny concluded, the price was too high." I was surprised at Johnny's attitude I would have thought a new quad bike would have tempted him. Yet he didn't waver under the prospects of a gift. My mobile rang. "Hello Sam." I answered calmly. "I thought I'd better leave." She said. "I didn't want to be in the middle of a feud." "It's okay Sam. A few heated exchanges between Johnny and Katie. Other than that it all ended reasonably." Sam enquired. "What was the outcome if you don't mind me asking?" "Neither of us will have Christmas with his mother." Sam confessed, "I was surprised at Johnny making a stand when Jenny offered him a new quad." "So was I to be quite honest, I suspect she will arrange for it to be delivered all the same. She's good at trying to buy people." The next morning at 7.30 am I arrived at the stables ready to start my first day. Sam was feeding the horses along with the other stable hands all young school leavers by the looks of them. Sam came across and took me into the tack room, taking me up a narrow staircase where anyone could have a break there was a kettle, microwave and a few chairs. "If you want a cup of tea Rob just help yourself," she said, kissing me. We then returned downstairs. "I must get on and feed the horses Rob," she said, running up the yard. "You start doing whatever. Don't frighten the horses." Okay, I replied. I fetched the ladders from the workshop and started cleaning the guttering out. They hadn't been done for years. There were over 50 stables; I swept up the mess I'd made putting the rubbish on the muck pile at the end of the yard. When the girls took the horses out to exercise I repaired each stable door while they were vacant. They had plenty of timber in stock just no one to use it. I found some unleaded paint and applied to finish them off. Although I was dyslexic it only seemed to really affect me, when I was stressed out and that had been most of the time lately. The stable yard had floodlights, which meant I could work after dark on simple tasks. It was three days before

Christmas and apart from being very cold it continually snowed. Mr Goldings arrived around 4 pm and came across to the stables. He walked up and down the yard. "Good gracious," he said you are quick I can see the difference you've made already, well done Rob." I packed the tools away and headed home. I hadn't seen much of Sam, only a glimpse occasionally the stables are certainly a busy place, people coming and going all the time. I went home.

Johnny was drying his eyes . . . "What's happened Johnny?" Mother came to the school today. It was embarrassing the headmaster summoned me to his office. Mother was in there drinking tea. I went ballistic." Something else I forgot to do. "I'm sorry. Johnny, that's my fault. I didn't notify the school regarding the situation." "It doesn't matter dad. The head sent me out of the office. I spoke to him after mother had gone and told him our side of the story. He was shocked and understood my behaviour entirely. I don't think she will dare come to school again," Johnny smiled continuing. "The headmaster would like to speak to you in the new term after Christmas." Of course, no more school now for a week or so. "I'd totally forgotten Johnny. I'm turning out to be a great father. I'm working tomorrow, then I'm home for a few days, will you be okay while I'm at work?" "No problem, I hate to mention it, but we are out of food." "Crumbs I forgot the shopping as well. We will have to eat out Johnny." "I have a confession dad. I tried to catch you at work and you'd already left. Sam said she'd sort something out. Sorry." "Oh great son she will think I'm a right idiot." "She won't dad I like Sam. It's a pity she's not my mother." "Hey steady on son. Don't get any wild ideas there it would be like marrying your mother all over again. I'm not getting involved with any rich women." "Oh yeah, dad, I see the way you to look at each other. I'm not stupid." He walked off into his bedroom. I checked the cupboards we were out of everything. Sure enough Sam arrived with arms full of groceries. Johnny went out to the range Rover and carried the bags in. "How much do I owe you Sam?" I enquired. "I will take it from your salary" she smiled. "You must think I'm a right idiot Sam." "No not really, just a man." "All men are disorganised." "Hey, hang on I'm not that bad." I protested. You owe me a meal anyway. Johnny came out from his bedroom. "Can you cook Sam?" Johnny enquired. "Yes, of course." "Let's put it to the test dad." I didn't know where to put myself, Johnny, I thought, will you shut up. I don't know what had come over him but he'd certainly taken a shine to Sam. "Oh well, I suppose if I cook it I will be able to eat it." she said, heading for the kitchen, "I'll help you." Johnny said, grinning at me. Starting to lay the table I just stood there in amazement my life was being taken over again by my son and Sam. Sam asked. Johnny. "Do you ride?" "No, I've never learnt." "Come with your father tomorrow you can spend the day at the stables with me. We will start to teach you how to ride properly if you'd like to of course?" "Yes please." "That's okay with you dad?" "Entirely up to you Johnny it's your decision if you want a sore ass." Sam corrected me quickly. "Not if you're taught properly, there's some nice young girls there you might like to meet." "Girls, no thanks, look what trouble dad got into." "Now there's a sensible lad, well said Johnny." I remarked. Sam started laughing. "I can't believe I'm cooking for you two, how the heck did I get conned into this." Johnny remarked, "It must be my charm, plus you fancy my dad." Johnny left the room, oblivious to what he said. I knew he was joking, but it hit home all the same. Sam looked across to me saying quietly. "That obvious?" I shrugged my shoulders. "How do you feel Rob?" Sam asked. "Scared to death to be quite honest, you frighten the life out of me." "Why?" Sam asked, leaning with her back against the sink. "Look who you are, you're well-to-do, you haven't got to worry where the next pounds coming from. I suspect you've never known a man with less than a million." "That's not quite true Rob I know you," she laughed. "The point is Rob. Do you want to be with me?" I pause for a moment, "Of course I do," I answered, and remarked, "what about your father and mother. They would murder you for socialising with someone like me." "I don't care what they think you are my choice, a very wise choice. If they can't realise that, they can go to hell." Sam was becoming angry and upset. I walked over to comfort her. "You must understand Sam. It's no fun being poor." "You survive." She answered. "Yes, that's all we do is survive. I would never be able to give you luxuries like you have at the moment."

"I'll tell you something very personal. Don't you ever repeat it to anybody." "Of course not," I replied. "I can't have children, the hospital carried out numerous tests, after I was badly trampled by a horse. There's something wrong inside. Now I'm older, I realise I would really like a child and never will conceive, the clock is ticking I'm nearly 26." "That doesn't matter to me. Sam I don't want a broody old mare." She punched me bursting into laughter, throwing her arms around my shoulders holding me close. Johnny peeped into the kitchen and then left. Sam remarked, "Johnny has just seen us holding each other." I replied, "does it matter now he knew before I did how we both felt Sam. Before we start world War three let's just take it steady and see how things progress for both our sakes. At least that way if for some unknown reason it doesn't work out, no one will get hurt." "Okay, she sighed if you're still unsure about me." "It's not that Sam, let's get my divorce and Johnny's security sorted first." "I see your point Rob we'll keep it to ourselves for now." "Johnny, promise not to tell anybody." We explained to him the reasons why.

You could tell from his expression he was really happy with the situation. We all sat down at the table and enjoyed the meal Sam had prepared. The conversation was light and jocular for the rest of the evening. We said goodbye to Sam and watched her disappear into the darkness. Johnny and I returned to the kitchen to wash up after the meal. My phone rang, "Hi Katie." She explained her mother's returning to London in the morning for her employer's Christmas party in the evening, would we collect the quad bike while Jenny was away. Katie enquired? "Okay," I said. With hesitation, "I'll be round after work." I hadn't purchased any presents for anybody not that I had any spare cash to splash out. Johnny came to work with me in the morning wearing his old jeans, thick jumper and jacket to keep warm. I could see Sam in the distance, talking to Caroline, the young stable girl, Johnny and I climbed out of the Land Rover. Caroline approached. "You must be Johnny she said in a sweet voice come with me, Miss Goldings has instructed me to take you in to the exercising arena. We have a horse waiting for you." Johnny looked at me for reassurance. "It's okay. Johnny, you'll be fine." I guessed Caroline wasn't much older than Johnny. I watched them both walk off into the distance. The wind was bitter, cutting across the yard drifting the snow. I wanted to avoid working out in these conditions. I checked the empty stable stalls for damage to the kick boards and panelling. I was never going to run short of work here horses can cause a lot of damage, especially when they get upset. I selected the tools I required from the workshop and started the internal repairs. Sam found me. "Hello you," which seemed to be her favourite saying. "Are you okay Rob?" "Yes, I'm fine, just a bit cold." I remarked, blowing into my hands. "Come with me see how Johnny is getting on." "Perhaps not, it will only make him nervous if he thinks I'm watching him." "He won't see us. We'll use the observation box and not put the lights on." "That's Sneaky Sam." I remarked. "Absolutely," she replied, smiling. We made our way round the back of the enclosure up the stairway into the observation box and sat just back from the glass. Caroline was standing in the middle of the ring with her whip. Johnny was trotting round on the back of quite a large black horse. We could hear Caroline shouting instructions to Johnny. Sam cuddled up to me on the bench, holding my hand. We were there for approximately half an hour watching Caroline put Johnny through his paces.

    Johnny looked rather funny wearing a hard hat and sitting on a horse, then without warning, the horse reared up and Johnny fell off into the sand. I rose to my feet quickly. Sam pulled me back down into my seat, "He'll be alright." Caroline was laughing as she walked across to where Johnny was laying. Caroline stretched out her hand. Johnny held and stood brushing off the sand we couldn't hear what they were saying to each other. Caroline removed her safety hat and kissed Johnny then smacked his backside with the whip. Now Sam stood up saying. "That is not professional." I chuckled, remarking Johnny didn't seem to mind, easing Sam down onto my lap. She placed her arm around my shoulder. I whispered in Sam's ear. "You certainly trained her well, I'm glad you didn't bring the whip the other day when you came round to see me." I kissed her cheek. She slapped my leg. We continue to watch Johnny under Caroline's supervision for a short while. Then Sam's phone rang. Caroline heard it and look towards the observation box. She could see nothing. We quickly left the building. I continued with my repairs and Sam went off. 4 PM came very quickly I packed my tools away. I hadn't seen Johnny at all other than watching his riding lessons and wondered what he was up to. I started walking round the yard, listening for his voice. I saw Caroline and Johnny coming from the hay store. Caroline caught sight of me and headed off in a different direction. Johnny had bits of hay all over his jacket. "Did you enjoy your riding lesson?" "Yes, dad, great fun." Sam came over, placing her arm on Johnny's shoulder. "Thanks Sam." Johnny said. "Would you like to continue with the lessons Johnny?" Sam enquired, plucking pieces of hay from his jacket and looking at me. "Yes please Sam. Or should I say mom?" "Shush that's not funny. Johnny if someone hears you." "Sorry," he replied. We all started walking back to the Land Rover. Sam removed a handkerchief from her pocket and wiped something from Johnny's face. He flinched. Sam whispered in his ear. Johnny quickly removed his handkerchief, and continued rubbing where Sam had started. We said goodbye to Sam and drove off. "I must call in at the shop on the way home. Grab some groceries." I remarked. "I must collect your quad bike Johnny from your mother's house." Johnny shrugged his shoulders, displaying his indifference. "Damn, I meant to ask Sam if I could borrow the horsebox to transport your quad home." We returned to the stables. I jumped out of the Land Rover and went round the corner. Sam was in a heated argument with a guy over something I couldn't quite hear. He started pushing Sam shouting. I jumped in between them and started pushing him. "Come on then mate try pushing me," he took a swing and missed, but I didn't, knocking him straight on his arse. Sam grabbed my arm. "Don't Rob." She pleaded. You come near this lady again and you'll answer to me. Out of the shadows came Mr Goldings. "What's going on here?" Sam turned to her father, saying "This gentleman owes us a great deal of money and he wants me to extend his credit further and I said no. Then he started to push me and Rob intervened." "Well Mr Jackson I suggest you get your horse off my property by the end of business tomorrow and don't come back." "I will sue for assault." "Please do Mr Jackson." Mr Goldings replied, "you assaulted my daughter and I saw you try to hit Rob. He was only defending himself. Now get off my property." Mr Goldings placed his arm around my shoulder, "Thank you Rob for looking after Samantha. You're not just our handyman, now you're her personal bodyguard as well." He chuckled. "I never did like that man Samantha. When Mr Jackson comes to collect his horse make sure you phone Rob he can monitor the situation. I will pay you extra Rob if you come in." "No problem Rupert I replied." Rupert smiled. "I didn't think it'd be a problem, if it involves Samantha." and he walking off. "Sam can I borrow the horsebox to run Johnny's new quad bike home. Jenny's gone to London. Katie said pop round and collect it tonight." "I'll come with you. I've finished for the night." We collected Johnny from the Land Rover. Sam drove the horsebox. Johnny sat in between us. When we arrived, the new orange quad bike was parked outside the garage. Sam turned the horsebox round. Johnny and I dropped the ramp. Sam stayed in the cab to make it look as if she was just helping us out. Katie appeared from the house carrying two wrapped presents. She passed the packages to Johnny kissed him on the cheek and then me. "A little something from me I do miss you both." I gave Katie a big hug. "Thanks. Katie you shouldn't have wasted your money. "It's not as if I'm broke. I have an account with over £50,000 from my father. Mother asked me to give you this Johnny." Katie removed an envelope from her coat. "There's £1000 in here to contribute towards buying clothes." Please accept it. Johnny said "Thanks." And slipped it into his jacket pocket. We pushed the quad into the back of the horsebox and strapped it down to stop it moving in transport. Katie walked to the front of the horsebox, while Johnny and I shut the tailgate, I heard Katie say "Thank you Samantha for helping dad and Johnny." She then turned and walked back to the house. Johnny and I climbed back into the horsebox and Sam drove off, saying "That was very nice of her." Sam expressed. "Very nice," "Katie has changed somehow" I remarked. We parked the horsebox on the side of the road and unloaded the bright orange quad I started it for Johnny saying "Drive very carefully down the track. I'll go back with Sam to collect the Land Rover." "Okay, dad." I watched Johnny drive off.

Sam started driving and changed direction, turning down the driveway to my deceased grandfather's farm. "Why are we going down here?" She didn't reply parking the horsebox outside the house. She took a set of keys out of her pocket and went to the front door, entering switching on the lights. She announced, "You are now looking at the new owner of Cranbury farm. My father purchased it in the auction he wants to expand the livery business." I stood there in amazement that was the last thing I was expecting to hear. Most of the old furniture had been left. Sam held my hand I was still speechless the house was freezing there'd been no heating on for some time. Sam grabbed some old newspaper screwing it into a ball and throwing in the old fireplace, along with some sticks and a few logs that had been left by the hearth. The dry wood soon caught alight. She then turned the light out, and sat on the carpet in front of the fire. I did likewise warming my hands, placing my arm around her. We looked into the flickering flames and watch the dancing shadows on the wall. It wasn't long before we were making love. I just hoped grandfather wasn't looking down on me shaking his head in disgust. Whatever spell Sam had cast over me was working, I just could not resist her. As we were leaving a police car pulled up behind the horsebox. The police officer came over. "What is your business here?" He questioned. He flashed his torch in both our faces. "I know you this is your grandfather's farm." Sam interrupted. "It is now my farm." "You are?" The officer enquired. "Samantha Goldings I own the stables at the end of the village. We are just checking the property is secure." The officer wrote down the registration of the horsebox, saying good night, he reversed his car and drove off. "That was a bit close for comfort Sam." "Doesn't matter I own the property." We drove off back to the stables. We kissed good night, I returned to the cabin. When I walked in, Johnny was on his mobile. I must, dad's home he said, quickly disconnecting the caller. "Who was that Johnny?" I asked. "Just an old school friend" he said. My intuition suspected there was a little more to it than that. I decided not to pursue the issue any further. We had all had a brilliant day and I didn't want to ruin it. Just as a precaution I thought I should have a little talk to Johnny man-to-man. Johnny. He looked up, "Have we ever discussed the birds and the bees?" "You mean sex dad, we've covered all aspects at school, including using condoms." Johnny laughed. Muttering "birds and the bees honestly dad, it's a bit late for that talk." I went into the kitchen to make a coffee and hide with embarrassment. The next morning, Christmas Eve, Johnny decided he would try his mother's present out around the wood. Sam phoned. Mr Jackson had arrived with the horsebox to collect his horse. I jumped in my Land Rover and drove over to the stables. The removal of his horse went smoothly and he caused no further disturbance. Sam and I went upstairs to have a coffee above the tack room. "My father questioned me after the police had contacted him, to confirm we actually owned Cranbury farm I explained we were just checking the property after dropping the quad bike off. I don't know whether he believed me or not." I could feel the rope tightening round my neck. Sam finished making the coffee and sat on my knee. "Father and my stepmother have gone off into London shopping." She placed her coffee on the table stood up and from the corner of the room. She carried two folded horse blankets and opened them on the floor then returned to the corner, taking a whip.

"I'm giving you the best Christmas present you've ever had. Take your clothes off," She ordered. Talk about kinky I thought. It must be right what they say about redheads I didn't argue. She pushed me on the floor removed her clothes and sat on top of me driving all my senses wild I'd never experienced before. Sam knew exactly how to ride me. Afterwards we just lay beside each other on the blankets until we started to get cold. We both dressed and scurried downstairs after hearing Rupert shouting. "Samantha where are you?" We had been above the tack room for over two hours. We both walked in to the yard like guilty children. "Did Mr Jackson collect his property?" "Yes, father, Rob was here no problem at all. I just made him a coffee before he went home." "Oh, okay, thanks for coming Rob and happy Christmas to you." "The same to you Rupert." I left in haste for my Land Rover. Rupert didn't look a happy bunny. Something had obviously upset him. I certainly wasn't after Miss whiplash had finish with me. I started for home; rubbing my leg where Sam had struck me with the whip, she said I'd remember the event. I walked into the cabin, only to hear a disturbance in Johnny's bedroom. I open the door and there was Johnny in bed with Caroline. I quickly closed the door and went to the kitchen. Like father like son, I shouldn't really be smiling. I couldn't imagine how embarrassed he felt. Johnny came into the kitchen, "Dad ah, sorry about that. I know you'll going to chew my ear off, please let Caroline leave first it's not her fault." Johnny pulled his T-shirt straight and returned to his bedroom. I made 3 drinks and called out to Johnny. "You two, I've made you coffee." I carried a tray into the front room. I sat down in my chair by the wood burner. Caroline a pretty girl with shoulder length dark hair nervously entered the room, looking rather embarrassed. Johnny followed closely. "Take a seat. I said your coffee is on the table help yourself to milk and sugar." "Thank you, Mr Jones." She said quietly. I hadn't seen Caroline since last year dad. I didn't realise she was working at the stables. She was in the year above me at school. Caroline finished her drink, saying to Johnny. "I must go. I'll see you after Christmas when you continue your lessons." I remarked, "Don't be a stranger, you're welcome any time." Caroline looked over to me, smiling "thank you." "I'll walk Caroline home dad." "Okay son." They both left I looked out of the window watching them walk slowly together, holding hands. Johnny returned. "Where does Caroline live, I enquired." "The other end of the wood. She lives in that black-and-white cottage with the thatched roof." "Oh, I know where you mean Johnny, what do her parents do?" "Her father is a lorry driver her mom just stops at home." "She's really nice" Johnny expressed. "Good for you son." "She looks a really nice girl treat her with respect, son." I was relieved he was dating a girl from a normal family. Not like his father. He had more chance of a successful relationship than me. "Don't worry dad, I'm being careful I do like her." "You and Sam okay?" "I'm worried Johnny, she is too good for me, when her family find out." "Stopped selling yourself short dad, you're as good as any man nobody's perfect." "No son but they are rich and that's one thing I'm not." "I don't think Sam is like that dad. I think she wants you just for who you are a kind nice person and a great dad." He smiled. "Thanks son." The phone rang. "Hi Katie you okay?" "No, dad. I'm scared." I stood up. "Why?" "I think there's someone in the house. I don't want to stop here tonight." "Stay where you are. I'll come and fetch you." Johnny said "I'll come." "Stop here Johnny I won't be long." I jumped in the old Land Rover and drove as quickly as I could to Katie she was watching from the window as I pulled up. She ran out into the drive and jumped in the Land Rover. "Dad, I'm scared." She clung to me. "We'd better get you some clothes." "No, she pleaded I'm not going back in inside. I'll sleep in what I'm wearing, or borrow one of your shirts for tonight." "I'll investigate Katie and get you some clothes. I'm sure it's just your imagination, being on your own in a big old house." "Don't go in there dad, please the place is evil." "Okay, okay, calm down." Without further discussion I drove Katie back to the cabin. She ran inside and embraced Johnny. She was trembling, something had put the fear of God in her.

I phoned the police told them what had happened and Katie was with me. If they could look round the property and grounds for anything suspicious would be appreciated. I went inside; Johnny had already made refreshments for everybody. Katie just shivered. I sat her in my chair by the wood burner. It was scorching hot, but still she shivered I crouched down in front of her, holding her hands. "No one's threatened you have they? You've had any weird phone calls?" "No dad no, it's just the bloody house. I hate it." I went into the kitchen and poured her a small glass of Scotch. "Here drink this Katie." She sipped, almost choking. She continued until she had emptied the glass. "I want to lay down now dad" she requested. "Your room is ready Katie always has been." "Thank you." She kissed me on the cheek. I quickly went to my bedroom and fetch my dressing gown I knocked on her door and passed it through. "Thanks," she replied. "What is going on dad? It's not like Katie. She's obviously scared of something or someone." I received a phone call back from the police saying they had searched around and could find nothing suspicious. I thanked them for their trouble and settled down into the armchair. "Some Christmas this is turning out to be Johnny." "I don't know it's not so bad were altogether. I have someone, you have someone who cares for us." "Keep your voice down Johnny remember Katie is in bed." "Sorry" he whispered smiling, continuing. "It is great dad. Johnny went to bed," I decided in light of the event I wasn't going to bed I would sleep in the chair with my shot gun across my lap. At least if we had any unwelcome visitors I could help them back out the door with both barrels. Approximately 4 am. Katie came out of her bedroom. I had fallen asleep in the chair. She whispered, "Dad, dad," I stirred. "What are you doing? Why are you sitting here with the gun?" "In case we had any unwelcome visitors." Katie went into the kitchen and made a drink and brought one back for me. "Do you feel better now love?" I asked. "I always feel safe when I'm with you" she smiled, returning to her room and closing the door. Morning had finally come. Katie came wandering out of her bedroom wearing my dressing gown, fully open, leaving nothing to the imagination. "Katie!" "Oh sorry," she quickly covered herself. Johnny staggered out of his room, rubbing his eyes. "What time is it?" "9 o'clock." Katie kissed me on the cheek, "Happy Christmas dad, I do love you." "I haven't got you a present Katie, sorry" I remarked feeling rather ashamed. "Doesn't matter dad." Johnny made some toast for everyone, I heard a vehicle outside. I looked out of the window. A police range Rover a male and female officer came to the door. "Mr Jones, Mr Robert Jones." "Yes. Could we come in please?" the police sergeant requested. Looking at Katie the sergeant continued your name is "Miss Katie Jones. Yes, why?" Katie replied. "You are Johnny Jones?" "Yes" Johnny replied. "What's this all about?" I asked. "I'll get to that in a minute sir." "Where were you all in the early hours on the 25th?" "All here officer." "We received a phone call from you, Mr Jones at 10:30 PM advising us of a possible intruder at your estranged wife's house and you had collected Miss Katie Jones to bring home to your premises." "That's correct officer." "We then went round the property ourselves could find no sign of a break-in. However, we returned in the morning at 8 a.m. and discovered there had been a break-in. We also found a gold coloured Porsche and a female body yet to be confirmed of Mrs Jenny Jones found slumped against her car on the driveway." I fell over into my chair in shock. Katie screamed. Johnny started crying. The female officer made everyone a drink. "Mr Jones can you think of anyone who could be responsible. Have you had a disagreement with anybody recently or your estranged wife for that matter?" "No, I don't think so. Wait a minute I remembered I did punch someone at work. I was protecting Samantha Goldings from being pushed by a man." "Oh yes. Were there any witnesses to the incident other than Miss Goldings?" "Yes, Mr. Goldings her father." "Do you know the man in question you hit?" "No but his name is Mr Jackson." I replied. "Mr Jones I'm afraid you will have to positively identify your estranged wife's body." Katie threw her arms around Johnny sobbing. The two officers left the family in utter devastation. I didn't know what to say or do to make everyone happy again; so much grief in such a short space of time. The children had been put through a mangle through no fault of their own.

"I'm going to identify Jenny's body. You two look after each other while I'm gone I'll be as quick as I can." They didn't answer. I grabbed my coat from the chair and jumped in the Land Rover and drove the 20 miles to the nearest morgue I entered the room, accompanied by a police officer. Jenny's body was covered on a stainless steel table. The attendant gently pulled the sheet exposing her face. Tears poured down my face. This is the first time I had felt anything for Jenny since we parted. The attendant replaced the white sheet. I was escorted away by the officer into a private room where I could gather my thoughts. I just couldn't stop the flow of tears. A member of the C.I.D came into the room, a Mr MacDonald he sat opposite. "I have spoken to Mr Goldings and his daughter. They both confirm your description of events at the stables. We are presently trying to locate Mr Jackson to question him. I'm afraid that's the only lead we have at the moment. Mr Jones, here's my card. If you think of anything else, contact me." I thanked Mr MacDonald and he left the room. I drove home very slowly when I arrived at the cabin. Sam's range Rover was parked outside. I went in to find Mr Goldings and Sam. She embraced me immediately. Rupert was sat in between Johnny and Katie talking calmly to them both, trying to help. "Thank you both for coming over to see us. I'm sorry if I've ruined your Christmas." Rupert glanced up to me looking over his spectacles. "You've ruined absolutely nothing." "No," Sam agreed. "We are only too happy to help if we can," she concluded. Rupert continued talking to Johnny and Katie. Sam and I went into the kitchen. She placed her hands softly on either cheek. "You okay Rob it must have been one hell of a shock, especially on Christmas day." She hugged me, once again. After about another hour Sam and Rupert said goodbye and left. Katie's mobile rang. She didn't recognise the number she answered, it was the press trying to get a story. I grabbed the phone and told them to piss off, then switched her phone off. Johnny's started to ring. This time it was Caroline. He went into his bedroom. A short while later he returned. "Dad he asked quietly. Caroline's parents have asked if I would like to go over there for the rest of the day. What do you think?" Just then my mobile rang again. It was the press. So I turned my mobile off. "Under the circumstances Johnny might be a good idea. Just leave your mobile off. Otherwise, the press will start chasing you for a comment. I'll take you. Will you be all right Katie left on your own for a minute?" She nodded, wiping her eyes. I drove Johnny over to Caroline's. Her father met us at the door. He shook my hand. "Please accept our condolences if I can be of any help, just ask." I thanked him and said. "Please keep the press away from Johnny." He agreed. I left returning as quickly as I could to Katie. She's the one that would be hurting the most. Unbeknown to me on my return Rupert had left some bottles of wine and three bottles of whiskey. Katie had started attacking the whiskey drinking; glass after glass. "That won't solve anything" I said. "I just want the pain to go away dad. She pleaded." I had a couple of glasses myself in the hope it would steady my nerves. We had, had nothing to eat all day.

Goodbye to Christmas! We hadn't even bothered with the turkey I placed the bird in the oven hoping we can eat something later. In the meantime I made some toast, hoping it would absorb some of the alcohol in Katie she was consuming. I place the toast in front of her on a plate. She took one or two bites and started giggling. "Perhaps you should go and rest Katie" I suggested. She laughed again. Nope. I tried to remove the bottle from her hand. "Leave me alone" she shouted. Just leave me alone. My dressing gown she was wearing had fully parted at the front a difficult situation should I close it for her? Or would she think I was trying to grope her? I decided to leave well alone. I thought the worst that would happen; she would pass out from consuming so much alcohol I returned to the kitchen. I turn my mobile back on. I had several missed calls. I didn't recognise any of the numbers so I presumed it was the press trying to get a story. There was one message from Johnny. He was going to stay the night at Caroline's. I thought in the circumstances with Katie in this state, not such a bad idea. In another two hours, the turkey would be cooked and at least I could make some sandwiches. I didn't bother preparing any vegetables. I thought it's just of waste of time. There was no one here to eat them apart from me. I decide to watch television, only to discover Jenny's murder was being mentioned. At least Mr MacDonald from C.I.D had asked everyone to stay away from the family and respect their privacy. They showed pictures of Jenny's house. I turned the television off and poured myself a glass of whiskey. Katie had gone to sleep in the chair for the time being, which I was quite thankful for. Just after 10 PM I saw lights coming towards the cabin. Sam had returned I wondered why, she came in carrying a bag. She looked across at Katie and noticed the empty bottle. "Oh dear Rob, you shouldn't have let her get in that state, she will have one hell of a hangover in the morning." Sam closed Katie's dressing gown. "Father agreed I can stop the night if you wish and help out." "Don't ruin your Christmas Sam." "You're not, my stepmother is driving me mad, make me a drink Rob" Sam remarked, sitting on the settee. "What would you like? we haven't much of a selection." "I'll have a large whiskey," she said, throwing her keys on the coffee table and removing her jacket, I returned with the open bottle of whiskey and glass placing on the table. Sam poured a very large glass. "Don't you start going silly on me Sam" I expressed. She removed her boots crossing her legs on the coffee table. "That reminds me;" She said. "We've had some intruders round the stables they slashed the tyres on the horsebox, we informed the police, they think it's all connected to this Jackson feller." "Marvellous" I expressed. "Will this nightmare ever end?" "Where's Johnny?" Sam asked. "The press tried to make contact. Caroline phoned and her parents offered to have him for the night. In fact, he's been there most of the day." "That was very kind" Sam remarked. "Yes, I thought so". Katie started to stir, "Mother is that you?" she was trying to focus. "No it's me, Sam." Okay, "Hi Sam. Katie giggled. Sam. Sam." "Yes Katie," "My mother's dead." "I know Katie Sam replied quietly." "I need a drink, dad, dad, dad," "No more Katie, I said firmly." "You bastard!" she shouted at the top of her voice. Sam lent over with the bottle and filled Katie's glass. "See, fuck you Katie shouted sipping the whiskey." "What are you doing Sam?" "Leave her alone Rob, let her get it out of her system now she's that far gone. She's had a shit day like the rest of us." Sam poured herself another large glass. I thought what the heck; I topped my own glass up as well. Katie emptied her glass. "More please." Sam topped it up again. I was beginning to feel a little lightheaded. I went into the kitchen to check on the turkey, finally cooked. I placed the turkey on the table in the kitchen. "Katie would you like some turkey?" I called out. "No, fuck the turkey." "You fancy any turkey Sam?" "No thanks Rob I've already eaten." I returned to the settee after snatching a leg and kitchen towel.

Sam kept filling Katie's glass. I was becoming rather concerned. I sat there quietly chewing on the turkey leg. I did consider throwing Katie into the shower and turning on the cold water. Another bottle of whiskey had been emptied. Katie tried to stand up, but obviously couldn't she was paralytic. I asked. "Where do you want to go Katie to bed?" "No, I don't I want to pee." "I'll take her Rob," Sam said, standing up. She placed her arm around Katie and they made their way to the loo. Neither of them steady on their feet. They both returned. Sam sat Katie back down in the chair and then went into the kitchen, returning with the last bottle of whiskey. This was certainly not helping matters in my opinion. I remarked to Sam. "Are you sure?" "Yes I am!" she snapped. "I did exactly the same thing when my mother died I know what she's going through." Sam, toped Katie's glass up again and her own right to the brim. I could see this all ending in a big disaster. In order to lessen the amount, they were consuming. I topped my own glass up to the top because once it was gone. That would be the end of it. I just hoped I could keep my wits about me until I could get Katie safely into bed. Hopefully she would sleep for the next eight hours at least. Katie started giggling again and in a slurred voice. "Sam." "Yes, Katie?" "You're fucking my dad. Mother said he's got a big dick." "Now you're talking silly Katie." Sam remarked. "Yes, you are." I commented. "You killed my mother!" I jumped to my feet. "That's enough Katie, don't be so bloody rude." Katie took another sip from her glass. "You're not my father. He's dead. Everybody is dead. I wish I was fucking dead." Katie was becoming more unreasonable and incoherent. "Come on Katie." I said, grabbing her arm. "I'm putting you to bed." "Fuck off, you pervert I saw you looking at my tits. Do you want to suck?" "Ignore her Rob." Sam said. "She'll soon be out of it. Then I'll put her to bed." I sat back down, sipping my whiskey. Sam patted my leg reassuringly she turned and kissed me on the cheek. "Whatever she says Rob just let it go over your head." Sam cuddled up to me, keeping one eye on Katie as she moved her head from side to side, then trying to take a sip from the glass, missing her mouth. It wouldn't be long before she passed out completely and we could all get to bed. I'd had enough of today. Finally, Sam helped Katie get into bed, there was still half a bottle of whisky left, and I replace the top and returned it to the kitchen, along with the dirty glasses. Sam returned, placing her arms around my waist from behind and lowering her head in between my shoulders. "I love you Rob". I turned around to face her we kissed passionately. Sam collected her night bag from the chair, and we went into my bedroom. We lay in bed holding each other. Sam whispered "I wish we could do this every night." There was no reason why not. I was now a single man. I lay on my back, looking at the ceiling wishing my mother and father were still alive. Sam placed her head on my chest. I kissed her fragrant head and confessed. "I love you Sam." She then rolled over on top of me. I caressed her breasts and we made love. We awoke after hearing a noise. I quickly dressed and Sam put on her dressing gown, we opened the bedroom door slowly. Light on in the front room and someone was in the kitchen. We looked in to see Katie finishing off the bottle of whiskey. She was naked. Sam approached her cautiously and removed the bottle, placing it on the table. Katie kissed Sam on the lips drew back and announced. She was a lesbian. Pulling the cord on Sam's dressing grown then eased the dressing gown over Sam shoulders, kissing Sam again fondling her. This was all too much for me. Why Sam didn't slap Katie's face I will never know. I couldn't watch I went into the front room and sat down. Sam came into the room, supporting Katie. Both were naked they continued kissing each other. I just couldn't believe my eyes. "What are you doing Sam this is ridiculous behaviour." "It's alright Rob, she is only experimenting, and it means nothing." This was a side of Sam; I was certainly not impressed with. I was beginning to suspect this lovely woman I'd fallen in love with was not all she seemed. Sam and Katie sat either side of me on the settee. "Why are you so embarrassed Rob?" Sam asked. "She is my daughter." "She's not." Sam corrected. "She is just a young girl experimenting with life." Katie placed my hand on her large breast. "Would you like to fuck me stepdad?" She slurred lowering my hand to the inside of her thigh. I stood up. This was too much for me I walked into the kitchen and drank the remainder of the whiskey. I looked in the cupboard for some pills. I discovered another bottle of whiskey. I'd obviously purchased at an earlier date. I couldn't stand the situation I wanted to escape. I open the bottle and drank heartily. Sam had taken Katie back to her bedroom. I returned to the front room I slumped on the settee. Sam returned to me. She could see by the expression on my face I was shocked and appalled. "Do you want me to leave?" Sam asked. "I don't know I'm confused." Sam put her dressing gown back on. "Did I shock you Rob?" "Yes!" I replied. "I used to be a lesbian Rob until I met you." I held my head. "I think I should dress and go home. Give you time to make up your mind" Sam concluded. "I do really love you Rob and I would never betray your trust I promise." "I don't want you to leave Sam."

I was beginning to understand Sam's past. I suppose we've all got skeletons in the cupboard we prefer not to escape. At least she's been upfront and honest; Sam and I went back to bed. Sam went off to sleep. I lay on my back, trying to analyse the situation. If Sam and I were to get married would she be faithful to me or would I be going down the same road all over again? Or was she really just a lesbian? Experimenting with me? What was I going to do with Katie, was she a real lesbian? Or just so blotto she didn't know what she was doing? I could hear movement again in the house. I got up to investigate slipping on my pants. The front room light I could hear someone being violently sick in the toilet. I peeped around the door. Katie still naked was washing her face then cleaned her teeth. She dried her face and turned to face me. "I'm sorry, I'm really sorry;" she placed her arms around my shoulders, pressing her breasts against my chest. It was almost morning birds singing in the trees. I helped Katie back to her bed. She held my hand and I stayed with her until she went to sleep. Sam woke up at 8 am scrambling to get dressed. "I must feed the horses;" she exclaimed kissed me on the cheek and ran out of the cabin. Shortly after my mobile rang it was Johnny. He asked if he could stay with Caroline for the rest of the day. I agreed. Let the boy enjoy himself. Why come back here and be miserable. 10:30 am Katie finally came out of her bedroom, holding her head as she entered the kitchen. I was clearing away I made a coffee and she sat at the kitchen table, she finally put a dressing gown

Charmed Log Cabin: Enchanted Life

on. I passed her a coffee. "Oh my head. She pleaded." "I can guess how you're feeling Katie." "No, you can't dad it is unimaginable." I made some dry toast, which she ate gingerly I need to go home dad to fetch some clothes. That's not possible. Katie it's still a crime scene. What am I going to do dad? We'll wash what you have here and make do. Katie staggered back to her bedroom, returning with her clothes. We turned the washing machine on and went into the front room. I phoned Mr MacDonald from C.I.D asked when we could gain access to the house so Katie could retrieve her clothes. "I'm afraid not at the moment, Mr Jones, forensic haven't finished. What I can do is send one of the PCs round to collect some garments providing forensics has cleared the area where they are." "That would be great." Two hours later a PC came to the door, leaving a suitcase. I carried it into Katie's bedroom and left her to dress. Mr MacDonald from the C.I.D phoned in the afternoon. "We have a breakthrough; we have eliminated Mr Jackson. Forensics have lifted some fingerprints which relate to immigrants, we have two in custody and are chasing two others." "Thank you very much for the update Mr MacDonald." Katie came back into the room. I explained what I'd been told she sat down and started to cry. I perched beside her on the edge of the settee and held her very close for a moment. I phoned Sam and relayed what I'd been told. She enquired "How's Katie this morning?" "She is distraught."

Sam asked, "Can you forgive me for what happened last night?" "Nothing to forgive Sam" everyone was off their head. Just a minute Katie wants to speak to you I handed the phone over. Katie said quietly. "I love you. I really do. Are you coming round later, Good, Good bye" Katie passed the phone back to me. "I will see you later Rob." "Okay." I replied. Katie enquired; "Was I really terrible last night?" "You'd had enough love." "You and Sam are seeing each other aren't you?" "Sort of" I replied, changing the subject. "I will make some turkey sandwiches Katie." I left the room quickly to avoid any further questioning regarding Sam. I left Katie attempting to eat something. Through my coat on and went outside, climbing the stairway to the canopy of the oak tree. The wind was fresh and the tree bear of foliage. I couldn't see very far because of the tall conifers that surrounded the cabin. I couldn't make arrangements to bury Jenny because of the ongoing investigation everything seemed to be in limbo. I just wanted to put everything behind me and get on with my life. I glanced across to my old tractor shrouded in its tarp watching the snow melt slowly with the water dripping off long icicles frozen to the sheet. I noticed Sam's range Rover pull up by the side of the cabin. Johnny and Caroline got out to my surprise. Johnny looked up and waved. "Hi dad" he shouted. Caroline waved. I acknowledge them. Sam came up to me, Johnny and Caroline went in the cabin. "Hello you." Sam said, leaning on the rail beside me. "Hi," I responded, "come on let's go in." I continued. "It's starting to get really chilly outside now. What about the horses who is feeding them?" "We bedded them down early today. Johnny and Caroline came to help." We entered the cabin. Caroline was sitting by Katie talking. Johnny had gone to change his clothes the place was absolutely packed. I'd never designed it for parties. Caroline came across to me, "Mr Jones, she said softly. My father has sent a present over for you; it's in the back of Sam's range Rover. Will you help me carry it?" "Sure." Sam through the keys to Caroline, we opened the tailgate. Bottles of Bacardi and coke plus 6 bottles of gin. "Your father shouldn't have" I remarked. Caroline smiled. "Well he didn't really, it's what is known as falling off the back of a lorry." She laughed. I knew exactly what she meant. I helped her carry the bottles into the kitchen thinking. I wish he hadn't I really don't want alcohol in the cabin. Caroline asked. "Mr Jones, would you mind very much If Johnny stayed at my house tonight? My father and mother are out for the evening and I would prefer not to be on my own in the house." Johnny came into the kitchen carrying a bag, gave me a hug. "Hi dad." "It looks like the decision already was made" I smiled. Caroline gave me a kiss on the cheek. Sam was preparing food with Katie, finally Katie had moved instead of sitting on the settee, continually thinking about past events, definitely a good sign. I drove Caroline and Johnny back to her house, her parents had already gone. I waited till they both went inside and put the lights on. Johnny came back to the door and waved. I turned the Land Rover around and headed for the cabin. The gritting Lorries didn't bother with the back lanes, so it was quite treacherous. There was going to be another frost tonight. I would have to stock up with wood. I parked by the side of Sam's range Rover, where I stored my logs. I collected an armful and went inside. Sam and Katie were still in the kitchen talking. I place the logs by the fire and went in to the kitchen. To my horror, they had opened a bottle of gin, sat at the kitchen table, facing each with a glass of gin. Sam looked across to me. Seeing the frown on my face. "We are only having one glass" smiling, "probably one or two with the meal?" I tried not to smile, but just couldn't help myself. "Come on grumpy sit with us." Katie remarked pushing out a chair with her foot for me to sit on. Don't look so worried dad Katie professed. She had certainly brightened up since Sam had arrived. I could smell the food cooking. Katie made me a Bacardi and coke and return to the table. Katie reached across and placed her hand on mine. "Okay, dad I know it was obvious you and Sam are an item. You're not going to throw your rattle out of the pram?" "No."

Katie approved. I breathed a sigh of relief. She continued, "we've decided to share you." I didn't know quite what that meant, and I really didn't want to hear the explanation. Katie and Sam served up the meal and we sat quietly eating. I went into the front room and switched on the television they were covering Jenny's murder again, saying they now had four people in custody and all indications were they were going to be charged with murder. "Katie shouted from the kitchen. It's about time you bought a dishwasher." I heard them both laugh. I shouted back. "I have you two!" Katie and Sam came into the front room. "What was on the news?" Katie asked. I explained. "Great Sam remarked." Katie then turned to face me. "I don't think I should call you dad any more." "Why Katie?" "Because it's not the truth. Would you be very upset if I called you Rob because dad at my age is a bit juvenile?" She had a point I suppose. "I agreed." Sam voiced, "she's over 18 Rob and dad does sound childish." "I suppose if it makes you happy and that's what matters." Katie then enquired. "Once this situation is all over I presume you will be asking Sam to marry you?" "Steady on, Katie" I exhaled. Sam looked across rather hurt. Katie continued, "you won't find anybody like Sam dad. Sorry Rob." "Don't push me Katie." She then sat back. Sam was still staring at me, searching for answers she wanted to hear. Sam reasoned. "Because of what happened last night, isn't it Rob?" "No, yes. I don't know." "We are discussing marriage when Jenny is not cold in her grave yet it all seems wrong to me" I explained. I continued "I know I love you to bits." She threw herself on my lap embracing me. I placed my arm around her waist while she rested her head on my shoulder, kissing my neck. Sam stood up after a few minutes, "I'm going home, Rob." "Why?" I asked, rather puzzled. "I thought you were going to stay the night." "No not tonight, I think we all need a little space." She kissed me on the cheek and Katie as she went. I was starting to feel very depressed. I was surprised Sam didn't stay or perhaps I'm expecting too much of her. Katie went into the kitchen, returning with a tray supporting three bottles my Bacardi and coke and a bottle of gin, she placed on the coffee table and poured us both a drink. "Rob," Katie said. "Don't lose Sam she is besotted with you." "I can't understand you. Katie I thought you really loved your mother." Katie shrugged her shoulders. "I think it was the shock of being told she was dead. You know how mother was and don't forget what she did to you Rob." She continued. "You owe her nothing. I thought you were my biological father and you're not. Yet you still stand by me after all that's happened." I moved over to the settee and sat by her, patting her leg and kissed on the cheek. "You will always be special to me Katie." She rested her head on my shoulder and we sat there watching the television for the rest of the evening. We both decided we were going to bed and hope tomorrow would be a better day. I kissed Katie Good night on the forehead and she went into her room. I turn the lights out and retired to mine. I couldn't help myself. I lifted my mobile from the bedside table phoning Sam. "Hello you." She answered "what's wrong?" "Nothing Sam I wanted to hear your voice. What time is it?" "It's just gone midnight. I just wanted to tell you I love you, I'm just a little mixed up at the moment." "I understand Rob and I love you too, I'm not feeling very well at the moment." "Okay Sam, I'll let you get some sleep. Sorry I disturbed you." "That's all right Rob. Good night." Katie knocked on my bedroom door can I come in Rob please. Yes, what's the matter? She sat on the side of my bed in her see-through nightie, "I'm scared. I don't want to be alone tonight. I can hear the wind howling outside and I feel cold." "I shouldn't do this really." I remarked, "come on, jump into bed." She slid in beside me and snuggled close to me. I lay on my back, looking at the ceiling, feeling the situation was totally wrong. I shouldn't have my stepdaughter in the same bed as me. We both finally dropped off to sleep morning soon arrived I was in bed on my own. Katie wasn't there. I could hear her in the kitchen. I dressed and went in. She had made me breakfast egg on toast. "Thank you for understanding how I felt Rob last night." She said, sitting down at the table, starting to eat her breakfast. My mobile rang Mr MacDonald from C.I.D "Good morning Mr Jones." He said. "We have finally charged the four immigrants with breaking and entering, and one of them with murder." "Thank you Mr MacDonald." "Miss Katie Jones, can return to the house. Our investigations are finished." I said thanks again and conveyed the information to Katie. "I don't have to move back there?" She asked. "Not if you don't want to Katie. You have your own bedroom here. Besides Jenny's parents own the property and will be selling it shortly." She smiled with relief, we decided to go over this morning and retrieve everything she wanted from the house and bring back here. We finished breakfast quickly, taking Katie over to the house. It was a bombsite inside. Her car was still outside undamaged; she quickly gathered her remaining possessions.

She then went on her hands and knees. Folding over a large rug and lifted three small floorboards, taking out her laptop. "They didn't get that Rob. Most of my coursework's on there plus loads of Private stuff" Katie said, smiling then concluded. She was going shopping and catch me later. I went home to the cabin I unloaded everything she had given me into her bedroom, which made it rather cramped, but she wouldn't be stopping here very often, when she went back to university, after the Christmas break. I realised I hadn't checked the post box virtually since I've erected I walked down the track and found it full of mail. After returning to the cabin I laid the letters out on the table. A lot had not any stamp on obviously been hand-delivered I struggled to read them, most were wishing me well I left out so Katie could see and read them. I wondered what personal stuff was on Katie's laptop. I wondered why she had taken so much trouble to conceal it. I wasn't connected to the Internet yet; I might still be able to retrieve some information. I felt rather guilty. Nevertheless, I plugged it in, password protected. I tried date of birth and it let me in. I waited for it to start up then went to the pictures which I found to be rather shocking. She was dancing naked with other girls kissing. There was even a picture of her mother being screwed by a bloke. So Katie was a lesbian. I quickly turned the laptop off and put it back in her bedroom. Katie phoned she had parked on the side of the track. She couldn't come any further because it was too rough for her car, would I fetch her. I jumped in the Land Rover and parked alongside her car. She opened the boot and proceeded to load groceries into the Land Rover. I turned the Land Rover around and we headed back for the cabin. She studied the mail I'd received and smiled. You are really loved by everyone in the village Rob. She said, gathering the letters together and stacking them on the shelf. She then places the groceries in various cupboards around the kitchen. Then went off into her bedroom to sort out the rest of her belongings. I received a phone call from Jenny's parents in South Africa, asking when the funeral was taking place. I explained they had not released Jenny's body yet and I would let them know immediately. I also made them aware of the conditions in the house after the burglary they were not concerned. They were just going to sell and dispose of it. They explained they had arranged for the funeral to be videoed rather than them make a long flight. They didn't see it making any difference if they were present or not. Totally typical of her parents cold and calculating. You could see where Jenny got her attitude from everything was pounds shillings and pence to them. Rupert phoned asking if I would like him to handle all the legal matters relating to any estate Jenny had, he would also arrange for a funeral director to contact me to organise the funeral. "I don't know how I will ever repay you Rupert I expressed." "It's my pleasure Rob just leave everything to me, I'll be in touch, goodbye." Rupert rang off. I felt as if I was betraying the man going behind his back, sleeping with his daughter. I think if he ever found out he would never forgive me. Katie came into the kitchen making us both a drink. "Rob I don't mean to be a pain I could really do with an Internet connection." "I know Katie, it was planned, and recent events thrown everything upside down I'll get right to it love." After New Year's Day I had a landline fitted to the cabin. We finally had a proper telephone the police released Jenny's body and the coroner gave me a death certificate. The funeral went ahead Jenny was laid to rest in the local churchyard. Some of the village attended, although some people were rather disgusted with her parents having the ceremonially videoed, rather than attend themselves. Jenny had planned ahead she'd already taken out an insurance policy covering her funeral expenses. Rupert discovered she had various amounts of money in different accounts totalling just over million. Which was a shock to me? She had not made a will so everything was coming to me; although we were separated we were still legally married. Rupert felt her parents, who were multimillionaires would have no further interest in fighting for such a small sum in their eyes he advised me. I just have to be patient while he finished all the legal stuff. Then the money would be transferred to my account in due course.

Johnny went back to school. Katie was preparing to return to university I was back at the stables, making various repairs to the property. I hadn't seen much of Sam. She almost seemed to be avoiding me. The most I got out of her at work was "Hello you." Her favourite saying, she didn't look very well. Or perhaps she decided it was all over between us. I needed to know where I stood. I saw Sam go into one of the stables. I followed her in. "Sam. What's the matter?" "Nothing" she replied "You're avoiding me why?" "No I am not." She snapped. "You haven't been well since Christmas, what's wrong with you?" "None of your bloody business get on with your work." "I presume it's over between us?" "I didn't say that I'm just too busy to be bothered with you at the moment." "Thanks." I walked off 4 o'clock came and I went home. Sam's attitude had changed. I walked into the cabin rather deflated. Katie had made tea; Johnny was in his bedroom finishing his homework. "Katie Do you know what's wrong with Sam?" "She's alright, isn't she?" I shrugged my shoulders. "I don't know she is just avoiding me. She hasn't been around for a while." Katie concluded. "I'll give her a call. See if I can find out anything." "No it's her decision if it's over, it's over. I didn't think it would work in the first place." I confessed. Katie turned round from the sink and hugged me. "Don't worry Rob I'm sure she'll explain when she's ready." "I suppose you're right Katie. I will miss you when you've gone back to university." "I may not go back Rob." "You must Katie it's your future." "I don't need a degree to work in Tesco's. That's probably where I'll end up there's not many good jobs out there, especially for women." "That's not true I assured." "I have straight A's from my exam results. I'm sure I could quit university save the expense. I just wanted to get on with my life and not sit with my head in a book for the next five or six years." Johnny ran into the kitchen, "Dad, dad, it's Sam. She's had an accident. She's in hospital." "Calm down Johnny how do you know?" "Caroline has just phoned me. Sam was riding a horse around the indoor arena. Caroline said she just collapsed and fell off." Without hesitation I threw on my coat jumped in the Land Rover and drove off to the hospital. I checked at reception. "You've just had Miss Samantha Goldings admitted." "She's still in emergency under examination are you a relative?" "No a work colleague." Rupert came to reception and saw me sitting across the way. "Do you know what happened to Sam Rob?" "No Rupert, Caroline phoned home notified me. I came straight over. Caroline said she just collapsed and fell off the horse. I have no more information than that." A doctor came to reception "Mr Goldings. Yes. We are admitting your daughter for observation overnight. It appears she may have fainted; she will be taken to the ward in the next few minutes if you wish to see her." Mr Goldings phone rang. He took the call outside; you could tell from his body language. He was not happy. He turned his phone off and came back into me. "Rob something very important, has happened I must attend. Will you stay here with Sam?" I answered, "Okay, of course." "Tell her I will come in later." "Okay." I was finally allowed to see Sam.

Sam smiled with excitement. I sat beside her in a chair. "Hello you." she smiled. "What's happened?" I continued. "Sam I know you fell off the horse. But why? Caroline said you were only . . ." "Oh Caroline told you she interrupted." "Yes. Didn't you want me to know?" I exclaimed I held her hand, looking into those beautiful hazel eyes? "I told the doctor not to tell my father what was wrong with me." "Why Sam he loves you, just like I love you." "I'm glad you said that Rob, the impossible as happened!" "what you mean. The impossible has happened." She whispered in my ear, "You have a broody old mare, I'm pregnant." "Oh no. Your father is going to kill me." "I'm not having an abortion." "Don't you dare Sam!" I remarked, "whatever it takes I'll standby you. Will you marry me Sam?" "I'll think about it." She smiled. Just don't say anything to father for the time being. It may be touch and go whether I can carry the baby full term because of my internal injuries." "No more sex" I sighed. She laughed "That serves you right for getting me in this state. Only you could pull off a miracle Rob and make my life complete." I saw Rupert come into the ward with Mrs Goldings the Dragon. "I'd better go Sam. Okay?" "I love you Rob," she said quietly, "be home tomorrow. Don't worry; leave it to me to sort these two out." I left her bedside and acknowledged Rupert and the Dragon I returned home. Johnny and Katie were all over me like a rash, trying to glean pieces of information from me. "Nothing serious, she just fainted." Katie placed my tea on the table. She kept it warm in the oven. "I bet she's pregnant Rob" Katie remarked. She looked at my face for a reaction. I tried not to smile. "She is I knew it" Katie said excitedly. "I'm saying nothing, neither are you." Johnny remarked "Oh blimey, we'll need a bigger cabin." I fought my way through the burnt remains of my tea. I poured myself a Bacardi and coke, and sat watching the television, Katie beside me on the settee. "I told you Rob there'd be an explanation." She smiled; Johnny had gone back into his bedroom. I wondered how long we could keep Sam's condition under wraps before it exploded in my face. The next morning at 10:30 am Sam returned to the stables in a taxi. She made a beeline for me, looked around and pulled me into an empty stable pushing me back against the wall, kissing me on the lips. We embraced for several minutes expressing our love for each other. "I haven't told them yet Rob I hope you haven't said anything to anybody." "Sam, we'll not keep this quiet for long, even Katie tweaked." "Oh God" Sam rubbed her forehead. "Katie will talk to Johnny. Johnny will talk to Caroline; it'll be common knowledge in seconds." "They promised they wouldn't say anything." "I hope you're right Rob. I must pick the right moment. I think father will be fine because he didn't like me being a lesbian, my stepmother on the other hand, will be a right cow and cause trouble I suspect." "Don't worry Sam. We will fight each battle as it comes along." I seemed to be a dab hand at the moment. She hugged me, once again, saying as she left the stable. "I will see you later." I finished work and drove home stopped at the letterbox to see if I had any mail. There were several letters which I took to the cabin. Katie had made the tea once again. I threw the letters on the side and started eating. "Shall I check the post Rob?" Katie enquired. "You can do love I'm sure it's only bills." "Here's one from the bank." "I suspect overdrawn," I commented. Katie opened and read the letter "Rob the bank manager wants to see you, 1.5 million pounds have been deposited into your account. They want to discuss investment options." "That's from your mother's estate, bloody hell. I exclaimed." "Rob, you realise you are now financially secure." "We all are Katie, not just me." "This is a cause for celebration." Katie announced pouring us both a glass of our favourite tipple. Katie and I were getting along far better since her mother died. Sam turned up and came in. Katie ran over to greet her with a hug, placing her hand on Sam's stomach. "Boy, or girl?" Sam turned crimson. I'm not pregnant. Yes, you are Katie, insisted. It's written all over your face. Leave her alone Katie I smiled. Have you told your father? No Sam replied, I think he knows he's just waiting for me to say something.

Katie announced to Sam. Rob is worth 1.5 million now. "Money doesn't matter Katie." Sam explained, "If you marry for money, like my stepmother and father. You'll be miserable, if you marry for love, money doesn't matter;" "I told you Rob" Katie expressed, "she was the girl for you." Caroline was in the bedroom, with Johnny, who had both overheard the conversation. They entered the room. Sam very firmly said to Caroline, "Don't you dare say anything."

"We're not stupid" Caroline remarked. "Everyone knows you're pregnant." "Everyone." Sam gasped. "Yes, everyone you're showing all the symptoms, sick in the morning at work. Even Mr Goldings suspects, he asked me to personally watch you, didn't do anything stupid at work." Sam sat down and exhaled "Rob please repair the track to the cabin. It's so rough it's worse than riding a horse coming to see you." "Okay Sam. No problem," "I'll order some stone, I'm not breaking any planning laws because it's not a permanent fixture. You still haven't answered my question." "What was that?" Sam enquired. "I'm rather preoccupied" she confessed. "Will you marry me?" "Of course, you silly man" Sam smiled, encouraging me to sit by her. The cabin door opened, standing in the doorway, was Rupert. "Can I come in Rob?" "Please do Rupert." He had mud on his shoes and suit. He'd obviously walked down the track. In his right-hand was a large bottle. Sam and I stood up Rupert removed his camel hair coat. Johnny and Caroline vanished back into the bedroom. Katie offered. "Would you like a coffee Rupert?" "No thank you. I think 6 glasses is more appropriate for this occasion," he said, looking at Katie over the top of his spectacles. "Father," Sam said "how do you know?" "I wasn't born yesterday Samantha, you showed the same symptoms as your mother when she was carrying. You are a bloody nightmare to live with," he smiled. "I was going to tell you, father" Sam assured. Rupert sat by the wood burner in my chair, releasing the cork on the champagne. Katie returned with a tray of glasses, Johnny and Caroline who were listening from the bedroom door returned to the front room. Rupert poured from the large bottle of champagne, filling every glass. Katie gave everyone a glass. No one knew whether to smile or cry. "I'm to blame for everything Rupert." "That's never a truer statement Rob." "No, it wasn't your fault Rob" Sam came to my rescue. "I chased him father." "That I believe Samantha when you want something you get it" he agreed. "A toast, I'm going to be a grandfather, I thought would never happen." "Father" Sam warned "it's not going to be straightforward. It could all end in disaster." "I might not be able to carry to full term." I'm fully aware of the situation Samantha." "How do you know father?" "I'm not a solicitor for nothing I have a way of obtaining information when it's important. You are very important to me Samantha." Everyone was listening intently to the conversation. What are your plans he asked with a smile? Sam and I looked at each other. "I thought so," he continued to smile. "This is what we're going to do, Caroline can run the stables; we do need someone to handle the accounting." Katie suggested. "I'd like the job." Rupert looked up. "Have any experience?" "I have straight A's in everything." "You're at university that wouldn't be practical, although," he concluded "when you finish university. There will be employment waiting for you." Katie topped everyone's glass up. I sat very quiet, expecting to be torn to shreds and it never happened. Sam held my hand and squeezed gently. "Your stepmother is not so impressed she suggested that you terminate the pregnancy whereupon we had a blazing row as you can imagine, she's flying off to Switzerland tomorrow to have her nervous breakdown." He grinned, continuing, "are you just living together, getting married?" "We're getting married father" Sam said, quickly. "Good," he replied if I didn't know better Rupert voiced. "I'd say God had a hand in planning recent events. I will have that coffee please Katie he said." Everyone started to relax. "A registry office marriage Sam?" "That's not important father, Rob and I being together is." "Good," he said. "I will sort out the reception." He insisted finishing his coffee and said to Sam "Give me a lift in your range Rover back to my car on the road. I'm plastered in mud and now you need to rest." They both left and I sat down and breathed a sigh of relief. Katie gave me a hug. "That wasn't so bad Rob." "No." I remarked, finishing my coffee. Johnny then approached the subject of a holiday. "Dad, someone has dropped out of the trip to Austria at school could I go?" "When is it son?" I enquired. "The end of next month Please dad I'd love to see Austria." "Yes, I don't see why not if you can arrange your passport in time." "I'll sort that out Rob" Katie assured. "I need another favour dad." "Go on while you're on a roll son and I'm in a good mood." Caroline's parents are away the same two weeks as me, could Caroline stay here rather than be alone in her parents' house?" Katie quickly responded. "Yes, she can, she can stop with me. I've decided I'm not going back to university. Other than to sit exams I can study just as well here on my laptop." "Katie, I'm not happy." I don't care Rob. I've made up my mind." "Then yes to the second request." "Thank you, Mr Jones" Caroline said. "Call me Rob, Caroline, like everyone else."

February soon arrived. I had repaired the track having numerous lorry loads of crushed slate delivered I levelled it with the old JCB at least everyone could drive to the cabin now, without being plastered in mud. The countryside was starting to come to life, including the old oak tree, shrouding my log cabin. Sam was in and out of hospital and doctors' surgeries trying to protect our unborn child. Everyone knew from the start. This could be a battle we lose in the end. We had a small engagement party, but decided to delay the wedding until after she had given birth to avoid any anxiety or stress. Caroline had stepped into Sam shoes. I continued with my handyman duties Katie continued her studies from home, which I wasn't happy about I still thought she should have attended university properly. It was now time for Johnny to leave for Austria. I drove him the short distance to school at 4 am to catch the school coach. We said our goodbyes and I returned home. Katie was in PJ's making a coffee and yawning. "I'm absolutely knackered." She proclaimed slumped at the kitchen table, trying to keep her eyes open while she sipped coffee. "I didn't finish till 1.30 am this morning I had to get my paper finished. I'm off back to bed," Katie announced, leaving the table. I didn't see the point in me going to bed; it would soon be time to go to work. When I arrived Sam greeted me. "Hello you." "How are you feeling Sam?" "Crap" she expressed kissing me. Caroline came across. "Shall I load my suitcase in your Land Rover Rob?" "Yes, then we won't forget it." "Perhaps you should go back into the house Sam and rest." "I'm bloody fed up of resting Rob I'm bored stupid, my stepmother is being a right bitch, father and my stepmother have been rowing constantly he should have never married her." "Go and lay down Sam." "Okay." She kissed me again and walked slowly back to the house. 4 o'clock came and Caroline was finishing off. Instructing the other stable hands what she wanted done. She seemed to take charge quite easily and had no problem in disciplining anybody who crossed her path. She was meticulous in her approach to her duties. She jumped in the old Land Rover with me and we started home. "Why do you keep this old Land Rover Rob?" She enquired. "Sentimental reasons I suppose, before I had any money it's all I could afford and she's never let me down." We arrived at the cabin. I carried Caroline's case inside. Katie was there to greet us. I placed Caroline's case in Johnny's bedroom and returned to the kitchen. After tea I poured myself my usual tipple, and sat watching TV. Katie took Caroline into her bedroom. I finally thought my life had sorted itself out and everything should be plain sailing from here on. At 9.30 pm I phoned Sam. "Hello you. Checking up on me again." "Yes." "I'm in bed. Don't worry; I'm watching television board stupid. I really want to feel you inside me. I want to feel your embrace, your breath on my breasts." "We can't Sam you could lose the baby." "I know," she replied. "I'm just fantasising. Once we've past the three months period, things may improve I hope." Sam rang off. I poured myself another drink. Katie and Caroline returned to the front room, giggling. Katie took my glass from my hand. Caroline is going to make you a very special drink. They wandered off into the kitchen still giggling almost as if they'd been drinking. They returned moments later with my glass filled. I don't think we should give it to him Katie, Caroline said concerned. I took a sip as they sat either side of me. It still tasted like Bacardi and Coke, just with a strange tang. They sat there looking at each other giggling. "What's so funny?" I enquired. They giggled even more Katie went to the window and drew the curtains.

My eyes started to go out of focus. I tried to get up and couldn't. I heard Caroline say "just a few more minutes." I could hear them still giggling as I tried to focus. Katie asked will he remember in the morning. Caroline said "No, He will just have a stinking headache." "Let's go and have a shower" Katie suggested .The two girls disappeared from focus I could hear the shower running then my eyes focused on two naked girls standing before me. I tried to focus properly, but I couldn't make out the faces. They were kissing each other as I wandered in and out of consciousness, I heard someone say. "Let's set up the video camera," then more giggling. I was frozen to the spot. No matter how hard I tried I couldn't move all that I could see was flashes of two girls dancing and occasionally kissing. The next thing I woke in bed with a very bad headache. Katie came into my bedroom carrying a coffee. I asked. Katie what was in that drink Caroline made me? "Just Bacardi and Coke and a mixture of fruit juices" Katie replied. "Is that all?" "Yes," she said allowing her garment to part showing me everything, then slowly closing with no urgency smiling. Caroline knocked on my bedroom door "Can I come in?" "Yes," I replied. "How you feeling Rob you were out of it last night," she said. Reinforcing Katie's story while looking at each other Caroline said "I'll go and make breakfast." Katie perched on the side of the bed, allowing her dressing gown to part again giving me full view over her breasts. I remarked "Katie cover yourself." She looked down grinning and said. "You've seen my breasts before Rob I'm not embarrassed neither should you be. Drink your coffee and get dressed. Breakfast will be ready shortly. She said leaving the room. I had a shower and dressed and headed for the kitchen. Just before entering I could hear Caroline and Katie talking. I peeped round the corner and they were kissing. Katie was stood behind Caroline, fondling her. They parted quickly on noticing me. I said nothing and sat at the table, wondering if every woman who worked at the stables was a lesbian. Still, that's none of my business as long as it doesn't affect my life. Caroline had prepared a lovely breakfast, bacon, eggs, fried bread all cooked properly. Unlike I'd received from Katie. "Apart from a stinking headache I do feel rather relaxed for a change," I remarked to them both. Katie and Caroline looked at each other and smiled we finished breakfast. The two girls washed up and then went out in Katie's mini. A short while after Sam arrived. I open the door for her as she held her tummy. "Hello you." "You don't look very well Rob?" "I feel alright apart from a headache. Caroline made me a drink last night I can't remember anything after that. How's my beautiful wife to be?" I asked. "Fat, I feel fat, I look fat." She complained and continued "I can't drink. I can't ride my horses." "Okay, I interrupted. I get the message." She smiled; "Don't drink so much Rob," she scolded. "If you can't remember what happened the next morning." I nodded in agreement. "I thought I should tell you, be careful. I don't trust Caroline. I gathered that this morning when I walked in the kitchen I replied. I saw Katie and her kissing." "Just leave them to it Rob. It won't affect you." "Yes, but she supposed to be Johnny's girlfriend" I pointed out. "Their relationship will fade out" Sam remarked then smiled. "There again, It may not if Johnny's anything like his father?" I placed a pillow in the middle of her back to try and ease her discomfort. "I'll be glad when this child is born. I want to rip your clothes off now. I'm sorry you're having such a miserable time Sam." She kissed me very tenderly; "It will all be worth it in the end Rob. We have a lifetime together. I just wish my real mother was alive to see how happy I am now."

Baby scan was on Monday. "Do we want to know what it is?" "No let's be surprised" I remarked. "I'd better go otherwise I'll be in bed with you and ruin everything." "Well we could go to bed as long as we didn't do anything." "That's as bad as having a packet of sweets and can't open." She laughed. "That reminds me. I must pick up some chocolate from the shop. I just can't get enough of it at the moment" she said getting into her range Rover. I went into Johnny's bedroom where Caroline was supposed to be sleeping. The bed hadn't been slept in. She must have stayed in Katie's bed last night I looked around the room. I could see nothing out of place. I went out into the wood and cut some timber for the fire. The temperature was certainly warming up, spring was really on the way the trees were budding and the undergrowth was thickening up, I returned to the cabin and peered through the window Caroline and Katie were kissing in the front room, fondling each other. I pulled away from the window and made a noise stacking the wood. When I entered the cabin they were sat on the settee pretending to watch television. They informed me they'd nipped to London to do a little shopping. Katie remarked she'd purchase more groceries. I asked her if she wanted to be reimbursed. "No Rob, its fine I'll cover it." The two of them went into the kitchen to prepare an evening meal. After we had eaten Caroline's phone rang. One of the stable hands had a problem with a horse. She asked Katie if she could borrow her car, although she had a driving licence. She hadn't purchased a vehicle for herself. Katie said yes. I remarked, "You realise it's only insured for yourself to drive Katie." Katie replied. "It's only just up the road Rob it won't hurt." Katie threw the keys to Caroline she left in a hurry. Katie was behaving very odd. She drew the curtains then went into her bedroom. I poured myself a drink from the already started bottle of Bacardi and sat watching television. I started to feel a bit strange again looked at my glass smelt my drink, I could see nothing wrong with it. I put my glass down and knocked on Katie's bedroom door.

Come in. She answered. She was sat at her dressing table in her dressing gown with her laptop in front of her looking at photographs she turned to me with her dressing gown open. Have a look at these photos Rob, they're interesting. I sat on the edge of her bed, looking to the screen, feeling lightheaded. I feel strange again Katie I confessed. I could barely focus on the photos. They were nudes of her and Caroline kissing and me sitting on the settee with my trousers missing, watching them. I'm going to bed. I remarked staggering from her bedroom into my own. I lay on top of the bed I hadn't the energy to undress. Katie came into the room. You have been drinking too much Rob again. I don't remember I muttered. Let me help you get undressed. I felt my clothes being removed and the bed clothes being placed over me, a warm body beside me. I felt my hand being placed on a breast and being kissed and fondled. Then there was a sensation of penetration I could hear sounds of pleasure as if it was Sam beside me. I awoke the next morning to find Katie beside me. My head was screaming in agony. She slid from underneath the bed clothes slipping on her dressing gown. "What are you doing Katie?" I questioned? "You were very ill last night Rob so I stayed with you. I was so worried" she explained. "I think you should stay home today Rob, you're not very well. I'll run Caroline to work." I sat on the edge of the bed. What the hell is going on? I couldn't understand why I am so ill I made my way into the kitchen and heard Katie's mini start and leave. I sat at the kitchen table, holding my head when I heard the door open, it was Sam. "What's going on Rob Caroline informed me you're drinking heavily last night." Sam saw the nearly finished bottle of Bacardi on the draining board. She went over and removed the top and smelt and tasted. "I recognise that smell and taste. Something been added Rob. You're being doped, reminds me of a product we use to calm horses." "All I can remember is going dizzy and being shown pictures. The rest is just fuzzy. I woke up this morning and Katie was in my bed," she said. I'd been ill all night? "She stopped with me." Sam was furious. Sam went into Katie's bedroom and switched on her laptop. "Do you know the password Rob?" I shrugged, "Try her date of birth," the password worked.

"Oh my God!" Sam shouted. "Look what they're doing to you, playing with you." Sam then went into Outlook and found messages from someone who wanted to purchase more photos. "Sam please calm down, it's bad for the baby." "The little bitch has got a scam going. No wonder you can't remember what's going on, the tranquiliser can be lethal to humans if not handled in the correct dosages." "Katie would know what to do Sam." "No, she wouldn't Caroline would though." Sam deleted all the photo files. "Better still." I voiced. I grabbed the laptop and threw it on the log burner. The laptop melted and burnt furiously. Sam packed Caroline's clothes, "I'll deal with her. You will have to deal with Katie." Sam held her tummy. "Are you feeling okay Sam?" "I will as soon as I've sacked that little bitch. I can't say anything to my father. He would have her thrown in jail, which would then involve us." I carried Caroline's case out to the range Rover. We kissed and she left. I went into the kitchen and emptied the Bacardi bottle down the drain. I was totally shocked. How could Katie become involved in producing pornography I wondered? I checked the other bottles of Bacardi, none of the tops had been touched nor had the Coke. I sat in the front room, sipping my coffee, trying to comprehend what had taken place. I looked across to the wood burner. The laptop had disappeared into oblivion. Katie returned ignored me and went straight into her bedroom, closing the door she almost immediately came straight out. "Where's my laptop Rob?" I pointed to the log burner. "No, oh no. Why?" "You know why, Katie." "Fuck you!" She stormed out of the cabin and drove off. She returned some hours later with a brand-new laptop went straight into her bedroom and slammed the door. In the meantime I had disconnected her Internet connection from her bedroom. She was totally up the creek without a paddle until I could get assurances, from her that she would never become involved in such activities again. I hadn't been as clever as I thought my modem was in the next bedroom and of course she could run her new laptop off Wi-Fi connection. Sam phoned, "Hello you." Those two words always made me smile. She continued "I have some good news baby and I are fine. They are very pleased with the scan results. Have you spoken to Katie?" Sam enquired. "She's in her bedroom." I explained "I'm waiting for her to come out and face me, which she will have to do sooner or later." "I, had to explain to father why I'd sacked Caroline. He understood the situation totally and agreed with my decision. He sends you his best wishes and hopes to see you soon," we said goodbye. I guessed I'd be cooking my own tea this evening. I made myself a cheese sandwich and a drink and settled down to watch television. Katie came out of her bedroom naked and went straight into the kitchen, made herself something to eat and return to her bedroom without acknowledging me whatsoever, just like her mother, I thought she was different I sighed. Katie appeared from her bedroom, and sat beside me on the settee. Still, with no clothes on. I was waiting for the blazing row instead. Katie turned to face me. "Rob please before we start rowing. Let me explain. I became involved when my mother invited me at the age of thirteen to play with women and make easy money. There's a big market out there for pornography. I'm sorry, I allowed Caroline to dope you that was stupid on my part and I've always been a lesbian. My mother always professed. She would have never married you if she hadn't been pregnant with me and apparently you're so good in bed, I was curious. I bribed Caroline to agree to make it possible for me to understand what mother was talking about. If you were my real father, I wouldn't have considered what we did. You were the first male I fucked and the last. I had to find out. Now I knew what she meant. I'm packing my bags in the morning and moving out, I'll find somewhere in London to live."

I felt sick and disgusted. "Thank you for telling me Katie, I couldn't allow you to continue producing pornographic material in the cabin." "Okay Rob, I understand." Katie kissed me on the cheek and return to her bedroom. I could hear are starting to pack I really didn't want her to go. I'd looked upon her as my daughter for 18 years. Her mother had twisted her mind, turning her into a sex slave just to make easy money. I went to bed trying to think of a solution to the problem.

Katie asked. "Can I come in Rob?" Foolishly? I said "Yes." She stood by the side of the bed with nothing on. "What are you doing Katie to yourself?" "Please, Rob before I go make love to me properly. So I know what it's like to be really loved." "I can't Katie you're my daughter." "I'm not Rob," she said slipping into my bed. "Give me something to remember you by." It wasn't hard to become interested. She had a beautiful body and she knew how to use it. It wasn't many seconds before I was aroused making love, God I'll hate myself in the morning. I awoke to find Katie was already up and ready to leave I helped Katie load her belongings in the car. "I'm really sorry to see you go Katie." She smiled. "It's for the best Rob. It's for the best." She kissed me on the cheek. "Mother was a fool to let you get away." I watched her drive away knowing I'd probably never see her again. I sat on the porch and shed a few tears then went back inside. There was a faint knock at the door. I opened Caroline was standing there, she said timidly. "Please don't slam the door in my face. I'd like to explain what happened." I invited her in. She removed her fur-lined coat, exposing her see- through white blouse short pink miniskirt, we sat on the settee. She twisted around to face me sitting on the edge, revealing she wasn't wearing any underwear. She knew I could plainly see. "First I must apologise Rob. I shouldn't have done what Katie asked. You were in no danger; chemistry was my top subject at school. Katie wanted me to dope you, she said she'd never been with a man she'd always been a lesbian. Her mother had always told her you were brilliant in bed. She wanted to experience the feeling. Katie is in love with you and always has been. That's why she wouldn't go with another man." "This is becoming a sick conversation by the minute Caroline." I expressed feeling erection in my trousers. "Once you were virtually unconscious we removed your clothes so she could play with you. I added a different substance to insure you could maintain a good erection." "This is absolutely disgusting. Caroline whatever possessed you." "I don't know. It has ruined my career. I'm so sorry, I'm really lucky I didn't end up in jail Sam just sacked me. I suppose you won't let me see Johnny?" "Once he finds out what's happened. I don't think he'll want anything to do with you. Do you?" "No I suppose not. How I'm going to explain to my father? I've lost my job." "I don't know." Caroline stood up; remarking. "I'd like to make it up to you." She could see the bulge in my trousers. She stepped closer, knowing full well I was aroused. She unzipped my trousers and slid her hand inside holding me. I wanted to pull away. Reasoning they've had fun at my expense. Why shouldn't I get my own back? With her free hand She unbuttoned her blouse lifted her miniskirt up and placed my hand between her legs. We stood there for a while she knew I couldn't resist any longer and finally she lay on the floor and we made love. She was moaning and groaning with pleasure. "Oh my God, she said you are good, don't stop please don't stop." After about half an hour we dressed. She kissed me tenderly on the cheek smiled, walking off into the distance. Sam turned up an hour later in her range Rover. I explained to her what Caroline had said, in fact, it wasn't really Caroline's fault. Katie had bribed her. "Oh." Sam remarked, "nevertheless, she shouldn't have done it." "When Johnny comes back off holiday. I don't know what to tell him, I'll keep the details a bit vague." "I agree." "Sam how's my baby?" Fine she smiled. "The doctors said if we were really careful. We could have a little fling" Without another word being spoken. We went to bed. Oh God that feels so good Sam expressed. An hour later we dressed and made coffee. I was absolutely knackered.

I felt like Casanova. "Oh, you don't know how that felt Rob." "I do Sam I was there." She laughed. "You wait till I get rid of this lump I'll ride you hard every day like my horses." Sam returned home. We hadn't discussed where we were going to live when we were married I presumed it would be here and working on that principle. I started preparing timber to build an extension to my bedroom for a nursery. Sam phoned "Hello you. I've decided to give Caroline a second chance. I don't think she would have done what she did if she hadn't been coerced by Katie." "I'm inclined to agree with you Sam I just thought I'd let you know. "Sam, while you're on the phone. I presume we will live in the cabin when were married?" I asked nervously. "I thought we would live at Cranbury farm once the house was modernised." "Oh," I replied. "You don't sound very happy Rob about that" Sam queried. "I was going to build a nursery extension to the cabin." "I suppose that would work it just seems more sensible for me to live on the farm, I thought, let's not fall out over where were going to live, she concluded, we'll discuss it at a later date." "Okay Sam, bye." I suppose she was being practical and I was just being sentimental, the thought of leaving my log cabin, which I put my heart and soul into building. Didn't see much point in building an extension I looked across to my tired old Land Rover and decided it was time she was retired, her final journey would be to the nearest Land Rover dealership to find her replacement.

I looked round all the models on arriving. I selected the model I wanted in black. Having a few extras fitted towing hitch and winch. I paid for the vehicle there and then. They said it would be delivered within a week. I looked myself up and down, and decided I looked like a tramp. So I gave myself a refit. Jeans, T-shirts, coats by the end of the day. I had spent nearly £80,000 on myself for a change. I felt good when I arrived back at the cabin. Caroline was waiting. "I just wanted to say thank you, thank you so much." She smiled. "It wasn't my decision Caroline Sam employs you, just don't do anything silly again and don't be influenced by anybody." "I shan't." "How long have you stood here?" "An hour and a half, it doesn't matter, she said, shivering." "Come on, have a coffee with me I will drive you home." "There's no need Rob I can walk." She sat by the log burner warming hands and drinking coffee. I went into the bedroom to change and try on some of my new clothes, new boots, jeans, T-shirt, jumper, returning to the front room Caroline looked me over. "Nice." She exclaimed "you look smart." "Thank you." Caroline stood up and adjusted my jumper and removed the tags. She then slid her hand down the top of my jeans. "No Caroline." I said. She continued until I was aroused. I didn't want her to stop. We went into the kitchen, she sat on the table, opening her blouse and pulling her miniskirt up out of the way she opened her legs for me to see everything I just couldn't stop myself. She moaned with pleasure. "Keep going, keep going." She pleaded; you're wonderful she clung to my neck for dear life. I finally pulled away and she tidied herself, placing her hands at the back of my neck easing me to her lips she kissed me tenderly. We sat drinking coffee. "Caroline I won't say anything to Johnny when he comes home the end of the week; just let the last few days drift into history." "Thank you." She flung her arms around me kissing me on the cheek. I gave Caroline a lift home and returned to the cabin, feeling a little uncomfortable in my new clothes and what had transpired over the last few days. Johnny returned off holiday and had a good time. I explained to him about Katie, although not in great detail Caroline and Johnny continued their relationship.

My new range Rover arrived. I parked my old Land Rover up by the tractor, Johnny and I went for a spin in the new vehicle. He was well impressed. He said it was a right bird puller as if I really needed any assistance in attracting trouble. Sam was becoming very large only one month left before she would

Charmed Log Cabin: Enchanted Life

give birth. I'd had a few emails from Katie telling me she was okay and she had return to university to complete her education and was no longer involved in the smutty side of life. Sam came round to the cabin and waddled in holding her back. We kissed and she sat down. Johnny joined us at the kitchen table. Sam announced the house at Cranbury farm was now fully renovated and we could move in, Johnny voiced politely. "I don't want to live there. I want to stay here, dad." I sighed "I'd like to stay here too Johnny." Sam started crying becoming very emotional. "I can't live here with the baby. I need more room. I need to be near my business." Johnny and I looked at each other. I moved round the table and comforted Sam. "Okay I'll move." It broke my heart, saying that. Johnny suggested. "Why don't Caroline and I live here shack up together if she wants to?" "You're a little young Johnny." "That's bullshit, dad, I've been fending for myself for nearly a year." Johnny took his mobile from his pocket. "Hi Caroline, how do you fancy living with me in the log cabin just me and you okay, speak to you later." "She said yes, dad. Besides, you're only 2 miles down the track." Sam continued to sob. "I'm splitting the family up." Johnny reached across the table, holding Sam's hand. "It really makes sense Sam; especially now Caroline is pregnant. Oh shit." Johnny went very quiet, realising he let the cat out of the bag. Sam looked up. We both looked at Johnny. "What did you just say Johnny?" "Oh well, you might as well know; Caroline is pregnant. It's no good shouting at me. I took precautions it just didn't work for some unknown reason. Sam smiled." "I can believe you Johnny. I was not supposed to conceive and look what your dad did to me. Like father like son." She remarked. Sam asked, "How far along is she?" "About a month. I don't know really possibly before I went on holiday." I asked Johnny "How you going to support yourself son?" "I'll have to get a job dad." "He smiled but I do have wealthy parents," he chuckled.

Sam and I went to look at the refurbished house everything inside was beautiful. Sam had spent a great deal of money on furnishings the nursery had been painted in a neutral colour because we didn't want to know the child's sex until it was born. "What do you think Rob?" Sam said, observing my expression. "It's lovely Sam." The surrounding land had been seeded by contractors. The farm buildings had been demolished and new stable blocks built, including a large enclosed exercising yard. "I would give you a hug Rob, but I can't get close enough." She smiled. I kissed her on the cheek. We were just about to leave the house when Sam screamed in pain. Her waters had broken baby was on the way. I phoned for an ambulance and she was shortly taken into hospital. I stayed by her bedside while she gave birth a six-hour heart wrenching event. She gripped my hand so tight it went numb. Sam gave birth to a boy, the midwife quickly checked him over, although born slightly premature. He was healthy. Sam held him, "Meet your son Rob." The baby was then taken away while they moved Sam into the maternity ward. I informed Rupert, who was ecstatic with the news. We settled for the name Jonathan. Six weeks after Jonathan was born. Sam and I were married in a registry office. Rupert had organised the reception he had a large marquee erected and all the villagers were invited to attend. Johnny was with Caroline, who was just starting to show she was pregnant. I had sent an invitation out to Katie. I'd even tried phoning her but she didn't answer. I just hoped wherever she was, she was safe and happy. Sam and I moved in to Cranbury farm. Johnny and Caroline moved into the log cabin. Everything seemed to be going well. Sam and I were very much in love. I was working in the stable yard and I heard a scream and so did everybody else Caroline was laying on the floor in one of the stables a horse had kicked her she was rushed to hospital in an ambulance. Unfortunately, the injury caused her to lose the baby. Caroline was devastated and so was Johnny. Sam visited Caroline regularly in the cabin to check she was alright. Johnny had finished school and was applying to go in the Navy. He said it was a good job with plenty of prospects. Caroline said it was nobody's fault but her own she had frightened the horse unintentionally. Caroline was off work for nearly 3 months, convalescing and hoped to start back shortly. Although Sam wasn't very keen on the idea of me contacting Katie she could understand my concern for her welfare. We had tried emailing her and phoning without any success. Someone had purchased Jenny's house.

Being nosy. I spoke to one of the builders. "Hi, I used to live here." I said. "We're under contract," he said, "to renovate, someone's purchased it; in a wheelchair we'd been told. Make one room into a large nursery suitable for wheel chair access." "Oh, you know the name?" "Yes, I think it's a Miss Jones." "Strange that's the same name as mine." "It's a pretty common name." The builder replied and I left. I called in to see Caroline. "Where's Johnny?" I enquired. "We're not getting on very well Rob since I've lost the baby. He thinks it was my fault." "I will have a talk to him Caroline, that's ridiculous." "Would you like a coffee Rob? You stay there love, I'll make it." "No it's okay, I need to move around." We both went into the kitchen. I told her about the work going on where Katie used to live. "Miss Jones has purchased it apparently she's in a wheelchair. She has a child or going to have a child I think. Have you heard anything from Katie since she left?" "No Rob, she just went right off the radar." "I had a few emails but nothing else," I replied. Johnny came into the cabin. "Hi dad." He made himself a coffee. "I'm leaving in two days to start my training in Portsmouth." I felt sorry for Caroline. She was getting a raw deal. "I might move back in with my parents Johnny when you go." Caroline remarked. He replied, "Please yourself." "I need a word with you. Outside son." The smile vanished from his face. "What the bloody hell do you think you're doing son?" "I don't know what you mean, dad." "Yes, you do, why you are you blaming Caroline losing the baby?" "Because she is a stupid cow, she shouldn't have been in with the horse on her own. Anyway it's all over. As far as I'm concerned." He stormed off. I went back into Caroline she'd heard what had been said. "I'm coming back to work tomorrow Rob. I'll move back into my parents' house you can have the cabin back then." "No, you stay here. I don't mind. Don't let him bully you Caroline," I instructed, "you've got my phone number ring me if you have a problem." She rested her hand on mine and smiled. "Thank you Rob" I left and drove home. I sat by the fire, talking to Sam and explained everything to her. She voiced "I knew something was wrong Rob perhaps things will improve when he goes into the Navy. Absence make the heart grow fonder." She smiled and you've been away too long, husband." Jonathan started crying. Sam went and fetched him. "Who's that then?" she said to Jonathan, sitting him on my knee. He immediately stopped crying. "See you have that effect on everybody Rob. Every time you hold Jonathan he doesn't cry." She made him a bottle fed and changed him and put him back in his cot. We then retired ourselves. The following morning, I went to the stables. Caroline came to work; I enquired how she got here. "I walked." She said. "I need the exercise I put on a little weight." I thought for a moment, "You can have my old Land Rover to use it's only sat there doing nothing." Caroline smiled "You sure Rob?" "Absolutely." Sam arrived with her range Rover with Jonathan in the back. I explained to her. I was letting Caroline use my old Land Rover, she thought it was a good idea. I took Caroline home in the evening, gave the keys to Caroline to the Land Rover and she started the engine, to make sure it hadn't a flat battery, I returned to Cranbury farm.

Sam introduced me to the new nanny. Sam could see the expression on my face. So, she took me aside. "What's up Rob?" "You don't know Sam, do you? When did you suddenly decide you needed a nanny? Probably a lesbian that's all you ever employ I suppose I'm still just the bloody handyman and needn't be consulted about my son's welfare." Sam had never seen me lose my rag she was searching my face with her eyes. "I've just married another fucking rich girl, who thinks she can do what she likes," before she could respond. I jumped in my range Rover and tore off down the drive, like my arse was on fire. Sam continually rang my mobile I didn't answer. This was our first argument. Sam had miscalculated my response. I turn my mobile off completely so I couldn't be tracked. I drove some distance out of the village and saw my old Land Rover parked in a layby. I pulled over behind it. Caroline was sat inside, shivering and crying. She's had a blazing row with Johnny. She sat in my warm range Rover I gave my handkerchief and told her to dry her eyes. "I don't know what to do Rob. I really don't. I tried everything, with Johnny, he won't listen. He just keeps blaming me for the baby." "You're not the only one with problems tonight love." I explained to her what had happened between me and Sam. "She never took a nanny on without consulting you Rob?" Caroline gasped. "She doesn't have to work." "That's the whole point. Caroline, I'll take you for a drink." We left my old Land Rover in the layby and drove off about 25 miles away from the village. I pulled off into a pub called the Robin Hood way out in the countryside. We just stepped out of the range Rover. Caroline's phone rang. "It's, Sam. Caroline asked panicking. What shall I say? I bet she's trying to find out where you are." "Just say you haven't seen me." "Okay if you're sure, but don't you get me the sack." "Switch on speakerphone Caroline." "Hi Caroline .I've just spoken to Johnny. He said he's leaving for Portsmouth tonight. He said you've gone out in Rob's Land Rover." "Yes." "Have you seen Rob anywhere?" "No. If you see him Caroline, tell him to ring me, it's very, very urgent." "Okay," "see you tomorrow, bye." "Turn your mobile off, Caroline otherwise you can be tracked." She did as I requested we went inside the pub. There were many people inside. We sat in a secluded corner and had a few drinks. "Johnny has gone Rob," "I heard. He's a fool, you're a lovely girl." Caroline lent against my shoulder for a while. We left the pub as it closed. Caroline switched on her phone to see if there were any messages. There were none, we sat in the layby by my old Land Rover. "What are you going to do Rob?" "I think I made a mistake myself. Can I stay in the cabin tonight Caroline?" She thought for a moment. "Are you sure that's the right decision? Shouldn't you go home?" "No I'm not running back; let her sweat for a while. It'll do her good." "Okay, calm down," she said, rubbing my leg. Caroline jumped in the old Land Rover and drove back to the cabin I followed parking my range Rover out of view. We went inside. There was a note from Johnny on the table stating quite clearly he'd finished with Caroline. She burst into tears. "Why isn't Johnny like you? You've only ever shown me kindness even when I drugged you. You were nice to me." I smiled. "If I remember you were very nice to me too." She grinned. "I remember everything." She made a coffee and we sat at the kitchen table. "Don't move out Caroline. I own this property and I say who lives here," she reached across and held my hand. "You better go home tonight, Rob. If you stay here I know what will happen." "I hope so." I replied. We went into the bedroom. She removed her clothes and lay on the bed waiting. We made love like possessed people. I couldn't get enough of her. She forced her breast into my mouth, "don't stop." She wrapped herself around me like a snake and wouldn't let go. Finally, with exhaustion we lay on the bed, panting like a couple of old dogs trying to catch our breath then dressed. "Okay, I'll go back and face the music." I kissed her tenderly on the lips; "I'll see you at work tomorrow love." She smiled. "Thanks Rob. You made my night," she saw me to the door. "I said switch your mobile on. If you're ever afraid give me a ring. You are special to me." "Okay, thanks," she waved. I drove back to Cranbury farm. Sam came running out throwing her arms around my neck, crying. "Wherever have you been Rob? I've been worried sick I'm sorry Rob. I should have talked to you first I'm just so used to giving orders and making decisions. I don't think about anybody else." "I gathered that, I don't care what you do with the bloody horses, but what happens to Jonathan you will consult me on." She agreed. I sent the nanny away. I'll have to struggle on my own somehow I don't want my marriage to fail. "I didn't think you were coming back. I nearly didn't. I was so angry. I'm not a rich spoilt bitch." She said, escorting me back into the house. She poured two drinks, and then disappeared for a moment returning with not a stitch of clothing on, I'm still in good shape Rob. Even after having a baby look. I stood up facing her. She placed my hand on her large breast and she unzipped my trousers released my belt and eased me down onto the floor.

She caressed her breasts. Then, placed one hand behind my neck, forcing my mouth onto her breast within an hour we were in bed repeating what had happened downstairs. At work the next morning I saw Caroline went upstairs to have a coffee above the tack room. "How did you get on last night Rob?" "We sorted things out." "That's good," she said, placing a hand on top of mine. "How you feeling today Caroline?" Okay I suppose. "Keep your chin up girl. There's more fish in the sea than ever get caught." "I know," she said, kissing me. I heard Sam's range Rover come into the yard. She fitted Jonathan in the pram and started going round the yard. Caroline and I came down and out into the yard. Sam looked over to us suspicious, as she pushed the pram. "Everything alright Caroline?" she enquired. "Yes thanks Sam." "Any problems?" "No There's nothing to worry about all the horses are exercised the other stable girls are dealing with any other issues." "See Sam." I voiced "you're redundant, Caroline has everything under control." "She's a real professional. Sam snapped and how the bloody hell would you know Rob." Just then Jonathan started crying. Sam lifted him from the pram he still wouldn't stopped crying. I went over took him off Sam and he stop immediately. Caroline laughed and walked off. "This is bloody ridiculous." Sam said, "how come you can stop him crying and I can't?" "You don't seem very happy. Sam?" "No, you'd been drinking last night, yes.

I called into a pub before I came home I needed some Dutch courage." "Not only that, she implied, there was powder on your T-shirt." "It was probably when the barmaid threw me on the floor and ravaged my body." I joked. "It's not funny, Rob." "It could have come from anywhere. Sam." "Well, it certainly wasn't mine." "Are you accusing me of fooling around Sam?" "No, no, I know you're not like that." I took Jonathan over to one of the stable doors and let him touch one of the horses he gurgled. Then, the horse stuck its tongue out and licked him under the chin. Sam stood watching. "You shouldn't do that Rob. It's not hygienic" She remarked folding her arms. I put him back in the pram under the covers. "Go home Sam and look after your son if you're really bored." "We could always have another one." "Not on your life," she scoffed, "I'll never conceive again." "Caroline" I called. She came over. "Could you look after Jonathan for about half an hour?" "Yes," she said, looking puzzled. "His bottle is in the Range Rover we won't be long. Come with me Sam." I grabbed her hand pulling her. "You can't leave Jonathan with Caroline." Sam protested. "I can and I have." "Where are we going?" I dragged her all the way into back of the hay barn, opened her blouse uncoupled her bra and pulled her jeans off, threw her in the hay. "Stop it, stop it you devil stop it. No, don't stop keep going, that's wonderful." We were there for about half an hour. "If you've free time on your hands I'll give you someone else to look after." Sam tidied herself red-faced. "Go home and prepare yourself to be a mother again." "You're being ridiculous, Rob, there's no chance."

A month past and Sam was feeling sick in the mornings she went to the doctors, it was confirmed she was pregnant. She rang me at the stables. "Jonathan is not a year old and I'm pregnant again." "I told you Sam." I laughed. "I hate you," she said. "This shouldn't be happening." "I'll stop you wandering round the bloody stables." "I love you Rob." "I love you too Sam" "And you are still not having a bloody nanny. Okay?" I was rather concerned. It was a little early to conceive again and to be quite honest; I didn't think she ever would. The doctor insisted she didn't work. It was okay to look after Jonathan but that was it. Rupert was over the moon of course the Dragon thought it was ridiculous, but I think Dragon's days were numbered if Rupert had anything to do with it. Winter had return with a vengeance. Johnny had found digs in Portsmouth and never came back to see Caroline. She still lived in the log cabin and occasionally I would go over and cut some timber for her to keep warm and for cooking. I drove past the old six bedroomed house. I stop looking up the drive. I saw a mini that resembled Katie's, mangled at the top of the drive. I turned into the drive and parked outside the house.

Katie's new mini, or what was left of it! I knocked on the door. It opened automatically. There sat in a wheelchair was, Katie. I just stared in silence. "Hello Rob. Is that really you?" "Katie, I'm afraid so. How, what happened?" "Come on in Rob go into the sitting room." She wheeled herself in. "Would you like a drink Rob?" "Yes please. I'm stunned." "Can you help yourself from the cabinet?" I poured myself a Bacardi and Coke. "Would you like anything Katie?" "No thanks." I sat. "What happened?" "I had an accident;" "I can see that from the state of the car. I've tried to phone you. I've emailed you, you never answered." "No I thought I'd done enough damage. My grandparents offered me this house and had it altered so I and my son had somewhere to live." "Wow. Wow your son? You're married?" "No; just then another woman comes into the room. Can you bring Robert down please Jane?" "Jane was a young Filipino who obviously lived there as well." "You look very confused Rob." Katie spoke softly and quietly, "I hear you and Sam have a son too?" "Yes." Jane returned with a young boy, not much younger than Jonathan. Jane sat Robert on Katie's lap. She turned the baby round so I could see his face. She kissed him on the cheek. "Meet your father Robert;" my hand was trembling, trying to hold the glass steady. "Can I have another drink Katie?" "Help yourself, Rob." I poured myself another large one. "Yes, you are the father." "This is the present you gave me when I left. Luckily I didn't lose him in the accident, but it was touch and go. I won't be able to walk for a long time. But they do think eventually I will recover." "Would you like to hold Robert?" "Yes please." I reached over and sat him on my lap. He didn't cry. "Are you alright financially? Katie." "Yes, the bus hit me it was their fault. I'm quite wealthy, thanks. I would rather have not had the accident." "Are you going to tell Sam?" "No, this is our secret Rob; no one will know who the real father is only me and you." "Robert obviously feels safe with you Rob. Just like I always did." I stood up and carried Robert back to Katie and placed him in her lap. I kissed her on the cheek. "It's good to see you Katie. Can I tell Sam and Caroline?" "Yes, they'd find out sooner or later I'm living here, but Robert is our secret." Katie asked where Johnny is. "He joined the Navy he lives in Portsmouth at the moment but I'm sure he'll come this way soon." "I hope so I'd like to see him." "I'd better go Katie." "Call in anytime Rob bring Sam if she'd like to come, I'd like to see your son, Robert and Jonathan should meet." She passed me a card from the sideboard. "Here's my new number. I know you're dying to ask, Jane lives with me. I pay her to look after me and Robert." Katie followed me to the door. I bent down and kissed her on the cheek before I left. I drove straight back to Cranbury farm. Tears were streaming down my cheeks. Sam met me at the door. "What's happened Rob?" "I've just seen Katie." "What?"

"She moved back into the old house, she's in a wheelchair Sam." Sam put her hand to her mouth. "Oh no, what happened. I explained everything to Sam." "She has a son?" "Yes." "She's married then." "No." "Who's the father?" "I don't know I didn't bother to ask." I pulled myself together kissed Sam goodbye and carried on to work. I saw Caroline and told the story. We both went above the tack room to have a drink. "I can't believe it." "Neither can I poor Katie," Caroline expressed. "Should I go and see her Rob?" "I don't see why not she's all alone apart from the nanny she employs to look after her and the baby." "What has she called the child?" "Robert." "Oh God." Caroline had already twigged "It's yours." "No." "It is Rob. I was there; don't forget. You are the father. She was plastered in semen by the time she'd finished with you." "Don't say anything to anyone Caroline please." "No, definitely not. That incident, I would prefer to forget, apart from when you laid me she smiled. I will never forget your tenderness." "Okay Caroline. Someone could hear us." "We won't speak of it again. Rob I'm short of firewood could you pop round and cut some for me please. Perhaps you should show me how to use a chainsaw, and then I could do it myself." "No chance that's bloody dangerous I don't want anything to happen to you. I'll pop round later." "Thanks." I went back to Cranbury farm. Sam came out to meet me carrying Jonathan.

"I've seen Katie Rob." "Have you?" "Yes. I took Jonathan round for her to see. I saw Robert as well. She has really calmed down. I think Robert is little younger than Jonathan by a month or so." We both walked back inside the house. "I've got to nip over to the cabin." "Why?" "Caroline needs firewood I shan't be long." "Please be careful Rob I don't like chainsaws." "Caroline asked me to teach her how to use one I refused." "No. You mustn't show her Rob Sam insisted." I kissed her on the cheek and I drove off to the cabin. I Fuelled and oiled the chainsaw and quickly cut a load of timber, stacking it by the side of the cabin. Caroline came home just before dark, she left the other stable hands to finish off settling the horses for the night. "Would you like a coffee Rob?" "Please I'm freezing out here." We went inside the wood burner was very low I stoked it up increasing the heat in the building. I was worried about the plumbing. Caroline made a coffee we seated at the table. "Sam has been to visit Katie already." "You're joking." "No, she took Jonathan round to show Katie and she saw Robert." "This is going to explode on us, Sam's not stupid Rob." My mobile rang. "Hi Sam." "Hello you. Are you going to be long Rob? I'm just having a coffee with Caroline and fixing a plumbing problem. Okay, don't be too long please." "I haven't got a plumbing problem Rob?" "I know I just didn't want to go home to quick too face an inquisition." Caroline reached across and rubbed the back of my hand. "You're naughty, sit and watch the telly Rob." I must change I smell like a horse. Caroline disappeared, I heard the shower running. She came into the front room, wearing her dressing gown, drawing the curtains. "You better go Rob." "Yes, I suppose you're right." "I think there is some plumbing that needs attention," she said, dropping her dressing gown, we caressed for a moment and Caroline said, smiling, remember. She sat on the table. She clung to me for dear life as we made love. My phone rang again. I struggled to get it out of my pocket before it rang off. "Yes Sam?" "What are you doing Rob?" "I told you fixing a plumbing problem in the shower I'm coming home in the next five minutes." She rang off. I continued kissing Caroline on the neck until we had finished. "Thank you for fixing my plumbing Rob." Caroline smiled, "please come and inspect my plumbing anytime." Caroline kissed me on the cheek and then said "Wait a minute, there's lipstick on your face." I had a quick wash. "Is there any make-up on my T shirt?" "No, you're fine." I drove back to Cranbury farm. "Sam was waiting for me on the doorstep, inspecting me." "What's the matter?" I asked. "I'm just checking you out." "Why?" Just in case you have any make-up or lipstick on you. "If I have, it's from you or when I kissed Katie goodbye, this morning." "Keep your voice down. Jonathan's asleep." We sat by the fire. "Rob you don't think Roberts your son?" "No. Why?" "You know what Katie did to you and she has called the child Robert." "I shouldn't think so Sam." "I know it's not your fault it happened when you were drugged I know you wouldn't cheat on me." "Do you want me to try and find out for you Sam?" "Aren't you curious Rob?" "No, I've got you." She hugged me trying to unzip my trousers. "Hey, you can't do that in your condition." "No but I could play around." "Not tonight Josephine," I gave her a big kiss on the lips. "You need to rest and look after my son or daughter." "Oh, you are a spoilsport." "If you really want to know who the father of Katie's baby is, I'll take her out tomorrow night for a drink and meal see if I can find out for you." "Please Rob it's driving me crazy. What happens if it turns out to be mine?" " It won't affect us because it wasn't your fault. At least, we will know Jonathan has a half-brother." "You sure you can trust me. Of course," Sam replied. I phoned, Katie. "Hi Katie, would you like to come with me for a meal tomorrow night? Okay then 7.30 pm. See you then bye." "There you are your ladyship. Thanks Rob." I saw Caroline at work the next morning, explained to her. Sam was on the case. "I told you Rob, she wasn't stupid. How about if we come round to the cabin for a meal with you, Yes, I'd like to see Katie 7.30pm. I went to collect Katie. I rang the newly fitted doorbell.

Katie wasn't in a wheelchair. But on crutches, wearing a white blouse and tight jeans. "Where are we going Rob a local pub?" "I thought you might like to see Caroline again." "Yes, that would be nice." "She's cooking us a meal," "she is a good cook, Rob." "You know Caroline was pregnant. Living with Johnny and she lost the baby?" "No. I'll just be a bit careful round the subject of babies." "Sure." I helped her into the range Rover. "This is nice Rob not bad at all." We drove off to the log cabin. I carried Katie inside because it would have been difficult for her to walk on the loose stones. Caroline and Katie greeted each other with a big hug. Katie walked slowly into the kitchen using her crutches I pulled a chair out for her and she sat down. Caroline continued cooking. I poured Katie a large scotch and placed it on the table. "Thanks this is nice seeing everyone again. I thought you'd all tell me to sod off to be quite honest, I guess there's more to this meal than meets the eye? I suppose Sam suspects Robert is your son?" "You've hit the nail on the head." "Just tell her it isn't. Only we three know the truth;" "she said she's not bothered. She just wants to know if Robert is Jonathan's half-brother." Caroline served the meal. Absolutely beautifully cooked roast duck potatoes greens and all the trimmings. "Johnny was mad, leaving you Caroline you're the best cook I've ever come across." "It's a pity Johnny didn't feel the same way about me." "I'm sorry Caroline;" Katie said "things haven't worked out for you." "It doesn't matter Katie, there's nothing I can do. How long before you'll walk again?" Katie Caroline asked. "I don't know I may never walk properly again. I suppose Rob told you I lost my child." "Yes, so sorry." "Thank you. Let's get our stories straight now where did we all go tonight?" "Just say I invited you round Rob. Sam won't mind you came round here and it is the truth." "Yes, good idea. Caroline, this is like old times." Katie voiced "Thank you for the meal, Caroline, that was wonderful." We all moved into the front room. "We might as well just tell Sam Robert is my son." "No!" Katie insisted. "I don't want Sam thinking she can start and organise my son's life, especially if she proved you're his father. She might be out to get custody of him, especially in my condition and reputation." "That had never crossed my mind." I expressed. "Me neither" Caroline voiced pouring everyone another drink. "Okay then, who's the father?" "Just say I was at a porn party having sex with several men and I don't know who the father is, she'll believe that." "Plausible" Caroline said. "When I get home we'll see if she accepts that. I'll tell her we had to get you completely pissed before you told us the truth." "That sounds okay" Katie remarked. Katie started drinking heavily. "I haven't been pissed, she said, since I was last here and I haven't had sex since you banged my brains out the morning before I left, I thought you'd never stop." "He is good, isn't he Katie?" Caroline confessed. Katie looked surprised at Caroline's remark. "Hey, you two will you stop it." I smiled. "So Rob's been banging your brains out." "No" Caroline smirked. "You bloody liar" Katie said laughing. "I won't say anything. Don't worry life is too short to start a war I realise that after my accident. My son, that's the most important thing to me in the world, I know Rob wouldn't take him off me." "No Katie, don't worry about me. It is really good to see you again Katie." "Yes" Caroline agreed, "why did you have the mini put on your drive it will never be any good anymore?" "Just to remind me of how lucky I am. Could you help me to the loo Caroline?" "Yes of course Katie." I sat there drinking my scotch slowly. I couldn't have too much I had to drive home. I wondered where they got to I called out. You two okay? I had no reply. I thought I'd better investigate the door was open on my old bedroom, on the bed was Caroline and Katie, fondling each other. "You can go home Rob and talk to Sam, I'll take Katie home" Caroline said. I left them to it. I drove home it was 10.30.pm.

Sam greeted me inspecting me. "What have you found out?" "To start with we went to the cabin. Caroline offered to cook us a meal and once we got Katie pissed she confessed she'd been to a porn party and got screwed by several men and she doesn't know who the father is, she doesn't care." "Oh. Sam smiled. That's a relief;" she had swallowed the story hook line and sinker. "I just wish we could mess around; shall we risk it?" Sam asked. "Definitely not I want you to have another good pregnancy." "You thought the first one was good?" We went to bed and played around nothing too vigorous.

Time was marching on. Sam had reached seven months and started to lose a little bit of blood. She was rushed into hospital where they brought the situation under control, but she would have to stop there for a while. Katie came to the rescue, allowing her nanny Jane to look after Jonathan. He spent a lot of time with Katie and Jane, her nanny, while I continued working. Caroline decided she was going to move out of the cabin and move in with Katie, they had become an item. I visited Sam every night in hospital and occasionally brought Jonathan with me to see his mother. The doctors informed Sam and I this would be the last child she could have her internal organs would not stand another pregnancy. We had a letter from Johnny saying the Navy didn't suit him and he'd gone to live with his grandparents in South Africa, which rather upset Sam and me. Katie was now just using a walking stick, rather than crutches. She had purchased herself a new car, a free lander, which was easier for her to get in and out of. I said goodbye to Sam in the hospital and drove home to Cranbury farm. Katie phoned to say Jonathan had gone to sleep and she didn't want to disturb him. He could stay the night with Robert. She was coming round to discuss one or two things with me. I poured myself a drink sat in front of the fire, realising I had been nothing but a disloyal bastard to

Sam. The tears ran down my cheeks I'd had a few by the time Katie arrived, Caroline came too. I let them in. They could see I was extremely upset, they sat either side of me on the settee trying to comfort me. Caroline made me a strong coffee. Katie held my hand. "This is probably not the best time to ask. Caroline and I have been talking. I'd like another child." "No, I've done enough damage. I have to live with my conscience, which I'm struggling with at the moment, find another man." "Yes, that would be very simple Katie professed. I've loved you Rob all my life in my own twisted way. I don't want just any man's child inside me, it must be yours." "I'm flattered Katie, but I just can't." "Robert is your son she said firmly. Give him a brother or sister?" "Go to a sperm bank. They will have hundreds of suitable men." Katie looked across to Caroline for ideas. Caroline confessed, "I'm pregnant again it's yours. The one I lost the first time round was yours." "What Caroline." I said in disbelief. "If you don't give Katie another child, I will have to inform Sam you've been fucking me at the cabin and carrying your child." I protested. "You wouldn't do that Caroline surely, please." "Katie removed her clothes and lay in front of the fire I lay on top of her. "Be gentle Rob I'm not completely healed. Oh God, I remember that feeling when you're inside me, lovely." Katie dressed and kissed me on the cheek. "Thank you Rob," Katie said as they left. I went and showered, almost tearing my skin off. I felt disgusted with myself for being such a pushover. I didn't want to lose Sam. I was trapped in my own stupidity. Sam had been in hospital for nearly a month. She was now eight months pregnant. The doctors decided to induce Sam rather than let her try and go the full term. They feared for her health and the baby which turned out to be a girl on delivery, perfectly formed and very healthy.

The surgeon made sure she couldn't conceive again. We named our daughter Christina after her deceased mother. I avoided visiting Katie after what took place. Caroline had resigned from the stables and Jane the nanny had gone. Caroline took over the position of nanny and lover. Sam had engaged another woman to manage the stables under her supervision 25 years old, blond. Her name was Jackie. Sam and I were getting on extremely well. Jonathan was becoming quite boisterous and Christina had her mother's hair and complexion. I occasionally went to the log cabin just to maintain and stop it falling into disrepair. I move my old tractor back to Cranbury farm along with the Land Rover. Johnny had met someone in South Africa and was considering marrying her. He'd said in the last letter I received out of the blue. I had a phone call from Katie asking if I would call in. I reluctantly went round. Her mini had gone from the drive finally scrapped I presume I knocked on the door. Caroline opened she was showing quite a bump. "Hi Rob, please come in." I went through into the sitting room. Katie was sat by the fire in the armchair with her walking stick propped against the arm. "Hi Katie." "Hello Rob." You wanted to speak to me. "Sit down Rob please." Caroline had gone upstairs. I could hear her playing with Robert. "Would you like a drink Rob?" "No thanks. Let's get down to business." "Oh, she exhaled, you're still angry with me aren't you?" "What did you expect Katie?" "I know." She started to cry. "I don't think you will ever forgive me." "I doubt it not after you threatened to ruin my marriage for your own selfish gains." "Well I'm being punished now Rob." "What do you mean?" "I've been diagnosed with cancer if they can't stop it they think I have two years left maximum, just long enough to bring my new child into the world." "Oh God," I embraced her. "I'm sorry Katie." We held each for a moment. Then I returned to my chair. "You have nothing to worry about. Caroline will look after Robert and the new baby. I'm making sure she is left sufficient funds when I pass on; if I do, of course." "I'd like that drink now please Katie." "Help yourself Rob." I poured myself a large Bacardi and Coke. "As much as you probably hate me Rob. I've loved you always and wanted to marry you but I know you would never have accepted me. All I'm asking you to do if the worst does happen. Help Caroline as much as you can, she loves you like I do." Caroline came into the room. "Robert has gone to sleep" she remarked, sitting on the settee. I looked over to her. "How you feeling Caroline?" "I'm okay thanks Rob. I suspect you don't like me either after what happened." "To be quite honest Caroline, if I wasn't married to Sam, I would have married you." She sat back in astonishment. "Why?" "I don't know, there's just something about you that attracts me." "Thank you Rob that's nice to hear." "That doesn't mean it excuses what you've done, the pair of you." "Can we please all be friends Rob?" Katie exclaimed, "let's make the most of what time we have left together." "Okay. I'm going to have a boy Rob." Caroline informed me, "I'm going to call him Julian because that's your middle name." "Please don't tell anyone Rob about my condition" Katie asked. "I just hope they can stop the cancer before it destroys me or harms my baby. "We met Sam the other day in the shop. She enquired. Who was the father of my child I told her I'd had artificial insemination," Caroline commented. "I don't think she believed me and I don't think she is convinced Robert isn't your child Rob. I know that, she has no proof to disclaim your stories." "Let's hope it remains that way for everyone's sake." I said goodbye to them both and left driving on to the stables.

 Jackie had just fallen off her horse and was limping back into the tack room. She removed her boot as I entered. "You okay Jackie?" "Yes, just hurt my ankle. That bloody horse doesn't like me. When training police horses I had my ankle trapped between a bus and the horse. It weakened my ankle. I have to strap it sometimes." "Oh, I didn't realise you worked for the police." "It was no fun" she smiled removing her sock. "Would you like a cuppa I offered?" "Yes, why not Rob?" We went upstairs to the top of the tack room. "You have a log cabin don't you Rob?" "Yes, I used to live there before I married Sam." "Yes, the girls were telling me all about what happened to you. Not a very nice experience. I should imagine" she said, placing a bandage round her ankle. "Would you like me to help?" "Thanks." I wrapped the bandage round taping it. "The reason I mention the cabin I'm looking for somewhere better to live. Would you consider renting it to me?" "I'll have a word with Sam when I get home it's out in the middle of nowhere." "That's even better, somewhere I won't be hassled." "It hasn't been lived in for quite some time Jackie." "I thought you owned the land and the cabin." "I do." "Why do you have to ask Sam?" "I don't really, just trying to keep the peace." "Oh, you're under the thumb." "No I'm not." I helped put her boot back on and we finished our coffee. "I'll see you tomorrow Jackie." "Okay, don't forget to discuss the cabin with Sam" she smirked. I went home thinking about Jackie I was unsure of her. I spoke to Sam. "Jackie is interested in living in the cabin. What do you think?" Sam shrugged her shoulders. "Up to you Rob you own it."

Christina was crying. Sam brought her into the living room, plonking her on my knee. She stopped crying immediately. "See you do bloody nothing and she shuts up, here you can feed her." "Okay." I sat there holding Christina and the bottle, and then patted her back. She burped, she was fine. "Do you want me to put her in her cot?" "No I'll do it." Sam returned to me. "You don't like Jackie do you?" "I don't know; you're not going to tell me she's a bloody lesbian?" "No." You actually employed a straight girl?" She punched me on the arm. "You have a thing about lesbians." "I should have I married one." Sam smiled. "I'm not a lesbian any more, stop branding me." " I'll tell you what I do fancy branding" Sam exclaimed, removing her clothes, laying on the rug in front of the fire. "Come on then, big boy" she smiled, "show me what you're made of?" "My pleasure your ladyship!" We played around for an hour or so then went to bed. I arrived at work early the next morning Jackie came straight over to me. "Well can I can't I? I want to get out of those bloody digs theyre a nightmare." "Okay, but you will have to give me a couple of days to get everything working down there again." "Okay, that's great." She kissed me on the cheek. "What's that for?" "Because I wanted to" she said. "You always do what you want to do?" "Absolutely!" she winked. Jackie walked off and went round the corner. Jasmine came running out, a young stable girl. "Mr Jones could I speak to you privately please?" "Yes, let's have a coffee." "No, I dare not if Jackie catches me." "Don't worry about Jackie." We went up into the tack room and I made Jasmine a coffee. "Please don't repeat this. I don't want the sack I love it here." She took out her mobile phone and showed me a video of Jackie whipping Sam's favourite horse. "What's she doing that for Jasmine?" "She blamed the horse for her falling off yesterday. It wasn't the horse's fault it was hers. She hit him so hard he started to bleed." "Leave the coffee, jump in my Range Rover." On the way through the village I saw Jane Katie's old nanny. I pulled over. "Hi Jane" She smiled. "Can I give you a lift?" "No thank you Mr Jones I'm catching the bus trying to find myself a job." "You may have one Jane, jump in my car." I carried on home to Cranbury farm. Sam came out to meet me. "What's up Rob? Why is Jasmine with you? What's going on?" "You know you said you wanted a nanny?" "Yes." "Here's a very good one!" "Why?" Jane took the children. "Come with me Jasmine and you Sam." We all went into the lounge. "Show Sam." Sam watched the video placing her hand over her mouth. "Oh no, what she doing? the silly woman." Jasmine then told Sam what had taken place. "My poor horse, father purchased him for me." "Now Sam, if you don't sack her I'm leaving the stables." Sam quickly put her riding gear on. Jasmine looked across to me a slim girl with dark brown hair and a freckled complexion. "Mr Jones, everyone at the stables is scared of Jackie. Nobody likes her. She even hit me with the whip." Jasmine showed Sam the mark. Sam remarked, "Thank you jasmine, for bringing this to my attention and don't worry, she'll be gone in a few minutes." I took Sam back to the stables. Sam showed Jackie the video then went to look at her horse. She could see the scarring on the horses back. "You are dismissed Jackie get off my property." Jackie went to her car and disappeared down the road. Sam threw her arms around my neck. "If you only knew how much I love you Rob." Jasmine blushed. Sam put her arm round Jasmine. "If you can ever find a man like him, marry him, but this one's mine." she smiled. She continued, "That reminds me, Mr Jones. What was this you said about taking on a nanny without discussing it with me first?" "Okay, I'm really sorry I could see how unhappy you were at home and missing the stables. I thought you could combine the two." "Definitely."

Sam went in to her horse Freddie and gave him a pat on the neck. "Jasmine," Sam called out. "Can you fetch some cream for these wounds?" "Yes, Mrs Jones." She returned within a few minutes. Sam treated her horse. Sam called out "Does anyone know where Vicky is?" "Here Sam." "I know you're only 18 Vicky, but you're very clever and good with my horses. Will you take charge for the time being, until I decide what I'm going to do?" "Yes, Sam." "You know my mobile number. Don't be frightened to ring if you have any questions." "Okay," Vicky's smile broadened. "Don't let me down, Vicky." "No Sam, I promise." "I will be checking" Sam smiled. "I know," Vicky said, running down the yard. We drove back to Cranbury farm to see Jane playing with the children in the living room. Sam placed her arm around my waist, watching through the window. "You don't know how happy you've made me today Rob." We hadn't been home long before the phone rang, a horse had kicked the door off one of the stables, Vicky had informed Sam. "No rest for the wicked, Rob can you go sort it out. I want to stay and talk to Jane," "Okay. I'm on my way." "Wait a minute," I turned round and she kissed me very passionately on the lips, "Okay, you can go" she smiled. I drove back to the stables quickly. Sure enough, there on the floor was the stable door. It didn't take too long to repair. Jasmine came over, "Mr Jones." "Call me Rob Jasmine everybody does." "Okay thank you." "Would you like a cup of coffee?" "Yes please." Jasmine ran off and made a coffee I joined her above the tack room. Vicky also came up, Vicky remarked Jackie was evil. "She treated the horses horribly Rob." "I saw for myself Vicky. You should have come to me sooner girls you're not here to be punished or frightened. If you ever see anything you don't like. You report to me or Sam and we'll sort the problem out." "Okay thanks Rob" they both expressed and gave me a hug. "Don't let Sam see you do that" I smiled. They giggled and return to work. I phoned Sam. "How are you getting along with Jane?" "She is marvellous; Jonathan loves her to bits so does Christina. I have a present for you when you come home." "What is it?" "Wait and see." I returned home sometime later I went into the dining room and we sat down to tea. Sam made a lovely roast with all the trimmings. "With your approval of course she smiled across the table I have asked Jane to move in." "Yes, that's a good idea. She's a nice girl. Where's my present?" "After tea be patient otherwise you wait longer." I helped Sam put everything away. She took me outside to the barn. She opened the door and there stood my old tractor completely overhauled and re-sprayed almost look like it had come out of the factory. "Wow. Sam" I remarked, looking round. I placed my arm around her waist and we walked back to the house. The children were asleep Jane had obviously tired them out. We lay in bed together, holding each other. Sam remarked "I wish I could give you another child." "Why?" "Because I love you so much." "I'm happy the way things are Sam I have you and that's the most important thing." I then remarked "I don't want a floppy saggy wife thank you, I like everything firm. I squeezed her breast." "I hope you're going to keep going now Rob, now you've started." "You try and stop me." "As if I would" she giggled. I slid my hand down her thigh . . .

Now that Jane had taken charge of the children, Sam could spend more time organising the new stables, Vicky was doing very well keeping control of the old premises. Vicky asked me if I would consider letting her and Jasmine rent my log cabin. I consulted Sam and she didn't see any reason why not. I went and checked the cabin out lit the wood burner turned the water on and checked everything out. I spent half a day with the chainsaw restocking the firewood pile. Vicky had her own little car her grandfather had purchased for her. Vicky and Jasmine could travel to work together. They paid a small amount of rent out of their meagre wages. Finally, the cabin was alive again.

Sam received a phone call at 9pm from Vicky. The power had gone off in the cabin. Vicky asked if I would have a look in the morning. I said to Sam if there was an electrical short because a squirrel has eaten through a cable it may cause a fire. I'd better check now, she agreed entirely. "Don't forget to take your torch Rob." Sam phoned Vicky back to tell her I was coming over. I made sure I got all my electrical equipment in the Range Rover. When I arrived Vicky was standing in the doorway in her PJ's, holding a torch. I went inside checked the fuse box. I replaced a fuse and the electric supply came back on. "Thank you Rob, sorry we bothered you, can I get you anything?" "I'll have a coffee with you before I go back home. Just in case it blows again then I know it's something else." "Okay". I sat by the old wood burner my favourite place, Jasmine came into the room. She'd stayed in bed reading a magazine with a torch. Vicky returned with my coffee. "How do you like living here girls." Jasmine remarked. "It's nice Rob its cosy and our parents aren't breathing down our neck." I waited for half an hour, had the girls switch every light on in the cabin just to make sure the fuse wouldn't blow again. "I take it you girls are an item." They looked at each other. "What you mean?" They asked grinning. "You know what I mean." "We're not saying anything Rob we're just good friends." "Would you like another coffee before you go?" Vicky enquired. Just then the fuse blew again. "Bloody hell" I said. I checked the fuse again. This time the trip switch. Jasmine got too close to the wood burner and her nightie ignited burning rapidly. Jasmine screamed. Without hesitation I ripped her nightie off burning my hand slightly. I stamped the flames out on the floor. She ran into the bedroom and grabbed her dressing gown. She returned moments later. "Are you burnt anywhere Jasmine?" "My side I think." "Would you mind if I had a look I have my first-aid box in the Range Rover?" I ran out and got it and returned she lay on her side on the settee, Vicky watched. Jasmine had a slight burn on the top of her hip. I put some cream on. Jasmine then sat up and put her arms around me embracing for security. "Thank you, thank you. I could have been burnt really bad."

"Yes, Vicky voiced you're our hero." "That's a valuable lesson girls watch your clothing around heat, especially if it's inflammable material." I returned to Cranbury farm and sat by the open fire with Sam. "I forgot to mention Rob, Mary, the Vicar's wife, came round today. Oh yes. Apparently her husband's been looking through the archives and where you built the cabin used to be an old barn." Sam laughed continuing, "apparently witches used to meet their and sacrificed children back in the dark ages. The building was burnt down by the locals." "So you think I'm a Warlock then Sam?" I laughed. "No, don't be silly. The legend has it. Whoever lives there is supposed to be charmed and get what they want." "Don't tell me you're taking up witchcraft Sam." "It makes you think Rob. We have had a lot happen lately."

What happens next is another story.

CHARMED LOG CABIN
AND WHITE WITCHES

ROBERT S. BAKER

Proglogue

Two uneventful years passed, everything ticking along nicely, Johnny was still in South Africa. Katie had beaten the cancer problem and had given birth to a girl named Nicky. Caroline had not been so fortunate. She miscarried again because of the internal injuries she suffered from the horse kicking her. Vicky and Jasmine were still in the cabin. Jonathan and Christina were doing well. I finally thought my life had settled. I spent more time at Cranbury farm working around the new stable block. Sam on the other hand, shifted between the two regularly, trying to keep control of everything.

Chapter 1

Discovery

I drove over to the old stables where Mr Goldings lived I could see Sam's range Rover parked up and I Started looking for her. I peered staring into the shadows of the empty stable to see her with another woman kissing each other. Sam looked over the woman's shoulder and saw me. The horror on her face at realising I'd seen something, will live with me for the rest of my life. "Rob please" Sam called out in despair. I felt a pain in my chest and the next I remember is waking up in hospital partially paralysed down one side. According to the doctors I'd had a mild stroke. Sam was sitting by my bedside I just glared to her, she was crying. "I'm so sorry Rob I'm so sorry she was just an old friend. We weren't doing anything really". The doctor could see I was upset and he asked Sam to leave. Katie came in to see me, just needing a walking stick to move around. My speech slurred but I managed to get Katie to understand what I'd seen and what had caused my stroke. I asked her to make sure the cabin was free. I wasn't going back to Cranbury farm I was going home. Katie offered to have me at her house. "No thanks". Katie asked the doctors to stop Sam getting near me, those were my instructions. Finally, with the aid of a walking stick I left the hospital. Katie collected me with Nicky asleep in the car and we returned to the cabin. Katie had told Sam to find other accommodation for her staff, effective immediately. Katie had gates assembled at the end of the drive. Sam tried to phone me but I blocked her phone calls and I wasn't answering the home phone. Even Rupert had tried and I blocked his number too. Katie helped me into the cabin. I gave her a key for the gate so she could come and help me or Caroline. I was still weak down my right side. Katie stoked the wood burner and made me a cup of coffee "What you going to do Rob?" "Live on my own, Katie" I slurred. "Sam said she wasn't doing anything Rob. You knew she was a lesbian before you married her" "I know Katie I don't learn do I love". She crouched down by the side of the armchair and gave me a hug. Caroline came in with Robert. She placed him on my knee because he was being grisly he stopped immediately. "I wish I knew how you did that Rob" Caroline remarked, continuing. "Robert looks exactly like you Rob." "I'm taking Robert home. Caroline you stay with Rob ensuring he's okay. I can manage on my own tonight" she said. Taking Robert off my lap "I must go, Nicky's asleep in the car." "Would you like me to stay Rob?" Caroline asked. I shrugged my shoulders. Caroline glanced towards Katie. "I'm not going to leave him in this state Katie" "No Caroline don't I don't trust him he may do something stupid". Katie left with Robert. "What would you like to eat Rob?" I held her hand "No thank you." Just then the door burst open and in ran Sam crying. She dropped to her knees in front of me "I'm so sorry Rob I am so sorry". She said hysterically "please forgive me" She tried to hold my hand I managed to say ".You betrayed my trust you were the one person in my life I trusted." Caroline helped Sam to the settee where she continued to sob. "You will have to give him time" Caroline remarked. "Don't you want to see your son and daughter Rob" she cried. I shook my head Sam cried even more. "Give him a few days Sam I'm sure he will come round he's all mixed up. I don't think you realised how much he loved you he worshipped the ground you walk on". Sam tried to kiss me on the cheek and I moved away. She went out of the door holding her head. "Caroline, will you collect my range Rover from the stables. If Sam gives you any trouble phone the police, I own the range rover it's nothing to do with them."

    Caroline collected my range Rover she went to Cranbury farm and bring back some of my clothes. Although Caroline did say Sam was crying and didn't want to give her anything. She also asked when I'd be coming home. Caroline told me she told Sam not soon the way I'm looking. Caroline used my range Rover to collect the shopping. Katie had decided she could manage on her own with Robert and Nicky. Katie had decided it's best if Caroline stayed with me until I was well enough to manage. Rupert had paid me a visit and apologised for his daughter's behaviour and what she'd done. Although she was his daughter he's ashamed of her behaviour. He hoped I would recover soon and consider giving Sam another chance he said. "She will not make the same mistake twice you have my word on that Rob". Caroline would sleep with me and we never played around I was just not interested. She held me close reassuring me that everything would be okay in the end. She cooked and cleaned and catered to my every need. I was sitting watching television. Caroline had made me bacon sandwiches and we sat down together. "I wish I had married you Caroline I don't think you would have cheated on me." "I don't know Rob a lot has happened everyone has made mistakes." "I'm sorry you lost the baby." "It's punishment Rob for all my sins and there'd been a few" we both smiled. I was beginning to talk properly, recovering rapidly. The doctor thought it would take longer before I'd be mobile. I kissed Caroline goodbye and thanked her for helping me when I was in need of a friend. Katie came to collect Caroline she had brought Jonathan and Christina plus Robert and Nicky with Jane the faithful nanny. Jonathan ran over and grabbed my leg. "daddy." I held Christina in my arms and give her a big kiss on the cheek. Robert looked on rather left out so I bent down and cuddled him, a tear came into Katie's eye. Katie watched the way Robert clung to me as if he knew I was his father. Nicky was still in the car seat in the back of Katie's Free Lander. I went over and touched her face she smiled. Katie said "come on we must go back now leave Rob to rest." I kissed all the children once again and watched them disappeared down the track.

Chapter 2
The truth

Katie padlocked the gate. Mr Goldings had to walk to the cabin he knocked and walked in. "Can I please talk to you Rob?" "Yes, take a seat". I owe you a lot Rob, you saved my life you turn my lesbian daughter into a mother which I thought would never happen. I'm ashamed of what's taken place." "It's not your fault Rupert." "No but it feels like it. Sam is in a state Rob she doesn't know what to do to make it right. Please talk to her give her chance to explain, she's banned from the stables. She's stuck at home I own everything and I say who comes on my property and who doesn't. I told her to stay at home and think about what she's done. Even Mrs Goldings is disgusted. If her real mother was alive she would kill her." "How did her mother die Rupert?" "Oddly enough a car accident similar to mine no one there to help her get out before it was too late." "Oh, I'm so sorry for you Rupert". He patted me on the shoulder standing up. "I'm going now Rob, just let Sam give you her side of the story please before you throw the towel in." "Okay Rupert." Rupert left. Sam knocked on the door a while later and let herself in. She looked physically ill as if she hadn't eaten for a month. "Would you like a cuppa Sam "No, she said." "You might as well I'm having one." "Okay then" she replied nervously. I made us a cuppa I sat in my armchair by the log burner. Sam sat on the settee with her head bowed slightly, clasping her hands resting on her knees. "Rupert's been to see me." "I know I asked him to." I could see the tears dripping down onto her knees. "Okay" I sighed. "Let me hear your side of the story." "I don't know where to begin." "I've heard that sentence before Sam from Jenny when she was lying just tell me the truth". I had no sympathy in my voice. "The woman you saw me with is an old girlfriend. She didn't know I was married I was just giving her a hug and a kiss goodbye then I saw you. I haven't been having an affair and I never will" She explained, "I told her I had two children and before I had chance to finish explaining to her. You saw me. I came running out and you had collapsed on the floor. I thought you'd had a heart attack I thought you were going to die Rob." "I wish I had." "Why?" "I don't want to live any more Sam." "Why were you in the stable with her if it was also innocent? You were my rock Sam my reason to live." "Don't say that Rob please I love you so much. The reason we were in the stables was in case father saw me with her he would have gone mad. She turned up out of the blue Rob. If I'd known she was coming to see me. I'd have told her not to bother." "I think I want to be on my own." "Don't say that Rob please I don't want to lose you." She came over and knelt by my chair holding my hand. "There's something else you should know Rob as well." I sighed "Go on" "I know Robert's your son." "How do you know that?" I started to feel pain in my chest again as the stress of the moment attacked my soul. Perhaps my wish was going to be granted and I was going to escape deceit and deception. Sam clung to me for dear life "Don't die Rob, don't die please." "My pills." Sam ran into the kitchen coming back with my pills and glass of water. I took a pill and the pain eased. "You haven't answered my question Sam" She said nervously "Jane told me." "That's the only proof you have?" "Jane said you've been round to see Robert." "No I went round to see Katie She had been diagnosed with cancer." "Oh, I didn't know" She burst into tears. "They removed the tumour with keyhole surgery." "Oh, I'm sorry Rob I didn't know." "No, Katie didn't want anybody to know and I would prefer you not to mention it again." "There was also talk of you being the father of Caroline's child." "That's true I fuck her twice a week and once on Sunday's just for good measure I laughed. "While you're on a roll Sam where did you get that information from?" "Just talk around the stables." "That's all you have to go on I don't think your father would be very pleased with you jumping to conclusions without evidence." "We're not speaking at the moment not much anyway." "I know he's rather annoyed with you Sam" "That's an understatement Rob please come home if not for me for the children they miss you terribly." "While we are on the subject who else am I fucking around the stables?" "Nobody Rob honestly, nobody I can't help myself I love you so much." "It looks like it I suspect if I hadn't caught you in the stable with that woman she'd have had your knickers off in two minutes." "I will never ever see her again Rob." "I'm going to bed Sam." "Can I come with you?" "That's not a good idea Sam." "Please just let me lay beside you the children are safe at home with Jane." I sighed "I'd like another coffee first." "I'll make it" Sam said rushing into the kitchen. I thought to myself perhaps I should have just owned up to everything but it was Katie's wish that Robert was kept out of this situation altogether. I did feel sorry for Robert and thought he was getting a raw deal. Sam returned. "There you are Rob." I sat beside her on the settee. She placed her arm around my shoulder and lent her head against mine.

"Please forgive me Rob I don't want to lose you." I didn't answer I didn't know what I wanted. I knew when I was in the cabin I was home it was mine. Sam remarked "Everyone misses you at the stables especially Jasmine and Vicky. " "I suspect they don't like it because they had to move out." "They were a little upset Rob but they understood you were ill and need complete rest although. I think they've been told what's happened because none of them look at me the same way anymore. I get the impression they're blaming me. Vicky and Jasmine want to know if they could come round to see you." "Yes that would be fine. They're nice girls or would you think I'd rip their knickers off." "No, don't be like that Rob I'm not accusing you of anything."

Chapter 3
Temptation

Sam came to bed with me and lay close by my side. She held me like it was the first time she'd ever held me. We kissed a little but we did nothing else she made breakfast before she left in the morning. I said "Just give me a few more days and I'll probably move back home." She clung to me like the world was ending. "I love you Rob I really do." She left with a broad smile on her face. The next morning, I went for a walk round the woodland. Summer was here, the bluebells were in bloom birds were singing and everything had come to life. I tried to start Johnny's old quad bike but the battery was flat. Around 5 o'clock I was sitting on the porch and heard people approaching. It was Vicky and Jasmine dressed identically in jeans and white T-shirts. "Hi Rob, how you feeling." They said together. "Hello girls nice to see you." They sat on the porch one either side of me. "Sam said we could come and say hello" Jasmine remarked. "I'm sorry you had to leave the cabin." "We understand Rob when you go back to live with Sam can we have it back please?" Vicky remarked. "You can move in now if you want to. I shall be stopping here for a little while longer." "Can we?" they exclaimed with excitement. They both kissed me on the cheek. "Here's the gate key." "We'll be back in a while just collect our clothes" Jasmine proclaimed. An hour later the girls returned, they'd gone shopping purchasing a load of groceries and a present for me a bottle of Bacardi and coke. "We know you like Bacardi we checked with Sam," "Does she know you're stopping here with me?" "Yes, she said it's okay, we could look after you." "She wasn't angry?" "No, she was very happy but she did warn me." Vicky confessed "You're only allowed one glass of Bacardi." "Oh did she" I smiled "yes." We all went inside, Vicky cooked the tea and we sat at the table "You're, a good cook Vicky." "I did start to train as a chef but I prefer horses Rob." After tea the girls both went and had a shower changed and returned to the front room in their PJ's, sitting either side of me on the settee I was watching television. Jasmine commented "I don't wear nighties any more after what happened last time." "Would you like a drink Rob" Vicky asked?

"Yes please I'll have a Bacardi and coke. I haven't had one for a long time." She ran into the kitchen and came back with a glass. "Don't you girls want one" "No thanks." "You're old enough aren't you?" Jasmine voiced, "I'm just 18 and Vicky's 19 we prefer white wine but only on weekends usually" they giggled. "We don't want to be prosecuted for being drunk in charge of a horse." I glanced across to the window saw Sam looking in She entered "Checking up on me Sam?" She went slightly red "No, well yes I want to check you're, okay." The girls stood up Sam indicated with the movement of her hand and voiced "You can sit down." Sam advised. "I've only let him have one glass Sam" Vicky assured. "When do I get the gate key Rob?" Sam enquired "When I get one cut I haven't a spare" Sam sat in my old armchair by the fire. "How are you feeling Rob?" "I'm okay just relaxing, Vicky made me a lovely tea." "Oh well if you're okay then" She said with a sigh. "I'll go home." She came across and kissed me on the cheek "Jonathan and Christina miss you Rob." "I know Sam let's not rush into anything please." "Okay." She went out of the door I stood up and went to the window I could see a torch shining on the crushed slate track as she made her way back to the road. Vicky voiced "excuse me for saying this Rob but I don't blame you everybody knows what happened around the stables. Nobody is really speaking to Sam. In fact, Mr Goldings has told me to ring him if she is found going around the stables." "Blimey." I remarked "He is upset." "You should have seen him arguing with Sam when he realised what had happened. I thought he was going to hit her he was so cross; you didn't deserve that sort of treatment Rob" Jasmine said fetching a bottle of wine opening placing two glasses on the coffee table. "Hey girls be careful don't drink too much its work tomorrow." "We know Rob." The girls finished off the bottle of wine it was 10 o'clock. "Well girls I'm off to bed I'll see you two in the morning." "Goodnight" they voiced. Around 11 o'clock the wind was howling and really blowing the trees. I heard an almighty crash, breaking glass. I got up quickly put on my pants, Vicky and Jasmine came out of their bedrooms. "What's happened girls?" "Something has just come through my window Rob" Vicky sobbed. Jasmine Started crying. I went in and looked at the damage a conifer branch had come through the window. "I'm afraid you girls will have to share tonight." "Can't we stay with you please Rob we are scared?" "You'll be all right in Jasmine's bedroom." "Please, that's really upset me;" Vicky voiced "Me too" Jasmine cried." We will be like sardines in my bed." "We don't care." We all went into my bedroom they slid into bed. One either side of me each turned to face me placing their arm across my chest for security.

Chapter 4
Explanation

6 am in the morning I awoke to Sam standing in the bedroom doorway with her arms folded and a face like thunder. The two girls were still sprawled all over me. "What's going on here then?" "Nothing we had some problems in the cabin last night a branch come through Vicky's window. The girls were scared half to death." The girls were rubbing their eyes and scurried out of the bedroom. Sam went and had a look at the broken window. She looked the girls over seeing if their PJ's were still buttoned up correctly. I got out of bed when she returned to see me with my underpants on. "I don't think I'm coming back to the farm." "Why? I catch you in bed with two pretty girls and you expect me not to be suspicious?" Vicky and Jasmine return after dressing quickly. "He's telling the truth Sam we didn't do anything wrong." I dressed the girls made breakfast for us all. "Sorry." Sam voiced to everyone. "It did look suspicious." "We know" Vicky said. "Were not like that Sam, Rob is a good friend and he saved us twice now from being hurt." The girls left for work. "Why don't you check the bed Sam" "Do I have to?" "Yes I insist." I grabbed her by the arm pulling her into the bedroom throwing off the sheets of the bed. "There you are, examined carefully. I don't want you to miss anything." I'd had enough I wasn't guilty yet I was still under suspicion. "It's over Sam fuck off back to your lesbian bitch and let me get on with my life." She burst into tears "stop it Rob stop it. You're tearing me apart I can't help it I love you so much I don't want anybody else to have you. It's no worse than you accusing me of messing around with that woman and I wasn't" "Who knows if I hadn't turned up when I did she could have been licking your nipples?" I paused and sighed "Let's calm down we're getting nowhere." I kissed her on the lips and we held each other for a moment. "Please come home Rob please." "In a few days Sam, I'm going to the glaziers this morning to pick up some panes of glass and repair the window. You go to work and I'll be in touch." Sam left I drove down to the glaziers picked up four panes of glass and repaired the window. The girls returned 5 o'clock "I've repaired your window Vicky" "Thanks Rob."

Jasmine went into the kitchen carrying two bottles of wine. Vicky made the tea and we all sat at the table. "Sam was mad this morning wasn't she Rob? I'm sorry if we caused you any trouble." "It's alright girls" I sighed. "I made her inspect the bed in case you two ravished my body." They giggled. "We wish". Vicky voiced almost choking on her glass of wine. "I hate been accused of something I haven't done Jasmine" said pouring herself another glass of wine. "Do you think she'll come around tonight Rob to check?" "Probably perhaps we should all dance naked round the front room and give her something to look at girls" they burst out laughing. "I'm only joking" I said quickly.

The door opened and in came Caroline in the pink miniskirt and see-through blouse. Vicky and Jasmine looked at each other and to me. "Hi Caroline" everyone voiced. "Hi could I have a word Rob." "Yes what's up love?" She sat on my knee placing her arm around my shoulder. "Katie's managing well with the children on her own. She thought it might be a good idea if I could have my old job back at the stables the extra cash would help me." "We could work together" Vicky voiced. "We are short staffed; it would take some of the responsibility off me". Caroline remarked "I could also watch Sam" "Were already doing that" the girls voiced. "But another set of eyes wouldn't go amiss" Jasmine said "Were not having Rob upset again by that bitch." "Hey steady on Jasmine" "well its right Rob you've only ever shown me kindness you don't deserve to be treated like shit." Everybody looked at Jasmine a timid girl that would say nothing to anyone yet was standing her ground on this point. Caroline smiled "You're in love with Rob Jasmine." Jasmine didn't respond. Even I was taken by surprise at Jasmine's comment "What do you think Rob?" "I can try Caroline are you short of money? "Things are a bit tight Katie helps me out." "You have a bank account Caroline?" "Yes why?" "Give me your account details." "Why?" "Just do as you are told girl." She stood up and removed her bank card from her purse. I phoned the bank "could you please transfer £5000 into this account, effective immediately please. There you are your all sorted love." Tears ran down Caroline's cheeks. "Rob why you owe me nothing" "I told you long ago you are special to me you help me when I was ill you're always there for me, you deserve something love. Girls, don't you ever repeat this to Sam or anybody else." They shook their heads in silence. Caroline dried her eyes. "Everybody loves you Rob" she said placing her arms around my neck and kissing me on the lips. "Is Katie short of money?" "No I don't think so her grandparents have sent some money over she has what she received from the accident I can't keep asking her for money it's embarrassing." "I understand Caroline I've been in that position myself."

We went into the front room before I could sit down, Vicky kissed me on the lips and so did Jasmine. "What was that for?" "We love you Rob we all do." The girls went into their bedrooms. Caroline and I sat on the settee sitting facing me still drying her eyes. "I will pay you back Rob." "No you won't you've had nearly as much shit in your life, as I have." "What upsets me the most Rob is I lost both the children you gave me. I know they would have been special." We hugged each other. Sam came in we lent back on the settee. Caroline tidied her short skirt. Sam looked at both our faces. "I'm glad you came Sam" "Why?" "Caroline needs a job." "Oh I don't know I suppose she could work down at Cranbury farm we are short-staffed." I rose to my feet and kissed Sam on the lips which took her by surprise. Caroline stood up "when can I Start Sam" "In the morning don't be late." "Thank you Sam" "Just, don't get up to anything stupid Caroline" "No I won't" Caroline left. "She's a nice girl Sam She looked after me when I was ill." We sat by each other on the settee. I placed my hand on her leg She smiled "Please come home Rob" she said softly. "The weekend Sam it's only three days." She hugged me. "Oh God I thought I'd lost you, every woman I see looks at you I want to scratch their eyes out. I never thought I could be this jealous" "If you look at another woman or man I'm gone for good Sam do I make myself clear?" Sam replied quickly "Yes, it will never happen I promise. Where are Vicky and Jasmine?" Sam asked "In their bedrooms probably taking all their clothes off just waiting for me to come in" I joked. She hit me hard on the shoulder. "That's not funny" then smiled. "Father will be over the moon even the Dragon was upset" we both laughed. "I would like to see that definitely be a sight for sore eyes" I remarked. "Would you like to?" Sam asked searching my eyes placing my free hand on her blouse against her breast. "No." I'm desperate to have you inside me Rob" "Next week, the longer I rest the better." She gave me a tender kiss and left.

Chapter 5
Back in the saddle

Vicky and Jasmine returned to the front room sat either side of me. "Wow" Jasmine voiced. "I thought there was going to be a blazing row when Sam caught Caroline here dressed the way she was you could see everything" "I know Vicky" replied. "I'm moving out the weekend girls, it will be all yours again." They both hugged me. "I'll be out of your hair." "We don't want you to go Rob we like being with you" Jasmine voiced holding my left hand and Vicky holding the right ". You are a lovely person." "Look what you did for Caroline" "Don't speak of that girls I'm not such a nice guy as you think I have so many skeletons in my closet I'm struggling to shut the door." I went and took a shower had a shave and tidied myself up I felt no end better I went into my bedroom to dress. There was a knock on the door. "Yes" the door opened Jasmine sat beside me on the bed, looking at the floor "What's the matter Jasmine" I said placing my arm around her shoulder "Nothing Rob. I just want to be with you." She started kissing my neck. "Hey Jasmine stop that do you know how old I am" "I don't care." "Sam could return any minute" "Vicky's watching the track." She eased me back onto the bed kissing me on the lips, neck and chest placing my hand on her breast. She released the knot on my towel holding me firmly. She rose to her feet removing her T-shirt and jeans and finally her pants. She lay on the bed; I was so aroused it was unbelievable we made love instantly. She was young and fresh and within 15 minutes it was all over I was so enchanted by her body. She sat up and dressed kissing me on the lips passionately. "Don't worry Rob I'm on the pill I won't be getting pregnant." "We shouldn't have done that Jasmine." "It's no worse than what Sam was doing to you I just wanted to show you that somebody else really loves you" She confessed. I dressed and went back into the front room Vicky was cooking. Jasmine was brushing her hair. Vicky looked across to me and smiled with approval. We watch television till 10:30 PM. The girls were drinking their wine and I was having a glass to of my favourite tipple. Vicky left the room and changed the sheets on my bed just to make sure Sam couldn't find any evidence. Vicky returned licking her finger and sticking it in the air. "That's one for you Rob" she smiled. "At least now Caroline has her job back she can watch Sam at Cranbury farm. We can watch at Mr Goldings she'll have nowhere to hide if she tries to pull a dirty trick on you again." I leant over and kissed Vicky on the lips. "Thank you" She smiled in appreciation. Vicky and Jasmine went into Jasmine's bedroom. Jasmine came out "Rob there's a problem in my bedroom." "What is it?" "I don't think the window will shut properly." "Okay I'll have a look" I went to leave the room and I saw Jasmine looking out of the front room window up the track. "Can you see somebody" I asked? "No just looking" I went into Jasmine's bedroom Vicky was laid naked on the bed. She grabbed my hand and pulled me down locking me in an embrace she placed one of my hands on her small firm breasts. "Vicky this is wrong." "No it isn't" "It's deceitful." "I don't care fuck me." She sat up releasing my jeans she held me tight and groaned with pleasure. "Oh you fill me it's so nice you're so gentle". We finished dressed and returned to the front room. Jasmine topped everybody's glass up and we all sat watching TV each held one of my hands. I didn't believe what had happened and I moan about Sam's little indiscretion I could write a book on the infidelity of my life. I even contemplated grabbing the shot gun and blowing my brains out. Every principle I lived by had been torn to shreds I was nothing but a dirty disgusting bastard who didn't deserve to live.

Saturday morning, I loaded my clothes into the range Rover and drove back to Cranbury farm. I parked outside Sam came running out of the house and flung her arms around my neck, pushing me back against the range Rover her smile was so broad she kept kissing me. I thought she was never going to stop "Steady on Sam where are the children?" "They've gone to their grandfathers for a week with Jane." "Why?" I asked holding her around the waist "We need some time alone she remarked as I carried my suitcase upstairs to the bedroom. "How are you feeling Rob?" I've missed you so much." Sam Started to unbutton her blouse. "Not now Sam I'm not in the mood." She held my hand against her chest "Will you never forgive me Rob?" "It's not that Sam I just wanted to get into bed first" I laughed. Once she'd realise what I said watching me undress quickly. She Started smiling commenting "That was cruel." She quickly undressed and we lay in bed beside each other. We stayed there for the rest of the morning caressing each other. Sam commented how wonderful Katie had been and Caroline helping her through this very stressful situation. I agreed with her they'd both been wonderful and our marriage may not have survived if it wasn't for those two. Sam thought it would be a good idea if I saw more of Robert. I asked "Why?" "He's so much like you Rob he hasn't got a father like our children I feel so sorry for him. I've told Katie to bring her children round to play with ours anytime." I smiled in appreciation. Sam remarked how wonderful she felt and relaxed. She'd lost over a stone in weight in the past month. Things Started to return to normality. Jenny's Porsche had been put in the garage at the old house. It hadn't been touched since she was murdered. I thought it was time it was disposed of I went round to see Katie. She opened the door and let me in and we sat by the fire. I offered her the Porsche she advised me she didn't want it I could sell it out of the way. I suddenly realised the children were missing "Where's Robert and Nicky?" "There at Mr Goldings stables with Jane they're having them for a week." I was flabbergasted. "I'm confused Katie what's going on?" "Nothing Rob, Mr Goldings said I could have a break from the children in thanks for all that Caroline and I had done to resolve your marriage issue. I took him up on his offer." I slumped in the chair in shock. Katie sat on my lap, placing her arm around my neck and kissing me tenderly on the lips ". What you doing Katie?" "Nothing I haven't done before" she smiled. "You can thank me properly now" "I'm not giving you another child." "I'm on the pill Rob to assist me with the pain after my accident. I just want you inside me it's a memory I just cannot put to the back of my mind". She placed her lips against mine then eased my hand onto her beautiful breast. We kissed and cuddled for a moment. She then stood up holding my hand "come with me Rob". We went into her bedroom. She removed her clothes very slowly exposing her beautifully formed breasts. She lay on the bed encouraging me to join her, she commented, feeling me enter her body "Be gentle Rob. Oh God, it's better than I remember" I rode her like I was a wild stallion after an hour. We lay beside each other. She slid on top of me forcing down on me not letting me rest she kissed me tenderly and finally beside me. "I wish you'd have married me Rob I would have never betrayed you like everyone else has". Perhaps she was right but it was too late now we dressed and returned to the living room. She came in a moment later carrying two cups of coffee. We sat and looked at each other each realising how much we loved each other for all Katie's faults. She was a lovely woman a figure to die for and she'd had two of my children. "No other man Rob has ever touched me or ever will I only want you inside me." I said goodbye and arranged for a Porsche dealership to collect Jenny's gold coloured Porsche after they had looked it over. They decided it was worth about £50,000 it only had 5,000 miles on the clock from new and was in immaculate condition. They would sell it on my behalf and take a percentage for handling the sale. I returned to Cranbury farm and went into the barn to look at my old tractor grandfather had left me. I spent some time getting it Started again. It'd been sat there for a while over a year since it was last run. Caroline heard the noise of the engine and came in to see what was going on. She placed her hand on my shoulder which made me jump. She smiled "Sorry how's things Rob with you and Sam." "Okay?"

Chapter 6
Trying to be faithful

Sam asked me if I would go over and cut some wood for Vicky and Jasmine. It was now October and there was a chill in the air. I cut two small trees down, block and split the timber ready for the fire and the Aga. I stacked it on the porch. Sam phoned "Rob how long are you going to be?" "Not long my beautiful wife, keep everything warm for me" "Don't I always Rob?". Life was good. Sam and I couldn't get enough of each other just like old times. I was about to leave when Vicky and Jasmine arrived at the cabin they offered me a drink so I went inside "Thanks Rob" Vicky voiced Jasmine had gone into her bedroom. I sat at the kitchen table drinking my coffee; Vicky went into the front room. Jasmine came into the kitchen wearing a very similar outfit to Caroline's short miniskirt see-through blouse no bra, leaving nothing to the imagination. Jasmine sat beside me sipping her coffee I think she was waiting for me to react, but I didn't. "I saw the way you looked at Caroline Rob and I thought you'd like to see me dress like her?" She slid my hand between her legs. I could feel she was not wearing any knickers. "You are pretty Jasmine and if I wasn't married and old enough to be your father, things may be different." Jasmine Started to cry quietly" "Hold me Rob." I reluctantly placed my arm around her shoulder. She lent her head against mine. Vicky shouted "Sam is coming." Jasmine ran off into the bedroom quickly changing back into her riding gear. Sam came in saw me sat at the kitchen table drinking coffee "Would you like a drink Sam?" Vicky enquired "Yes I'll have one thank you." We finished our coffee. Sam jumped in my range Rover and we went home. I received a phone call early next morning from the Porsche dealership saying they had sold Jenny's Porsche. They could either pay the money direct into my account or if I wished I could collect the cheque for £45,000. I asked them to pay it straight into my bank account. I started walking round the stables at Cranbury farm. Sam and Caroline were mucking out. I had decided that I was going to purchase a second hand car for Caroline. She could have had my old Land Rover but it was a little expensive to run and wasn't in the best of shape. I didn't know how Sam would react to the idea. I took Sam aside Caroline kept glancing up wondering what we were talking about. "Sam my love I just received a phone call saying they've sold the Porsche. I'd like to buy Caroline a second hand car how would you feel about that?" She looked at me rather Startled "Why would you want to do that Rob?" "I don't know, I think she works hard and if it wasn't for her we wouldn't be together now it was Caroline that convinced me to give you a second chance." "Really I didn't know that Rob" Sam remarked surprised. "It's your money just don't spend too much" She smiled. "We'll only be gone for an hour" "No longer she's need here" Sam insisted. I called across the yard "Caroline, with me." Caroline Started walking towards me, looking rather puzzled and worried Sam passed patting her on the shoulder "What's the matter Rob" she asked. "Jump into my range Rover you're coming with me young lady." She sat rather nervously, she was about to speak and I put my finger to my lips, you could tell she was worried after travelling 10 miles out of the village. There was a small second-hand car dealership I pulled over "Don't go too mad pick the one you like." She stared at me in disbelief, placing her hand to her mouth. "Why Rob?" I indicated with my hand to walk around I rested against my range Rover with my arms folded watching her walk around looking back to me for a reaction. A car salesman came out and showed her around various little models. She came running over to me "There's a 1.0 Hyundai over their Rob It's really nice, small and it will be cheap for me to run are you sure Rob? What's this all about?" I put my arm around her shoulder and kissed her on the cheek we went to look at the car. It wasn't very old low mileage and came with 12 month's warranty for £5000, including 12 month's road tax. I also arranged 12 month's insurance for her at the same time. It would be delivered early next week we set off back to Cranbury farm. Caroline was crying ". Why Rob Why are you doing this for me?" "Because I can and you're special to me. You know I love you. Don't worry about Sam I asked her first". We arrived at Cranbury farm. Caroline jumped out of the range Rover ran across to Sam and gave her a big hug "Thank you so much Sam." Sam smiled "It's Rob you have to thank it's his money" "You really lucky Sam you've married a wonderful man; you are so lucky" Caroline voiced running off down the yard. Sam grabbed my arm and gave me a cuddle. "You are unbelievable Rob." I held Sam's hand taking her into the feed store. Closed the door pulling her jeans and knickers off, opened her blouse and released her bra and sat her on the feed bin we caressed there for a while. We were intoxicated with each other and I never wanted to let her go. She tidied herself slightly red-faced I remarked "Now we've christened the new farm" Caroline said opening the door "Can I feed the horses now you two are finished." We both went slightly red smiled and walked off across the yard hand-in-hand.

Chapter 7
Tragedy strikes

Rupert and Bethany his wife, who we always called the Dragon, had become besotted with the children. They spent more time with them than they ever did with us. That included Robert and Nicky everything was perfect. Bethany wanted to take Jonathan and Robert to Disney in France as a Christmas present. Sam discussed the proposal with me and I couldn't see any harm in the adventure. Katie thought it was a good idea too and was rather surprised that Robert had been invited. The two families appeared to gel, it would be a two-day trip for the boys. We all decided the girls were too young and wouldn't appreciate it until they were older. Rupert took them to the airport. Sam and I were working around the stables. Caroline was having her coffee break listening to the radio she came screaming out in the yard in hysterics. We all ran over to see what was wrong she had dropped on her knees in an uncontrollable state "Rob, Sam" she cried, "The aeroplane has exploded it had been hijacked by terrorists. We all collapsed around Caroline for a moment. Katie came screaming into the yard carrying Nicky "Rob Oh Rob my son" We all went to the house and turn the television on. There were images of parts of aeroplane floating in the channel. Rupert phoned, crying down the phone. "I'm trying to get confirmation it's their plane I'll let you know as soon as I have some information." He put the phone down. Caroline said she would go and finish the horses off, still crying. We were all in total shock. Rupert came to join us at Cranbury farm. We all hugged each other. Jane had taken Nicky upstairs to play with Christina, trying to keep them away from the distress Rupert confirmed. It was the airline the children were on with Bethany that exploded. We all sat there drinking I asked Rupert if he'd like to stay here the night he said "No thanks." He wanted to go home Time seemed to stand still. I held Katie and Sam in my arms sitting by the fire. I'd suffered a double loss both my sons were dead.

I suppose I must thank my lucky Stars I still had two daughters. None of us went to bed that night we just stayed by the fire drinking alcohol and then coffee. The next morning, we staggered out into the yard. The horses would have to be fed what ever happened? We found Caroline asleep in one of the stables. She'd stayed all night keeping control, seeing to the welfare of the horses, we gently woke her to go into the house and grab something to eat and drink. We thanked her for her hard work. Sam gave her a big cuddle. She told us to go back in the house. She'd manage on her own. We both kissed Caroline on the cheek and left her to it. The local postman arrived with an armful of mail. Most of the letters hadn't a stamp on them. He expressed his condolences and handed them over. Most of the mail was from the villagers. Katie and Sam held their daughters, Jane made everyone breakfast trying not to cry. Rupert contacted us after using all his influential power to gain as much information as he could. He said no one would have known what happened. It was a massive explosion and the chances of any bodies being recovered were very slim.

A month passed and diving teams had been down to the bottom of the sea. There were very few fragments of the plane left, only the wings. The main body of the plane was in shreds. Katie had gone home with Nicky. Christmas came and went. All of the stable staff rallied round to ensure everything ran smoothly to avoid disturbing Sam and myself. We slowly eased back into our daily duties. I decided life is like Russian roulette, you never know which Chamber has the bullet in. A service was held at St Michael's Church in the middle of the village another heart wrenching experience. We were now in the middle of May, spring was well underway. Sam and I sat by the fire, our favourite place on the carpet. We held each other very close.

Chapter 8
Another Child

"Rob I want another child I know I can never replace Jonathan I'm going to see a specialist tomorrow to see if there's any way I can conceive again." "Sam that's silly you'll kill yourself in the process." "I don't care Rob I want another child." Katie knocked and came in carrying Nicky. She sat in the chair. "I'm going to have another child Rob." Sam looked across to Katie. I looked at them both. "We've just been discussing that option Katie I'm going to a specialist tomorrow to see if there's any way I can conceive again." "What are you going to do Katie have artificial insemination?" Sam asked. "No I want Rob to make love to me Robert was his son" "I bloody knew it; you lying cow why didn't you come straight out and tell us?" "In case you tried to take him off me." "Why would I want to do that?" Katie shrugged her shoulders, "I wasn't going to risk losing my son." Jane came down and took Nicky upstairs to play with Christina. I just wanted to find a big hole and fall in it. My world was exploding in front of me "What you going to do Sam if you can't conceive again?" "I don't know." She started to cry. "It's no bloody good crying, you silly bitch! There's always a solution to a problem" Katie had become cold and calculated as if her soul had been torn out. I just sat back in astonishment "What are you suggesting Katie" "It's quite simple, you let me use Rob and I'll find you a surrogate mother. Do we have a deal that's if the specialist says you can't conceive again?" "Yes" Sam smiled. "Just a minute you two don't I get consulted or have a say in any fucking thing around here or am I just a stud for hire?" I couldn't believe what they were considering my two sons were dead somewhere in the sea. Sam placed her arm around me saying softly "You do it for me Rob you know I may not conceive again?" I shrugged my shoulders. Katie went home with Nicky, smiling. We went to bed and never spoke a word. I think Sam realised I wasn't very keen on the idea, but she was determined to have her own way whatever the cost. She went to the specialist the next morning who confirmed there was no chance she could carry again. She returned home and phoned Katie, who came straight round. I was outside repairing one of the stable doors. Caroline's phone rang. She headed for the house I followed wondering what's going on behind my back. I walked in to find Katie, Caroline and Sam all sitting in the living room. They all glanced at me, looking a little guilty. "Sit down Rob." Sam said "Funny how I wasn't invited to this meeting don't I count for anything Sam?" "Don't be like that Rob please just listen to what we're going to say then tell me what you think." She came over and perched on the arm of the chair putting her arm around my shoulder. Katie spoke sipping from her glass of wine. "Sam can't conceive again I want another child, so does Sam. Caroline doesn't know whether she can carry again but is willing to try if you're in agreement." Her words were cold and precise this was old Katie in action. Caroline suggested an alternative. "There is Jasmine She is madly in love with Rob I'm sure she'd do anything for him if I can't carry a baby" I voiced with concern. "How would you feel about giving up your child" "The honest answer is I don't know Rob? I would really have to sit down and think about it." Sam kissed me on the cheek reassuringly "How do you feel Sam about me sleeping with somebody else?" "I wouldn't be very happy but I would put up with it for a baby and that would be the only reason" she said downing a large glass of whiskey. Caroline suggested "Do you want me to talk with Jasmine?" Katie voiced "If you're unsure Caroline you can hand the baby over then we have to consider Jasmine and take her view on the idea. Better still, it should come from Sam. She may be more sympathetic to her." I was not happy with any of their ideas. What is wrong with just having a daughter I was perfectly happy with Christina. Sam instructed Caroline to fetch Jasmine we sat looking at each other like we were involved in a business deal instead of romance, love and offspring Caroline returned with Jasmine. Jasmine looked frightened to death. She'd obviously thought she was in trouble. She was trembling as she sat down in the armchair. Sam smiled kneeling in front of her, placing her hands on Jasmine's knees "Don't worry Jasmine you're not in trouble we want to ask you a question. If you're not really interested that's fine. But if you consider going ahead with our proposal you must understand the consequences." Jasmine looked puzzled as we left the room apart from Sam and Jasmine and listened intently from the door. We could hear the muffled conversation we heard Sam's raised voice "Thank you thank you so much Jasmine." Caroline took Jasmine back to work. Sam explained to us Jasmine was happy to carry our child. She would receive £10,000 from Sam and all the support she needed and would come and live with us during the pregnancy. Sam and Katie hugged each other. Caroline sat with her head slightly bowed. Once again she had missed out. Perhaps for the best I couldn't imagine her giving up my children. I thought I should give Caroline another present one she's always wanted I was being hired out as a bloody stud I might as well practice I thought. I went back out into the yard leaving Katie and Sam to arrange what was taking place. Caroline came out of the house Joined me in the yard we went into the feed shed and closed the door and put the lights on. "I couldn't give up a child conceived with you Rob I just couldn't I love you too much." "I'm glad you didn't get involved Caroline you suffered enough in your life and to take a child from you is something I couldn't do." We hugged and kissed each other passionately for a moment. "Caroline if you'd like to try for another child to have as your own." She placed a hand over my mouth "Quickly someone's coming sit on the feed bin over there and I'll sit on this one. So it looks as if were just talking." "Oh yes." Sam said opening the door. "What are you two doing having a shag?" She said folding her arms. "Does it look like it you silly bitch, were not even near each other were just talking things over. Like you're planning my bloody life, again I'm going I've had enough." Sam tried to grab my arm. Caroline came running out of the feed shed and jumped in her car and drove off following me in my range Rover. Sam rang my mobile I answered. "Yes" "I'm sorry Rob I shouldn't have said that, please come back I'm just upset with everything. I don't want you sleeping with anybody else." "It's your bloody idea Sam not mine why you can't be satisfied with Christina, She's a lovely daughter." "I don't know Rob." She cried. "I want you to have a son" "I don't need a son and you can't guarantee the sex anyway." I hung up and drove round to the cabin Vicky and Jasmine who were sat on the porch. They invited me for a drink then I left and returned home. I found Sam sat by the fire drying her eyes. "I phoned Caroline and apologised." "Rob she came back. I shouldn't have said that to her or you I'm just so frustrated with the whole situation, why am I a barren cow?" I held her very tightly in my arms and expressed my love for her.

Chapter 9
What does the future hold?

Sam and I lay in bed together. She explained to me that Katie had been on the phone wanting to know when she could have me. She wanted to get on with being pregnant again. Sam sighed She really didn't like the idea but she had agreed to it in principle. I was not to tell Sam when I slept with Katie. She would just try and shut it out of her mind. She was also unsure of Jasmine whether she'd be able to give up a baby. Sam held me very tight, kissing my neck, expressing her love and wish she'd never thought of the idea of having another child. I was perfectly happy with the way things were. I'd heard through the grapevine that Rupert was seeing another woman half his age and he was having a whale of a time. Mind you anything was better than the Dragon he had before, but I shouldn't speak ill of the dead. It was Saturday morning I got up and said I was going to the stables at Mr Goldings just to check things out there I called in to see Katie. Caroline was there too I could hear Nicky upstairs playing in her room we sat and had coffee and I explained to her. Sam didn't want to know when we slept together. I was not to mention it and neither was Katie. Katie agreed. She parted her dressing gown and lay on the floor with her legs apart, holding her breasts. "Come on Rob get inside me I love you." We caressed and cuddled and finally made love. Caroline was watching from the door unbeknown to me at the time. She came into the room as we finished carrying a fresh tray of coffee. She sat quietly on the settee. Katie looked over to her and nudged her arm indicating lay on the floor. She shook her head slowly. I went and sat by her and holding her very close she pressed her head against my shoulder. I placed my hand gently on her covered breast then release the buttons on her blouse sliding my hand on her breast. She Started to kiss me and we lay on the floor Katie sat in the chair watching everything we caressed and cuddled and finally I penetrated she cried out "Oh my God, keep going." We dressed and continued drinking coffee. No one had really spoken a word it all seemed to come quite naturally what was taking place. I stood up to leave and they both kissed me. "I love you Rob" Katie professed. Caroline walked me to the door and she embraced me kissing me tenderly and passionately like she always did. "I love you Rob." I left without saying another word and carried on to Goldings stables checking the stable doors and the general state of the buildings. I then called round to the cabin asked Vicky and Jasmine if I could take a shower before I went home. They knew exactly what had taken place and agreed. I stood in the shower trying to wash away my sins. I wondered what God would say if I ever met him. Suddenly the shower curtain slid open, Vicky and Jasmine entered naked, they washed me down as if I was a horse. I became aroused, lifting Jasmine up and pushing her back against the wall of the shower and penetrated her and then I moved on to Vicky did exactly the same to her. They smiled, enjoying the experience. We dried each other and dressed returning to the front room. I had a Bacardi and coke and the girls had a glass of wine. I finally went home Sam was sitting by the fire. She looked up to me and could see the guilt all over my face. She jumped to her feet and embraced me Starting to cry "It's all my fault Rob me and my stupid ideas. I love you with all my heart I don't want another child." I eased her away and kissed her passionately on the lips. Christina was now at infant school. Sam and I plodded on with our usual duties but each night we would express our love for each other. Katie became pregnant. Caroline didn't, her life had been ruined by a horse. Sam and I never spoke about Katie's pregnancy and when she conceived. Sam explained to Jasmine that she no longer wants another child. She was happy with Christina. There was a hole in our life that was once filled by Jonathan. Sam had come to realise that another child would not replace him. What we did have was each other, which was becoming more special every day. Summer was here once again we finally met Rupert's girlfriend she was only 25 and he was nearly 65. A leggy shoulder length brunette that had more plastic in her than a Lego brick. She was now living with Rupert, Sam and I were convinced She was nothing but a gold digger. Sam had, had several conversations with her father trying to make him understand he was being used. He couldn't grasp the real reason why a 25-year-old woman would be with a 65-year-old man. He had told Sam not to worry Cranbury farm was hers. He had already signed over the deeds so whatever happened she would not be left out. Her father told Sam he and Jennifer were trying for a child. I went over to Mr Goldings stables to make a repair to a stable after Vicky had phoned. Jasmine came over and offered to make me a coffee we sat up above the tack room talking "What you think to Jennifer Rob?" "I don't know the girl and don't want to" Vicky came up "Hello Rob." She kissed me on the cheek. Vicky's phone rang "Yes I'll be down straightaway; that's Jennifer she wants to ride a horse this should be good for a laugh." Vicky smiled. Jennifer was riding around on a grey horse in the arena. Vicky and I were watching from the side. She pulled up alongside Vicky and I signalling with her hand and said "Go away girl I want to speak to Rob" I whispered "In Vicky's ear video out of sight." She nodded understanding what I'd said. Jennifer dismounted and lent close to me on the railings. I pressed the record button on my mobile. Jennifer's blouse was unbuttoned just below her bra so her silicon filled tits bulged out "Rupert and I are trying for a baby but he's fucking useless in bed and I think he's firing blanks. You've come from a poor background like me, you married the daughter I just got the fucking old man" she sniggered. "I don't see how I can help you Jennifer?" "I'll show you Rob come with me." I followed her to the hay store she looked around to check no one was watching. She pulled me inside then dropped her riding britches and knickers unbuttoned her blouse and released her front coupling bra. Her tits stuck out like train buffers, she reached for my zip on my trousers. I backed away "No thanks" "You say anything Rob and I'll tell Rupert you tried to rape me he'll believe me before he believes you" she claimed. I walked up the yard Vicky and Jasmine grabbed my arm pulled me into the tack room and led me upstairs "What an old cow" Jasmine commented. I didn't realise that not only Vicky had videoed everything so did Jasmine. I had her voice on my mobile. I took the mobiles from them and headed back to Cranbury farm "Sam" I shouted. She came running across the yard we went in the house "Look at this Sam." Sam watched the two videos and listened to my recording .She phoned her father asking him to call in at Cranbury farm. We had something very important for him to see. 4.30 pm Rupert arrived. He walked into the house I asked him to sit down on the settee. He looked very worried Sam was sat in the other chair, holding the mobiles. "Rupert, you've known me for a long time and we've been through some problems together." He was one of the few men in this world I would trust. "I'm going to show you two videos and voice recording made by two independent people. "I know you Rob you wouldn't tell me any lies." Sam crouched placing her hand on her father's knee. He played the recordings and listened to what was said. He lent back on the settee with tears in his eyes. "I've been a stupid old fool thank you Rob for your honesty and stop me making a further fool of myself." Sam went into the kitchen and made a coffee we sat and talk for an hour then he went home. Sam joined me on the settee "She would have let you Rob and you didn't" Sam embraced me. Jennifer had vanished by morning I went over to Mr Goldings stables and returned the girls mobiles plus giving them £50 each for saving my neck. We all went up into the tack room for a coffee. "You don't have to pay us Rob we'd do anything for you." "Just take it as a present for your hard work and loyalty."

Chapter 10
Security camera footage

Life had returned to some normality Rupert had recovered from his disastrous relationship and was now dating a woman in her 50s a nice lady called Nicole. She enjoyed riding horses and never interfered with anything. she hadn't an unpleasant bone in her body I don't think. Out of the blue I received a phone call from Mr MacDonald C.I.D, he asked if he could come and see myself Sam and Katie at Cranbury farm. He said he'd already spoken to Mr Goldings who would attend as well. "What's this all about Mr MacDonald?" "I prefer not to discuss the matter on the phone I'll see you at 10 o'clock this morning." I informed Sam and phoned Katie, who was now struggling with the pregnancy. Everyone turned up and we went into the living room. Mr MacDonald explained a security camera at the airport had footage of Bethany Goldings. Getting into the back of a lorry after going through departure accompanied with two children, believed to be Robert and Jonathan. The only reason this camera was checked is because something went missing in that area relating to baggage. We all sat in silence. We allowed Mr Goldings to speak for us all. Katie was holding her stomach obviously in much discomfort and shock like the rest of us. "You are saying that my wife and the two children are alive and they never boarded the aeroplane?" "They were at the time of the footage" Katie screamed in pain. Her unborn child was on the way an ambulance collected her and she left for the hospital. Jane took care of Nicky Mr MacDonald continued. "We have alerted all police forces around the world we are still trying to find out what lorry was in the airport security area. How Mrs Goldings pulled it off is a puzzle to everyone please believe me I am going to do everything within my power to find these children and of course your wife Mr Goldings. "Do you have any idea where she might go?" "She has relations in Ireland and also in Norway." "That's great. Please speak to no one about this we don't want to panic anyone. I can only apologise the footage wasn't checked sooner on that camera, although it is somewhere the public should never be under normal circumstances and we presumed she was on the aeroplane" Sam was absolutely ecstatic and also upset at the same time. Mr Goldings just sat and held his head and voiced. "My wife had several accounts the day of the plane crash I noticed one had been closed there was over a hundred thousand pounds in it. It completely slipped my mind once I heard about the plane crash." "That now confirms our suspicions Mr Golding." "I'm sorry I just thought she placed it somewhere else and not told me." "Please find the children I hope they're all right" Sam cried "Whoever was involved in this kidnapping was very clever, was Mrs Goldings particularly interested in the two boys?" Rupert replied "Bethany was besotted with them. She would have had them move in and live with us if she could." Mr MacDonald left assuring us he would let us know the minute he had any news. We then left ourselves to see Katie in hospital when we arrived they had delivered the baby a 6 pound boy, born quite premature but fine. Katie was sitting up in bed. We explained everything that had been said and Nicky would be staying with us until she came out of hospital. Sam held the tiny new born remarking "He looks like his father" she smiled. Sam gently handed Katie's son back to her. "What are you going to call him Katie?" "Julian, his father's middle name." Sam glanced to me and hugged me. Much to my surprise Sam was not upset or angry. I think she was just over the moon knowing that Jonathan hopefully would be found and the tatters of our life would be put back together. The only other person that was told about the missing children was Caroline. She was extremely happy to hear the news. Katie returned home two weeks later, after the hospital was happy with Julian's progress. Sam gave Caroline a week off work with full pay to help Katie with the new born and look after Nicky. Sam went and saw Katie quite often holding Julian brought a smile to her face. Katie agreed with Sam that all our children should be good friends and I should play a big part in their lives. Time seemed to move slowly while we waited for information on Robert and Jonathan. Mr MacDonald informed us the lorry they were transported in was from Ireland. He presumed they were somewhere there he said. Bethany would think no one was looking for them so they might be easy to find. I went to see Julian with Sam. Sam would hold him as if he was hers. Katie was starting to feel ill and it was discovered the cancer had returned with a vengeance. It had now progressed to a stage where it was no longer curable. She had six months at the most to live she just hoped she would still be alive when Robert was found.

An old gypsy woman looking about a hundred years old came to Cranbury farm trying to sell bunches of heather. Sam and I listened to her stories. She knew about the old building burnt down hundreds of years ago in the wood she said. "Some of our ancestors used to practice magic there and anyone who was ill would stay in the building and slowly recover." I gave her a £20 note she looked into my eyes. "You are the blessed one you have lived in the wood I see the mark on you". Sam looked me over from top to bottom "I don't see anything." The old woman held my arm "Look she said look". Sam looked there was a six sided hexagram on my arm "What does it mean?" "It means my dear you have married a very special person who always helps those in need." The gypsy woman hobbled along with her walking stick down the drive "Can I give you a lift?" I shouted. "No" she called back "You can't come where I'm going" Sam remarked. "She is right about one thing you are special to me anyway and you always help people and everybody seems to love you." I phoned Vicky explained to her that I needed to move Katie into the cabin would she and Jasmine mind sharing "Of course not Rob we don't mind." My biggest problem would be convincing Katie to leave the house and live in the cabin. I thought Jane would look after Nicky during the day because Katie couldn't cope in her present condition. Sam and I jumped in the range Rover and tore off to Katie's house. Katie was already dressed sitting in the living room holding Julian in her arms "That took you long enough to get here." We looked confused I said. "You're not going to believe this Katie we may be able to save your life". Katie smiled. "I've seen the old gypsy lady selling heather she told me to get ready you'd be coming for me." Sam and I looked at each other in astonishment. Something was going on here we didn't understand I ran upstairs and dismantled the cot. Sam packed a suitcase for Katie. I thought I was going to have one hell of a time trying to get Katie out of the house or even believe what I'm suggesting. We drove off quickly to the cabin. We helped Katie in my old bedroom along with the cot. We placed everything she would need to feed Julian in the kitchen. Sam assured her she would come every day and make sure she was okay and we were only a phone call away. We would bring Nicky every day to see her. Katie held my hand. "I always knew you were special Rob don't let me die without seeing Robert one more time." "I will stay Rob I'll phone you later to pick me up." I drove away with a heavy heart, wondering whether the old gypsy lady was telling the truth. I didn't want Katie to die and I was desperate to see Robert and Jonathan again. Another month had passed. Katie had not improved nor got any worse Vicky and Jasmine helped her as much as they could, Nicky and Christina had become very close Sam watched the two girls playing. We had converted a bedroom into a playroom for the children upstairs. I went up and stood by her she placed her arm around my shoulders. "It's lovely to watch the children play Rob". Vicky rang we feared the worst. "You're not going to believe this Rob Katie's sitting in the front room watching television with Julian." "Were coming over." We jumped into the range Rover driving to the cabin we walked in to see Katie feeding

Julian. "My son is blessed look he has your mark." Sure enough on his arm was a very faint hexagram. "The old lady came to see me today." "When? I was here most of the day apart from when I went to the shop to buy some nappies before I went home" Sam remarked. "That's when she came she told me I wouldn't die and it was thanks to Rob and all his children would carry the mark and they would always be safe. "I know Robert and Jonathan are safe," she said not to worry they would soon be home. Sam and I looked at each other and so did the girls in disbelief. Katie was starting to look good. "I'm Starving is there anything to eat in this place?" She smiled. Vicky asked "What would you like Katie." "One of Rob's favourite egg sandwiches please." Vicky made her four sandwiches. She ate them like she'd never eaten before, we all watched in astonishment. Whatever was going on was working and I didn't care whether it was down to the old gypsy lady or God himself, providing Katie recovered and the children were returned. Sam and I went home. We checked Christina's arms and sure enough there was a mark. Thank God she didn't check Nicky's. I would have an awful lot of explaining to do.

Mr MacDonald informed me they had found evidence that Mrs Goldings and the two children had been in an old cottage in Northern Ireland. But had since moved on, he didn't think it would be long before he found them. We would just have to be patient a little while longer everyone was working as hard as they can he assured us. I conveyed the information to Katie, who was improving every day. Even the doctors had no explanation for her remarkable recovery from a death sentence. Julian was coming on too, now three months old. Sam commented he looked the splitting image of Rob. Sam passed him over for me to hold saying "meet your father Julian." I looked to Sam's face there was no pain just happiness. We just seemed to be one big family. Caroline had faithfully run the stables. Sam suggested I take her out for a meal as a special treat. Without her working in the background we could have lost a lot of business. Sam went to see Caroline and told her I was taking her out for a meal as a special thank you. For holding everything together while we were preoccupied. Sam took me aside and sat me down on the settee. "Rob my love I want you to do something for me." She looked me straight in the eyes and held both my hands. "I want you to sleep with Caroline. I want you to give her another child that is my present to her from us both." "You can't be serious you would never forgive me besides she can't have any children." "I've seen the old gypsy lady again it was her suggestion Rob. She confirmed what Katie had said. Jonathan will be returned soon unharmed, we are going to be one big family those were her words and I believe her Rob." I shook my head in disbelief at what Sam was suggesting. "You are to pick up Caroline 7.30pm this evening. Don't worry I love you so much, nothing will ever part us." Sam showed me her arm. She had the same mark on it as me. I left the house after changing and kissing Sam goodbye. I drove over to Katie's house and collected Caroline. We drove out into the countryside to a nice quiet pub and had a lovely meal we sat in the car park talking before driving home. "Thank you for everything Caroline the stables would not have survived without you." She smiled sweetly and held my hand we kissed a little. We went inside Katie's house Caroline made me a coffee and we sat in front of the fire "Sam told me to sleep with you Rob." I couldn't believe my ears. "Why would she say something like that any other time she would have killed me?" "I don't know Caroline what's going on?" "You don't think she's trying to get a divorce Rob?" "No it's probably that bloody old gypsy woman she's been talking to put ideas in her head but I must confess the old gypsy woman saved Katie's life." Caroline stood up and removed her pink blouse and skirt. She uncoupled her bra and removed her pants. I remove my clothes quickly she sat on the carpet holding me close and we lay side-by-side on the carpet kissing and caressing. It wasn't long before we were making love, not just once but twice. I couldn't stop myself. I'd never made love to someone for so long in my life. I just didn't want to stop. Caroline was clinging to me begging for more. We enjoyed each other every time we had come together, but never so much as now. We lay beside each other totally exhausted "If I'm not pregnant now Rob I never will be." She commented. I heard the clock chime midnight and I mounted her again "Oh God" she cried out "that's wonderful." It was 2 o'clock in the morning before I arrived home. Sam was sitting in the living room waiting for me. She held my hand and led me to the bedroom never once asking about the evening and what happened.

Chapter 11
Grasping the situation

I dressed and looked out of the bedroom window I could see Caroline working with the horses. Sam stood behind me with her hands on my shoulders. She kissed me gently on the neck professing she loved me. I turn and kissed her on the lips and we showered to together. She looked for the mark on her arm it had gone. Sam dressed and we went down for breakfast, Christina was asking where Jonathan was. Sam did her best to explain he was on a long holiday trying to shield Christina from the pain and reality of the situation. It was almost like Robert and Jonathan had vanished into thin air. All we had was the old gypsy lady's prediction they would be found and it wouldn't be too long. How does one measure the length of time when loved ones are missing? Katie was recovering in leaps and bounds. I wondered what price we would have to pay in the end for what had taken place. Rupert was really starting to show his age and the stress of recent events was pulling him down. Sam and I had talked to him assuring we were not blaming him for what had happened. We went out into the yard. Sam embraced Caroline like a daughter instead of her usual keep your distance attitude. There was a lot going on I didn't understand Sam suggested that I learn to ride and made Caroline teach me. I was not impressed with the idea of being jogged about on the back of an animal that could suddenly decide to charge off in any direction and likely to drop you in a pile of cow muck. Sam's reason was we could ride together in the summer. It would also assist with exercising the horses. Johnny was doing very well in South Africa. His grandparents had died within a week of each other leaving the majority of their estate to him and the business which they had been training him for. £3 million was transferred into Katie's account and a trust fund had been set up for the children. Johnny was upset with his grandparents and the way they had excluded me from the will. He transferred 3 million into my account as far as he was concerned. I'd been treated unfairly by everyone and promised to fly over to England once he had all the business affairs in order. He sent his love to everybody.

Charmed Log Cabin: Enchanted Life

Another month had passed still no news on the children and everyone was becoming rather frustrated with the situation, including Mr MacDonald, but he did promise to keep looking. I couldn't imagine another Christmas knowing Jonathan and Robert were still out there and not with us. Caroline and Sam came across to me with a mug of coffee while I worked on repairing a feeding trough in the stable. Sam informed me Caroline was pregnant without a glint of remorse for asking me to sleep with Caroline. They had become very close. Katie moved back into her house cured of cancer, so the old gypsy woman was right about the cabin. Vicky and Jasmine continue to live in the cabin. On Saturday morning Sam and I rode through the wood with our horses trying to dodge the branches. We stopped outside the cabin. We dismounted and tied the horses up, Vicky and Jasmine came out to greet us. We went inside to have a coffee Vicky remarked "I didn't know you could ride Rob?" Sam took Jasmine into the front room and was having a private conversation with her. Vicky and I looked on wondering what was going on Vicky remarked. "Jasmine hasn't seen anybody since she slept with you neither of us for that matter she is in love with you Rob we all are." I shrugged my shoulders "I don't know why, Vicky I'm over 40 showing my age." "It's not your age Rob or the way you look. It's what you are as a person that drives us wild I think you are possessed by magic." I smiled "You haven't been smoking cannabis in here" I joked. Sam and Jasmine returned to the kitchen then Sam took Vicky into the front room. I whispered in Jasmine's ear "What's going on?" She smiled and sipped her coffee sliding her free hand on my trouser leg I removed it quickly. "Sam will see stop it". Sam returned to the kitchen, glanced to me and smiled we finished our coffee and left riding back to the stables "What was all that about Sam? Why were you talking to Vicky and Jasmine privately? What is it you don't want me to know?" She turned to face me draping her arms over my shoulders and tenderly kissing me, "Nothing for you to worry about Rob just girl talk."

Rupert had taken semi-retirement from his law firm and was spending most of his time at home trying to work out where Bethany could have possibly gone with Jonathan and Robert. His girlfriend Nicole had fallen in love with Christina, who had now started school and would fetch her and take her to school every day. Nicole was a wealthy woman in her own right she didn't need anybody to support her. She owned a printing firm in London and didn't work anymore, all her free time she would spend with the children. Vicky was teaching Christina to ride under her supervision when she stayed with Nicole and Rupert he would spoil her, but we didn't mind it was his granddaughter and she made him happy. Katie would allow Nicky her daughter to stay with Christina sometimes but was rather worried about her disappearing like Robert.

Sam finished work early, said she was going to cook a special meal and would be at 8:30 PM I was to come home early enough to wash and change. I thought to myself at the time that was very odd. Usually we sat in the kitchen grabbing a quick snack. Perhaps she was trying to surprise me. Caroline had also left early which was unlike her. By 8:15 PM I was washed changed had a shave and returned to the living room sitting in front of the fire with my Bacardi and coke. I heard a knock at the door and Sam shouted "I'll go." I could hear people talking at the door much to my surprise in walked Jasmine and Vicky I stood up. The two of them were wearing see-through blouses with barely a button done up and miniskirts so short you could almost describe them as a belt, they looked stunning. I offered them a drink and they sat down. Sam called out. "I'm just going to change I won't be a minute." Sam came down wearing similar to the girls' outfit which was totally out of character for her. The girls looked nervous. We went in for the meal that Sam had cooked we sat around the large dining table me at one end Sam at the other and the two girls either side. I voiced. "This is a surprise I didn't know Sam had invited you." Sam spoke up. "That's what I was talking to them about in the cabin, we don't have many visitors and I thought the two girls had been so good I should invite them." We finished the meal, Vicky and Jasmine thanked Sam for a lovely meal. I went off into the lounge and poured everyone another drink. I sat in the middle of the settee looking into the fire my favourite pastime. Sam was in the doorway with Vicky and Jasmine adjusting their clothing. I called to them ". I've made you a drink come sit down". Vicky and Jasmine sat either side of me. Sam sat in the armchair crossing her legs giving me full view of her thigh. I also noticed she had unbuttoned her blouse and parted it slightly exposing her breasts. Jasmine nervously placed her hand on my leg looked across to Sam who slowly shook her head and Jasmine removed her hand. I was wondering what was going on here. I saw Vicky and Jasmine both had faint hexagrams on the back of their hand. Sam's had reappeared only this time on her thigh but very faint. The girls were chatting to Sam. I just sat in the middle listening to the conversation which was mainly about horses. At 10.30 PM the girls were leaving each kiss me on the cheek and did the same to Sam and left. I poured myself another drink and sat in my armchair. Sam returned to her armchair opposite side the fireplace "What was all that about Sam?" "I don't know what you mean Rob," she said softly" "Come off it Sam you're showing me everything and so were the girls. I suppose you want me to fuck them too?" "I didn't say that Rob." She smiled. "Or are they bloody lesbians that you want to play with?" "Don't be ridiculous I made you a promise and I'm keeping it don't you like the way I'm dressed? Wouldn't you like to take me to bed?" she said standing up removing her knickers?" "Any time I would take you to bed, you are my wife I love you and you only." "Let's not argue Rob it was a pleasant meal and the girls enjoyed themselves" Sam moved from her chair and sat on my lap. She was all over me like a rash slipping my hand between her legs and we finally retired to bed. The next morning, I called in to see Katie and spent some time with Julian, we went into the living room. Katie came in carrying a tray, no longer needing a walking stick. She sat opposite me pouring the coffee "How you feeling now Katie, you look marvellous." "Wonderful Rob wonderful I feel like 18 all over again. It was very kind of you to give Caroline another baby. She told me that Sam had approved. That was a shock." "I can't understand what's going on Katie she had Jasmine and Vicky round for dinner, she even showed them how to dress to try and entice me, I'm confused." "It is a bit strange Rob she will let you sleep with me. We did make a beautiful child didn't we." "Yes, he's lovely." She moved over and sat on my lap. "I don't mind sharing you if I can't have you all to myself." She smiled, kissing my neck.

Chapter 12
Where are Robert and Jonathan

Mr MacDonald had contacted me to say they now thought the children were somewhere in France and he wasn't very impressed with the French police. They appeared to be dragging their feet but rest assured he was doing everything within his power to resolve the situation. He said it may be a case we have to let the press loose, but would prefer not to encase it endangered the welfare of the children. I thanked him for his update and relayed the information to Sam. She held me close and cried on my shoulder. She dried her eyes and we carried on working around the stables. Caroline was starting to show she was pregnant. Sam had banned her from going into any stables unaccompanied and if she felt ill in the slightest way she was to stop work immediately and report to her. This was a new side to Sam. I couldn't get over how much care she was taking of Caroline if anyone deserved help it was Caroline she really was a lovely person. Christina was doing extremely well at school must have been given intelligence from her mother I decided the same went for Nicky. At least they should do well in later life I concluded. Sam asked me to take one of the horses for a ride and give it some exercise I rode across the fields out into the countryside. Spring was here again buttercups cowslips and my favourite bluebells in the wood out in the middle of nowhere. I came across the old gypsy woman. I dismounted and greeted her "Are you well?" She looked me over with her glazed eyes that held a million stories of things that have happened and things to come; she remarked "Katie recovered I told you it would work." "Do you know where Robert and Jonathan are? Can you not help us?" She lowered herself down to sat on the style in the hedgerow and thought for a moment "You may not believe this Chosen One but they are safe and you do have my word you will see them again but not just yet. There are things they have to learn before they come home". I gave her another £20 note from my pocket "Bless you" she said climbing over the style. I looked at my horse for reassurance I'd spoken to the gypsy woman. I looked around I couldn't see any sign of her She had vanished into thin air. I mounted my horse and continued riding around the perimeter of the property. I cut through into my wood and Started to ride past the cabin. I noticed on one of the roof tiles a hexagram faintly burnt into the timber. I looked at my arm they were identical. I trotted on back to the stable not telling Sam about meeting the gypsy woman again and what had happened. We heard Caroline cry out. We ran over to one of the stables a horse had stood on her foot, we all sighed with relief. Sam scolded her for being in there on her own. Sam took her into the house to examine her foot. I calmed the horse which was more like the size of an elephant, a member of the Shire horse family and weighed a considerable amount. Caroline came hobbling back from the house, Sam asked me to take her to the doctors just to make sure nothing was broken. We went in my range Rover. Caroline reached over and placed my hand on her stomach "Thank you Rob this is our creation". The doctor had given her the all clear but told her to rest. I phoned Sam and suggested we ask Vicky and Jasmine if Caroline could stay in the cabin to protect the baby during her remaining pregnancy. Sam thought it was a brilliant idea. Caroline was not so happy about the idea but conceded she didn't want to lose her unborn child again. I spoke to Vicky "Can Caroline stay with you in the cabin for the remainder of her pregnancy" Vicky replied "She is our sister of course she can". I spoke to Katie and explained my reasons she thought it was a good idea too. We called round to Katie's house and collected some clothes for Caroline and drove her to the cabin. I went into my old bedroom and she laid on the bed to rest. I kissed her gently on the lips. "Vicky will drop you off to work in the morning when you had chance to rest and if you're still not feeling well just collect your car and come back to the cabin." I drove back slowly to Cranbury farm trying to analyse what Vicky had said: our sister? To my knowledge they weren't related I shook my head trying to work out what was going on. Whatever power the cabin had was well beyond my comprehension, the old gypsy lady seemed to know everything yet gave very little information away. Sam arranged for Jasmine to help Caroline with her workload. Caroline was really starting to struggle so Sam decided she could no longer work with the horses until she had given birth. She was sent back to the cabin to stay there until it was time. Sam also told her she would not lose any pay not to worry about money. Sam was being generous almost like me, which I thought didn't come naturally to her. Something had changed her for better or worse I was undecided for the moment. What did strike me as very odd Sam would encourage Jasmine to work in the same area as me? I was working in a stable in the shadow, Sam was stood across the yard and Jasmine was close to the door looking towards Sam. Sam put her finger to her lips then lifted three fingers up to

Jasmine. Then on her blouse, counting three buttons down, and then she indicated part the blouse and go into the stable with me. I was absolutely shocked, what's going on. Why is Sam doing this? Sure enough in walked Jasmine. She had undone a further three buttons on her blouse and had parted it giving me full view of the top of her breasts before she could say anything. I walked out of the stable Sam looked at me with a concerned expression she suspected I'd seen something. I walked to my range Rover jumped in and drove off. Sam phoned "Where you going Rob what's the matter?" "I'm just going for a ride to the wholesalers. I need some screws of a different size okay?" I turn the phone off. I didn't give her chance to reply and she didn't ring back. I called in to see Katie. We sat drinking coffee. I explained to her what I'd seen. She moved over and sat on my lap, telling me how much she loved me "It's obvious she wants you to make Jasmine pregnant." "Why?" "Perhaps she really does want another child but is too afraid to mention it to you?" "Where's Julian?" "He's asleep having his nap he's a wonderful son I love him to bits I just wish Robert was home to share these moments" she sighed. I kissed Katie goodbye and return to Cranbury farm. Vicky was talking to Sam. Vicky looked over Sam shoulder and told her I'd returned. Sam was fiddling with Vicky's clothes they both come across to me. Sam had a guilty expression on her face. "I want you to go with Vicky and exercise two horses Rob take the usual route round the perimeter of the property please." "No I won't I've got more important things to do than mess about with bloody horse." I said walking off into the stable where I was working before. Sam came bursting in through the door. Grabbed my arm "I run the stables not you Rob." I'd never seen her look so angry. "I'll tell you what Sam, here's the screwdriver there's the screws fix it you're fucking self I'm off and while we're on the subject nice try with Jasmine but it didn't work." Sam's face went white now she knew I had seen her instructing Jasmine. She didn't know what to say as I walked out of the stable. Vicky came running over to me as I was about to get in my range Rover. "Don't go Rob, it's my fault and Jasmine's we just wanted to be with you and Sam was being so nice to us" Jasmine came running across from the shadows. Sam joined us with tears in her eyes "Come on let's go in the house we need to talk" she said quietly. I poured myself a large Bacardi and coke and sat in my armchair. I was bloody fuming to say the least. Sam poured the girls a drink then sat opposite in her armchair. The girls sat on the settee with their heads bowed as if at school waiting for punishment to be handed out. Sam glanced up from her glass "It's my entire fault Rob I should have talked to you first." "We've been down this road before Sam." Before she could speak I walked out of the door jumped in my range Rover and drove off. My phone rang it was Sam I didn't bother to answer, Vicky tried and so did Jasmine. I didn't answer any of the calls. I noticed a miss call from Caroline and a message she'd been taken into hospital her baby was on the way she hadn't carried seven months so its survival could be touch and go. I drove to the hospital and was allowed in to see her. The child was in intensive care. But other than that it was fine. I held her hand and sat by the side of her bed "Are you okay Caroline, how's the baby?" She gripped my hand tightly "He will be fine Rob" she smiled. Sam walked in carrying a bouquet of flowers. The nurse took them from her to place in water I stood up so Sam could sit down. Sam held my hand tightly we talked with Caroline for a while. We both kissed her goodbye and walked out into the hospital car park. Sam held both my hands then flung her arms around my neck holding me close "Don't leave me Rob please. I know I make mistakes just don't leave me I couldn't bear it." We went home in our separate vehicles we sat in front of the fire on the carpet. Sam placed her arm around my shoulder. "Vicky and Jasmine are really upset they think you don't like them anymore." I sighed heavily. "It's not that Sam. I love you I don't want to be unfaithful and you shouldn't be encouraging it, why are you?" She lent her head on my shoulder. "I don't really understand myself Rob." "I think I'm going to set fire to the cabin tomorrow burn the bloody thing to the ground." Sam said alarmed. "You mustn't don't do that please the old gypsy said whoever damages the cabin will die." "Your, seeing the gypsy woman then?" "Yes, quite often, actually, she told me you would never leave me and if I wanted another child in the family, Vicky or Jasmine would accommodate." "You're not the only one that seen her recently either. I did across the fields she appeared then vanished, I know that sounds ridiculous." "What's going on Rob I don't understand." Sam received a phone call from Vicky. Jasmine had locked herself in the bedroom and was threatening to kill herself. Sam called up to Jane to tell her we have to go out could she hold the fort. She grabbed my hand and explained to me on the way to the cabin. I was horrified, the thought that I could have that effect on someone, we burst into the cabin "Where is she Vicky." "In her bedroom Rob." Sam knocked on the door asking Jasmine to let her in and we could talk things through. There was no reply. I pushed Sam aside and kicked the lock on the door breaking in. Jasmine was on the bed; I picked her up in my arms and held her close. She placed her arms around my neck crying inconsolably. Sam stood and watched and so did Vicky. I kissed her gently on the cheek and told Jasmine I would always love her. "It's my fault Rob it's all my fault." Sam and Vicky went to make a drink and left me talking to Jasmine. She eventually dried her eyes and came into the front room. She sat beside me on the settee. Sam stood there with tears in her eyes watching how I handled the situation. I made Jasmine promise me she wouldn't do anything silly again and they could both come to dinner next week. I looked up to Sam and she approved. We left the girls in the cabin and slowly drove home. "Now you see why I love you Rob, you haven't an evil bone in your body only love." I received a phone call from Mr MacDonald C.I.D they now knew where the children were. Cuba, this had now become a diplomatic problem because of no extradition treaty he would keep us posted. I phoned to make sure Katie knew what was going on and Rupert who had already got divorce proceedings underway against his wife. He had also arranged for a private investigator to travel into Cuba to see what he can find out unbeknown to the police.

Chapter 13
Total deception

Another week came to a close. Sam had arranged for Vicky and Jasmine to come Saturday evening at 8 o'clock. Jane had taken Christina to her grandparents for the weekend and gone for the weekend herself. Sam cooked the meal I placed the wineglasses on the table and bottle of wine for the girls. We were going to try and make this very special for them, Sam went up to change. The girls arrived and I let them in. Once again they were wearing extremely short skirts and see-through blouses with obviously no bra underneath. I was a little annoyed at their dress sense you could clearly see their nipples and their breasts through the material. I took them into the lounge and poured them a drink. They both sat on the settee not wearing knickers. Sam returned to the front room she was dressed virtually identically I could see her breasts through her see-through top. I felt like walking out of the room but decided just play along and see where this is heading. Sam sat in the armchair I sat in mine I can see quite clearly. Sam wasn't wearing any knickers, she smiled sweetly at me drinking her wine and playing with our wedding ring on her finger. I could see this marriage ending before the night was out something was going on here and I didn't understand. If Sam and I were on our own and she dressed like that I wouldn't have cared less, in the presence of the two girls I was disgusted. The meal went off without a hitch just general chit-chat. We returned to the lounge after we had eaten. Sam pushed herself close to me in the doorway kissing me on the lips passionately sliding my hand beneath her short skirt to make sure I knew she wasn't wearing anything. Sam seated in the usual armchair the girls on the settee and me in the other armchair sipping our favourite drink. I really wanted to stand up and give Sam a real roasting but I didn't want to upset the girls and have a repeat performance of a suicide attempt. I was damn sure I was going to burn Sam's ears off once they'd gone. Sam then rose to her feet pulling something from her waist, a shiny Star "Girls, watch this." I laughed "What you think you're going to do with that." "I'm going to make you the happiest man in the world" I continued drinking from my glass while Sam spun the Star in front of my eyes. The girls watched intently then all I could hear was Sam's voice. "Stand up Rob, take all your clothes off, you will do exactly as I tell you, you can hear you can see, you cannot fight my instructions." "Can I hold it Sam" "Yes Vicky?" Sam instructed Jasmine to lay on the floor open her blouse and lift her skirt up. Sam returned to her chair. "Rob, make love to Jasmine now quickly." I felt myself compelled to do as she commanded when I had finished I stood up. "Rest Rob return to your chair and rest, Vicky lay on the floor open your blouse and lift your skirt up. Make love to Vicky Rob now quickly." I did as I was ordered not having the power to stop myself when I had finished I stood up. "Rest Rob, Vicky Jasmine, home it's done" Sam laid herself on the floor after an hour. "Make love to me Rob now". I proceeded to do as I was ordered then I suddenly awoke lying on top of Sam close to the fireplace. She was kissing me passionately I shook my head. "What is the matter Rob?" I moved away from Sam realising I was naked. Sam remarked. "Don't you want me anymore?" I just couldn't remember taking my clothes off. I couldn't remember getting on top of Sam. She came across to me. "Come on Rob, one more time make love to me." She kissed me tenderly pressing her breasts tight against my chest, allowing her hand to encourage me and we made love on the carpet beside the fire. Sam made some coffee afterwards and sat in her armchair. "Why did you dress like that Sam? What happened to the girls?" "Don't you remember Rob? We had a lovely meal chatting for a while and they went home." "I'm rather disappointed with the way you dressed in front of company Sam." "I was just trying to get you excited for later" she smiled. We went to bed and she was all over me riding me like she would one of her horses. I couldn't understand she went on and on and on wanting more and more and more, finally she let me sleep she bought me breakfast in bed which I thought was very odd. This was definitely the first time that had happened. I asked what was the reason she responded, "because of what we did last night." She said I performed wonderfully she'd never had such good sex from me before She wanted the same again tonight. She was feeding me up in preparation. I asked "What happened last night? I have gaps in my memory." She smiled sitting beside me on the bed "Let's just say your performance was outstanding" she chuckled. I'd never seen her this way before, yes we'd had great sex always but she'd never commented before so excited on my performance. I finished my breakfast and dressed. I drove over to Katie's house Caroline was now, back there with her new son. Katie let me in and I sat in the armchair in the living room. Caroline came down carrying her new son and placed him in my lap, "Meet your son Rob. Stephen a bonny little chap."

"Thank you so much Rob for giving me this child, I'm now complete." She smiled. She went back upstairs with him. Katie sat on my lap. I told her everything that had happened last night and my lapse of memory again very similar experience to when they had drugged me. Katie thought for a moment and then responded "You were hypnotised by Sam. I bet you were made to have sex with the two girls and then with Sam, so you wouldn't realise it was somebody else." I sat there in horror I'd really been conned and by my own wife. Caroline who had entered the room before the conversation had finished commented. "Jasmine is on the pill and so is Vicky I wouldn't lose any sleep over it Rob, she moaned about what we did to you." "Why would Sam allow this to happen she's gone completely weird?" Katie professed getting up and pouring me a large Bacardi and coke and returning to my lap. Caroline sat in the other chair looking rather left out. I suggested to Katie we all sit on the settee then I could put my arm round each of them. She agreed and we moved. Katie remarked "You'll soon have a bloody harem" laughing. After about half an hour I left and returned to Cranbury farm. I sat in my armchair looking into the fire. Sam came in. "You don't look very happy Rob what can possibly be the matter?" "Where's the pendant?" Sam replied "What pendant?" Sam looked worried. "Come off it Sam, I wasn't born yesterday." "Oh you mean this." She removed the pendant from the inside of her belt. She nervously handed it to me, I examined it closely then placed it against the symbol on my arm they were identical. Sam flopped down into her armchair holding her head in her hands. She started to cry. "I'm sorry Rob." "You better tell me what happened last night and the bloody truth Sam. I've had enough of being lied to all the time." I poured myself a Bacardi. Sam explained everything that had happened. I exhaled "Oh bloody hell is that the whole truth Sam?" She nodded. "It was the gypsy woman she told me what to do, because I couldn't get you to do it any other way. She said it was important if I wanted to see Jonathan and Robert again." She was obviously telling the truth by the state she was in I encourage her to come and sit on my lap. I embraced her and told her I loved her. I didn't understand what the gypsy woman was trying to achieve and I really didn't want to bloody know but I did want Robert and Jonathan back. I explained to Sam we would just have to play along for the time being. We didn't want to jeopardise any chance of the children been returned. I almost felt that this was a set up from the very beginning. Everything that had happened was linked to the cabin and its history. Jasmine and Vicky came to work as usual. They never pestered me anymore and seemed quite content just to carry on with their work. I couldn't see any obvious signs after a month of Vicky and Jasmine being pregnant. For some unknown reason Vicky and

Jasmine both handed in their notice at the same time. Saying they were leaving to work somewhere else. Sam and I wondered what was going on they both seem to be so very happy working here. Whatever had attracted them to me had obviously gone. Sam had put the pendant in her jewellery box upstairs she didn't want to carry it with her. Neither of us had seen any signs of the old gypsy woman either. Caroline had started back at the stables. Stephen was being cared for by Jane during the day.

Sam employed two new girls from the village. The press tried to grab the story from us regarding the missing children they managed to take some photos of me and Sam and Katie. Fortunately, Rupert used the law to have them banned from entering the property which took the pressure off us. The cabin was now empty again I went over and prepared it for the approaching winter. I had the local garage collect Johnny's quad bike and get it running so we could use it round the stables which was very handy when you had to cross fields. Time was marching on Caroline had taken charge of the new girls training them to do the job properly. Sam and Caroline still remained very close. Sam took great pleasure in pushing the pushchair around the stables with Stephen in it. Caroline didn't mind she was that sort of girl. One of the new girls approach me with a broken catch her name was Josephine, tall thin lass very slim build freckled complexion with ginger hair "Rob could you fix this please." I took it from her hand and said "Leave it to me". Rupert had divorced his wife and was preparing to marry Nicole she was the best thing that ever happened to him. I'd never seen him so happy. Katie came into the yard in her free Lander "Have you heard the news, have you heard the news" She shouted. The new stable girls looked on in bewilderment Caroline Sam and I join Katie "They had found Jonathan and Robert in Cuba and within the next 2 to 3 weeks they would be brought home." We all held each other crying. I received a phone call from Mr McDonald apologising for how long it took to find them but at least they were on the way home in due course. The children were fit and healthy. Mr Goldings ex-wife had been arrested and also been extradited to the UK to face charges of kidnapping. She also had an accomplice a Mr Rafferty from Ireland. He too was being extradited to face criminal charges we just couldn't believe the news. The newspapers went wild trying to phone us for a story. Rupert came to the rescue and gave a press conference at his home to keep the pressure of the rest of us. The clock was ticking and it was finally counting down in our favour. We went to bed that evening a very happy couple. Sam reached over to her jewellery box and discovered the pendant had vanished. She searched and searched but it wasn't there. Sam made passionate love to me and we slept like we've never slept before peace had finally reached the household, my life was finally going to settle down and drift into an uneventful history. I went riding the next morning around the perimeter of the property with snowdrop my favourite horse. Much to my horror I saw the old gypsy woman sitting on the style. I dismounted and approached her. "I told you Chosen One, that the children would be returned." "Why did you give Sam that pendant to hypnotise me?" I protested. "Vicky and Jasmine are both with child you will never see them again. We have other plans for them and your payment to the spirits for the return of your children." "Why didn't you just tell me that in the beginning we could have had my two sons back long ago" "Both of the girls offered theirselves to you unreservedly and you turned them away." I gave the old gypsy woman a £50 note she climbed over the style again and vanished. I rode back to the stables very slowly. Sam approached me seeing the expression on my face of bewilderment. I dismounted she searched my face with a beautiful hazel eyes. "You have seen the gypsy woman haven't you?" I explained to Sam what she told me and everything had been planned beyond our control. There were things in heaven and earth that we didn't understand and could not comprehend. Caroline took the horse from me. Sam and I walked up the yard arm in arm, while she rested her head on my shoulder. Mr MacDonald thought it may be prudent for Jane to come to London and meet the children at the airport. Out of sight of the press, slipping them out the back in a police car and bring the children back to us at Cranbury farm. He would also position a police car at the top of the drive. Stopping any press coming down to the house to give us absolute privacy while we accustomed the children back into our lives. He thought the press, once they saw Mrs Goldings and her lover coming through the airport, would be totally distracted away from the children if all went to plan. The day had finally arrived the day we've been waiting for what appeared to be a lifetime. A police car collected Jane early in the morning and drove her to London airport. Caroline stopped at home with her own child and Nicky and Julian at Katie's house. We watched television. The media were everywhere. You could see Mr MacDonald waiting in the airport with a dozen officers keeping the public and the press back. The plane finally touched down, Mrs Goldings and her lover had blankets over their head as the cameramen focused on them being escorted from the airport. Mr MacDonald's plan had worked. Rupert joined us at the house waiting to see the return of his grandchild. Robert and Jonathan entered the house standing side-by-side in identical suits and looked like they were twins. Neither Sam nor Katie knew which was which. Everyone stood for a moment Staring at each other then, Robert Started crying "mum" running to Katie and Jonathan did the same to Sam. They'd grown so much in the time they been away.

Within a few months, Robert and Jonathan had readjusted to their familiar surroundings. Our lives were now complete again both Jonathan and Robert had symbols of hexagram on their arm identical to their father. Rupert married Nicole and had a lavish party to celebrate the return of Robert and Jonathan and his wedding combined. On the roadside far away from the party stood the old gypsy woman who waved then faded away. Rupert announced he had purchased a property in Switzerland where he was going to spend his retirement with his new wife Nicole. He said the property was big enough for all the children to visit him at once for holidays. Sam and I could have his house Redbrick farm which consisted of 16 bedrooms and take over his livery business altogether. He still owned the legal firm although he didn't play much of a part in it any more. Sam, Katie and Caroline had a meeting amongst themselves unbeknown to me. I went into the house at Cranbury farm and found the three of them together. Sam asked me to sit down and listen to their proposal. They had decided because I was the father of all the children, it only seems sensible we all live together. I asked "Whose idea was this?" "Mine originally" Sam remarked sitting on the arm of my chair, placing her arm around my shoulder "We all love you Rob. The children love you and if we are altogether then no one loses out." I looked very confused "Sam I thought you didn't want me near anybody else?" "All our lives are so intertwined and I've shared you with Katie and Caroline before so nothing will have changed, you will still be my husband and always will. Please agree it really does make sense." I sighed "I must confess I do love you all in different ways but I am concerned about jealousy setting in and ruining everything for everyone." "That will never happen we are all content." There was a knock at the door.

Chapter 14
A power from the past

Sam went to answer it was the old gypsy lady "Can I come in please I need to speak to you all." She hobbled in the lounge we all stood looking at her. She started transforming into a beautiful woman. Sam screamed "Mother!" There standing before us all in white was Sam's mother. Everybody stepped away in fear. She started to speak "My daughter come to me." Sam ran over and held her mother. "I have waited a long time to hold you again Samantha. Sit down everyone I want to explain everything to you. Many years ago white witch's lived where Rob built the log cabin. They practiced magic only to heal people. But to the rest of the world a witch is a witch they were all murdered. The chain of events we put in motion made Rob restore our house and in return I gave him you my daughter. Everything that happened to each and every one of you was planned by me and my sisters." Katie asked "What happens now?" "You will all live together as planned. Caroline, your dream will come true, Rob will give you another child in time it will be a daughter. Samantha as wife of the Chosen One you will control the household "Will I ever see you again Mother?" "I'm always with you Samantha and occasionally you will see me. I shall be moving into the log cabin my new home with my sisters. Rob will stay in the cabin one night on the full moon to maintain his youth and strength because of his purity of heart." She kissed Sam on the forehead and vanished. Sam collapsed in the chair crying everyone came to support her. "So your mother planned everything" I remarked. We all sat round the fire trying to grasp what had taken place our future was planned whether we liked it or not. Caroline was smiling at the thought of having another child in the future.

Nearly a month had passed. Rupert had left for Switzerland with his new wife. We all said our goodbyes and wished them well. Sam made plans to move everybody in to the house Sam reminded me that I must go to the cabin on the night of the full moon, which was tomorrow. Everything appeared to be going extremely well but I was rather concerned about what was going to happen to me in the cabin. Although Sam had assured me her mother would never hurt me. The next day passed quickly and I arrived at the cabin at 5:30 PM I entered the cabin. The log burner was already alight and the cabin was warm. I went into the kitchen and poured myself a Bacardi and coke. I sat in the front room watching television trying to anticipate what was going to take place. I could smell something cooking in the kitchen which seemed rather odd, considering I hadn't prepared anything. So I went back into the kitchen to investigate the smell. There was Christina Sam's mother in a long white gown, her red hair just like her daughter cascaded down to the curve of the spine. Her complexion was pure in every form. I stood there in amazement how she had managed to get past me and prepare a meal without me hearing anything. She turned and smiled. "I can feel your tension and anxiety Rob. Don't be Rob you are safe with me. I have seen the way you have loved Samantha and fulfilled her with happiness" she approached me and kiss me on the lips. I pulled away in shock. She smiled "Don't be afraid." "You are Rupert's wife and my wife's mother". She placed the meal on the kitchen table. I had to admit it smelt absolutely wonderful although some of the vegetables I didn't recognise. "In answer to your question I am not Rupert's wife, since I am supposedly dead. You are correct, Samantha is my daughter and I am her mother kissing you will make no difference to either of them. I am your strength and life giver, eat your food Rob." I seated myself at the table. The meat was tender the vegetables although not recognised tasted absolutely wonderful.

I cleared my plate without any difficulty although I did feel a little strange. Christina poured me a glass of wine from a strange coloured bottle "Drink Rob drink please" she insisted. "Sit by the fire and relax I will attend to you in a moment." I could see shadows of people in the room all coming to look at me. I concluded. I must be hallucinating. No silly noises or scary faces as you would see on a horror film just pleasant figures flying around looking at me and occasionally, one would touch my hair then another would touch my cheek. The touch was not cold nor warm just pleasant. After about half an hour Christina entered the room. She was no longer dressed in white she was almost dressed like Sam would dress white blouse, black skirt and shoes. She held out her hand "Sit with me Rob we need to talk." We moved and seated ourselves on the settee. She snapped her fingers and the television went out. That's the best remote-control I've ever seen I was becoming scared. She held my hand, I didn't resist for fear of the consequences. "Calm down Rob relax you are safe you are the Chosen One for that very reason you are pure of heart and that's why we chose you to be the father of the new covenant." "You mean just a sex machine to father babies for you?" "No it's what's inside you, you hurt no one you help everyone. That is why you were chosen we didn't think anyone existed like you anymore. We have been searching for a long time and when we discovered what Jenny had done to you. We disposed of her she didn't deserve a second chance." "Oh, I sighed. You have that sort of power to give and take life?" "Yes." "You didn't do a very good job with Samantha she was a bloody lesbian" "It's better she was a lesbian than sleeping with men contaminating her body." We were keeping her for the man we chose, we knew once she had slept with you. She would never want to be a lesbian anymore and the same applies to Katie and Caroline. They are no longer interested only in you." "Wow this takes some understanding, what happened to Vicky and Jasmine?" Christina waved her hand around in a circle I could see Jasmine and Vicky holding their children in their arms "They're your daughters yes they both had girls. They are healthy and safe the Start of our new generation, be warned Rob I can hear your thoughts. You are wondering whether I am real touch me, unbutton my blouse and touch my breast. See if you can feel my heart". My hand trembled doing as she commanded I pressed my hand against her chest. I could feel her heartbeat. I was shocked. "You are alive." She smiled "Of course I am. I can be anything I want, a spirit, flesh and blood". I quickly re-buttoned her blouse and removed my hands. This woman was frightening the bloody life out of me. My mind then wondered what Sam was doing and would she be angry if I took her mother to bed. Christina laughed. "Let me show you Rob." she waved her hand in a circle again and there was a vision of Sam playing with the children along with Katie and Caroline. "And in answer to your question, she wouldn't mind, and neither would I." She held my hand and led me into my bedroom. She snapped her fingers and all her clothes fell to the floor. My God I'd never seen a figure like that in my life. She snapped her fingers again and all my clothes just fell off. We both stood there naked looking at each other. I immediately had an erection. She lay on the bed poised we kissed and caressed each other then I penetrated her warm body. She was unbelievable, obviously not from this world. I'd never had a woman like this before we lay beside each other still holding each other kissing. "You are the Chosen One you may take me any time you want I am yours forever. I will maintain you, keep you fit and well, so we can share an eternity together." She laughed "I know why my daughter loves you". She moved herself on top of me I held her lovely shaped breasts. She didn't stop until the early hours. We went in the shower together then dressed and returned to the kitchen. She snapped her fingers and there was a cup of coffee in front of me. Whatever I thought she could make it happen if she chose to. Caroline came into my mind and what we had done on this table. Christina smiled. "Remember Rob I can read your thoughts." My mind then wondered how she'd become a witch "In answer to your thought one of my ancestors many years ago was killed and burnt at the stake. So when I had my accident I was immediately taken to become what I am now. The only sad part was leaving behind Samantha she suffered a lot until we found you to make her life complete." "Could you make it so she could have a child again?" "No that is not her task she will be the mother of everyone in the house. She has two beautiful children and she is satisfied with that." Christina placed her arms around my neck and kissed me tenderly on the lips "Even now you try to make things right for my daughter. Your heart is pure and we are blessed to have you". Christina snapped her fingers her clothes drop to the floor. She sat herself on the table inviting me. I entered her body once more she enchanted me. It was nearly daybreak when we'd finished. "It's time for me to go Chosen One" She kissed me tenderly on the lips "see you the next full moon." She smiled and vanished.

I returned home Sam and Caroline were round the stables. They both came over to greet me each kissing me on the cheek. Sam voiced "Tell us what happened did you enjoy yourself, look at your hair. It's gone black all the grey his gone, you look younger somehow." Caroline agreed. "You are different I don't know quite how you are different." "Come on make me a coffee in the house and I'll talk to you all." We went inside. Katie, Caroline and Sam sat on the settee I relaxed in the armchair facing them all they listened intently to everything I had to say. I did miss out the part where I slept with her mother.

I didn't want to hurt Sam's feelings they were surprised that her mother could wave her hand and see what we were all doing. I explained to them quite clearly her mother had the power to give life and take it so not to be messed with, or try to deceive her because she can read your thoughts. The girls were horrified. "So we have no private thoughts?" Caroline voiced. Katie remarked. "That's bloody unfair". Sam came over and sat on the arm of my chair placing her arm around my shoulder. "I shouldn't think any of you should have unpleasant thoughts about the situation considering Katie. You wouldn't be here if it wasn't for my mother and you Caroline would have lost your child." They all agreed. One way or another spirits had saved them so thinking on kind thoughts about them was very unfair. We all knew there was a price to pay. Sam remarked "We must go and continue looking after the horses Rob. You should stop in the house and rest" Katie came over to me and sat on my knee. "This is wonderful Rob I finally get to live with you and have sex wonderful sex you make me so happy." She said placing my hand on her covered breast and encouraging me to take her to bed, she kissed me all over. "God sex is so great with you now I'm properly healed. Oh God, keep going. Go on, go on." I was finally allowed to rest. Sam came in the afternoon and woke me up "Come on sleepy you're in my bed tonight". I was beginning to feel like a piece of meat. I wondered if I could stand up to the demands being placed upon me what I thought was every man's dream. In reality it may become a bloody nightmare. At 11 o'clock Sam took me to bed after saying good night to everyone. Sam moved on top of me. "Oh my God it's bigger, what did she do to you in the cabin". Within 10 minutes Sam had climaxed twice and she rolled off "I can't take any more that is just too good." She professed kissing me on the lips. Finally, I was allowed to go to sleep. I awoke in the morning to find the sheets had been removed and Caroline, Katie and Sam looking me over deciding whether my penis had grown, I covered myself up quickly. "What do you think you're doing?" They all laughed. "Just checking the goods haven't been tampered with and by the looks of it, it has." "Does this mean I will actually be allowed to sleep?" Caroline remarked "I will tell you girls later." they giggled. I got dressed and had breakfast and went out into the yard summer was here once again. I went over to Cranbury farm to see if everything was okay. Sam was already there. "Meet the new stable girls Rob" "What happened to the last two you hired?" "They weren't very good with the horses Caroline did try to teach them but they just couldn't get the hang of it." I looked at them both thinking I was seeing things "You're twins?"

"Yes" they voiced together "My name is Julie and my sister is Juliet." "Before you asked Rob yes, they are lesbians and I'm letting them live in the house for the time being until we can find them other accommodation." Julie and Juliet kissed each other and walked off across the yard. I shook my head in disbelief trying not to laugh. Sam slapped me across the shoulder "I'm gonna tell your mother about you next full moon for hitting me I laughed." I kissed Sam goodbye and went back to where we were living now. I made a name plaque Redbrick farm. That's what it used to be called originally I thought it was only proper to give its original name back. I screwed the plaque with the burnt in name and a picture of a horse to the fence at the end of the drive. I then went up above the tack room for cup of coffee. Caroline joined me passionately kissing me on the lips as she always did. This was one woman that could drive me wild I don't know why, but she always did. I held her covered breasts in my hands. She stood there smiling in front of me as I released her riding britches. She grabbed a blanket and cast it open on the wooden floor laying, down. I lowered my trousers and pants. She stared. "Oh my God be gentle". I slowly penetrated, her nails dug into my back. She pressed her lips against mine and pulled me closer. She wrapped her legs around me pulling me in even more. We finished and dressed. She clung to me kissing me passionately "That was wonderful you've never done that to me before and it's never felt like that. If that was heaven, I'll have it every day please." I stayed out in the yard for the rest of the day. Sam came home. Caroline went over to talk to her they both went in the house. I went in a little later myself and flopped in my armchair by the fire. All three girls were on the settee staring at me. Suddenly Christina her mother walked into the room dressed in white. Sam went to move towards her. Christina stretched out her hand indicating stay where you are and Sam sat back down, Christina sat on the arm of my chair placed her arm on my shoulder and kissed me passionately. She glared at the three girls. "None of you will sleep with the Chosen One for a whole calendar month. Samantha removed those thoughts from your mind. Why did you employ lesbians?" "Well mother they are good with horses." "Is that all Samantha" I glared at Sam "you weren't going to cheat on me Sam after you promised?" "She dares not Rob I am watching." Sam voiced quickly. "I can't help what comes into my mind just because I think something it doesn't mean I'm going to do it." "If they are still working for you by the full moon I will replace you daughter, do you understand me Samantha" She said very sternly "Yes mother. Yes." The reality of her power was now coming to light. Perhaps Sam didn't have any interest in the two new girls she'd taken on. Perhaps it was just a passing thought, but her mother had sensed it "Do you realise how privileged you three are to be chosen to even be in the same room as the Chosen One". Christina then glared at Katie "You would be ill-advised to think that Katie with the snap of my fingers you will be dead, do you want the cancer to return?" Katie slowly shook her head. This woman meant business "Because you are new in the fold I will overlook your indiscretions this time but not again do you understand me" they all voiced. Yes, together. To be quite honest she petrified me. She gently kissed me on the lips the girls watched she rose to her feet and walked out of the room. "Sam whatever possessed you to cross your mother and me for that matter". "I wasn't doing anything Rob. I may have had the odd thought but nothing serious and I would never cheat on you." "Don't even have the odd thought Sam you won't get away with it If your mother doesn't deal with you. I certainly would, it would be over for us forever." Sam Started to cry so did Caroline. Katie had tears in her eyes but she refused to cry.

Chapter 15
The power of Christina

It was the night of the full moon. I drove down to the cabin at 5:30 PM poured myself a drink the log burner had been lit. I sat in the front room watching television wondering what the hell was going to happen tonight and would I survive or would any of us in the end. I could smell cooking in the kitchen again and presumed Christina had arrived. I went in to see for all her beauty she was a force to be reckoned with and I certainly wasn't going to cross her path. She approached me placing her arms around my neck and embraced me, I responded likewise. She placed my meal on the table and sat beside me pouring from a strange coloured bottle again a large glass of its substance, "Eat and drink Rob enjoy your meal." she kissed me on the cheek. I asked nervously. "Why were you so hard on the girls?" She stroked my cheek. "You are so wonderful those three do not deserve you" I finished my meal and went into the front room. I was almost scared to think I felt petrified in her presence. She came into the front room dressed in pink from head to toe her blue eyes pierced my very soul. She sat close to me holding my hand. "Don't let those three bully you Chosen One, you are in charge they must do as you request or answer to me" "You were very hard on Sam Christina". She squeezed my hand then lent forward and pressed her lips against mine then slid her hand round the back of my neck, pulling me closer. I had to respond, her intoxicating presence gave me little choice in the matter. "Samantha should know better I placed her in a position of authority and if she abused her position, I'm afraid I will remove her. It is not just me that makes these decisions. It is the collective the covenant we cannot have anyone who does not follow the rules." "Surely Christina you would not destroy your own daughter. We all make mistakes in life she can't help what she was in the past. Please be tolerant, but just don't let her make a mistake, correct it before it happens." The lighting went dim and the room filled with spirits gently touching my face and head my whole body. "You are truly pure hearted and kind all my sisters love you and they are envious of my fortunate position having you to hold". Christina laughed, unbuttoning her blouse releasing her bra and removed it. "I will fill your appetite until you can feast no more. I read your thoughts and I am flattered by them." She held my hand and led me to the bedroom with the snap of her fingers. The rest of her garments disappeared, she lay poised on the bed and snapped her fingers and my clothes fell to the floor "Are you pleased with what we've done to your body?" "Yes I feel stronger and more invigorated although the girls think" Christina interrupted. "It does not matter what they think come to me lay upon me and take your pleasure." I did not hesitate with her invitation, she could do things to me that no other woman could, she knew exactly how to please me. We showered before daybreak I washed her breasts gently with the sponge and press my lips against hers. We left the shower. She snapped her fingers and we were dried and dressed within the blink of an eye. She was now wearing her white robe as we entered the kitchen. She snapped her fingers again and a coffee was on the table waiting for me. "I must go in a minute Chosen One until the next full moon remember what I told you, take charge, you are the Chosen One not them". She kissed me tenderly on the lips and disappeared. I returned to Redbrick farm and went straight into the house and sat at the kitchen table. Katie cooked me breakfast she didn't look very happy "What is wrong Katie love?" "I don't know Rob. I thought this was all going to be wonderful now I'm scared to think anything" I finish my breakfast and we went into the lounge. Katie sat on my lap cuddling close to me. I kissed her tenderly "I love you Rob take me to bed, show me you still love me". I picked her up in my arms without any trouble at all I was strong, she felt as light as a feather in my arms. She smiled as we climbed the stairs looking into my eyes anticipating what was to come. She undressed quickly and lay on the bed. I remove my clothes and slid onto her gently caressing and then penetrated her. She inhaled deeply "Oh God I've never ever felt like this before" she kissed me frantically she pulled my head down onto her breast. I lay beside her she moved on me and gently eased herself down "I can feel you inside me you are filling my body with everything I want." The next morning, I drove to Cranbury farm. Sam was already there, Julie and Juliet had gone, there were now two new girls. The girls approached me and so did Sam by her facial expression I could tell she was not happy "This is Nicola and Tinkerbell they've been recommended by someone we know Christina. They were told to come to the stables to work". Both girls had long black hair, good figures and beautiful complexion. They both held their hands out for me to shake and I saw the hexagram on their hands. Sam looked across to me. We both knew Christina had sent the girls but what was the reason? I could see Sam felt threatened. Even the horses were nervous around these two girls, although they didn't play up when they were ridden. I embraced Sam passionately reinforcing my love for her. She held me tightly "What are we going to do Rob I'm scared, mother is taking over my whole life." "I'll bet they're not lesbians." Sam slapped me on the shoulder hard. "I promised you I would never cheat on you with anybody and I've never broken that promise Rob." I placed my arm around her waist and went inside one of the stables. It was November and the wind chill was quite severe. I pulled her riding britches down and removed them and lay in the straw and started to make love to her. Sam opened her eyes and looked over my shoulder Nicola and Tinkerbell were stood looking over the door as we made love. When they realised Sam had seen them they moved away. Sam whispered in my ear what she had seen, I look back and they'd gone for sure we dressed and held each other. "We are being watched whatever we do Rob can't you speak to Christina. This is so "unfair". I sighed heavily "I did speak to her concerning you and told her to give you a fair chance. This may be a way of controlling the situation without actually punishing you. I think if any lesbians came to the stables those two would eat them for breakfast they do look fit." Sam turned my head to face her. "You don't fancy those two Rob?" "No I was just stating the obvious." We walked back out into the yard when I heard my favourite horse snowdrop neighing, we walked over to the stable door the horse placed his head against mine. "Even the bloody horses love you Rob." Sam commented. I saddled snowdrop although it was very cold. I went for a ride around the perimeter of the property. I hadn't got very far before I heard two horses coming up from behind me. It was Nicola and Tinkerbell they came either side of me "You are the Chosen One. I am honoured to be in your presence" remarked Nicola. So, am I Tinkerbell voiced? "We're truly privileged to be chosen by Christina to be in your presence. I cannot wait for the full moon. I galloped off ahead, I wondered what they meant. I returned to the stables very cold, Nicola took my horse and put him back in the stable. Sam came across to me "You're freezing Rob come with me I'll make you a coffee". We went inside the little room that had been set aside to make refreshments. I held my mug in both hands finally feeling the warmth penetrate my skin. I thought the only way I could bring all this unhappiness to an end would be for me to die for everyone's sake.

Chapter 16
The gift

It was full moon time again. I arrived at 5:30 PM my glass of Bacardi and Coke was waiting for me on the kitchen table. I went into the front room. The television was already on. I returned to the kitchen a few minutes later after smelling the food cooking Christina was there in her white robe. She placed my meal on the table as usual and gave me a glass of her special drink. "Tonight is very special Rob. You have a gift coming unblemished and untouched by anyone." I finish my meal and went into the front room. Christina accompanied me remaining in her white robe the spirits entered the room as the lights dimmed. This time Christina told me to stand, she snapped her fingers and all my clothes vanished. The spirits finally went but the lights stayed dim the front door opened and in walked Tinkerbell and Nicola in white robes "Come my children." Christina snapped her fingers again and their robes vanished. I thought my very soul was going to burst into flames as each kissed me in turn. "Take them Rob take them." We went into my bedroom. They both lay upon the bed. I positioned myself between them they turned towards me kissing me all over. Nicola moved on top of me and lowered herself down very gingerly. "You are my first Chosen One". Panting within anticipation it was all over quickly I couldn't control myself. Tinkerbell did exactly the same. "You are the only Chosen One for me" They lay beside me holding me close. I lay on Nicole kissing her all over and penetrated her. She smiled "Oh Chosen One you honour me." Tinkerbell whispered in my ear "Don't forget me Chosen One." I rested for a few minutes and then mounted Tinkerbell, riding her like a wild stallion. I lay exhausted between the two of them. They caressed me gently and we finally went into the shower and I washed their bodies. We stepped out of the shower and Christina snapped her fingers and we were all dressed again. She clapped her hands. "Go children you have been loved and blessed." They left after each kissing me on the cheek. I returned to the settee where another glass of my favourite tipple waited. Christina sat beside me still in her white robe, she snapped her fingers and she was naked. She wasn't going to miss out on any fun that was sure, she snapped her fingers again and I was naked. She watched my erection grow as I looked at her beautiful body. I was surprised I could become interested in such a short time after the two girls. Whatever she was feeding me and giving me to drink supplied me energy beyond my comprehension. We went back into the bedroom and I rode her until daybreak. We quickly showered and she vanished. I drove home slowly to Redbrick farm. Sam was waiting for me on the doorstep she took me inside and sat me down. She handed me a Bacardi and coke which I thought was rather early to start drinking at 8:30 AM in the morning. Caroline and Katie came into the room crying and sat on the settee, Sam had tears in her eyes. Katie knelt down before me. "Rob" she said sniffling, I just received a phone call from South Africa. Johnny was on his way to the airport to come and see you he was involved in a car accident he didn't survive." The tears streamed down my cheeks I couldn't comprehend what had taken place. I hadn't seen him for a long time and finally was about to then he's taken from me. I drank my Bacardi and dried my eyes. We all cuddled each other trying to find solace. I arrange for Johnny's body to be flown over and to be buried in the local churchyard beside his mother, we had a very Private Service just family members. We all returned to Redbrick farm each grabbing our favourite drink and sitting quietly. The children had never met Johnny so in order to shield them from any pain. We arranged for them with Jane the nanny to be flown out to Switzerland to stay with their grandfather. He was over the moon yet saddened by the death of Johnny. The full moon had come again. I went to the cabin in haste I wanted bloody answers and I wasn't going to take any crap anymore. Sam had warned me not to push my luck but I didn't care I entered the cabin. My drink was waiting for me. I sat waiting for the smell of cooking food. I waited for over an hour and still there was no smell of cooking food. We seem to have a routine which was now no longer in place. Christina finally appeared in her white robe, I stood up. She showed me the palm of a hand which forced me to sit back down she could see the anger written all over my face. "Why did you allow this to happen to Jonny Christina, he was of my blood my son." She poured me a drink from her bottle "Drink this and I will tell you the truth." I emptied down my throat as if it was a drain with the tears streaming down my face. She encouraged me to move to the settee, she waved a hand across my face and dried my tears. The lights went dim and all the spirits entered and quickly vanished. Christina's beautiful blue eyes shone and sparkled like diamonds. She held my hand. "You will not like what I'm going to tell you but it's the truth. You must believe me Chosen One. I am not permitted to lie to you". She held me tightly in her arms I did not respond,

I could feel the pain fading away in my body. "This must be our secret Rob. You must not tell anyone else. Johnny was not your son otherwise we would have protected him." "What." I shouted, pushing her away from me. Christina spoke calmly. "You knew Jenny was deceitful. You actually saw Johnny's father on Katie's laptop in that very bedroom over there. He was just one of many lovers she had, we very often watched her perform sexual acts with men." "She told me he was mine and Katie was hers and her boyfriend." "She really didn't want Johnny but she knew you did and she knew you would do everything in your power to have him. That is when we intervened putting the idea in your grandfather's mind to change his will and leave you the woodland. You are a good carpenter and we knew you would build our home." I flopped back on the settee in shock. I didn't realise Christina had been watching for that long. She knew everything Katie and Jenny had done nothing escaped her knowledge. She snapped her fingers and I could smell the cooking "Come and eat something Rob." The spirits returned and surrounded me once again. I sat and ate my meal she stood beside me with one hand on my shoulder. We didn't sleep together as we usually did. We returned to the front room "You will become extremely wealthy Rob. Johnny made a will before he died although he was extremely young. He left everything to you to share amongst the family you should have £200 million in the next few months when his estate is closed down. He loved you as his father." I burst into tears again once again the spirits returned and Christina held me close. The pain drifted away to some degree. They made it more tolerable for me to understand and accept the truth. I held Christina and kissed her tenderly on the lips and thanked her for her patience with me. She smiled. "You do not have my foresight you are human and were not aware of what had taken place in the past. She placed her hand on my forehead and I drifted off to sleep. I awoke the next morning she had gone. I drove back to Redbrick farm and explained to the others except I miss the part out he wasn't my son. Rupert phoned to ask if the children can stop another two weeks they were having such good fun. Katie, Caroline and Sam took it in turn speaking to the children. They all told the children their father sends his love.

Sam Started to feel ill and we didn't know why. The doctor could find nothing wrong with her he concluded it's down to exhaustion and overworking. Katie looked after her while Caroline managed the stables at Redbrick farm. I went out to Cranbury farm to check everything was running properly. Nicola and Tinkerbell appeared to be on top of everything. But of course they were using magic to do half their work. They both came over to me as I got out of the range Rover and kissed me on the cheek telling me all the chores had been done, including some of the repairs. Of course it makes all the difference if you can snap your fingers and something is fixed. It's a pity I hadn't that gift I thought my life would be so much simpler. We went to have a coffee Christmas had been and gone. We were now at the end of January the air was still fresh with a slight chill, we sat drinking Tinkerbell reached across and put her hand on mine. "Does everybody love you as we love you Chosen One?" "I don't understand what's going on girls everything just seems to happen to me." I said shrugging my shoulders. Nicola also reached across placing her hand on top of Tinkerbell's. "We are yours for the taking Chosen One." "I think you would have to consult Christina first you don't want to get on the wrong side of her." Both of their mugs of coffee rose from the table and were emptied in their laps they ran out of the room screaming and went to get changed. I smiled to myself thinking Christina is watching and they got their answer. I looked into the top of my coffee the shape of a heart appeared and I saw Christina's face in the swirling liquid then vanished. I shook my head with a smile in total disbelief. I went back out into the yard jumped into the range Rover and drove off back to Redbrick farm. I went up to see Sam I held her hand and kissed. She smiled at me sweetly "Can you ask my mother to make me better Rob please on your next full moon visit". I kissed her on the forehead and told her I would. I went back downstairs. Katie was on her computer looking at photographs. I thought Christina would not approve of. I sat by her and warned her she could be in trouble. I recognised some of the photos and wondered if she had copies of old hard drive before I trashed it in the fire. I asked. "Did you keep copies of everything I tried to destroy?" She smiled of course I'm not that stupid I have copies of everything." "Do you still have the pictures of your mom having sex with them fellers". Katie looked at me rather Startled "When did you see that Rob?" "When you left me with your laptop after collecting it from the house, I had a nose." "Yes it's on my hard drive somewhere mother used to make me video everything so she could bribe them later on if she wanted to and if they were wealthy enough." "Is there no end to your mother's talents?" Katie laughed. "No not really she was a right cow." I sat beside her on the settee slowly scrolling through loads of photos of her naked with girls and her mother naked with men. She then played a video of her mother making love to three men. I couldn't believe what I was seeing how could this have taken place and I didn't know? She then scrolled across two pictures of me sat on the settee with my trousers missing and Katie touching me. She quickly moved on and then went into movies where I appeared again, Katie bouncing up and down on me. "Sorry Rob I'm not like that now." She then downloaded another movie of her mother, suddenly Christina appeared on the screen and the laptop burst into flames. Katie threw it straight into the fire and it disintegrated immediately "Oh shit, I'm going to die" Katie professed. I placed my arm around her shoulder "No, you won't I know why you are allowed to show me those photos". Katie turned to face me with a puzzled expression on her face. I just planted a kiss on her lips to avoid any questioning. She hugged me we held each other. Sam came downstairs and sat by the fire. She saw the remains of Katie's laptop. She looked across confused. "It caught fire Sam" Katie expressed. "I feel wonderful I'm going out to see my horses". Obviously Christina had something to do with her recovery like she controlled everything else in our lives. Katie was shivering in fear wondering if she was going to die for looking at lesbian porn. She threw all the copies on the DVD's in the fire. I did try to reassure her but I don't think it had any effect, Katie shed a tear. "I don't have a picture of my mother anymore I know she was a bitch, but she was still my mother." I glanced to the mantelpiece there was a picture of her mother in a gold frame "Look Katie" I pointed. She looked to the mantelpiece a broad smile came across her face. She stood up and took it off the mantelpiece, she called out. "Thank you Christina, I'm sorry". Katie ran off upstairs clutching the photo against her chest. Christina did have a heart I decided she wasn't all rules and regulations. Perhaps there is hope for us all yet. The children had returned from Switzerland and went to their respective schools on a daily basis. The full moon appeared again and I returned to the cabin. I waited for some time for Christina to appear. Instead, the door opened and in walked Nicola and Tinkerbell. "Why are you here girls?" Nicola spoke. "We've come to apologise Chosen One for our indiscretion at the stables. We presumed you could take us anytime. But Christina told us only when we had her permission.

We are to serve your meal and wait upon your every command". The girls scurried around preparing my meal and pouring my wine. It didn't take many seconds when you only have to snap your fingers to make things happen. I had my fill and returned to the settee, they sat either side of me. I did not make any advances to either of them fearing Christina's wrath if I miss read the signs. The girls were still dressed in their riding gear so I naturally presumed this was strictly a no touch policy.

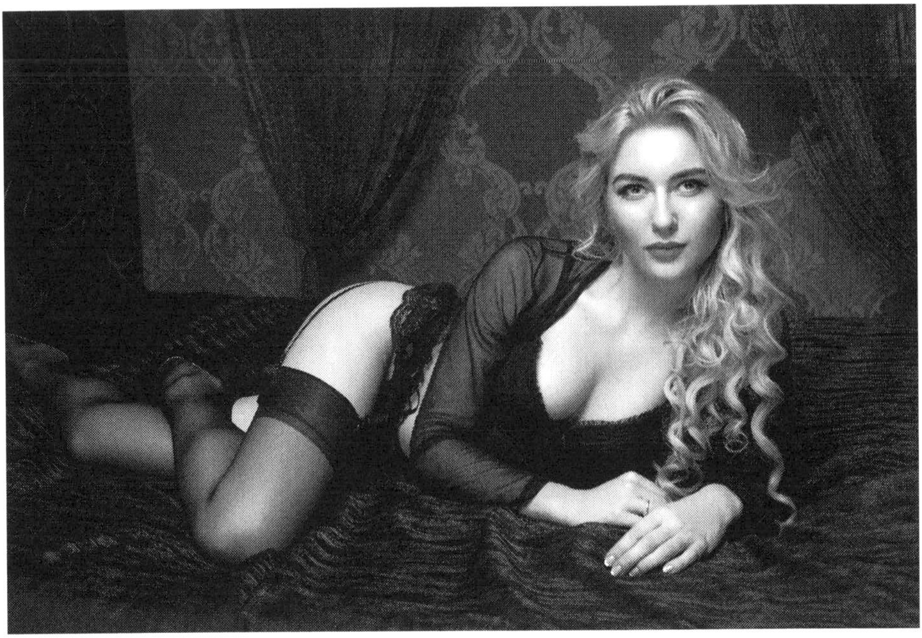

Chapter 17
Personal servants

Christina appeared the two girls stood up and bowed their heads. She came over to them and embraced them both. "I have a task for you two. You are the personal property of the Chosen One you will do everything he asks without question. Do you understand me girls? You will live here so the Chosen One can come to rest and be waited on". They nodded. Christina led me into the kitchen "I will not punish Katie I allowed her to show you those pictures so you really understood what had been going on." I embraced her and kissed her passionately leading her into my bedroom. I snapped my fingers and her clothes fell off. "I just don't believe it." Christina smiled at my surprise. "Your powers are limited and will only work in the cabin for the time being. I don't want you going off killing somebody if you get angry. All you have to do is think of what you want and snap your fingers I can see from what you've done to me. I know exactly what you want" she smiled. I started to make love to her. She moaned with pleasure. I caressed her breasts kissed her neck. I was all over her. We showered. She said kissing me tenderly on the lips "You could have had two young girls yet you chose me, I'm honoured." "I have something to confess Christina." She placed her finger on my lips "I already know how you feel about me you honour me greatly and I will always be yours and yours alone". We returned to the front room. The girls were still sat on the settee. "I'm leaving now I have other duties to perform, do not disappoint me girls." "We won't Christina". Christina vanished. Tinkerbell voiced. "How can we serve you Chosen One?" "The first thing you can do girls is call me Rob. If you call me Chosen One and somebody hears you it will only cause problems." They nodded in agreement. "Would you like a drink Rob" Nicola asked. "Yes please I'll have a coffee" Nicola snapped her fingers and it appeared on the coffee table that took all the excitement out of having a coffee. Now I could snap my own fingers having servants seemed a little silly. The girls sat like statues unsure of what I wanted or what to do. "Relax girls." The lights dimmed in the cabin and the spirits returned they went all round me and the two girls. They stayed for half an hour if not more and then vanished, and full lighting returned. The girls got up and went into the kitchen came back with a bottle of Bacardi and Coke and a bottle of wine. They poured me a glass and themselves. They had suddenly become more human. They each placed a hand on my leg. I switched the television on and we sat there relaxing enjoying the evening. We were watching a nature programme, suddenly the channel changed to romance. I flicked it back and it changed back again. I looked at the girls they were grinning it was them. "I'm going to bed". I started walking to the bedroom. They followed I snapped my fingers and my clothes fell off. I smiled, thinking to myself, that's an easy way to get undressed. The girls snapped their fingers and their clothes fell off. They climbed in either side of me and hugged me. I could feel their hands sliding up and down my chest and legs. I could see the clear sky through my window the Stars were twinkling very bright. I lay on top of Nicola, she accepted me without question she was young and fresh she held me tight. Tinkerbell was kissing me all over I moved over onto the top of Tinkerbell. They both had lovely firm breasts and both girls were there to be plucked like ripe fruit. I lay in the middle of them. They caressed me and kissed me until I fell asleep. By daybreak they had gone to work. I went into the kitchen and thought of eggs, beans and toast. I snapped my fingers and it appeared on a plate piping hot. I don't think I could ever get used to doing that. But it was far easier than struggling with the bloody tin opener. I drove directly to Cranbury farm. The girls were busy snapping their fingers while they weren't being watched all the work was done quickly and efficiently. Sam turned up "Hello you." I hadn't heard that for a long time. We embraced each other. I saddled snowdrop and went for a ride. I felt good this morning I don't know why I just did. Someone was approaching, Nicola and Tinkerbell came galloping up behind me and drew alongside Tinkerbell voiced "Did we please you last night Rob?" Nicola studied my expression "Of course girls you both pleased me very much." Their smile broadened and they galloped off ahead. I suddenly felt the urge to ride to the cabin I had no idea why snowdrop took off like his backside was on fire. We worked our way through the wood until I came to the oak tree. I dismounted and went into the cabin. Caroline was inside." What are you doing here Caroline" "I want to know why she killed my unborn children?" She was sat at the kitchen table crying. I placed my arm around her shoulder "Let me talk to Christina. I'm sure there's an explanation." Almost before I'd finished speaking Christina appeared "Why Christina, why did you kill my unborn children?" These thoughts must be festering in Caroline's mind for a long time and now she couldn't hold her pain back any longer she needed some answers. "Come with me Caroline sit beside me on the settee." They went into the front room by now Caroline was crying uncontrollably. "Both of your children had died inside you Caroline." Christina waved a hand in a circle a picture formed. Caroline Stared. "We only have so much power Caroline. We can stop cancer but we can't replace an arm and if you look at the pictures closely you will see the babies have become detached inside and that's why they aborted. The first one was caused by the horse kicking and your second child because of the damage hadn't properly repaired from the first one. It was nothing to do with me or the covenant it was just beyond our power to help you." Caroline flung her arms around Christina. "I'm so sorry I thought you'd killed my unborn." "What I can tell you Caroline, you are fit and well, dry your eyes and settle yourself and I'm sure the Chosen One will give you another child." Christina glanced to me and smiled. She then held Caroline's head in her hands. "Your pain has gone look forward and all will be well. There is also one thing I should mention Jane is leaving you in two weeks don't be alarmed. I have a new nanny from the covenant who will assist you all." Christina vanished. I sat beside Caroline and embraced her. "I'm sorry Rob I didn't mean to cause you a problem." "You haven't Caroline you have always been special to me. Come with me". She followed me into the bedroom. I snapped my fingers and her clothes fell away. She stood there in astonishment. I invited her to lie on the bed, her smile broadened as we made love she knew she was going to receive something. She'd longed for a daughter as foretold by Christina many months ago. We showered together and I snap my fingers again and we were dressed "You have powers Rob"? "Don't repeat it to anyone Caroline the powers I have are secret and must be kept, don't jeopardise your chance of having a daughter by being loose tongued". She shook her head slowly from side to side and embraced me again. We both mounted snowdrop he was not impressed with the idea but tolerated it all the same. I dropped off Caroline at the end of the track. She jumped in her car I'd bought her and drove away a very happy woman. I rode back to Cranbury farm wondering who Christina was going to select as the new nanny. We had become totally dependent on Jane she knew how we lived. I left my horse at Cranbury stables. Tinkerbell took him from me and placed him back in his stable. I drove back to Redbrick farm and called Jane down to see me in my private room. She came in and sat down "You're leaving us Jane"? She looked surprised at my comment. "How did you know Rob? I haven't handed in my notice yet." "We have ways of finding things out Jane you have been a loyal person to this family and I don't really want you to go." "I must go Rob I'm getting on in years. I have to find a husband and have children of my own." I sighed heavily. "I understand Jane I may know someone who can help you in the Philippines find your true love." She smiled and left my room. I was determined to help in any way I could.

Chapter 18

The new nanny

I went to the cabin to see Nicola and Tinkerbell. They greeted me with a kiss we sat with refreshments on the coffee table. "We know why you have come it has already been arranged Jane will marry an accountant and she will have two children, a boy and a girl". I kiss them both and thanked them. I returned home and gathered Sam, Katie and Caroline into the living room to explain what I knew. They were shocked. I also informed them that Christina was providing the next nanny. Katie voiced "The children don't need a nanny now Rob" "I'm afraid we will in nine months." Caroline went bright red Sam and Katie embraced her. "She will give birth to a daughter as foretold by Christina". We said goodbye to Jane and I placed £10,000 in her bank account as a gift from us all. The next morning there was a knock at the door. Katie answered, "I'm the new nanny sent by Christina." Katie let her in showing her into the living room where I was sitting in my armchair she stood before me. I almost spilled my coffee when I looked at her she couldn't have been a day over 17 "What's your qualifications and how old are you?" "I'm 17 in your years. I'm fully qualified" she passed her paperwork to Katie who stood there in absolute silence, realising the girl was the splitting image of her mother at that age. We all wondered what was going on here. "And your name is" "Jenny" I dropped my cup, Katie felt onto the settee. Sam walked in after taking the children to school and stared in astonishment. "Meet the new nanny Sam, this is Jenny." Sam collapsed beside Katie. Christina appeared "Is there a problem?" Christina said placing her arm around Jenny's shoulder. Katie voiced "How could she possibly have all these qualification she's not even out of nappies herself?" Christina laughed. "You have no idea, do you woman? She has been bringing up children for the last 30 years around the world. Do not be fooled by her looks. She is far more qualified than anyone of you in this room to care for a child. Yes, I know her name is the same as your dead wife Rob and yes, she does look like your dead wife, but they are not the same person do I make myself clear." "Crystal" I replied. Katie and Sam nodded in agreement. "Before I go, Jenny is pure and untouched by man or woman. The only person in this house who may touch her is the Chosen One anyone else will feel my displeasure". Christina vanished. "Let me show you round Jenny" Sam offered. "No thank you I already know the place inside out. I've been here before". She bent over and kissed me on the cheek "Thank you Chosen One I'm honoured to be in your presence." She snapped her fingers and vanished. I advised Sam and Katie not to mess with her. "It looks like she has a lot of power similar to Christina". I heard a voice "You're correct Chosen One". Katie exhaled "Oh shit." Sam came over and sat on the arm of my chair putting her arm around my shoulder, looking very concerned. I commented "Now we have our own Mary Poppins" "I heard that Chosen One". We all looked at each other alarmed. Could we not hold a conversation in private anymore? Caroline came in from the stables could see the concern all over our faces before she could speak. Jenny appeared in front of her. Caroline flinched. Jenny then placed her hand on Caroline's stomach "Oh good, she is progressing nicely". Jenny vanished. "I think we'd all better go and have a look at the horses don't you" Sam suggested. "Yes" they all voiced. We walked out to the stables went up above the tack room "That's the new nanny Rob?" Caroline queried. I nodded in response "Better still" Sam remarked. "Let's go to Cranbury farm to finish our conversation", we all agreed. We all jumped in my range Rover and I drove off. We went into the house and removed the dust sheets from the settee and chairs. Sam lit the fire quickly "What are we going to do?" Sam enquired. Katie voiced "Rip her knickers off Rob and get her pregnant quick, she might then be taken away." "I hope she just didn't hear what you said Katie". It was decided amongst us all to be careful what we said at Redbrick farm. One thing we knew for sure the children couldn't pull a fast one on her or perhaps she was here to groom them for their assignments later in life, who knows the real reason. We return to Redbrick farm. It was just 1 o'clock the dinner table was laid. The food was on the table as we walked in. "I've prepared your meal Chosen One". Before I could reply she had vanished. We were so used to having snacks this was an absolute shock and we were all very impressed. The food was absolutely gorgeous. "Jenny" I called out. She appeared by my chair at the dining table "Thank you for a lovely meal". She smiled, every movement reminded me of Jenny, she was wearing a knee length blue skirt and a white blouse with a blue jacket her long golden hair was tied in a ponytail. She was very tidy and precise. She snapped her fingers and desert appeared in front of everyone. She walked out of the room glanced back and smiled at me then continued walking. Nobody spoke a word just enjoyed the desert in front of us, strawberries and cream. We walked into the living room. Jenny entered the dining room snapped her fingers and everything was cleared. I kissed her gently on the cheek. "Thank you that was lovely." I invited her to join me in the cabin. She thought for a moment. "Yes I would like to see the cabin you built for my sisters your praises are sung in many countries." She joined me in the range Rover sitting very prim and proper occasionally she would glance to me when she thought I wasn't looking. On our arrival Nicola and Tinkerbell greeted us at the door. She hugged them both as if she'd known them all her life. I sat in my old armchair by the log burner while the three girls sat on the settee chatting. Tinkerbell whispered something in Jenny's ear. Christina appeared. The three girls immediately jumped to their feet and bowed to Christina. Christina looked across to me sitting on my own, drinking my glass of Bacardi and Coke. She slowly shook her head removing the glass from my hand and leading me into the bedroom. She snapped her fingers and we were naked. She caressed me like no other woman and we professed our love for each other. We showered and return to the front room. The three girls were standing in a line. "What were your instructions girls? I felt the loneliness of the Chosen One it's your fault, nobody else's." They bowed their heads. "If it happens again you know the consequences, you will all be banished to the dark place from which there is no return". I stood there, absolutely stunned. I hadn't really felt lonely I thought or perhaps Christina could feel things I couldn't. She kissed me tenderly on the lips and vanished. The three girls ran over to me "Take us, punish us, we are sorry. We don't want to go to the dark place where there's no return" I seated myself by the log burner and continued to drink my Bacardi after having sex with Christina. I didn't think there was anybody to match Christina. Her face appeared in my Bacardi with a broad smile. She must off read my thoughts. I rose to my feet and indicated to Jenny we were going home to Redbrick farm. It was a full moon tomorrow night and I would have to return to the cabin. Jenny went off upstairs and I went into the kitchen to make myself a coffee. I sat in the armchair pondering what to do next. Summer was here again and I took snowdrop from the stable and rode him around the perimeter of the farm. He was a lovely horse gentle and kind always looked after me and never threw me off in any cow muck. I heard a horse approaching from behind. I looked round and it was Sam. She drew alongside me we kissed professing our love for each other "Well did you?" Sam questioned. "I know what you mean, no" I said dismounting. Sam dismounted as well. We tied the horses in the hedgerow and we embraced once again expressing our love for each other. These moments seem to become few and far between with our hectic lifestyle. We lay in the mowing grass and we caressed reaffirming our love. Later in the day we returned to Redbrick farm.

Jenny greeted us "Samantha, you are to accompany the Chosen One on the full moon to the log cabin. Christina wishes to talk to you both." "Why?" Sam enquired concerned "All will be revealed at the right time. It's a full moon tomorrow. I will be coming with you". Katie had overheard the conversation coming over to us. "I don't like the sound of that. She's never asked for you before Sam". "No, it does seem odd, something else for me to worry about now." I placed my arm around both their shoulders and eased them closer to me. "Don't worry, I'll be there I will protect you." "Against my mother, I don't think so" Sam remarked. "I'll go and talk to Jenny and see if I can retrieve more information. I called out, "Jenny come in my office please." Before I had chance to sit at my desk Jenny appeared. She stood in front my desk facing me. "You called Chosen One?" "Sit down Jenny." Jenny seated herself in the chair. I walk round from my chair and perched on the edge of my desk. I was not convinced this wasn't Jenny my ex-wife just transformed into a younger model but I must be careful what I think, Christina can monitor everything. "What is planned for Sam on the full moon? I think I'm entitled to know as the Chosen One." Jenny rose to her feet. "It is for Christina to explain she is your spiritual wife and sees to your every need. We are here just to help her take care of the Chosen One."

Chapter 19
Confrontation

The night of the full moon Sam, Jenny and I drove to the log cabin. We entered nervously. We had no idea what we were walking into and Christina was already there. So were Tinkerbell and Nicola. Christina embraced Sam. The front room had been altered there were now two settees and three other armchairs. Christina indicated for us all to sit the lights dimmed and the spirits entered concentrating on Sam more than anyone else. This went on for about half an hour then the lighting returned to normal and the spirits disappeared. Christina stood up to face us all. "Sisters you know why we are here." "Yes." they all voiced. "Samantha my daughter you continue to have unacceptable thoughts when you are near other women. You are the Chosen One's wife you dishonour him you are to love him and love him only" Sam Started to cry. "What can I do, I cannot change what I think it doesn't mean that I will have an affair." I glared at Sam I felt hurt inside. I didn't think she thought like that anymore, tears came to my eyes and I moved away from her and sat by the log burner. She looked across to me with her hazel eyes filled with tears. "Now I feel your love for the Chosen One." Christina claimed continuing. "You should feel like that all the time for the Chosen One as I do and all my sisters in this room, you have a twisted mind daughter. If we cannot correct your thoughts and desires, then you will be disposed of. You are not worthy of being included in the covenant. Even Katie who was a pure lesbian no longer thinks of women but only of the Chosen One. You shame me daughter." The spirits returned engulfing Sam and she vanished. I jumped to my feet alarmed. "What you done?" "She has been taken for rehabilitation if possible she will return on the next full moon if they can repair her thoughts. If not, she has been thrown in the dark place. I feel your pain Chosen One your loyalty to her is beyond comprehension. She does not deserve you." Christina embraced me tears run down my cheeks. Christina kissed me tenderly and I felt the pain go away. She dried my eyes with the movement of her hand. The other sisters group round kissing me tenderly on the cheek. "It has been decided I shall remain flesh and blood until the next full moon and live with the Chosen One to satisfy his needs while Samantha is absent". We drove back to Redbrick farm. Katie and Caroline put their hands to their mouth when they realised Sam wasn't with us and Christina was, they wanted answers to many questions but feared the consequences of doing so. Christina spoke "Sit down all of you. I hear your thoughts and questions. Samantha has been taken away by my sisters to remove the impure thoughts of women from her mind. If we cannot she will not return". Jenny went over and touched the stomach of Caroline. She smiled and looked to Christina. I just sat in my armchair wondering how the hell I got myself in this mess and how I was going to get out of it and the rest of the family. Christina picked up on my thoughts "There is no escape Chosen One, we made you what you are youthful virile with the strength of four men". Christina turned to face Katie. "You truly love the Chosen One with your heart and soul you honour him. We are surprised and pleased". Katie smiled "I have always loved you Rob even as a child, kind and loving, he gives himself to everyone without reservation." Katie moved to the arm of my chair and placed her arm around my shoulder, kissing me tenderly "I will always love him. I'm surprised Samantha doesn't feel the same way all the time." I retired to bed it was nearly two in the morning, Christina joined me. She slid her body on top of mine. I was wondering if she could ever get pregnant. Christina picked up my thought. "To answer your question only if I chose to and I would have to be flesh and blood for the whole nine months. I would need all my sisters to agree to the pregnancy in order to transform". She eased her breast against my lips as she lowered herself onto me. She caressed tenderly leaving none of my senses untouched, if this was Paradise I wanted to be there for the rest of my life. We awoke to a knock on the bedroom door. Jenny entered. She snapped her fingers and two trays appeared with breakfast. Christina and I sat beside each other in bed eating. I couldn't stop myself glancing across to her lovely breasts. She smiled at my thought. "My daughter is a fool, how could she possibly have impure thoughts? I feel your love for me it caresses my being." Jenny knocked and entered. She snapped her fingers and the trays vanished and so did she. "I hear your thoughts Chosen One take me. I want you inside me." We started to make love again. She sent me to places I'd never been before. I dressed and went to Cranbury farm leaving Christina. Katie explained to the children that Sam had to go away for a month to rest. Nicola and Tinkerbell had carried out the usual chores attending to the horses. I saddled snowdrop and rode him to the cabin. I walked inside with a heavy sigh made myself a coffee and sat in my usual armchair. Jenny appeared which rather Startled me "Chosen One why are you so sad? My sisters will not harm Samantha if she really loves you like we all do." She came across to me and sat on my lap placing her arm around my shoulder which I didn't expect her to do. She kissed me gently on the cheek and then on the lips. "Why haven't you taken me to bed? Like all my sisters? Is it because I look like your dead wife? I'm still a virgin I have never been with a man and I have been given to you yet you still do not take me?" I didn't reply, to be quite honest my whole life just appeared to be making love to women. The things I used to enjoy hunting making things all appear to have drifted into history and now I'm just a stud. It is very true what they say, you can have too much of a good thing. Christina was the one that drove me wild. She had a way of holding and touching me like no other woman "I'm surprised you came to see me Jenny I thought it would have been Christina?" "She wants you to like me and understand I'm not here to harm you, only to help. I know you don't like me reading your thoughts but it is the way we are. We read each other's thoughts". I stood up supporting Jenny in my arms then lowered her to her feet. I snap my fingers and her clothes vanished her smile broadened, so did mine. I carried her into my bedroom and placed her on the bed as my clothes fell away. I kissed and caressed her finally penetrating an expression of excitement eclipsed her face. Everything about her reminded me of my ex-wife I would make sure she would remember this day. An hour later we were still making love her soft breasts moved with every thrust. She moved like a wild animal trying to escape but she was trapped. I finally lay beside her. She turned to me gently kissing my neck. "Thank you Chosen One she gasped I am now content and complete". She vanished. I dressed and returned to my chair. I heard snowdrop neigh I went out onto the porch and stroked his forehead. "Sorry my old mate I'm neglecting you." We slowly trotted off towards Cranbury farm. The smell of hay being made in the field drifting in the air. I was missing Sam I really did love her although when you consider my infidelity. You could easily come to a different conclusion. I hoped God was listening he would make sure she was returned. It was the time of the full moon again. I was petrified Sam would not come back. Jenny, Christina and I drove to the cabin. We entered my glass of Bacardi was by the wood burner. I seated myself in the armchair Tinkerbell and Nicola appeared we were all here waiting for the outcome whether Christina already knew or not I didn't know. The spirits entered the room gliding around Christina a horrified expression came across her face. Then Sam reappeared looking 10 years younger, more beautiful than I'd ever seen her look before if that was possible, her hazel eyes shone like diamonds. A spirit figure appeared in a haze "Christina you are pregnant." Christina sat down on the settee looking astonished at the confirmation of her condition. The spirit figure continued "This cannot be, we would not allow it." She gasped "Never in 1000 years has this happened to a sister without approval from us all. I will consult the covenant on what we are going to do with you Christina". Sam embraced me. "I thought I'd never see you again Rob." She sat on my lap, kissing me tenderly Christina sat very quiet. "Sam remarked that will teach you to play around with my husband mother he always performs the impossible" Sam went to the kitchen and made a coffee for me. "Here my lovely husband a properly made coffee." She smiled, returning to sit on my lap. Jenny seated by Christina watching Sam kissing me. She seemed jealous of Sam's advances Christina had obviously read her thoughts "Remove those thoughts Jenny or I will punish you." Jenny snapped her fingers and disappeared. "What are you going to do now Christina?" I asked, looking across to her. "I don't know Chosen One, I suspect I'll have to stay in the cabin until I give birth, your effect on me was greater than I realised. I did want your child inside me and perhaps that's the reason I became pregnant. It will be up to the sisters what happens to me." We left Christina and returned home to Redbrick farm. Jenny was not there only Caroline and Katie. They greeted Sam as if she been away for years. They stared at her in amazement at her restored youth. We told them what had happened to Christina and they laughed, remarking it served her right. Sam and I decided to go to Cranbury farm and go for a ride me on snowdrop and Sam and Freddie her favourite horse. Tinkerbell saddled both for us with a click of her fingers. The horses shied with the sudden attachment of their saddle and bridle we rode across the fields in late September. The air was still warm. We dismounted by the style where I'd seen the old gypsy lady we embraced each other "God Sam you do look good" I remarked unzipping her riding jacket we lay in the grass caressing each other as we made love. I realise she was different somehow more loving everything was fresh about her as if she'd been reborn. She lay there arching her back, encouraging me to penetrate her further. We were intoxicated with each other. It felt like I was almost sleeping with a different woman. Even the stretchmarks she moaned about for so long after giving birth to our two children had gone. She was tight and firm all over. We rode through the wood to the cabin and entered. Christina wasn't there. We made ourselves a coffee a spirit appeared shrouded in a mist "Chosen One, we have taken Christina away. Don't worry, the unborn child is safe you have done us a great service bring Katie and Caroline on the next full moon. We have a gift for them both and then we shall vanish from your life for a while". Before we could question her the mist vanished. Sam and I hugged each other "Finally over Rob it's over everything will become normal". Sam and I rode back to Cranbury farm Nicola took the horses from us and we drove back to Redbrick farm. We rushed in the house and informed Katie and Caroline. The next full moon came and we all drove to the log cabin. We entered and seated ourselves. We were the only ones there Nicola and Tinkerbell had not turned up as they usually did neither had Jenny. I snapped my fingers and everybody was given their favourite drink, which was a shock to Katie. She'd never seen me do it before. The spirits entered the room they encircled Katie and Caroline it went very dark and when the light returned their youth had returned. They looked 10 years younger. Katie ran to the mirror in the bathroom "Is this really me Rob" I nodded. Caroline went to look at herself. "I don't believe how good I look." The mist appeared again. "Chosen One we are entrusting you with new abilities until we return, so you can watch over your family and punish them if they disobey you. Be warned it is a great responsibility do not command in anger for the consequences could be fatal. We are always with you Chosen One, have no fear we will be watching you and listening. You will all maintain your youth and age very slowly your children will become part of the covenant as they mature and be sent to different countries around the world. Your sons will sire new generations providing they maintain their purity". The spirit vanished. We all looked at each other with part sadness and part relief we drove home to Brickyard farm. We sat down to have another drink. I snapped my fingers and the glasses appeared on the table with everyone's favourite tipple my powers now worked beyond the cabin. I snapped my fingers, looking at Katie and her clothes fell off. She "screamed" in shock. I snapped my fingers again and she was dressed. She moved over to me and slapped me on the arm "Can't you wait till later" she smiled. Sam sat on the arm of my chair holding my hand we sat there with a sense of relief but wondered what the future held for us?

Chapter 20
The stables

We needed more staff and urgently. I couldn't use my powers all the time because of the public being present and seeing what was going on. Caroline was doing her best although she was pregnant. I spoke to Sam suggesting I go to the log cabin and see if I can acquire some help from the witches she didn't like the idea. It had taken us quite a while to get rid of them and we didn't really want them interfering in our life again, but she confessed she couldn't see any alternative. Very often we would train young girls and then they would leave to either get married or go into the racing scene where the pay was better. Looking after horses is not so glamorous as it sounds either up to your neck in manure or trying to avoid them biting or kicking you. I drove to the cabin on the next full moon. I entered nervously much to my surprise the log burner was lit and there was a glass of Bacardi and Coke waiting for me. I flopped into my old chair exhausted although I had been given a great deal more strength than I should have for a normal man. Working 15 hour days, would bring the best person to their knees eventually. I could see the television was on although there was no sound. I moved over and sat on the settee and looked at the screen, a picture of Christina appeared. She smiled sweetly at me and showed me her bump. "I cannot travel to you Chosen One because of the love inside me. I know you are struggling with your business and I know you want me to send more sisters to your aid. Are you sure you really want them their Chosen One?" I shrugged my shoulders "I've really got to do something Caroline is with child. Sam is on her knees with exhaustion we have to do something". Christina smiled sweetly "I wish I could be with you my love I will send you four sisters use them wisely. When I've given birth to our wonderful child I will return to you." "Will you allow me to see my son or daughter?" "You will have a daughter my love. She will be very special she will have a gift like no others. Because of the joining between us two and of course you will hold her. I will bring her with me so you may bless her with a kiss. I must go now Chosen One, my sisters will be with you shortly." The screen went blank. I poured myself another drink and wondered whether we'd made the right decision or just brought a load more grief to bear. The four sisters appeared they looked around the cabin and then returned to me. They looked virtually identical as if they were two sets of twins all in white robes with long black hair cascading down their backs. None of them looked over 18 but we've been fooled before by guessing the age of a sister. They bowed their heads before me standing in a line and they introduced themselves to me "My name is Jackie." She continued. "This is Susan, Rebecca and Tracey. We are honoured to be selected to work with the Chosen One. There is great envy among the sisters all want to be in your presence." "You will live here girls do you all know about horses and how to look after them"? "Yes Chosen One we know everything we need to know, you go home and rest and we will attend to your every request". I drove home to Redbrick farm wondering whether I'd made the right decision. The door was already open and Sam standing there waiting for me. She grabbed my arm and pulled me into the living room. There standing in a white robe was Jenny. "I've been sent by Christina to apologise to the Chosen One for my unforgivable behaviour. You affect me like no other person Chosen One. I couldn't control my feelings in the cabin for you, please forgive me and allow me to stay and look after Caroline and her unborn child." She went down on her knees bent her head in front of me. Sam Caroline and Katie sat on the settee, looking on. I looked across to them they shrugged their shoulders "You can stay Jenny stand up." I kissed her gently on the cheek "No more reading our minds and repeating our thoughts unless you read something serious, then tell me only do you understand." She nodded in agreement. Jenny moved over to Caroline who stood up immediately. Jenny placed her hand on Caroline's stomach and unborn child. Jenny glowed brilliant white everybody panicked for a moment, wondering what was taking place. Jenny smiled. "I have repositioned the baby it was trying to leave the womb too early like the others." Caroline embraced her. "Thank you Jenny I don't want to lose this child." "Don't worry Caroline you will not lose the baby. I am here to make sure it does not happen. Jenny smiled and continued "Thank you all for giving me a second chance to prove my worthiness as the Chosen One's servant". Jenny snapped her fingers and she vanished. We all sat down again. Caroline commented "I feel better inside already more comfortable than I've been for ages". Katie voiced. "How did you get on at the log cabin Rob"? They all listened intently. "I saw Christina on the television screen. Believe it or not she can't travel because of her condition." They all smiled. "We have four new witches living in the log cabin." I told them the girls their names". Sam asked concerned "Are there any conditions attached?" "No Christina said I was in charge and that's all she really said, we are having a daughter and she will bring her to see me when she can travel".

Jenny appeared, inviting us in to the dining room. She had prepared a lavish meal although only with a flick of her fingers. We all smiled. After dinner, Sam and I went for a walk in the cool night air of early spring. "Do you think we've done the right thing Rob by inviting the witches back?" Just look at yourself Sam you are absolutely stunning and beautiful, you haven't aged a bit". She smiled in appreciation of my comment. "I didn't think you noticed me anymore Rob." "I know I don't complement you very often Sam but you are my rock and I love you, above all others," I smiled. She rested her head on my shoulder as we slowly strolled around the yard. Moments like this were very few and far between. If it wasn't the horses, it was something wrong with the children they were all becoming young adults slowly. We retired quite early in evening. The next morning, we started walking round the yard all the work had been done. Sam stood there put her hand to her mouth in astonishment. There was nothing left to do. We jumped in my range Rover went to Cranbury farm the same had taken place there. There was nothing to do. Jackie brought snowdrop out and Rebecca led Freddie out all saddled and ready to ride. They bowed to me I had to tell them not to do in case the public saw them and I also told them to call me Rob in public otherwise be too many questions asked. They understood my reasons why Sam and I went for a ride around the property holding hands. It Started to rain and we dismounted I snap my fingers and a large umbrella covered us. The horses shied slightly, but then calmed. Sam kissed me passionately "You're wonderful and gentle". We waited until the shower had stopped. I snapped my fingers and the umbrella vanished. We rode on slowly talking things over and confirming our love for each other. You can't buy moments like this, I thought peace and tranquillity. That's all I wanted and to be with Sam. We rode past the cabin through the wood. I commented to Sam "Have you ever thought the cabin is bigger inside than it looks from the outside?" "Yes I've suspected that for a long time Rob". We rode back to Cranbury farm. Rebecca took my horse and Susan took Sam's. Sam commented "I don't look at women the same way anymore Rob. Not like I used to". I smiled and kissed her on the cheek. I must confess I thought to myself that had crossed my mind with all these pretty girls around the stables. I wondered if it would become a temptation for her, but not from what she's just said. We drove back to Redbrick farm. Caroline was sitting on the settee appearing to be in discomfort. Sam approached her quickly "Are you alright Caroline?" "No" I called out "Jenny where are you?" Jenny appeared. "I've been as quick as I can I had to return to the realm to bring back some medicine for Caroline." Caroline drank quickly her discomfort subsided almost immediately. Jenny looked worried. "She must not work Chosen One. It is not good for her, make her stay in bed. She will not listen to me." "Go to bed Caroline and do as you are bloody told; you are carrying my daughter" Jenny helped her upstairs to bed. Sam and I sat down to have a coffee I snapped my fingers and they appeared in front of us. "Don't lose your temper Rob, you could accidentally think something and cause a great deal of harm." Sam lent forward placing her hand on mine. "Let Jenny deal with Caroline she's more qualified than us." Jenny appeared in front of me "I have no time to explain take us to the cabin. It is a matter of life or death." I carried Caroline to the range Rover. Sam jumped in with me. I drove as quickly and as carefully as I could to the cabin. I carried Caroline into my bedroom "Leave us Rob, leave us". Jenny instructed Sam and me to return to the front room. I snapped my fingers and our favourite drinks appeared the lights went dim and all the spirits appeared. They swirled round me and Sam and then went into the bedroom. We could hear Caroline screaming in agony. I wanted to go in and so did Sam but we know we could do nothing if we did. Katie arrived coming in. We told what had happened. She started to cry poor Caroline "She deserves better luck than this". It all went very quiet for a long time we thought we had lost Caroline and the baby. Then we heard a cry of a new born baby. Jenny carried the baby into the front room and the spirits surrounded the child, each one appeared to touch it and then vanish. There must have been hundreds of spirits there seemed hours before they had finished. Jenny spoke "Meet your daughter Rob she is now well and healthy thanks to my sisters" "What about Caroline." I asked quickly "She survives; she has been taken to the realm by the sisters so she may make a full recovery. I will look after her child until she returns. What will you be calling your daughter?" "Margaret, after Caroline's mother."

We all returned to Redbrick farm. Jenny took the new-born upstairs. Katie, Sam and I stayed in the living room talking. Katie dried her eyes "How could this possibly happen Rob they said she was going to have a daughter. They didn't say she was nearly going to die in the process." "I suspect it's all the stress of trying to keep the stables going she pushed herself too hard like she always did. It's our fault she's in this state". Sam Started to shed a tear. "I should have realised Rob I just left her to it". We all sat down feeling guilty. Jenny appeared. "Margaret is sleeping soundly do not concern yourselves with Caroline. She will recover but it will take two months at least. The sisters are caring and loving she is honoured to be taken to the realm." I rose from my chair and embraced Jenny kissing her passionately on the lips. "Thank you

Jenny we could have had a total disaster on our hands without your presence." Katie and Sam rose to their feet and kissed her also on the cheek and gave a hug in appreciation of her skill in saving the baby and Caroline. Sam voiced. "Sleep with the Chosen One tonight as a reward". Jenny's smile broadened. "You honour me Samantha with your gift. Unfortunately, I must stay with the child to feed her and care for her in the first few days." "When you are happy Margaret is safe then you may take my husband for one night." Jenny embraced Sam. "I look forward to that time". She vanished. The television screen flashed and flickered and we all sat and watched Christina's face appear. "My daughter you are thinking like a leader and showing your generosity I'm pleased". She then showed us Caroline lying suspended in the air with hundreds of spirits encircling her she wasn't moving. We all stared on in horror, fearing the worst. Christina continued. "It is thanks to Jenny, realising something terrible had gone wrong inside that saved Caroline's life and your new daughter, Margaret." Christina then showed me her stomach displaying her pregnant state. "It will not be long now Chosen One and I love you truly for this present" She smiled and the picture vanished. I snapped my fingers and everybody had a drink again. Katie sighed. "Just when I thought everything was going well this has to happen to us." I moved over and sat between them on the settee. Sam suggested that we all sleep in the one bed and hold each other tonight, which made Katie smile. We went to bed and we all huddled together nobody was interested in making love. We were all too concerned with the day's events. It was almost like part of us had died. It all seems so strange about Caroline not being present, none of us had realised how much she meant to us until she wasn't there.

Chapter 21
Waiting for Caroline to come home

I went to the cabin taking Jenny with me. Margaret was safe and out of danger being watched by Katie. It was the night of the full moon. I held her hand and we entered the cabin we sat on the settee. She snapped her fingers and drinks appeared in front of us. The television flickered and flashed Christina appeared with a broad smile on her face holding a new daughter in her arms. "Look Chosen One your daughter what will you call her"? It had never crossed my mind I would be asked to name a daughter that belonged to a woman from the realm, I replied. "How would you feel about Star, Christina?" Her smile broadened that is a beautiful name I agree entirely." "When will I see you again Christina?" "Very soon my love very soon" The television screen went blank Jenny and I Started to kiss and cuddle. She was looking forward to her reward. I held her hand and took her into my bedroom. She snapped her fingers and both our clothes fell off. We made passionate love for most of the night at 7 AM we showered and went into the kitchen. She snapped her fingers and my breakfast was on the table. She sat beside me kissing my neck and cheek. She held me round the waist ". I'm in love with you Chosen One I cannot help myself." I turned to face her "I love you too Jenny. You have a wonderful body and a very tender touch". Her smile broadened pleased with my comments we returned back to Redbrick farm. Sam greeted Jenny with a kiss on the forehead and a cuddle. She knew what had taken place with her approval. Sam and I drove over to Cranbury farm to see what was going on. Jackie and Susan had completed all the work including the repairs we were redundant everything was obviously running very smoothly, which was a relief. Sam thanked the two girls for their efforts and we return to Redbrick farm. We seated ourselves in the living room. Suddenly, Caroline appeared and so did Christina and the new baby Star. Caroline looked like she was 18 again. She hadn't a blemish on her. Jenny brought Margaret down and placed her in Caroline's arms. She sat down and cried overjoyed with the outcome. Christina approached me "Your daughter Chosen One". She handed the little child over to me carefully. You could clearly see the hexagram on her arm. Christina kissed me gently on the lips. Katie was sitting with Caroline, holding Margaret. Christina said it was time for her to go but would return soon, we could keep the four stable girls she had provided for a little while longer but not indefinitely. Jenny entered the room embracing Christina and looking at Star. Then Christina and Star vanished. It was good to have Caroline back. Jenny would look after the baby during the day and Caroline returned to work with the horses, something she loved and enjoyed the spirits had been really kind to her. She said they had restored her youth and repaired the damage inside. We all maintained our youth ageing slower than any other normal person. Two months had passed and it was the night of the full moon. I drove to the cabin on my own. Jackie Susan, Rebecca and Tracey were never present on my full moon visit nights or if they were I couldn't see them. Christina appeared. She embraced me passionately "Where is Star" I asked? "She is safe Chosen One she is with the sisters who dote over her all the time preparing her for her future". Christina prepared me a meal and afterwards we sat on the settee together discussing what we were going to do in the future. She told me that I would live forever but not in this world I would be transported to the realm but not for many years. Sam, Caroline and Katie would also be transported to the realm when it was time to leave this world. In the meantime, we would enjoy each other's company every full moon. I asked if I would be able to hold anyone in the realm along with Katie, Caroline and Sam. She smiled sweetly "Nothing will change Chosen One just a different place in a different time where we can continue living with each other until time itself ends. Some of my sisters are over 10,000 years old. Every hundred years we renew ourselves with ancient magic that has been passed down over the centuries. You will enjoy travelling with the snap of your fingers." She laid her head on my shoulder and we drifted off to sleep.

We awoke to the presence of someone else in the log cabin Jenny had arrived. We sat up as the spirits engulfed her they then disappeared. She stood before Christina with her head slightly bowed "Oh dear Christina remarked, you are pregnant how could this possibly happen." She then smiled "How could it possibly happen to me?" "Please let me stay with the Chosen One and look after the children. Margaret will be over 12 months old before it is time for me to give birth. All should be well by then. I am truly blessed I am carrying a daughter of the Chosen One." I stood up and held her close to my chest kissed her tenderly on the forehead and then on the lips reaffirming my love for her. Christina voiced. "You may stay until you have given birth then you must return to the realm." "Thank you Christina, thank you" "You realise you cannot travel any more by the click of your fingers it could harm the unborn child Jenny." "I know Christina I will have to travel back with Chosen One in the range Rover such a primitive way of travelling" she sighed "What ever happened to Nicola and Tinkerbell Christina?" I asked snapping my fingers making a coffee she laughed and so did Jenny "What happens to all women who get close to you. You should have don't touch stamped on your forehead". She said turning to kiss me sweetly on the lips. She waved her hand and a picture formed Nicola and Tinkerbell were both carrying daughters in their arms. Christina picked up my thoughts of her enlarged breasts, she smiled. "They are for your daughter Star not for you Chosen One." She smiled and kissed me again. I must return to Star to feed her. She kissed me on the lips and vanished. Jenny seated herself beside me placing her arm around my shoulder and kissing me softly on the lips "We are truly blessed. I dream of you every night and the way you entered my body. I wanted your child inside me, although I was not supposed to until permitted by my sisters but they understand what you do to a woman and they are pleased with the outcome". We slowly drove back to Redbrick farm. Sam greeted Jenny as a daughter in the living room. "I've an announcement" Jenny said softly. "I'm with child." Caroline, Katie and Sam embraced her and congratulated her on her condition. Jenny went upstairs to tend to her duties. I asked them to sit down and I explained to them what happens to us in time, how we would be transported to a new realm our lives would continue there. They all smiled but hoped it wouldn't be too soon. Katie came over and sat on my lap. "You haven't been in my bed for at least a week why not? I love you with all my heart". Caroline remarked "You have not laid a hand on me since I returned from the realm and I have never looked this attractive in my life before, why?" "Must I make love to you all the time do you not realise I love you more than life itself. But when we do come together, you will remember the event." They smiled.

Chapter 22
Not as I'd planned

I drove to Cranbury farm snowdrop was looking over the top of the door to me. Susan brought him out ready saddled. I kissed her on the cheek and mounted snowdrop and trotted off around the property. I wondered if I'd really lost interest in sex altogether or was there other forces controlling what took place. I decided it was pointless me trying to work things out. I neither had the knowledge or the ability to understand much when it came to magic and spirits. Both the stables were being run so efficiently by the four spirits I had time to think and relax and so did Sam. Most of the male customers drooled over the four girls who used their charm to make us even more money. Without overstepping the mark of actually becoming involved with anyone. One could almost call it a right torment and I was glad I wasn't involved although I knew I could take anyone of them to bed. Should I choose to I just didn't want to ruin a good thing, and decided to keep everything strictly business. Sam galloped up from behind me and pulled Freddie up alongside Snowdrop. "You are troubled Rob what's the matter". I reached across and held her hand and squeeze gently. "Things haven't turned out Sam the way I wanted them to for us. I didn't want to sleep with all these other women I just wanted you." I Started to cry thinking of all the sins I committed and the pain and suffering all my love ones had endured. Sam grabbed the reins of Snowdrop as I fell off my horse. I awoke to find myself in the cabin in bed. Sam, Caroline and Katie were at my bedside I can see the spirits touching me but I just didn't want to go on. Christina appeared in my bedroom looking very alarmed "This should not have happened to the Chosen One." There were so many tears from everyone I thought the cabin would be flooded. I convalesced for six weeks staying in the cabin. Sam stayed with me all the time, Christina would pay daily visits after attending to Star her daughter. I was broken I had no will to live nothing I'd wanted in life had really worked out. Jenny my first wife betrayed me. Sam was the best thing that ever happened to me and she has to share me which I thought was unfair. Caroline had never done anyone any harm had suffered more than most. Katie one minute was my daughter and the next my stepdaughter and finally my lover. This is not what I wanted out of life why am I being punished. Christina could read all my thoughts. She stood over me crying with my pain I could hear Sam and Christina talking. "My daughter I think you are going to lose him from this world he will not respond to the spirits until we get him into the realm." Caroline entered the room carrying Margaret in her arms. "This is your daughter Rob you would leave her without a father? You're a selfish bastard, stop feeling sorry for your bloody self you can't even be bothered to fuck me. I'm leaving if you haven't by the end of the week. Do you get the message you so called Chosen One?" I had never seen Caroline so angry she placed Margaret on the bed I sat up and held her. Sam and Christina looked on in horror at what Caroline had said to me the Chosen One. Caroline then took Margaret from my hands and stormed out of the bedroom. The spirits returned enhancing my body and mind. Christina started to smile "That is not the way to speak to the Chosen One but it worked he's mending". Christina and Sam held each other in astonishment. I started to dress myself and went into the front room. Christina snapped her fingers and a plate of food was on the coffee table waiting for me to enjoy. I ate heartily and started to feel better in myself. Caroline had gone back to Redbrick farm. After a further week of convalescing I felt my old self. Caroline entered the cabin wearing a see-through blouse no bra short miniskirt and no knickers. She sat beside me on the settee "Well I'm waiting and you better be good." I snapped my fingers and she was naked, her body had truly been transformed there was not a blemish on it. I held her hand and we went into the bedroom. She jumped onto the bed parted her legs "I'm waiting". I lay on top of her kissed her tenderly and entered her body. She gasped "My God, come on ride me, fuck me." This was a whole new Caroline. Two hours later we were still entangled her tenderness her passion she wasn't going to let me go. She was going to wear me into the ground and make me realise how much I loved her and she loved me. I lay beside her exhausted she rolled over on to me "Is that all you're going to give me"? She teased me until I was fully erect and then started to ride me like no other woman. Finally, she let me rest. She lay beside me kissing me tenderly "I love you Rob. I always have, don't you dare leave me". We showered and dressed. I snapped my fingers and food was on the table. The sun was shining through the window casting shadows from the trees, dancing on the walls as they moved in the breeze. We seated ourselves at the table enjoying the food. Caroline then remarked "Do you remember the table Rob or would it be too much for an old man to handle?" I lifted her onto the table throwing the plates on the floor, ripped her blouse open and thrust. She hung onto my neck how dare she question my ability? I thought I will show you. I thrust hard and fast she bit my shoulder hanging on the dear life "That's great, don't stop." We showered again I snapped my fingers and she was dressed. We kissed and held each other "Now that's the Rob I remember." She smiled holding my hand. We drove back to Redbrick farm. Everyone was there to greet me. Caroline ran upstairs to change. Jenny was starting to show she was pregnant. I sat in the armchair by the fire Katie came and sat on my lap "You're with me tonight my love". I looked across to Sam who came across and sat on the arm of the chair and kissed me on the forehead with approval. I was still trying to live with my guilt but everyone else seemed to be perfectly happy with the situation. So I suppose I mustn't moan or feel sorry for myself

    The next morning, I drove over to Cranbury farm I wanted to see snowdrop. Susan informed me Snowdrop had been playing up ever since I'd fell off him. He saw me approaching and neighed, nodding his head. He placed his head over the stable door and gently against mine. I said to him "It wasn't your fault I fell off Snowdrop." Susan placed her hand on my shoulder then kissed me on the cheek. "You are special Chosen One". She snapped her fingers and Snowdrop was ready to ride. He came out of the stable and stood ready for me to ride him. I mounted and we went around the property. I patted his neck and he shook his head. Susan galloped up from behind and stopped alongside "Christina has instructed me to ride with you Chosen One, she doesn't want anything to happen to you". Summer was here and the air humid, we talked as we rode along together. She explained to me she had never left the realm until Christina instructed her to come here. She was enjoying the experience although she didn't like the men who leered at her when they came to ride their horses. "We are only allowed one man and that has to be the Chosen One". I pointed out she was extremely attractive and any red-blooded man would want to possess her. She smiled, shaking her head. We continue riding we cut through my woodland the bluebells filled the air with scent the primroses were growing in clumps in places, you would think nothing could grow. We stopped at the cabin and went inside to have a coffee we sat at the table. I snapped my fingers and the drinks appeared. We sat there talking about horses then finally got onto the subject of feelings. She explained to me although she came from the realm they do have feelings they can be hurt just like a human being because that's where they all descended from. She started to shed a tear as she told me about the way some of her sisters had been tortured for practising magic many centuries ago and they were only ever trying to help people with their illnesses and were totally misunderstood. She couldn't imagine what it must feel like to be burnt at the stake alive. "You realise you'll be the only man allowed in the realm, you are so privileged when you leave this world. Once you are there we can breed without complications of travelling. A man has never been in the realm and you will have your choice of unseen beautiful women." She reached across and placed her hand on mine. We left the cabin and rode back to Cranbury farm. Sam was waiting for me she looked at my face and then Susan's very suspiciously. We dismounted and Susan took snowdrop back to the stable. "You haven't Rob?" "I haven't what?" I knew exactly what she was getting at but thought can't I just go for a nice ride with a beautiful girl and not rip her knickers off "Ye of little faith woman". Sam smiled holding my arm and we walked up the yard. I heard a scream from snowdrop's stable. I ran over a man in there trying to kiss Susan and open her blouse. The rage that filled my body was unbelievable. I didn't have to touch him I just stared at him, his feet left the ground. I looked out of the open stable door and he was propelled 20 yards across the concrete yard and fell on his back. He screamed in agony. I shouted "Come here again and I will break you in half." Susan tidied herself and came out into the yard. She kissed me tenderly on the cheek. Sam came running over, she said "You realise Rob you glowed white. I thought you were going to kill him." "It did cross my mind Sam; no one will hurt my wives" She looked at me curiously trying to comprehend what I'd just said. I kissed Sam goodbye and Susan driving to the churchyard and look at Jenny's grave and Johnny's. I wondered how things would have worked out if they were still alive. I shed a few tears and drove to the log cabin. I went inside snapped my fingers and a Bacardi and Coke appeared, snap my fingers again and the log burner was lit. Christina appeared in her white robe "Are you having depressing thoughts again Chosen One? I feel your pain. You must not dwell on such things these events were set in stone long before either you or I were born. The universe is planned by a greater power than either of us possess." She held my hand encouraging me to sit by her on the settee. She held me close. "I sense the love you have for everyone". We kissed a little. "How is Star? Christina. I haven't seen her for ages. Why don't you bring her with you Sometimes?" Christina waved her hand and there was Star playing with other female children. I had fathered all the children they appeared to look identical as if they had come from the same mother. Sam entered the cabin looking rather flustered and out of breath. "What is wrong Samantha?" Christina said standing up and embracing her. "You know I look after the Chosen One. He will come to no harm. Why are you so worried about him?" "Unlike you mother I cannot read his mind and when he wasn't at Redbrick farm after nearly killing someone I panicked and feared the worst." "I am here daughter to take away his pain. I am aware of everything he does and I will never stop watching him because he is my true love." "He's my husband mother not yours." "He is everyone's husband daughter and don't you forget it do I make myself clear?" I walked out of the cabin jumped in my range Rover and drove off. I'd had a bloody enough of this situation.

I drove for miles and miles. The further I got away the better I felt. Christina appeared in the passenger seat looking very alarmed. "Where are you going Chosen One?" "Getting away from you bloody lot." I pulled over into a layby. "Well you get out I've had enough." Christina sat there very quiet, whether she feared my anger would produce such an emotion that would enabled me to harm her I don't know but she didn't move or speak. She then quietly remarked "It was only a mother and daughter disagreement. It's inevitable when two women love the same man so much. Please return to the cabin. Sam is heartbroken and needs your tender touch" Christina vanished. I drove back to the cabin. Sam's range Rover was still there. She looked out of the window to see me pull up and ran out almost ripping the door off the vehicle trying to reach me. I jumped out and we embraced and went inside. I snapped my fingers and both of our favourite drinks appeared on the coffee table. We sat there caressing each other trying to make light of what had happened. I could tell from Sam's expression she was really worried about me "Sam my love, you are my heart and soul. I will always want you and always be with you that is my promise to you." She flung her arms around my neck crying on my shoulder. "I don't like this situation any more than you do Rob but is better than losing you altogether".

The next full moon came and I went to the cabin. Christina didn't appear but Susan did and I was confused. She prepared my food and drink "Where is Christina?" "She thinks she has offended you and asked me to take her place which is an honour for me to serve you and you saved me which proves your love for me." Susan had not changed from her riding gear it must have been a last-minute decision by Christina not to come. Susan and I talked most of the evening discussing what the future held and my concerns. She was a lovely person to talk to we seem to get along really well. I was determined not to turn it into another rip her clothes off and ravish her body situation like with everyone else. The most we did was kiss and hold hands. I awoke the next morning to find Susan had gone. I decided to stay there for the rest of the day. I wanted some peace and quiet. About 12:30 PM Sam arrived in her range Rover and came in "Why didn't you come home this morning Rob?" "Well I had these 10 women to have sex with and I just needed the rest" I smiled. She remarked smiling sitting by me. "In your dreams, No, seriously, why didn't you come home?" "Just wanted to rest my love and think things through, you're going to have to control your temper Sam around your mother." "I know I just suddenly had a fit of jealousy. You are my husband and I really don't want to share you" "You now know how I feel I only want to be with you." Sam left kissing me on the cheek. A short while later I heard horses approaching. It was Susan on her own horse and leading Snowdrop by the reins to the cabin. I greeted her and Snowdrop as usual, he placed his head on my shoulder "That horse really loves you Rob" Susan commented dismounting. She came in and we had a coffee "I thought you might like to ride back to the stables with him. That man who tried it on with me yesterday took his horse away this morning. He has a broken arm he didn't even speak to me." She smiled. I jumped on Snowdrops back and we trotted off towards Cranbury farm Susan rode alongside me. She had a beautiful smile and a very kind personality but I was keeping myself in check. I was not going to ruin this relationship. I needed a friend to talk to and the minute I took her to bed I knew that would be over. We returned to Cranbury farm Susan took my horse.

Chapter 23
A shocking discovery

I returned to Redbrick farm Sam and Katie were seated on the settee. When I entered the living room Jenny was perched on the arm of my chair. I seated myself looking at the worried expressions on everyone's faces. Jenny placed her arm around my shoulder. "We have a problem Chosen One. I have just been explaining to Katie and Sam. Robert and Jonathan are showing homosexual tendencies. I suspect it is because both of their mothers are contaminated we know it is not from you the Chosen One". Sam and Katie looked at each other and to me. I exhaled. Sam had tears in her eyes and so did Katie. This was totally unexpected and I had no idea how to deal with the situation "Would they not grow out of it Jenny? Because they are barely teenagers" I said snapping my fingers and a large glass of my favourite tipple appeared. "That is a good question Chosen One we feel it is highly unlikely because it is part of their chemistry." "Perhaps we should introduce them to girl's take them to a nightclub or a strip club, even if I have to, to a prostitute." Jenny sighed. "I have encouraged them myself to see our beautiful stable girls. I even instructed my sisters to make slight advances towards the boys to see if they showed any signs of interest which they should do at their present age." Jenny stood up and sat between Sam and Katie who had been silent and placed an arm around each of their shoulders. "That was the last thing I expected to hear." I remarked emptying my glass. Katie and Sam were wiping their eyes with a handkerchief. "What will happen to them"? "They will lose their protection to start with, Christina will not allow homosexuals to be protected and it wouldn't be just her decision. It will be the sisters too." Katie remarked becoming angry. "What proof do you have?" Jenny waved her hand in a circle the boys appeared in there with two boys kissing other boys and fondling each other. I snap my fingers and the vision disappeared. Jenny could see the anger on my face. "Calm yourself Chosen One please, you could kill them with your thoughts." Sam and Katie glared at me in fear of what I might inadvertently do. "Is there no one in this house who is not contaminated" I shouted. I rose to my feet leaving the house, jumping in the range Rover. Heading for the cabin perhaps they thought I was running away. That was not the case I knew if I stayed there. I would administer punishment on the two boys I needed to calm down and think of a solution calmly. I entered the cabin, snapped my fingers, a drink appeared and the wood burner was lit. I sat in my armchair fuming instead of calming down I was becoming more livid. Christina appeared. She sat herself on the settee and patted the other seat for me to join her. I did as she requested. She placed my head against her chest "You were wise to leave Chosen One, it's a difficult situation and you could have made a decision you would regret for the rest of your life." "What am I to do Christina"? "The decision has already been made Rob, Katie and Sam, decided to send them to live with their grandfather in Switzerland. Don't worry about Stephen he is not affected but Julian will be. We suspected this may be a problem from the outset." Sam entered the cabin heartbroken. Christina embraced her daughter and eased the pain as much as she could. She guided Sam to the settee to sit in between us. Sam flung her arms around me. "Don't kill him Rob he's your son." "I had no intentions of doing that Sam you think so little of me that I would actually kill my own son?" "I don't know what to think anymore Rob." Christina advised "At least while there in Switzerland they will be away from the contaminated environment which has affected them. They are too young to be helped by us yet, but it may be possible to do the same as we did to you Sam when they are older." Sam turned to her mother and embraced her, crying on her shoulder. Christina rubbed her back trying to ease the pain. "I explained to my father." Sam sobbed. "What was going on with the boy's. He said he'd try his best to cure the problem and where he lived there was no chance of them meeting those people. I will miss him terribly Rob." "I think you have made a wise decision." Christina remarked. Katie entered the cabin with tears streaming down her cheeks. "I managed to get them on a late flight. They didn't want to go but I didn't give them a bloody choice." She was angry, she slapped my face, everybody looked shocked. "Don't you dare kill my son you bastard." Christina immediately raised her hand and Katie curled up on the floor in extreme agony. "How dare you strike the Chosen One he has no intention of touching his sons. Why do you think he is here talking to me? although we could with a single thought kill them both and you." She said looking at Sam and Katie with her face glowing white. I said. "Enough." I helped Katie to her feet. She threw her arms around my neck crying. I eased her onto the settee and I sat in my armchair by the wood burner. I snapped my fingers and everyone had their favourite drink on the coffee table and mine by the fire. I stared into the flames watching them dance on the back of the fire. Christina was talking to Sam and Katie. Katie came across and kissed me where she'd hit me on the cheek. "I am sorry Rob I should have realised you wouldn't kill your own son." You and Sam go home. I am staying to talk to Christina privately we have much to discuss." My voice had gone ice cold and they knew as they left the cabin I was angry. Sam started back towards me then changed her mind looking at the expression on my face they both left. I moved over to sit by Christina again. She touched my face where I'd been struck and the pain went away. "Will my daughters be affected?" "No, no Chosen One they are safe the boys may be cured yet do not give up hope we have sisters in Switzerland who will work on them to improve and repair their affliction." I embraced her, kissing her tenderly on the lips. I wondered what else was going to go wrong. There was a knock on the cabin door. Susan entered in a beautiful red long dress. Christina smiled, inviting her to sit beside us on the settee. "I sent for her Rob. I know you're fond of her and you like talking to Susan. She is yours for the taking Chosen One like all my sisters." "I thought you lived here yet I never see you?" Christina laughed and so did Susan. "We are living here, you just can't see us." She kissed me softly on the lips, Christina voiced. "You are afraid to touch her Chosen One you think you will lose her if you do, that's a strange thought Chosen One. Now I understand you don't want to make her pregnant and lose her, that is a very honourable thought." Susan kissed me again and held my hand. Christina held my other hand and they both lent their heads against my shoulders "This is such an honour Chosen One" Susan voiced. Christina stood up holding my hand "Come with me. You are full of tension and stress not of your making". She led me into the bedroom. "I have longed for this moment since giving birth to your daughter." She snapped her fingers and we were both naked. She eased me down onto the bed lying on top of me. Her breasts were still large because of her breast-feeding she teased my mouth with one and then the other she lowered herself down onto me. She caressed me and teased me until a smile came on my face again. She lay on her back inviting me. We made love again she was absolutely wonderful. Just before daybreak we showered, Susan was still there. She had prepared breakfast. Christina said "I must go but Susan will stay with you today. Remember you can sleep with her if you wish she is yours Chosen One." Christina vanished. Susan sat by me at the kitchen table her brown eyes pierced my soul. Every time I glanced to her I was desperate to take her to bed but feared she would become pregnant and be taken away. She had obviously read my thoughts. She snapped her fingers and her clothes fell away. I Stared at this unblemished body, beautifully formed I felt my body exploding inside desperate to take her so I snapped my fingers quick and she was dressed. She looked on disappointed hoping I would take advantage. She re-seated herself beside me "Chosen One please take me." I thought for a moment. Condom's came to my mind why I hadn't thought of it before I don't know. I snapped my fingers and they appeared on the table. She looked at them curiously. I grabbed a packet and her hand, her smile broadened when she realised we were heading for the bedroom. I snap my fingers and she lay on the bed naked I penetrated her lovely body. I kissed and caressed her. We showered and dressed. She sat beside me on the settee "Why did you do that Chosen One?" Because I don't want you pregnant I don't want to lose you. I love you I want to enjoy you forever." Susan smiled "I don't think Christina is going to be very happy if you don't make me pregnant". Christina appeared holding the use condom "What is this? you dishonour Susan. She wants your child inside her. That is the sole purpose." We went into the front room I sat in my armchair staring at Christina and Susan. "I am the Chosen One. I will decide when Susan becomes pregnant. You told me she was mine and to do with as I please. It pleases me not to make her pregnant yet". Christina exhaled. She was about to open her mouth. I snapped my fingers and thought of a coil as a contraceptive. Susan flinched as it located itself. Christina Stared at me in astonishment. "You cannot do that Chosen One my sisters will not approve." "Susan is special to me and I choose not to make her pregnant for the time being. Talk to your sisters I'm sure they will agree." "They agree Chosen One but for only one calendar year. It is a waste of your seed". Christina conceded. "I have plenty and if your comment is correct then why you aren't pregnant again?" I smiled. Christina vanished. I grabbed Susan's hand pulling her into the bedroom. I snapped my fingers and we were both naked "Now we can make love properly." I said smiling "Oh yes Chosen One I feel the difference." We stayed in bed for the rest of the morning. I'd finally managed to get my own way over something that was important to me, we showered and dressed. Susan snapped her fingers and lunch was on the table. "You honour me Chosen One by wanting me for a long time if you get bored with me I will go and you can have another sister." I rose to my feet and embraced her. "You are not to be treated that way I will never get rid of you. Sam and Katie entered the cabin. Susan vanished. I think she was feeling she would only be in the way I sat in my armchair. Katie kissed me on the cheek and so did Sam and seated them on the settee. "What are we going to do Rob. What did Christina have to say after we'd gone?" Sam asked "We will just have to wait and see how they turn out. Christina feels as they mature and with the right guidance it may not be a problem although they cannot allow them to breed with any of the sisters in the future. The covenant cannot afford any contamination. But there is no reason why they cannot lead a normal life like anyone else." Katie smiled "At least they can live like normal human beings not like us. I am really sorry I hit you last night and doubted you would not look after your son." Sam exhaled "I never considered myself to be damaged goods Rob." "It doesn't matter Sam, your daughter is fine she will join the sisters and so will Vicky. It is only the boys that have a problem and you can't conceive anymore so there is no chance of you producing anymore offspring." I explained snapping my fingers and glasses of wine appeared for everyone. Sam moved across to me kissing me on the lips then returning to the settee "What about me?" Katie asked "You don't want any more children do you Katie?" "No I'm on the pill I just want you to fuck my brains out every day and twice on Sundays" she smiled. We heard horses approaching. We all stood at the window looking out, Susan on her horse bringing snowdrop. Katie and Sam went back to Redbrick farm after kissing me on the cheek. Susan entered the cabin after tying the horses to the guard rail. I grabbed her around the waist kissing her passionately on the lips and neck. She smiled, enjoying the attention. I carried her in my arms into the kitchen snapped my fingers and she was naked. I placed her on the kitchen table and entered her body. We kissed and cuddled I stroked her lovely breasts with my hand. I couldn't understand what attracted me so much to Susan and really didn't care. We enjoyed each other for an hour. We showered and I snapped my fingers we were dried and dressed "Chosen One, there are three other sisters here yet you focus your attention solely on me?" I looked around and the three other sisters appeared, and then vanished. "You mean they are watching us make love?" "Of course, they are waiting to be taken like me. They want to experience the same feeling and long to be taken to your bed." She smiled. I had never realised I was always being watched. We rode back slowly to Cranbury farm Susan took Snowdrop back to his stable. Sam came across to me after getting out of the range Rover she had been to the school and explained to them. We had decided the boys were going to finish their education in Switzerland. The headmaster was not impressed but he could do nothing about it. She kissed me tenderly on the lips searching my face with those beautiful hazel eyes. "Do you still love me Rob?" "That is a real stupid question Sam whatever possessed you to ask that?" "I don't know Rob I feel like I'm losing you." "What did I tell you, you are my wife and I will never let you go, regardless of what you think or what happens providing you never betray me." She smiled, gently kissing me on the lips. "I will always love you Rob. I thought you wouldn't want me because I'm damaged goods and what has happened to Jonathan. I thought you would blame me for everything." I picked her up in my arms. She smiled sweetly. I kissed her as we walked across the yard. I threw her into the loose hay snapped my fingers and she was naked and we made love. She tidied herself afterwards plucking pieces of hay from her hair. Her smile was so broad with satisfaction and confirmation that I still loved her. We walked hand-in-hand looking into each stable and stroking the horses as we passed. Although I loved so many people she was my first love the woman that turned my life around when I was in so much trouble all those years ago.

What happens next is another story.

CHARMED LOG CABIN
AND THE REALM

ROBERT S. BAKER

Chapter 1
Is There a Solution

Twelve months had drifted into history. Robert and Jonathan were still in Switzerland and the reports we received back were not very favourable; they were still showing homosexual tendencies. A meeting had been scheduled by Christina on the next full moon to discuss solutions to the situation, which in her eyes were unacceptable. Katie and Sam accompanied me, leaving Caroline at home to look after the children. We drove to the cabin with a heavy heart and on our arrival, the cabin door was open. We all entered, wondering what was going on. Coffee was already on the table waiting for us in the front room. Everyone seated themselves, me by the log burner.

Then, Christina appeared in her white robe. "The sisters and I have decided it is time for you to see the future and meet all the other sisters." Before we had chance to argue, we'd vanished, travelling in a mist, then the next second we were in a new log cabin, far larger than the one I constructed. Everyone stood in amazement gazing around I looked out of the window. We were in the middle of a forest with the largest trees I'd ever seen similar to the Redwood. Christina smiled as she read our thoughts. Although Sam and Caroline had been to the realm before they had never seen this place, it all looked brand-new. Christina walked out of the cabin, saying "Follow me." We did exactly as we were requested. We walked through the forest filled with unfamiliar aromas, although very pleasant and calming. We entered a clearing not far away Sam held my hand and so did Katie. Although this was a very pleasurable experience, there was still an element of fear in everybody's mind. Christina indicated to sit on the grass and wait.

The sun was shining brightly, casting shadows of the large trees onto the grass. Christina clapped her hands and suddenly this large grassed area was filled with sisters all in white robes. Christina called out "Children of the Chosen One, come." Suddenly I was surrounded by my offspring all daughters and their mothers. Tears filled my eyes as I held each one of them close. Christina called out again to the sisters "Can you all feel the love?" The thousand or more sisters called out "Yes, we feel the love." Christina lifted Star into her arms "You honoured our daughter even more Chosen One." The symbol of the star where I'd kissed her on the forehead had appeared. All the sisters bowed for as far as I could see. I wanted to live here, everything seemed at peace, no horses no argumentative customers and no worldly problems what more could anyone wish for?

Christina sat down in the grass by me. She clapped her hands and the children were taken away by their mothers. Jenny glanced back, I jumped to my feet and ran across to her kissing her on the lips and gave her a big hug. "What did you call our daughter?" "Miracle, because it was a miracle you slept with me." I returned to sit by Christina with a heavy sigh, dreading the next few minutes and what the conversation would entail. Sam reached for my hand. Katie held Sam's hand. "The sisters and I have decided to try and remove the unacceptable thoughts from your sons. We cannot guarantee success but we will try because you are the Chosen One" Christina voiced. I sighed with relief. She then continued "If we fail they will be destroyed, if we succeed they will not be part of the covenant. Although they can continue to lead a normal human life the choice is yours." She snapped her fingers. We had returned to my log cabin minus Christina. "Well girls what's your view?" I asked, sitting in my old armchair. Katie and Sam seated themselves on the settee looking at each other and then me. "I would sooner they stay as they are Rob." Katie voiced "It's better than a death sentence." "I must agree with Katie, Rob." Sam remarked. "It doesn't matter if they're gay as long as they're happy." Susan came into the log cabin, everyone greeted her and looked surprised that she had turned up. Katie patted the seat on the settee indicating come and sit by us. "I know what you've been discussing." Susan sighed "It must be a difficult decision for you all to make deciding the future of a love one." She held both Sam and Katie's hand. I thought hard for a moment I didn't like the situation. I didn't want to risk the sisters trying to fix the problem and if they couldn't the alternative was death. "So, we're all in agreement then. Leave them alone, you never know we may have a miracle." Sam and Katie smiled in approval of what I'd said. Sam came over and kissed me tenderly on the lips. Christina returned "I don't agree with your decision Chosen One but we will honour it." She vanished. Obviously, not happy, even Susan's expression was one of disappointment. She snapped her fingers and disappeared. We all looked at each other. "We've definitely upset the sisters" I commented. I snapped my fingers and everyone had their favourite drink in front of them on the coffee table. Katie looked across to me worried. "You don't think they'll just do what they like anyway Rob?" I shrugged my shoulders I didn't know what would happen.

I sat between them on the settee, placing my arms round their shoulders and they lent their heads against me.

We dropped Katie off at Redbrick farm. Sam and I continued to Cranbury farm. Susan and Jackie already had our horses prepared. Snowdrop looked as I jumped out of the Range Rover. I took my reins from Susan. She said coldly "My coil has been removed I wish you to make me pregnant so I can return to the realm." I stared at her in surprise with her changing attitude towards me. She saw the anger in my expression. I jumped on Snowdrop and rode off with Sam on Freddie. Sam asked "What was all that about? She didn't look very happy Rob." "That's an understatement Sam." I remarked, glancing back at Susan. Sam and I rode on.

Suddenly, with no warning, I was in a mist. Christina held my hand and within seconds we were in Switzerland. "Prepare yourself Chosen One." "What are we doing here Christina?" "Look to the floor Chosen One. Observe quietly they have the power to kill us both." I looked over a bale of hay in the loft down onto the floor. There was Robert and Jonathan in black robes kissing and cuddling other men. I snapped my fingers and Christina and I were outside the building. I raised my hand in the air and waved a circle shape over the wooden barn. I then thought of fire and the whole place burst into flames. Christina placed her hand to her mouth in shock. No one could escape everyone was destroyed with the timber barn a total inferno. She grabbed my hand quickly and snapped her fingers, so we were transported in the woodlands some distance away. We could still see the flames, Christina snapped her fingers again and I was transported to the realm, to the new log cabin and placed in bed. Christina had conveyed a message to Susan to tell Sam I was taken ill. And that's why I'd been transported from the horse and would return home shortly. Christina sat beside me on the bed holding my hand "Do realise what you've done Chosen One? You have destroyed your sons and all the filth they were practising with the black arts. I didn't realise you had that power Chosen One yet. Your anger must have been great." The tears ran down my cheeks. Had I made the right decision? How could I ever face Katie and Sam again without them realising I was responsible. Christina dried my tears with a wave of her hand. The spirits entered the cabin hundreds each embracing my body. Christina kissed me tenderly.

Chapter 2
Going Home

Christina transported me back to Redbrick farm, not in the house, but by the stables. She kissed me on the lips. "Will you be alright Chosen One? You should have stayed with us for a day longer giving yourself more chance to compose yourself." I kissed her on the cheek and headed for the front door. I entered the living room. Katie and Sam were on the settee crying, they ran over embracing me. "Do you know what happened? Rob our sons are dead." Katie said sobbing. "How?" I asked surprised. Flopping into my armchair with tears running down my face. Sam spoke up "According to my father they'd sneaked out and were involved in black magic. That's probably why the sisters wanted us to let them cure them if they could" she cried, continuing. "Apparently there was a gas explosion in an old barn and everybody was killed." Christina appeared and so did Jenny. They wrapped their arms around Sam and Katie trying to take the pain away. Caroline was upstairs with the children trying to console them. Jenny went upstairs to help with the children's pain. Christina sat on the settee and held Sam and Katie in her arms, looking across to me with sadness written all over her face. Katie asked sobbing "You didn't kill our children Christina?" "No, it was certainly nothing to do with me." Which in reality was the truth. I'd carried out the punishment and I have to live with the fact, for the rest of my life, which could well turn out to be an eternity. I stood up and headed for the door saying "I'm going out for some fresh air." I walked down looking into the stables at the happy, contented horses. I then went into the tack room and upstairs to make myself a coffee. I sat there looking into my cup suddenly Susan appeared. She went down onto her knees and bent her head. "Chosen One you honour the sisterhood, you sacrificed your own children in order to banish the filth. There is no greater honour than to serve you." She was dressed in pure white with her beautiful black hair cascading down her spine. Her hypnotic brown eyes looked into mine. "The sisters have said I'm yours forever if you'll have me? I'm not worthy to be in your presence." I held her hands and smiled pulling her close encouraging her to sit on my knee. I placed my arm around her waist. She kissed my neck gently I finish my coffee and we walked along in the moonlight hand-in-hand. At least I had Susan to talk to now for as long as I wanted. We sat under the willow tree at the end of the garden on a large swing. There was a chill in the air and I removed my jacket and placed it around her shoulders. She smiled and cuddled close. "Chosen One I love you, I've always loved you from the first day I saw you. I want your child inside me. Only when you give me permission that has been agreed with all the sisters I'm a gift for you as long as you want me." I kissed her gently on the forehead and told her I would want her forever. I was not impressed with having a quick mating session and then probably never see them again. If I ever made it to the realm permanently there should be changes made where no one is left out. Sam came from the house with a torch, we could see her approaching. Susan snapped her fingers and disappeared. Sam seated herself beside me leaning her head on my shoulder holding my hand. "Why is your jacket on the floor Rob? You'll catch a chill." She remarked, picking it up. I put my jacket back on Sam and cuddled up to me. "What are we going to do Rob? Everything is falling apart again." "Just do what we always do love, soldier on and recover". I remarked holding her by the hand and slowly walking back to the house.

It would be several months before Robert and Jonathan's remains would be released from ongoing investigations. We also had to explain why our two sons were out there in the first place which was rather distasteful. Katie had, had a conversation with Christina wondering whether it would be possible for Julian to be treated before he went the same way as Robert. Christina's response was she would talk to the sisters, although she felt there could be a security risk for the sisters, taking such a young child to the realm, who might convey his experience when he returned. She didn't discount the idea altogether. There was no problem with Stephen, he took every opportunity to squeeze Christina's boobs. She refused to let him sit on her lap in the end, commenting "He's worse than his father" with a broad smile. Caroline was relieved.

I drove to Cranbury farm. Summer had arrived, the daffodils were in flower all the way down the driveway at Redbrick farm and Cranbury farm. It was beautiful to see. Susan came running over to me. I looked at her in disbelief. "What have you done to your hair your beautiful black hair?" "I thought you would prefer me as a blonde and it's still the same length" she remarked, kissing me on the cheek. "You're beautiful, which ever colour hair you have." I commented as she spun around. Sam turned up in her Range Rover jumped out and looked at Susan "Whatever you done to yourself?" Jackie looked on from the stable door and then walked across to join us looking identical in physical appearance to Susan. Other than the colour of her hair she snapped her fingers and her hair turned blonde. She snapped fingers again and it returned to black "There's nothing remarkable in doing that." she scoffed, turned immediately around and headed back to the stables. "She's got a bee in her pants." I remarked. Susan commented. "It's because you haven't slept with her in all the time she's been here." Sam laughed. "You mean you missed a girl, you're slipping, it must be your age my love." Sam saw my expression change. She ran across the yard laughing. I ran after her picked her up in my arms and took her in to the hay barn, throwing her onto the soft hay. I snapped my fingers she was naked, her smile broadened with anticipation. It's been a long time since we last made love with all the problems that have been ongoing. She held me tight and confirmed her love for me. I snapped my fingers again and she was dressed. She walked out of the barn pulling bits of hay out of her hair jumped in her Range Rover and waved goodbye with a broad smile. I went over to the stable where Jackie was working. She looked at my expression and thought she would be punished. I snapped my fingers and her clothes fell away. I lay her on the bedding straw and made love to her for the first time, she cried out "Oh wonderful." She stood up, tidying herself. I smacked her backside, "Don't be impatient" I remarked with a broad smile leaving the stable. I kissed her goodbye and prepared myself to go to the cabin. It was the night of the full moon.

I parked outside the cabin with my Range Rover and entered. My Bacardi and Coke was by the log burner. The television was on and I could smell cooking. I went into the kitchen Christina was there in a long blue dress. I seated myself after kissing Christina on the lips. Christina remarked. "We were very fortunate Rob. There was an old gas cylinder in the barn, it covered up everything you did" she seated herself beside me placing one hand on my shoulder and pouring me a drink. "I don't think Sam or Katie suspect any involvement from the spirits. It doesn't look like the Swiss police have found anything of interest to bring charges against anyone else either". We went through into the front room and sat on the settee. "You made Jackie happy today Rob." Christina smiled. "She has asked for permission to have sex with you again. She just can't get over the experience. "What did you do to her? That you haven't done to me." Christina smiled undoing the buttons at the front of her dress allowing her cleavage to be seen. "Would you like another child Christina?" "No, I just want you to take me to bed. I am perfectly happy with Star she is a beautiful daughter and loved by everyone". She held my hand leading me to the bedroom snapping her fingers, so all our clothes vanished. I lay beside her on the bed and we embraced each other with great passion. We showered I washed her smooth skin. I suddenly became aroused again. Lifting her from the floor I penetrated her again, forcing her back against the shower wall. She held me enjoying the experience. I commented. "You should have another child".

We dressed with the snap of her fingers and went into the kitchen. She snapped her fingers and a coffee appeared on the table. She held my hand searching my expression with her beautiful blue sparkling eyes. "You do want me to have another child? I will consult my sisters yet I can't understand, there are far more beautiful girls in the covenant who dream of these moments yet you choose me why?" She placed her hand to her mouth. "I feel the love inside you, it caresses my very being. You truly do love me equally to Samantha." She snapped her fingers with excitement her blue dress fell away. She seated herself on the table. "Take me Chosen One, take me". We showered again then seated ourselves on the settee. She held me close, kissing my neck and lips. The spirits entered the room and engulfed us both. I felt exhilarated and lifted. Christina's smile broadened. She called out "Thank you sisters for your understanding." The spirits vanished. "They have given permission, Chosen One for me to carry another child of yours." Her smile was so broad it was unbelievable the happiness that glowed from her face with the anticipation of carrying another child "I know I'm pregnant. I can feel your seed planting itself and growing. I must go Chosen One; Susan will care for your needs." Christina snapped her fingers and vanished with a blink of an eye. Susan had appeared still with her long blonde hair tied in a ponytail and wearing her riding gear. She snapped her fingers and it was transformed into a beautiful white dress, she seated herself beside me snapping their fingers again and my favourite tipple was on the coffee table. She held my hands. Her smile was broad and pleasing. Jackie suddenly appeared with Rebecca and Tracey. Tracy voiced. "You have taken Susan and Jackie. What is wrong with Rebecca and me?" I rose to my feet. "You do not dictate to me. I will take you each when I am ready and not before." The three girls dropped to their knees and bowed their heads. "We are sorry Chosen One, please forgive our indiscretion but we are desperate to have you inside us. We have waited over a year for your attention." Susan held my arm encouraging me to sit down. The girls rose to their feet with their heads still bowed. Jenny appeared in her white robe. "How dare you three make demands on the Chosen One. I think I will send you all to the dark place. You do not deserve to belong in the covenant be gone now." Jenny shouted. The three girls vanished. Jenny sat beside me and Susan. I asked. "How is Miracle?" Jenny held my hand and smiled. "She is wonderful Chosen One, a gift truly to be proud of." Jenny snapped her fingers and Susan vanished. I looked very alarmed. Jenny smiled. "Don't worry Chosen One she has not been harmed and neither have the other three. I can understand their desperation to be with you."

Chapter 3
The Funeral

There was little left of either Jonathan or Robert you could fit there remains in a shoebox. We arranged for a cremation it seemed to be the only sensible way of dealing with the situation although the Swiss police had separated the remains using DNA. I snapped my fingers and I was dressed in black. The ceremony was Private and only members of the family attended. Rupert and Nicole did not attend. They had a few health issues which I've been meaning to talk to Christina about to see if she could help. I shed a few tears as the guilt chewed away at my soul. We returned to Redbrick farm. No one really spoke just stared into space in disbelief when the reality hit home. I excused myself and went to Cranbury farm.

It was now December and cold, there hadn't been as much snow as in previous years, although the bitter wind tried to cut you in half. I went over to Snowdrop's stable and found him dead on the floor. Susan ran over to join me and explained she didn't bother me because of the funeral. She didn't want to give me any more heartbreak. I ran to the Range Rover and drove to the cabin. I was crying more for losing my horse than my sons which is a terrible thing to say. I went inside snapped my fingers and a pint glass of Bacardi and Coke appeared. I sat there drinking until I was virtually unconscious. I could see the television flickering and Christina looking alarmed; then, I must have passed out. The next thing I remember is gaining consciousness in my bed. Susan was standing over me her tears dripped onto the blankets. She held my hand and the room appeared to be engulfed in a mist and suddenly I was in the realm. Inside the new wonderfully built log cabin, which you could almost describe as a mansion. I opened my eyes and Christina was sitting by my bedside. The spirits were whirling around my head finally disappearing. Christina encouraged me to sit up. "Listen, Chosen One, listen." I could hear a horse neighing I didn't think they had animals in the realm. I jumped to my feet and ran outside. It was Snowdrop saddled and ready to ride. I looked back to the cabin. Christina was standing on the porch with a broad smile; her beautiful blue eyes betrayed nothing but love. Snowdrop rested his head on my shoulder. Christina snapped her fingers and another horse came trotting in from the forest; pure white, it had never occurred to me, although it should have done, that Christina rode horses. She mounted her horse, her white gown settled against the horse's flesh, blending in. I mounted Snowdrop this was definitely Snowdrop not an imitation, he had certain mannerisms that were his own. We rode together through the forest on a well-worn trail just wide enough for two horses to travel side-by-side. We held hands discussing recent events. We dismounted by a lake the scenery here was spectacular. It really took some believing we sat on the shoreline and held each other. "You know I'm carrying your child Chosen One. It will be a female child." I placed my hand gently on her stomach and kissed her passionately. "Thank you for saving Snowdrop I didn't think you bothered with animals?" "If they are important and kind, and we knew how important Snowdrop is to you. So he will live here awaiting your arrival" she remarked, rising to her feet and mounting her horse. I did likewise. "It's time Chosen One for you to go back. Sam has discovered Snowdrop is dead and Susan has told her what happened and where you are." We rode back she kissed me, remarking. "You can come here whenever you please Chosen One, the sisters have agreed. You have full access to all your powers. This also includes reading people's minds, careful how you judge people when you read their thoughts do not act in haste." She snapped her fingers and I was back in my old cabin. Sam was waiting for me. She embraced me. "I'm sorry about Snowdrop Rob" she cried. I eased her away from me and smiled "Snowdrop is happy and safe he is with the sisters I've just been for a ride on him." She searched my expression with her hazel eyes finally smiling after she absorbed what I'd just said. "I thought I'd lost you Rob," she hugged me again. "Stay with me tonight here Sam." Her smile broadened. I snapped my fingers and two meals were on the kitchen table with two glasses of wine. "We don't have many moments together Sam like we used to when we first met; life has become so complicated." I snapped my fingers and her black dress changed into a beautiful blue skirt and white blouse. She looked herself up and down and was surprised. We went into the kitchen and sat and had a quiet meal together. We returned to the front room. Sam phoned home to tell them she was staying with me tonight here. We kissed each other and cuddled, watching TV with glasses of our favourite tipple on the coffee table. Now this is how I wanted life to be, just Sam and I not all the other complications that seem to have attached themselves. I could hear Sam's thoughts of how much she really loved me and wished the same as I did although she didn't say it. She also hoped I would make love to her tonight she wanted to be held in my arms. I could hear Susan's thoughts longing to be held by me. Suddenly my mind was flooded with everyone I'd slept with wanting the same attention. Christina warned me to be careful how I controlled the information I was receiving. This was a whole new ballgame and very difficult to control. Rather than snap my fingers I eased Sam away from me slightly and unbuttoned her blouse one button at a time, her mine was going wild with anticipation begging me to continue. I kissed the top of her breasts and her neck and released her bra. I held her breasts gently in my hands then finally held her hand and led her to the bedroom. I didn't snap my fingers again. I removed her blouse and released her skirt and finally removing her pants. She held me passionately savouring every second of the moment. I finally eased her down onto the bed and we made love which seemed to go on for hours. This was a moment I would cherish I didn't care if the other sisters were watching somewhere in the shadows. Sam was my wife and always would be and she was the one I wanted above all others to love. I had learnt a valuable lesson having the ability to snap your fingers make things happen, took all the magic out of preparation for real lovemaking and it was something I would not forget in the future.

    I awoke to the smell of cooking. Sam wasn't beside me, so I went into the kitchen after dressing. She had prepared us bacon and eggs for breakfast. She greeted me with a passionate kiss. "Oh Rob I will never forget last night it was special it felt different like I was the only one in your life." I smiled, seating myself at the table and so did Sam. "You are the only one in my life Sam in my mind there never will be a woman to replace you." "I wish I could give you another child Rob especially now Jonathan has gone from our lives" Sam sighed. "That's not important Sam we have each other, that's all that matters to me". We drove to Cranbury farm after breakfast. Sam had arranged unbeknown to me for Snowdrop to be buried not taken to the knacker's yard. He was in a field close to the stables she also arranged for a plaque to be made honouring the horse I loved so much. I received a phone call from Caroline telling me she had problems with her car and was broken down between the two farms. I left Sam at Cranbury farm and went to see what the problem was with Caroline, halfway through the village. She was parked on the side of the road with the car bonnet up. "I'm sorry Rob, to bother you but it just won't go." She had left Margaret with Katie at home and was coming to Cranbury farm just to check on the horses. I told her to leave it there and I would arrange for it to be collected. I decided we needed new vehicles. I was worth over £200 million so spending a few quid on cars would not even dent my wallet. Caroline jumped in the Range Rover I asked her what her favourite colour is. She looked at me rather puzzled. "Blue" she answered. I phoned Sam and asked her the same question and also Katie. I immediately drove off to the Land Rover dealership still with Caroline in the Range Rover the salesman came across to me. "You know all the vehicles we have at Redbrick farm you supplied them apart from one." "I want the best Range Rovers, all diesel if you give me a fair price now on the others, they are in the same condition as mine". "Yes, Mr Jones, we would be very interested and thank you for coming back to us." "One must be blue." Caroline smiled. "One must be crimson, mine is black and the last one white." We agreed the figures and I paid for them there and then. They also arranged for Caroline's car to be collected and scrapped out of the way. It would only take seven days to get new vehicles to us so Caroline wouldn't have to suffer too long without a vehicle. Caroline phoned Sam and Katie telling them what I'd done. I could hear them screaming down the phone at each other. I didn't see the point in not spending the money. I didn't know how long I would be on this earth. So I might as well enjoy it while I had it and make as many people happy along the way; everyone works so hard yet seem to have little reward for their efforts.

Chapter 4
My Surprise

Everyone had received their new vehicles. I also had our own diesel tank fitted to save running miles to a garage all the time to fill up which was appreciated. I missed riding Snowdrop and often went to Cranbury farm looking over his stable door just to check he wasn't there anymore. It's funny how you can fall in love with an animal that means almost more to you than anyone else. When I arrived I noticed Snowdrop's stable door was closed. Susan came across to me and explained Jackie was pregnant and has returned to the realm but she'd ask Christina to replace her with another sister. I asked why Snowdrop's stable doors were closed Susan shrugged her shoulders. "I have no idea Rob" and walked off, which was unlike her. I went across to investigate. I opened the top half of the door and staggered backwards in astonishment as Snowdrop placed his head over the top of the door and "Neighed". Rebecca and Tracey shouted surprise they ran over and picked me up off the floor as the tears streamed down my face. "Is it really you Snowdrop"? He moved his head up and down I went over to him and he rested his head on my shoulder as usual. There was no doubt in my mind this was Snowdrop I turned to face Rebecca and Tracey. "HOW, WHAT?" "This is our gift to you Chosen One we begged Christina and the sisters to return Snowdrop to make you happy again." "This was your idea?" "Yes Chosen One I hope you're not angry with us?" "Angry, how could I possibly be angry at such a loving gesture and returning my favourite horse?" I kissed them both on the lips and I kissed Snowdrop, he shook his head. I placed my arm around the waist of each girl. "You will come to the cabin tonight and receive your reward". Rebecca and Tracey smiled "Thank you Chosen One." I snapped my fingers and Snowdrop was saddled we rode around the property. Snowdrop paused and looked at his grave then trotted on I didn't realise how much these moments of solitude really meant. Just me and Snowdrop I phoned Sam and explained to her what the girls had done. She was ecstatic and said they needed rewarding. I advised Sam I'd already planned their reward. She knew exactly what I meant and knew it would eventually take place but realised she was number one in my life and that would not change. I went to the cabin that evening Tracey and Rebecca were already there preparing my meal and refreshment. I seated myself at the kitchen table and enjoyed the food they had prepared, although with the click of their fingers. We then moved into the front room I sat on the settee and they sat either side of me. They were in their white robes which I thought looked rather boring I could hear their thoughts, wondering who would be taken first and what it would be like to make love. I snapped my fingers and Tracey was dressed in a red mini skirt and white blouse and for Rebecca I changed the miniskirt colour to blue with a white blouse They looked at what I'd done to them both tidied their skirts not wishing to reveal too much leg, although I'd made it almost impossible considering the length the skirts. I snapped my fingers again and my favourite tipple appeared. I could hear their passing thoughts to one another becoming more excited as the evening progressed. I placed my hand on each one's leg. Tracey was thinking I will explode in a minute I want him to take me. I stood up and reached for Tracey's hand and led her into the bedroom. She was about to snap her fingers to undress and I waved my finger from side to side. I then kissed her and unbuttoned her blouse and then released her skirt and removed her pants. I eased her down onto the bed and penetrated her, caressing her breasts lips and neck. After an hour we showered we returned to the front room. Rebecca was sat on the settee looking very nervous. I heard the thoughts between the two girls again Tracey was telling Rebecca how wonderful it felt to be loved and not to be afraid. I led Rebecca into the bedroom and did the same to her. We returned to the front room the smile on their faces was so broad. I heard their thoughts again they wanted more they wanted to experience it all over again. I grabbed both their hands and led them into the bedroom again. This time I snapped my fingers and their clothes all fell away and mine we spent the rest of the night there. When I awoke in the morning they had gone. I showered and dressed snapped my fingers and breakfast was on the table. I sat quietly sipping my coffee and eating my bacon and eggs. Sam entered and came and sat by me kissing me on the cheek. I snapped my fingers and a coffee was made for her. I could hear her thoughts, wondering whether she should mention about me sleeping with the two girls last night. I could feel the anger in her mind although her smile betrayed a different story. Reading people's minds was no asset you could feel how much you'd hurt someone without them speaking a word. I finished my breakfast and kissed her on the lips telling her once more how much I loved her. I then picked up Caroline's thoughts. She was desperate for new clothes, but didn't want to ask me or try and borrow money from any other member of the household. This was not what I wanted to hear from a member of the family concerned about such a trivial matter and would not cost a great deal of money. I kissed Sam once again and said "I must go to Redbrick farm." She continued on to Cranbury farm. I went inside my private room opened the safe and removed £2000. I called out returning to the living room. "Caroline where are you"? She came running downstairs, looking rather worried. I kissed her on the forehead and then passionately on the lips. "You are a silly girl stop worrying, talk to me you know I love you." She searched my expression wondering what I meant. I grabbed her hand and placed the £2000 in her palm. "How did you know Rob? Has somebody been saying something to you about the way I'm dressed?" She protested. I eased her onto my lap and gave her a big hug. "It's been a long time Rob since you've held me like this I didn't think you wanted me anymore?" I sighed. I immediately placed her across my knee and slapped her backside, then turned her the right way up back onto my lap. "That hurt Rob. What was that for?" She protested. "How many times have I told you you're special? how many times do I have to tell you I love you?" Tears came into her eyes and she held me close. "It's alright for Sam and Katie they have their own money, I don't and I don't want to ask anybody. I know I have my wages but it isn't much." Katie came downstairs hearing the commotion, seeing tears in Caroline's eyes. "What's going on?" I phoned Sam. "Sam, get your arse in this house now." I was becoming angry. Katie sat down quietly, I could hear her thoughts panicking wondering what was going on. Sam came running in "What's wrong Rob?" I pointed to the settee "Sit there". The colour drained from Sam's face as she sat down seeing Caroline drying her tears. "Sam, Katie. You are selfish bitches you both have money of your own. Caroline has nothing except what she's paid by you Sam which is bloody peanuts. I don't know why she bothers to work for you. She was desperate to buy new clothes and was too scared to ask either of you to help her out with money and she is a member of this family. Katie you sit on your fat arse and do nothing all day. It's about time you started helping around here." Katie stared on in horror at what had been said, which was the truth and she knew it; the most she ever did was look after the children, when it suited her. I heard her thoughts "Bastard Who Do You Think You Are?" I looked at her hands and her long manicured fingernails. I snapped my fingers and they all fell off. Every fingernail was cut right back. She screamed in horror running off upstairs. I then turned to Sam. "Well what are you going to do about the situation Sam?" She couldn't speak for a moment after seeing what I'd done to Katie. She shrugged her shoulders. "I can only say sorry Rob I didn't realise." Jenny appeared. "Christina sent me before the situation gets out of hand and you do something you'll going to regret Chosen One. She feels your anger and so do I. Katie deserved what you did to her I will stay. Take Caroline to the cabin, she desperately needs your love." Sam stood up and embraced Caroline. "I didn't realise, I'm sorry Caroline." I voiced angrily "You're my wife Sam, Katie I've known all my life. How do you think Caroline feels just being treated as an outsider? and no thanks to you or her upstairs, the situation hasn't improved. "Go Chosen One, go now." Jenny insisted. Sam burst into tears. "I wouldn't leave you in charge of a wheelbarrow let alone this family. If it's not a fucking horse you're not interested." I picked Caroline up in my arms and walked out of the house. I placed her in my Range Rover and headed for the cabin. "You shouldn't have said those things Rob. They were really hurtful to Sam and Katie". "That's what happens when you marry rich arrogant bitches." She placed her hand on my leg. "Calm yourself Rob please you're frightening me." I smiled. "I'm sorry love. I don't know why I got so angry but I felt your pain and when I read your thoughts." "You what, you can read my thoughts, everyone's?" I nodded. "That's how I found out you were short of money and scared to ask anybody for help." Caroline exhaled. I could hear her thoughts worrying what was happening to Sam and Katie. We entered the cabin. I snapped my fingers and the lights came on and drinks were on the coffee table, our favourite tipple. Jenny appeared. "Chosen One your punishment did not fit the crime. I know Katie called you a bastard in her mind, but she didn't actually say it. Sam just didn't realise, an innocent mistake. I have replaced Katie's nails and she has promised to do more in the house. Sam has doubled Caroline's wages, so this situation should not arise again." I moved over on the settee and patted the seat. Jenny seated herself. I snapped my fingers and she was dressed in a mini skirt and blouse. I did the same to Caroline. I placed my arm around their shoulders and kissed them both on the cheek. "I have to return to the realm Chosen One." "Not until I tell you, you're not going." Jenny stared at me in bewilderment. "Why have you dressed me in such a style?" Caroline laughed. "If you don't know by now Jenny, you never will." "Oh dear, I should be getting back Chosen One." "No, I haven't finished with you yet don't you want to be in the presence of the Chosen One and please him? I'm sure Christina would have something to say about that." Her smile broadened. Christina appeared on the television screen, smiling, "You never cease to amaze me Chosen One you may take Jenny to your bed. Katie and Sam are really doing some soul-searching this evening and coming to terms with the mistakes they've made. Just remember Chosen One control your temper. I wish I could be with you to enjoy the moment." She then showed me her pregnant state and the screen went blank. "There you are Jenny it's sorted". I smiled kissing her on the lips. I held their hands and escorted them to my bedroom and made love to them both right until the early hours. Jenny voiced at 6 am "I must go Chosen One." "Not until 7.30 am Jenny." I eased myself on top of her again. Caroline was still asleep. 7.30 am came and passed, Jenny did not complain. She kissed me goodbye at 8 o'clock and vanished. Caroline was just waking up. "Oh, I feel wonderful I'll make us some breakfast Rob." "No need Caroline, it's already done and don't dress." I smiled. We went into the kitchen and ate our breakfast. I then eased her onto the table, a place she was very familiar with. We made love again caressing each other and reaffirming how much we wanted each other. We showered and dressed and returned to Redbrick farm. I sat in my old armchair. Caroline ran upstairs to change and then go shopping with the money I had given her. Sam came in to see me. "I didn't know you could read our minds Rob. Jenny told me last night. Katie is absolutely horrified and scared to death of you." "I'm fully aware of the situation Sam. Jenny filled me in last night." Sam sat herself on my lap. "Are you still angry with me?" "No, you have corrected the problem that's all that matters." Caroline came running downstairs and out of the front door, she was off shopping something she'd longed to-do for a while.

Chapter 5
Three New Stable Girls

Katie was not speaking; she was avoiding me altogether. I left her to get on with it. It was spring I could see the early morning mist lifting as I left the house. I drove to Cranbury farm. Susan came across and greeted me with a kiss on the cheek. We have three new sisters Rob. The sisters came towards me, all blondes. They each held their hand out for me to shake and introduced themselves. "My name is Summer" "I am Autumn." "I am Spring we are honoured to work for the Chosen One." Susan quickly corrected them. "You must call the Chosen One Rob in public. I've told you, off to work girls." Susan linked her arm in mine and obviously read my thoughts that I preferred her with black hair, it immediately changed. We went into the little room to have coffee. She snapped her fingers and it was made. "You have spent little time with me Rob are you becoming bored with me?" That bloody sentence was driving me mad everybody seemed to use it the minute I wasn't ripping their knickers off. Susan picked up on my thought "Sorry Chosen One, Rob". She went to leave and I grabbed her hand, pulling her onto my lap and placing my hand around her waist. She smiled, enjoying the embrace. "Let's go for a ride this morning together." Before we'd had chance to return to the yard, Snowdrop was ready, and so was a horse for Susan. We rode out of the yard and along past Snowdrop's grave he paused as usual for a moment and then trotted on. Susan commented. "I hope I look as good as those three sisters when I'm 2000 years old." I stopped Snowdrop immediately. Susan turned her horse around and joined me. "Did I hear you correctly Susan?" "Yes, you know how old Jackie was when you slept with her?" "No, she was only 18, I thought or 19 perhaps 20?" Susan laughed. "She is 4000 years old." "Blimey the best pair of tits I've played with for a long time." Susan laughed so much. She almost fell off her horse. We rode on "How old are you, then Susan?" "Only 1000 years old and barely out of my nappies." She laughed. I was trying to analyse all the information; none of the women I had slept with appeared to be over 18, or in their 20s. I reached across and held her hand. She smiled, enjoying the attention. We called in at the cabin and made a coffee. I could hear Susan's thoughts. She was concerned about my comment regarding Jackie's boobs. She unbuttoned her blouse and exposed them. "What's wrong with these two Rob?" She remarked, looking at them both. I kissed both her breasts. "They looked wonderful to me Susan." "Are they not big enough Rob I'm sure I could make them bigger if it pleases you?" I laughed "You silly girl you're lovely just the way you are. I don't want you to change a thing, but please keep your hair black it does suit you." I buttoned her blouse up. Her expression was one of disappointment. I kissed her tenderly on the lips and explained to her how special she was and I didn't need to rip your clothes off every five minutes. I just wanted her with me.

We rode back to Cranbury farm holding hands. I left Snowdrop with Susan and drove back to Redbrick farm and went into the house. As I entered the living room, Katie was about to scurry upstairs. "Katie sit down I want to talk to you." She froze on the spot. I walked over and held her hand easing her back to my chair and sitting her on my lap. Her head was bowed and didn't look at me. I gently turned her face until I could see her eyes. I then kissed her on the lips. She did not respond I sighed. "Come on Katie, what's wrong?" "You scare me Rob I think you're going to kill me. I want to leave I want to live somewhere else." "So you're no longer in love with me, then?" "I didn't say that Rob I just don't want to die when you get angry you could do anything." "This is not like you Katie you would normally stand and fight, not run away." "How can I possibly fight you, you can snap your fingers and I'm dead. Or my children for that matter I've already lost Robert." "Do you think so little of me Katie that I would harm someone I love and have loved all my life?" I could feel her trembling sitting on my lap. I could hear her unsettled thoughts of wondering what to do. She wanted to kiss me and hold me close but feared the consequences; her mind was totally mixed up. "You haven't made love to me for nearly a month, so you must be fed up with me and the way I am." I was trying not to become angry it all boiled down to not receiving enough attention. I just couldn't be everywhere at once. "You've known me all my life Rob. I've always been a self-centred bitch." She placed her arm around my neck and her head against mine." "Well I suppose we better pack your bags then and you can return to your old house." That really sent her mind into overdrive trying to think of a way of saving face and not moving out. "Perhaps I'll stay a little longer and see how things work out." I carried her upstairs she smiled, instead of going into her bedroom we went into the shower. I eased her to her feet and unbuttoned her dress. I could sense the excitement in her mind. I snapped my fingers and I was naked, but continued to undress her slowly. Her thoughts were screaming for me to hurry up. We finally stepped into the shower and allowed the water to flow over us both. She held my erection lifting herself and gripping me with her legs around my waist. I carried her from the shower snapped my fingers and were dry. I then carried on into her bedroom and made love to her all over again. She then rolled over to face me. "I'm sorry Rob, I do love Caroline, but if she won't talk to us about her problems, we cannot help really." "I know Katie it won't happen again don't worry." With the snap of my fingers we were both dressed. The smile had returned to Katie's face she just wanted reassurance. She was still someone special in my life which I was happy to prove to her.

I transported myself to the realm I needed to understand and find out more about this place that exists but doesn't. It's an awful lot for a simple minded person to absorb. I materialised in my new cabin. Christina was there to greet me displaying her pregnant state she hugged me and gave me a kiss. "You want to understand the realm?" She smiled. "At least find out where it begins and ends". "That would be impossible. There is no beginning and there is no end. Only where we are now in time, you could walk for the next thousand years and never find the end. Just accept what it is and enjoy the gift of life." I went into the kitchen there was no cooker, no kettle or a fridge. Christina laughed sitting in a chair, holding her stomach. "Just think of what you want Chosen One and snap your fingers and no you can't have that in my state" she smiled. I snapped my fingers and a coffee appeared Christina said she would rest and left the cabin. I drank my coffee and thought of Snowdrop and snapped my fingers, much to my surprise he appeared outside the cabin saddled and ready to go. I went out onto the porch and as usual he placed his head on my shoulder. Perhaps I should have married my horse it would have been simpler.

We rode through the forest slowly taking in everything I could see it was almost like home from home. I couldn't get over how all the trees seemed to stretch into the clouds. I came into a clearing just green grass and no people I had seen no animals either, other than Snowdrop. I carried on riding across the open space the air smelt so fresh. I then suddenly realised there were no flies or bugs. I dismounted and stamped my foot on the ground just to make sure it was real Snowdrop looked as confused as I did. I could pick up Christina my daughter's thoughts. I waved my hand in a small circle and could see her outside the college in a heated argument with a group of young men trying to get her in a van. I snapped my fingers and I materialised behind a tree just 20 m from her. I walked over she was surprised to see me. "Dad" she called out. The boys jumped in the van and drove off. I snapped my fingers and the engine burst into flames. I thought that'll put you out of action lads, she linked her arm in mine same complexion as her mother and beautiful long red hair. "What were they trying to make you do?" "Oh, nothing dad just wanted to give me a lift home and I wouldn't go." I kissed her on the forehead. "That was sensible Christina." "Where's your car dad, you can give me a lift home". Oh shit, I thought "It's in the college car park". We walked slowly. I listened to all the things she was studying in college we entered the car park and I could see my Range Rover and how it got there I don't know. Then I heard a voice in my head. "Me, Chosen One", Jenny had come to my rescue. I didn't know I could move objects from place to place, there's an awful lot I don't know yet I decided as we arrived home. A short while later Christina ran in and kissed her mother and explained to her what had happened. Sam looked across to me rather worried after Christina had told her the young lads van caught fire. I just smiled and sat in my armchair. Sam came over and sat on my lap. "Rob, she is allowed to have boyfriends." "They weren't boyfriends my love. They just wanted to have a gangbang and that's not going to happen to our daughter." I responded firmly. "Really" Sam put her hand to her mouth. "I forget you can read minds; as much as I don't like you doing that I'm glad you did Rob." "You think they'll try it again?" "I'll be watching Sam, have no fear, no one will touch our daughter or they will feel my anger." Sam had decided she would have a talk to Christina although she didn't say it I read her mind. She kissed me on the cheek and went upstairs.

I snapped my fingers and I was back with Snowdrop in the realm who had been patiently waiting for me, I mounted Snowdrop. Jenny rode over and pulled up alongside me. She smiled. I bent over and kissed her. "Thank you Jenny, you saved my skin and an awful lot of explaining". "You are welcome Chosen One, you must watch Christina your daughter, she is extremely attractive and will be a target for young men. But don't worry Chosen One we will help you too." "Jenny do you think there's anything we can do to help Rupert and Nicole Sam's parents their health hasn't been good of late?" "I will talk to the sisters for you, but they already know your thoughts Chosen One, which are always kind. You must remember we all die sooner or later accept here." We trotted along, heading back to the cabin. Jenny's beautiful blonde hair move gracefully in the wind I could see her smiling, reading my thoughts about her. We dismounted and went into the cabin before she had chance to say another word. I scooped her up in my arms and went straight to the bedroom. I was desperate to make love to her and snapped my fingers so she was naked on the bed. I read her thoughts of pleasure and enjoying the experience. She loved me and wanted to be my wife and have me every day to make love to her. We sat in the large front room. My mind had been so preoccupied with Jenny making love and enjoying her company.

Chapter 6
Abducted Daughter

I had failed to pick up the thoughts of Sam. Jenny realised something was wrong and waved her hand. There was an image of Sam parked outside a nightclub, trying to find Christina our daughter. I snapped my fingers; I was standing beside Sam's Range Rover. "Rob I can't find Christina." Christina's thoughts came to my mind. She was in the back of a red van heading away with her hands tied I could see through her eyes. There were several guys drinking and laughing. One man and his hand down the top of her pants playing, with the other had his hand inside her blouse, kissing and playing with her breasts. "Go home Sam I'll find her." I could see her being dragged into an old building. I now understand why I didn't pick up her thoughts before, a slight bump was on her forehead she'd been made unconscious. The rage that filled my body was almost intolerable. Sam could see me starting to glow white "Rob you're glowing, don't in public." Susan came to join us "Chosen One be careful how you use your gift, have all the facts before you act. Although I can see the same as you I will stay with Sam."

Christina was screaming the men were removing her clothing. I snapped my fingers and within seconds I was there outside the building. I ripped the door off with my bare hands I had so much power. I entered to see one man with his hand between her legs and two others playing with her breasts kissing her. The four men saw me ran towards me. One of the men removed a gun and shot me in the shoulder. I just kept going forward. He shot me again in the chest. I snapped my fingers and all four men burst into flames. Christina was watching in horror crying. I snapped my fingers and her bondage released. I snapped my fingers again and she was dressed. I staggered towards her, she clung for security screaming. "Dad, you're bleeding." I gripped Christina with my last breath and thought of the realm.

I was immediately transported there with Christina my daughter. My wish had been granted. I awoke to find myself in bed healed and my daughter sitting by my bedside. I could see her hexagram on the back of her hand. When she realised I'd gained consciousness she hugged me. "Oh, dad I love you." Her tears dripped on to the blankets. How I survived the attack I don't know I had no pain and no scarring from where the bullets hit me. I embraced her. "Are you alright my love?" She nodded. "I'm fine, dad." Jenny appeared and placed her arm around Christina. I sighed. "I suppose I'm in real trouble with the sisters and I have a lot of explaining to do." I said, sitting up in bed. I then realised my daughter was dressed in a white robe. She had her mother's beautiful hazel eyes that only betrayed love and kindness. Jenny smiled. "No Chosen One your daughter has known for a long time you were special our secret is safe with her. Don't worry Chosen One. Sam is perfectly happy she knows where Christina is and what took place." I joked. "I wouldn't have thought you'd have liked that sort of attire?" "It's all the fashion here, dad" she joked. "Please thank the sisters for saving my life." Jenny placed her hand on mine. "We have thousands of years to spend with you Chosen One we weren't prepared to let your life end prematurely." I dressed and went into the large front room snapped my fingers and two meals appeared on the table. My daughter looked on in amazement. I invited her to sit by me and enjoy the food. Jenny had explained everything to her and she understood how important it was that no one else found out because she would become one in time and will lead a wonderful life, which she said she was looking forward to. Jenny told me telepathically that Christina, Sam's mother had purposely stayed out of the way not wishing to alarm my daughter. She hadn't been told fully my position, she'd only been informed I was special and helped all the sisters. In their opinion she was still too young to understand and accept the situation fully. Jenny snapped her fingers and my daughters clothing had been replaced with a more suitable outfit, black skirt and blouse ready to return to my time, my daughter flinched. "I'll never get used to that dad. Just think of your clothes and they appear." Jenny advised "Hold your father's hand tightly and remember say nothing outside of the family you have a special gift to come do not abuse it". I held Christina's hand tightly and snapped my fingers and we were back at Redbrick farm.

Sam, Katie and Caroline were all there to greet us. Sam embraced her daughter fearing she'd never see her again. She looked over to me with her tear filled eyes and smiled. She kissed Christina on the cheek after checking she was okay and moved over to me and sat on my lap in my armchair. "Oh God, Rob I thought you were gone for good. Susan has been very good. She has kept me informed of everything and how badly you were hurt. You saved our daughter like you always save everyone here. Oh God, I love you so much." Christina ran off upstairs. Katie came over and perched on the arm of my chair "It's been all over the news Rob it was a good job. Susan set fire to their van otherwise Christina's DNA would have been in there and we'd have a load of explaining to do". I sighed. "Yes, I must thank Susan for covering my tracks but after I'd been shot the only thing I could think of was making sure Christina was safe, before I died." Sam stared so did Caroline and Katie. "You're not dead are you?" "It felt like it I'm not Superman" Sam unbuttoned my shirt. "He still has a heart I can feel it" Susan appeared. "The Chosen One did not die it was very close, but we managed to save him"

She smiled. I stood up and embraced Susan for clearing up the mess I'd made and so did the others. Susan snapped her fingers and disappeared I went upstairs and knocked on Christina's door. She told me to enter. I sat on her bed watching her brush her lovely long hair after she'd taken a shower. "Christina my love what happened the other day don't you ever mention it to anyone". "I know dad don't worry Jenny explained everything and the consequences should I slip up. I don't want to go to the dark place." She smiled sitting herself on my lap, placing her arms around my shoulder and kissing me on the cheek. "Now get out of my bedroom I want to dress please dad." I left her bedroom closing the door, feeling more relieved and settled. I just hoped she wouldn't mess up, although she'd always been a very sensible daughter and I hoped it continued to be that way.

I went downstairs and told everyone I would ride Snowdrop, spring was here the daffodils were in bloom and the small orchard at the side was preparing to blossom. I drove to Cranbury farm Susan greeted me, holding Snowdrop by the reins and her own horse. "I thought I would come with you Rob this morning if you don't mind?" "Of course not Susan you know I love being with you" she smiled. We rode out of the yard and across the fields I reached over and held her hand. We eventually ended up at the cabin having a coffee. The television suddenly flickered, flashed. Christina appeared holding her new daughter. "My beloved the Chosen One your daughter, what will you call her? She is only three hours old" Christina's smile was full of love Susan cuddled me. "I would like to call her Passion after the way her mother treats me." I heard Christina call out sisters meet the new child of the covenant, Passion. "You honour me again Chosen One". The screen went blank I could hear the thoughts racing through Susan's mind. I held her hand then lifted her in my arms, kissing her softly on the lips and walking into my bedroom. I undressed her slowly savouring every button until she was wearing nothing. I snapped my fingers and my clothes fell away. I eased her onto the bed. I caressed her breasts, kissed her neck, kissed her all over and finally penetrated receiving that exhilarating feeling. We finally fell asleep. We showered; I washed her all over and finally I snapped my fingers and we were dried and dressed. She kissed me tenderly "Rob I can't wait to carry your child like the other sisters, you bring so much joy and happiness to everyone but I am content to be your servant and receive your passion."

We slowly rode back to Cranbury farm and I kissed Susan goodbye. I drove to the cabin and snapped my fingers I was back in the realm at the new log cabin the sisters had built for me. Christina was already inside seated, breast-feeding our new daughter. She glanced up to me as I entered "I knew you would come." She finished feeding Passion and passed her to me I kissed her on the forehead. Immediately a hexagram appeared where my lips had touched her. The spirits entered the room surrounding me and Passion. I passed my daughter back to Christina. Two sisters entered the cabin and I passed Passion to them and they left after kissing me on the cheek. Christina stood up and embraced me. "We have another wonderful daughter and you blessed her with your kiss of approval. Do you like what the sisters have done look?" She said, waving her hand and a full-length mirror appeared? I looked at myself not a day over 25, this is ridiculous I thought how would I explain this in my time. Christina read my thoughts. "Don't worry Chosen One. The only people that will really notice are your family the rest of the world will think nothing of it. You must go back to your time now I have things to do." She kissed me on the lips walking out of the door.

I snapped my fingers and I was back in my old cabin. I drove back to Redbrick farm and entered the living room. Katie was sitting on the settee reading a magazine. She glanced up to me. "What have they done to you? You look so young." I seated myself in my armchair snapped my fingers for a coffee. Katie came over and sat on my lap. "What else have they improved Rob?" She smiled, kissing me tenderly on the lips. Her thoughts were wondering if I would take her to bed. She voiced. "You know what I'm thinking Rob. What are you going to do about it?" "Nothing I'm drinking my coffee thanks" I was trying not to laugh. She started kissing my neck and playing with my ears. She was doing everything she could think of to try and arouse me she wanted to be the first one to try my new body out which I was saving for Sam. She stood up frustrated sitting back on the settee and continued to read her magazine. I smiled "Later love I have things to do." I drove over to Cranbury farm. Sam was talking to Susan they both looked across to me and stared. Sam approached cautiously unsure if it was really me. She didn't speak. She gently placed her hand on my cheek searching with those beautiful hazel eyes for an explanation. "Aren't you impressed Sam?" "I don't know I like my husband the way he was I'll be fighting every woman off from here to London and back." "How do you think I felt all these years having the prettiest wife in the world and wondering how long I'd managed to keep her?" She smiled hugging me. "Am I really that important to you Rob?" I scooped her up in my arms and kissed her passionately on the lips. "Put me down everyone's watching." "Not on your life Mrs. you're coming with me" "Not the hay store Rob it gets in my hair, please." I went around the corner out of sight of everybody snapped my fingers and we were in the cabin. I carried her through into the bedroom and threw her on the bed snapped my fingers and we were naked. "Look at your body your all muscle and be careful what you're doing with that thing" She smiled. She just couldn't control herself and neither could I. I had more power, strength and energy than ever before I finally lay beside her. She rolled over to face me and eventually we went into the shower. I gently washed her and she did the same me. I snapped my fingers and we were dried and dressed. We had a coffee before leaving. We walked back to Cranbury farm hand-in-hand through the wood and across the fields. She knew how much I loved her, leaving no doubt in her mind we drove back to Redbrick farm.

There was a police car parked outside. We went in a policewoman was interviewing my daughter Christina. They had found a locket in the red van destroyed by fire. Christina was quick thinking on her feet and said she'd lost it at a dance the other night. The police were happy with her answer and presume the men and the van had been involved in the theft. It must be a gang-related incident and obviously they fell out with each other and the four were murdered.

Chapter 7
Just Another Problem

The police officer left and thanked us for our time. Christina ran over and embraced me. "Do you think they believed my story dad?" I smiled kissing her on the forehead "You did just fine love." She ran off upstairs. I turned to Sam. "I think we were bloody lucky there". She nodded in agreement. Katie came downstairs looking rather flustered. "I've been trying to ring Nicky but she's not answering her mobile, Rob can you see if you can pick her thoughts up and find out where she is?" I laughed sitting down in my armchair. "You actually want me to read someone's thoughts and you've been moaning about it for months". "Yes, well, please." The smile drained from my face I was seeing things I didn't want to see. Nicky was at Glastonbury smoking pot. "Let me see Rob, let me see". Katie insisted. I waved my hand in a circle. Sam and Katie stared on in horror seeing Nicky dancing away smoking pot and kissing two young men. "You know where this is going to end up. Katie she'll be pregnant next" "The little bitch she told me she was going to stay with her friend for the week." Katie was stamping her feet in anger "Fetch her back Rob, please." "I can't Katie I wouldn't trust her with knowing about my powers she'd blab it everywhere." Katie flopped down onto the settee. "What am I going to do with her Rob she's very naughty. I don't want her to ruin her life." Sam placed her arm around my shoulder. Jenny appeared. "Oh dear, what a naughty girl! The solution is Chosen One; you transport yourself and Katie behind the refreshment tent I will send your range Rover and leave it just down the road from the gate." Katie jumped to her feet excited about the whole idea. She hugged Jenny. "Thank you Jenny for coming to help me. That little bitch will get one hell of a surprise when I've finished with her, I will teach her to lie to me." Katie said. Jenny advised. "It's a little late to start punishing Nicky, this is your own fault for lack of discipline in the earlier years." Katie looked to the floor knowing Jenny had spoken the truth. She had been very laid-back when it came to discipline. "Are we ready then?" I asked. Katie nodded, gripping my hand so tight, almost stopping the circulation. Jenny said "Wait, you stand out like a sore thumb dressed like that." She snapped her fingers and we were both dressed in denim's.

I snapped my fingers and we materialised behind the drinks tent, there was no one there. Katie and I held hands, slowly walking round the side. We glanced across to the back of another large marquee and there was Nicky with a man kissing her she was topless and with his hand down her jeans. The expression on Katie's face was one of outrage I'd never seen her like that before. We ran over Katie grabbed Nicky's arm. I hit the guy under the jaw and he was knocked out. The expression on Nicky's face being caught in the act was shock. Katie said angrily. "Put your bloody top on girl you're coming with me." Nicky didn't argue. She dressed very quickly. We walked up through the gate no one saying another word until we got in the Range Rover that was waiting for me. Katie started "You deceitful little bitch, how dare you, lie to me." Nicky was crying saying how sorry she was. I drove back to Bristol listening to Katie and Nicky arguing. I then went onto the M4 heading home it took nearly 3 hours. Katie was still shouting at Nicky when we parked up. Nicky ran into the house and straight up to her bedroom. I placed my arm around Katie. She showed me what she'd taken off Nicky; ecstasy pills and pot. "No wonder he was having a wonderful time with my daughter, he drugged her". Sam was sitting on the settee, I sat in my armchair. Katie came to me sitting on my lap crying. "You'll have to face the fact Katie love. If Nicky didn't want to take the drugs she wouldn't have." I remarked calmly. Sam looked on very concerned. Caroline came downstairs remarking "Nicky's having a shower crying." Katie sobbed. "She's turning out like I used to be, nothing but a bloody slag and it's my fault like Jenny said." "Jenny reappeared. "I can try and straighten her mind out for you Katie." Katie jumped to her feet embracing Jenny. "Please Jenny, I don't want to lose my daughter." "I'll talk to her whatever you hear do not disturb us." Jenny instructed. Jenny went upstairs we were all waiting to hear a blazing row. I snapped my fingers and everyone had their favourite drink.

It was now 3 o'clock in the morning and Jenny had been up there at least two hours. Jenny finally came downstairs and seated herself on my lap. "It's done just don't mention what happened again. She is still a virgin so don't worry." Jenny rose to her feet. Katie, Caroline and Sam both hugged her in appreciation. "I have wiped her mind of the incident and I have planted a thought in her mind. She will reject boys, girls and drugs until she is a lot older providing it works, hopefully by that time she would have joined the covenant. Remember Katie, discipline her otherwise you will lose everything". Katie voiced. "You really are a super nanny." Jenny smiled, snapping her fingers and vanished. We all sat down. I snapped my fingers and another drink appeared for everyone. Sam came over sitting on the arm of the chair she unbuttoned my denim shirt encouraging me to stand up. "Look at this you two." I was now on display; Katie and Caroline stared. "Mr fit" Caroline whistled. Katie remarked. "I want some of that." Sam whispered something to Katie and Caroline and they both said together "Really" Katie said "Me first." I grabbed Sam's hand then lifted her over my shoulder turned to face Katie and Caroline slapping Sam's backside, "This one tonight girls." They laughed. I carried Sam up to bed, snapped my fingers and we were both naked. We climbed into bed, cuddled each other and drifted off to sleep.

Breakfast was chaotic as usual. Mothers and children trying to get ready for school or college. I walked along the stables at Redbrick farm looking for any damage. Nicky came running over to me she was the splitting image of her mother, long blonde cascading hair, beautiful complexion and good figure. Such a prize for any young man and that was the trouble. I thought to myself a few years ago I was chasing anything that looked like that. But when it's your daughter the shoe is on the other foot it's not so funny. "Dad." She grabbed my hand I turned to face her. She kissed me on the cheek. "I just wanted to tell you dad, I love you." "I love you too Nicky, just behave yourself love." She ran back up the yard and jumped into the Range Rover with Katie and the other children and drove off. Caroline walked down the yard and went straight into the tack room. I followed and discovered she gone upstairs. I continued following her, she was sitting up there crying. She quickly dried her eyes. "What's the matter Caroline" I asked sitting by her. "I think you died when you were shot, look how the sisters have changed you. You couldn't do that to a normal human being." I placed my arm around her shoulder and kissed her on the cheek. "Does it matter I'm still here in whatever form. I must confess I've had my suspicions too." She turned and embraced me. Susan appeared. "You did not die Rob. We have powers that you could not even comprehend." I could turn Caroline into a goat with a snap of my fingers you want me to show you?" She said, staring at Caroline. "Okay Susan you've made your point." I said frostily. Susan placed her hand either side of Caroline's head she glowed white. "There you are Caroline no more silly thoughts". Susan snapped her fingers and my shirt vanished "There you are Caroline have a look at that." Susan smiled. "My sisters really did enhance your figure." Caroline laughed and so did Susan both gently rubbing the palm of their hand down my chest. I snapped my fingers and my denim shirt was replaced. Susan snapped her fingers and disappeared. "Come on you let's get some work done." I remarked to Caroline, walking downstairs.

I drove to Cranbury farm and went to Snowdrop's stable. He placed his head on my shoulder as he usually did. Thinking to myself we buried you my old friend and your here alive and well. Susan came across to me and stuck me with a pin in the backside. "What was that for?" "I just wanted to check if you are alive or dead." She jabbed me again I grabbed her arm. "That's enough I feel it." I suddenly felt a burning sensation in my hand I released her arm "Do you get the message Chosen One?" "I put my hands up, okay I get the message, alive." I smiled. Susan snapped her fingers and Snowdrop was saddled, she brought him out of the stable and the new stable girl Spring, brought Susan's horse.

Summer was almost over again. Years seemed to come and go quickly these days. I mounted Snowdrop and Susan mounted hers. We rode out of the yard and as usual Snowdrop paused at his grave and then carried on walking. "Why does Snowdrop do that stop every time he passes his grave?" "Out of respect and gratitude for being given a new life." "He understands she remarked." "Of course just because he's a horse it doesn't mean he's not intelligent, every form of life has intelligence and understanding." I reached across and held Susan's hand as we gently rode along. I decided it was quite a lovely morning so I dismounted. Susan looked on puzzled. I indicated for her to do the same. She tied the horses up to a branch on an ash tree. I snapped my fingers and a large blanket was on the grass. Susan seated herself and watched a flask of coffee appeared. "This is romantic Chosen One." She smiled. I poured two coffees, passing one to Susan. I watched the sun make her black hair shine as she rested back on one elbow, I could see her trying not to smile as I undressed her in my mind. "I feel neglected." She casually said lying on the blanket. I kissed her tenderly on the lips and undid her riding britches. She was about to snap her fingers and I said "Don't." I finally penetrated her. "Oh sisters if you could only feel this." She said softly, gently placing her hands around my neck, pulling me closer. We were still kissing and cuddling when I heard a horse approaching. It was Sam. Susan snapped her fingers and we were fully dressed before Sam reached us. Sam looked down at the two of us on the blanket. "When you finished fucking my husband Susan there's work to be done." Susan didn't move, suddenly Sam's horse reared up and she slid off. Susan tried not to grin. Sam picked herself up. "Bloody horse". She muttered. I rose to my feet and snapped my fingers and she was clean. Susan jumped on her horse and headed back for the stables. "It's alright for some, romantic picnic. I don't get that bloody treatment." Sam protested. I could feel the rage in her mind and the pain at what she'd seen wishing it was her and only her. "Look at me Rob I'm starting to look old, my tits are sagging my firmness is going away. "I'm even getting grey hair." She cried. I could feel her desperation. I must do something for her. I embraced her, although I'd always told her she was my first love it wasn't enough. She needed to feel good and look good. Christina appeared grabbing Sam's hand "Come daughter I feel your pain". Christina and Sam vanished.

I rode back to the stables, returning Snowdrop and Sam's horse Freddie. Susan approached "That was nasty Susan making Freddie throw Sam." Susan bowed her head. "I apologise Chosen One. I just didn't like what she said, I thought it was unfair you are everyone's husband to share." "You must understand Susan she is flesh and blood. She's not a sister who accepts these things as normal and above all she is my wife. Don't you forget it!" Susan put the horses away and I drove to the cabin. I needed a little solitude for a while. I sat watching the television with my Bacardi and Coke desperately trying to resolve the situation that was impossible. Whatever I do causes somebody pain, it had to stop. I removed my gun from the cabinet in my bedroom and sat out on the porch. I placed both barrels under my chin and pulled the trigger. Nothing happened. I checked the gun was loaded and repeated the process. It still wouldn't fire. I threw the gun on the porch and both barrels discharged making me jump. I removed a can of petrol from the back of my Range Rover emptied over the porch. I threw five or six matches down and it would not ignite I sat on the edge of the porch and cried. There was no escape. I was trapped. Jenny appeared picked up the shot gun and snapped it in half with her bare hands. She snapped her fingers and the spilt petrol was removed from the porch. "Oh Chosen One" she said, sitting beside me. "Why do you despair? your heart is big enough for us all to enjoy, you take too much notice of what you're reading in people's minds. Most things are just trivial and forgotten. Samantha will be returned shortly with all her body defects repaired. So, she will be perfectly happy."

Jenny and I went back inside and Sam reappeared. "Look at me Rob I feel wonderful again, no more grey hair, even my boobs are firm again." I smiled and walked over and kissed her on the cheek and sat back down in my armchair. Sam could sense something was going on. She could smell petrol. She looked outside and saw the shot gun broken in half. She ran back inside and looked at me and then to Jenny. "Oh no, it's what I said to you this morning isn't it?" Jenny stared at Sam and nodded. "If you really love your husband Sam, you would understand he loves you for what you are not the way you look, your vanity would have killed him if we hadn't intervened." "Then we would have all lost a very precious person. Someone we have been searching for as long as I can remember. He was willing to sacrifice his life for you." Christina appeared.

"What are we going to do with you Chosen One you take everything to heart" "This is your fault daughter of mine. You are such a disappointment." Sam looked horrified at her mother's comment. "If this happens again Samantha we will take the Chosen One away from you and he will live in the realm forever where he will be treated with respect and love." Sam had collapsed on the settee crying as the reality of the situation sunk in. Jenny and Christina kissed me on the cheek and vanished. I snapped my fingers and two coffee's appeared. I moved over and sat beside Sam she searched my face with her beautiful hazel eyes. "I was only doing it for you Rob I'm always scared of losing you. I just wanted to be attractive, so you'd notice me." "I've never stopped noticing you Sam from the day you walked into my life." I stood up and reached for her hand and we went out of the cabin to my Range Rover. I snapped my fingers and the twisted shot gun vanished.

We returned to Redbrick farm. Sam received a phone call from her father telling her he had beaten the cancer and Nicole's hips no longer troubled her. She said goodbye to her father and told him she loved him and missed him. She then turned to me "You asked the sisters didn't you, to help my father and Nicole?" Sam searched my expression for a reaction. I smiled. "I did ask and they said they'd do what they could." I moved over into my armchair.

I suddenly heard someone crying for help. I snapped my fingers and materialised out of sight of a police car overturned and on fire just outside the village. There was a policewoman trapped inside, the fire was intense and the door was jammed after being struck by another vehicle. I grabbed the frame of the door and ripped it off quickly uncoupled the seatbelt of the young officer and lifted her to safety. I used my mobile to phone the police, fire brigade and ambulance. The young woman was barely conscious she had banged her head severely as the vehicle rolled. The police turned up first and a few minutes later the ambulance and finally the fire brigade. Sam heard the sirens and had driven through the village to see what had happened. Finding me, holding the young woman in my arms and being taken into the ambulance. I gave a statement to the police and they thanked me very much for saving her life. Apparently she was chasing a speeding motorist and lost control on the corner. Sam came over to join me. "Are you alright Rob?" "Yes, I'm fine Sam thanks, you can take me home." Sam drove me back to Redbrick farm. "You heard her crying Rob and she was not a sister or a member of our family?" "Yes, I can hear anyone's thoughts, especially if they're in trouble" We went back inside and I plonked myself in my chair, Sam sat on my lap teasing "You're my little hero." A few minutes later the press were knocking on the door asking for an interview. I explained to them I just happened to be in the area and saw the policewoman trapped in her car. They took one or two photos and went away. A week passed and there was someone at the door. Katie answered, I heard her say. "Please come in". It was the young police officer who I rescued dressed in her uniform. I stood up to greet her, her name was Fiona Collins. I invited her to sit down and Katie made us a coffee. She explained. She was chasing someone and lost it on the corner, a stupid mistake she said and thanked me very much for saving her life. "Before I go could I have a look at the horses?" "Yes." I replied standing to my feet. "I'll come with you." We went into the yard and slowly walked along looking in each stable then I took her into the enclosed arena to watch Caroline exercising a horse. I could hear her thoughts she wished she could ride. I asked. "Do you ride" "No but I would love to." I called Caroline over. "Meet Fiona, she's the young lady I rescued from the car, they shook hands. "Do you think you could give some free lessons to Fiona?" "Of course no problem, when can you come?" Fiona went slightly red-faced. "I couldn't impose, I haven't any riding gear." Caroline smiled. "Rob will arrange that for you" "If you're sure it's not too much trouble Mr Jones." Fiona smiled. "Call me Rob". "Okay Rob, I'm not on duty tomorrow is that convenient for you Caroline?" "Yes, around 10 o'clock, Rob will fetch your riding gear then you can come ready to ride." I walked off. "Rob" Fiona called. "Don't you want to know my size"? Caroline laughed. "He already does". I glanced back and smiled. Fiona looked very puzzled. I returned after going round the corner out of sight and snapping my fingers, boots, britches, blouse and jacket plus a hard hat. I returned to Caroline and Fiona. Fiona put her hand to her mouth. "It's all brand-new". She checked the sizes on the labels. "How did you know?" "Come on, I'll see you back to your car." Fiona was about to leave and Sam pulled up in her Range Rover. I introduced them and explained to Sam what I'd arranged for Fiona "That's fine Rob." Sam replied. We watched Fiona drive away in her police car. "Okay Rob, what's all that about?" Sam asked, looking rather suspicious. "Well I thought I'd take her to bed but give her a few riding lessons first. That's what you want to hear, isn't it Sam?" Before she could answer I snapped my fingers and I was in the realm. The one place I could go to escape the inquisition. I walked into the new cabin and there was Christina with Passion and Star. I pick Star up in my arms and gave her a big hug. "Daddy, daddy" she pointed at me. Christina smiled. "Yes, that your daddy." I sat beside her on the settee. After she'd finished breastfeeding Passion I sat her on my knee. Christina placed her arm around my shoulder. "You are troubled my love? It's my stupid daughter again. Will that girl never learn?" Two of the sisters came in taking Star and Passion from me. "Bye-bye, Daddy" Star waved. I waved back. "See you soon." "Perhaps you should come here permanently Chosen One and leave that ungrateful daughter of mine." "What about Caroline and Katie? they are as bad in their own way" I sighed, wondering what the hell to do. Jenny entered the room she sat beside me and Christina. "This can't go on Rob. You will destroy yourself trying to please everyone and achieving absolutely nothing. They are the most ungrateful people I've ever come across." Jenny expressed. Christina agreed. "Stay here for the week Rob let them do without you. You're not there for their convenience anyway." Christina snapped her fingers and I heard Snowdrop neigh outside. I looked out of the window and it was him with another white horse ready saddled. Jenny snapped her fingers and I was in my riding gear and so was she. Christina kissed me goodbye and told me to relax and enjoy myself. I asked. "Where is Miracle?" "She is with the sisters learning her craft like all your other children that are of age. You have brought great joy to the realm having children here." We rode off slowly through the forest. I stopped, seeing someone sitting on a tree stump in what appeared to be a long blue gown. Jenny remarked "That is a sister of great gift. She is one of the eldest here almost a founding member she is very pleased with our choice of man." We rode on. We left the forest and went around the large lake of clean freshwater. We went up a mountain track until we were surrounded by snow. I didn't feel cold in the slightest, which was rather surprising we continued until we went through the clouds and everything was blue as if we were in an aeroplane. I felt exhilarated and refreshed. Every-time I looked at Jenny I could see my dead wife in her which bugged me. Jenny had picked up my thoughts. "You loved her a great deal didn't you Rob?" "Yes, until I discovered what she was doing." "That must have been soul destroying." She remarked, reaching across and holding my hand. "I know you love me because I can feel it although you fear I will hurt you like your deceased wife. That will never happen Chosen One you were the first man to ever touch me and you will be the last." I smiled at her comment "You are really a gift to have with me Jenny, so understanding and generous with your love."

Chapter 8
Trouble at Home

The week had passed by quickly. I'd enjoyed every moment and the thought of returning to my time didn't impress me in the slightest. I snapped my fingers and I was standing in the yard at Redbrick farm. As I approached the front door. I could hear the three of them rowing over who was to blame for me not being there. I walked in they went quiet. Sam moved out of my armchair and approached me. I pushed her away with my thought. She dropped down onto the settee by Katie and Caroline. I seated myself and made myself a Bacardi and Coke and looked at the three. "I remember a sentence that came from your mouth Sam, there would be no jealousy. We would live in harmony and you two agreed with her." I drank from my glass studying their expressions. "Christina has suggested I move to the realm and leave you lot to it." "No, no Rob, don't please". Sam replied quickly. Katie followed and so did Caroline. None wanted me to go. "Well then, what is your solution?" They all looked at each other. "It's all because we want you to ourselves, we don't want to share you. We know you can do nothing about it, but we can't help the way we feel" Katie said. Sam and Caroline agreed that was the main reason. Sam remarked "I know you'll take Fiona to bed if she stays around here too long." Caroline spoke up. "Does it matter who he fucks, he hasn't left us and he takes us all to bed and treats everyone the same. We all know he loves you Sam above everyone else because you are his real wife." "That's the first sensible thing that's been said this evening. You either all share me or I'll be taken to the realm whether I like it or you like it." It was not my idea of a solution because nothing had changed and nothing would change. Well we were controlled by the covenant. The upside was we still had each other and as long as we played ball that would not change. Christina appeared, seating herself on my lap and then passionately kissing my neck. She then glared at Sam, Katie and Caroline. "We've had one of these talks before and this one will be the last one. If you can't control yourselves and understand and accept the situation then the Chosen One will live in the realm, and never return to see any of you. Or perhaps just dispose of you and bring in three more sisters to please the Chosen One." Sam stood up I could feel her anger. "You call yourself my mother and you treat me like dirt. You fuck my husband. You let other women fuck my husband and I'm supposed to think that's okay." "Sit down daughter before you embarrass yourself any further with your lies. Let's see how much you really love your husband. Remember the stable incident Samantha?" Sam looked alarmed. "You'd been in that stable 15 minutes before Rob arrived." Christina made a circle with her hand and a film appeared on the wall showing what really took place. Everyone stared, Christina gave a commentary "She was kissing the other woman and fondling her breasts. The other woman had her hand down Samantha's top, you then heard Rob's Range Rover turn into the yard and you quickly tidied yourselves but stayed in there hoping you wouldn't be seen. And again the other day while Rob was away Samantha" Sam looked horrified "The same woman you promised never to see again. You kissed her in the stables at Cranbury farm, but you did nothing else, and she left." I glared at Sam she bowed her head and cried inconsolably. "The only reason you are still alive Samantha is because the Chosen One wishes it. If I had my way you would be gone daughter, you are a disgrace". Katie and Caroline looked on horrified "How could you be so stupid Sam?" Katie voiced. "Rob is wonderful to you he treats you like a queen and you do that to him. "I'm sorry I had to show you Chosen One she thinks she is cleverer than us. We have been watching her every second of every day like everyone else in this household" Christina said, snapping their fingers and providing me with a drink of my favourite tipple. "Chosen One, I hear your thoughts. Don't do that." They all stared at me. The woman Sam had been seeing was driving along a country road. I steered her car into the path of an oncoming lorry. "You can attend her bloody funeral now you bitch. We are finished." I snapped my fingers and transported myself to my own log cabin. The spirits surrounded me trying to absorb the pain I was suffering. Susan entered the cabin in her white robe and seated herself by me on the settee. "How can humans be so cruel to each other" She held my head against her chest. My mobile rang it was Katie she was crying. "Don't leave me Rob I've done nothing to you neither has Caroline. We both love you. Christina's taken Sam away we don't know where." I sighed. "I'll be home soon my love don't worry." "We love you Rob we both do" and she rang off. "Where has Christina taken Sam?" "Christina made Sam phone her father and arranged to stay there for a month to rest." I sighed with relief at least Christina hadn't killed her. "Don't worry Chosen One I can run the stables with one hand tied behind my back." She laughed, and then kissed me softly on the lips. "Oh, I wish I was your wife, your real wife. What a luxury that would be to have you in my bed every night". I held her close in my arms and told how much I loved her. She snapped her fingers and disappeared. I drove back to Redbrick farm and went straight to bed on my own. I awoke to Katie bringing me breakfast in bed all made by her own hands. Caroline had gone out to look after the horses. "Come on sleepy" I sat up in bed. Katie placed the tray on the bed then lent forward, exposing her breasts kissing me on the lips. "Remember when I used to do that to you Rob in the cabin?" She smiled. I smiled back. "Oh yes, I remember everything about you my love." "I told you, you should have married me Rob". She left the room commenting "I must get dressed I have to take the children to school". I waited till she'd left the room snapped my fingers and removed the burnt toast, uncooked bacon and runny eggs. It made me smile. She was never intended to be a cook but she tried and that goes a long way in my book. I finished breakfast and dressed wondering how our children had ever survived with her cooking. I went out into the yard noticing a car I hadn't seen before. I went into the arena. Caroline was in there teaching Fiona to ride. Caroline came across to me. "How is she getting on Caroline?" "She's very good Rob I don't think I can teach her anything else, she certainly handles the horses well and how are you feeling this morning Rob?" I sighed. "I'm okay I don't know what will become of Sam and it is maybe all over." Fiona came alongside she had beautiful shoulder length brown hair and a beautiful smile. "Have you ridden outside yet Fiona?" "No Rob" "Are you busy this morning?" "No, I don't think so. Why?" "Come with me, I'll take you to our other establishment at Cranbury farm and take you for a ride around the property." "Are you sure you're not too busy and you don't mind." "I'm the boss I can do what the bloody hell I like." I laughed. Caroline smiled as Fiona glanced to her. "It will be one hell of a ride Fiona one you won't forget". I looked at Caroline, who was trying not to laugh. I knew exactly what she meant and that wasn't my intention. I commented as she got into my Range Rover "It is taxed and insured." She smiled.

We arrived at Cranbury farm. Susan as usual in her efficiency had brought out Snowdrop and one of the other horses. I kissed Susan on the cheek. "Thank you my love." She smiled in appreciation helping Fiona to mount the horse. We trotted off around the property. "You have a lot of pretty stable girls working for you Rob. Your wife must really have to watch you" she smiled. "You are correct and she does, although she's in Switzerland at the moment with her father" "Who is watching you now then?" she joked continuing "Excuse me for saying so Rob, you are extremely handsome and I'm glad I'm not your wife having to fight off all these women" she said, looking slightly embarrassed at her own comment. I didn't reply I was listening to her thoughts. She fancied me but was unsure of how to approach without seeming too keen, but didn't want to leave me in any doubt she was interested. We had a pleasant ride. I avoided going anywhere near the cabin and we returned to the stables. Susan took the horses and I gave her a ride back to Redbrick farm. She thanked me for my time and all that I'd done for her. I told her she could come anytime she wanted and continue to ride, providing we had a spare horse. She softly kissed me on the cheek and said goodbye and drove off. My mind was preoccupied with Sam. I could see her sitting on the top of a cliff, looking out into the wilderness searching for ideas on how she could repair our marriage and feeling deep remorse for being involved with the other woman. I snapped my fingers and I was sitting by Sam, which startled her. Sam's hazel eyes filled with tears. I kissed her gently on the lips. "I still love you Sam and always will." "I can't ask you to forgive me again Rob. You trusted me and I let you down." "You want a divorce then?" "No I want to end it all I don't want to live". "I will certainly not let you kill yourself". We embraced passionately. She pulled away slightly searching my expression "Do you still really want me Rob?" "Only if you promise again to behave yourself and you keep your promises this time" She cried inconsolably. I held her in my arms "You stay here with your father for the rest of the month and relax and we'll start afresh when you come home. Okay?" She nodded. There was no way I could let her go. Considering all my indiscretions she hadn't even scratched the surface of being unfaithful. I held her for a little while longer then kissed her goodbye, snapped my fingers and I was home at Redbrick farm.

I walked into the living room and sat in my armchair. Katie come across and sat on my lap. "I missed you Rob you went to Switzerland to see Sam?" "How do you know"? "Sam's lipstick is on your cheek". Katie laughed. "She's okay, very upset with the situation like everyone else." Katie kissed me tenderly on the lips. "I love you Rob. I always have." Caroline came into the room and sat on the settee. I eased Katie up and sat by Caroline and Katie joined us on the settee. I placed my arm around them both. "What a fucking life this has turned out to be we go from one disaster to the next." Christina appeared. "So you're going to give my daughter another chance Chosen One?" "Yes, I've been fucking everything I can lay my hands on for your benefit and she's done virtually nothing wrong." Christina exhaled. "You really think I want to harm my own daughter? You are the Chosen One, and the future of the covenant is in your hands. You are the key to our survival and I'm not prepared to sacrifice the realm for one person." I was becoming angry. I thought sit down Christina and she sat immediately, her face filled with fear as I started to glow white. Sam and Caroline moved away. "If anything happens to Sam I will kill you Christina. It is for me to decide her fate as her husband not you". "Yes Chosen One I will insure she is kept safe" Christina snapped her fingers and vanished. Caroline and Katie re-seated themselves after I stopped glowing white. "Bloody hell Rob you told her." Katie remarked. Caroline held my hand. "Calm yourself Rob please your frightening me." I kissed them both on the cheek and snapped my fingers and there were three meals on the table in front of us and three glasses of wine. Katie nervously asked. "Do you want one of us to sleep with you tonight for company?" "No I want both of you" I smiled. They both grinned. We finished eating and I snapped my fingers and the coffee appeared. We all retired to bed. I snapped my fingers and they were both naked. "Come on girls take your pleasure. No fighting these plenty for both." I just rolled on my back and left them to it. By 3 o'clock in the morning they had worn themselves out. "Oh God, that's wonderful". Katie professed. "I just can't take any more." "Nor me I'm absolutely knackered and it's still hard." Caroline remarked. They both cuddled up to me and we went to sleep. Early the next morning I awoke to Caroline coming in the bedroom carrying a tray. I sat up and she placed the tray on my lap. "Last night was wonderful I feel a whole new woman this morning." She kissed me on the cheek and left to deal with the horses. Katie came in dressed and kissed me on the lips. "I've never had sex that good before, mind you it's always good with you. I must get the children ready for school. I'll see you later." She smiled. Christina appeared. "Are you still angry with me Chosen One?" "No, I feel quite good this morning. You should know you can read my mind." "Not always, especially when you're annoyed like you were last night". She snapped her fingers and her clothes vanished. She slid into my bed. "I thought you might need to relax a little more". I lay there. "Take your pleasure woman". She looked at me strangely then we made love after an hour she rolled off. "I can't take any more of that I must be getting old." She smiled. She kissed me on the cheek and snapped her fingers and disappeared. I showered, dressed and went downstairs had a quick cup of coffee and went out into the yard, realising Fiona's car was parked. I went into the arena and she was riding around on one of the horses with Caroline instructing her. Caroline came over and kissed me on the cheek. "I'm not sure if she's coming for the horse riding or just to see you. That's all she seems to talk about is you. I think she's got the hots for you Rob." Caroline said, patting me on the head.

Chapter 9
What to Do

Fiona rode over to where I was talking to Caroline. She smiled and dismounted. Caroline took the reins of the horse and commented. "I think you've finished riding this one for today. Perhaps you should try the other one." I watched Caroline walk off trying to stop laughing. She was becoming very mischievous although, was always a bundle of fun she didn't particularly care who I slept with as long as I didn't forget her. "I'm going to Cranbury farm would you like to come?" "Yes, if you don't mind Rob." "I presume you're going riding again today?" I nodded. She jumped in my Range Rover with me and we went to Cranbury farm. Susan already had the horses ready on our arrival. She helped Fiona into the saddle and we trotted off. "You will have to let me pay for some of my lessons Rob, otherwise your think I'm taking advantage of your kindness." I smiled. "There's no need but if it makes you feel better, you can always give Caroline a tip for her trouble. It's her training that made you a good rider nothing else." "You're very fond of Caroline Rob?" Definitely she's been a good and loyal friend to the family". "I think you're fine she is in love with you Rob. Oh, perhaps I shouldn't have said that, I apologise. It's none of my business." "You can say what you like to me Fiona and yes I know Caroline is in love with me. She always has been." I smiled. Fiona looked on in astonishment at my reply. "Does your wife know?" "Of course she's not worried either. I love lots of people." I could hear Fiona's thoughts trying to understand what was going on, her little mind was working overtime "And you all live in the same house?" "Of course, let's find out something about you then, are you married seeing someone have children?" I knew the answers already but I thought I would put her on the spot. "No I'm not married, no one would have me. I haven't any children, and I'm not seeing anyone, I'm very boring really. I haven't had this much fun for ages." "Do you fancy a coffee?" "Where?" She said looking around for a building. "Follow me." Snowdrop picked up the pace and we slowly weaved our way through my wood to the log cabin. "I didn't know this was here Rob." "I built this many years ago to live in when my first wife was murdered." "Oh I remember the case, I'm sorry for your loss". She said dismounting. We went inside, "Take a seat on the settee I'll make the coffee. How do you like it?" "A little milk, little sugar and not too strong, please. I snapped my fingers and carried in the mugs of coffee. "That was quick I didn't even hear the kettle" she smiled continuing. "This is nice and cosy; do you spend much time here?" "Quite a bit actually I come to escape everybody." I could hear her little mind ticking over, wondering if I'd had affairs and brought all the women here to make love to. I was trying not to smile if she only knew the truth. I thought she was trying to figure out how to encourage me to kiss her without seeming too forward. We finished our coffee and we mounted our horses and continued slowly through the wood. She thought about falling off hoping I would hold her in my arms, but then decided it might be too painful falling off such a big horse. The poor girl was struggling to come up with a solution to her dilemma. I would not encourage her in the slightest. It would have to be her idea and her decision alone to take matters further. We finally reached Cranbury farm and dismounted. Susan took the horses from us and kissed me on the cheek. Fiona commented. "Do all the women around here kiss you every time they see you?" "Why not? it doesn't harm anybody." Summer and Spring came over to me two beautiful blondes and each kissed me on the cheek and walked off. Fiona shook her head in disbelief walked over close to me. She sniffed my jacket. "What's the matter do I smell bad or something?" I asked. "No, no, sorry I just can't understand why those two girls just kissed you for no apparent reason." Not understanding what was going on was driving her crazy. We jumped back into my Range Rover and drove steadily back to Redbrick farm. As soon as we arrived she thanked me very much and ran over to Caroline. I could see them both chatting, I listened. "Why do all the women round here kiss Rob?" Fiona asked Caroline. "You don't know Fiona we're all his wives." "You're joking" "Of course" Caroline laughed. I thought to myself, be careful Caroline, you'll let the cat out of the bag in a minute. "He must be really a nice guy for all these girls to like him" Fiona said, staring up the yard towards me, checking to see where I was. Caroline replied. "You wait till you get him in the sack, you'll see why everybody loves him." "You actually sleep with him. What about his wife?" "She joins in as well." Caroline burst out laughing. She couldn't maintain a straight face any longer but all that, she said, was the truth little did Fiona know. "You're pulling my leg Caroline." By this time Caroline was bent double laughing. Fiona walked back over to me by her car. "Bye Fiona" I said as she jumped in and drove off. Caroline came over to me trying to stop laughing the tears were streaming down her face. She placed her hand on my shoulder. "I'm sorry Rob I'm sure you heard the conversation I just couldn't resist it." I remarked "Just be careful Caroline, once a copper always a copper." She nodded in agreement and walked back down the yard drying her eyes. I went into the house and sat in my usual armchair with my Bacardi. Susan appeared. "Don't forget it's the full moon tonight Chosen One." She snapped her fingers and disappeared again. I looked at the clock on the wall. It was almost 5:30 PM. I jumped in the Range Rover and went to the log cabin. Christina was already there, she'd made my food and drink. Afterwards we sat in the front room talking things over, she informed me that her daughter Samantha was feeling a lot better and coming to terms with the situation. Christina said "Someone's coming down the drive Rob I'll disappear. It's a policewoman you been seeing." I switched the television on and sat quietly drinking my Bacardi I could hear Fiona's thoughts, wondering if I was having an affair. I was trying to stop laughing. I heard her footsteps on the porch. I saw her glimpse through the window then pulled back as I looked up. I snapped my fingers and I was round the back of the cabin. I sneaked around to the front and saw her peering through the window. "Can I help you?" "It's not what it looks like Rob." She said nervously. "I'd better go." "Would you like a coffee? There's a chill in the air and the fires warm, you're welcome to come in." I said approaching her and opening the door. She nervously stepped inside and removed her fleece lined jacket. "Search the place Fiona you obviously think something is going on here. Perhaps I'm a drug baron" I laughed sarcastically. She went into every room to find them empty "Are you happy now?" I went into the kitchen and made a coffee and returned to the front room. She was sitting by the fire in my old chair warming herself. "I think you owe me an explanation Fiona please" I said, passing her the mug of coffee. I then said. "Here's my mobile, phone the police and tell them where you are in case you feel threatened." She was shaking. I didn't know whether it was from the cold or fear. I passed my mobile, she pushed it away. "I don't need to ring anybody. I'm just a nosy bugger you intrigue me and I know you're not short of money. I brought you up on the police computer to have you checked out. You don't have a criminal record." She finished her coffee quickly and stood up. "I'd better go I'm sorry, you could report me for this." "You still haven't answered my question. Why did you come in the first place?" "Oh I don't know." I move towards her "Because I wanted to do this." She kissed me tenderly on the lips and ran out of the door. Christina reappeared "That's a strange one, she wanted to kiss you and she wanted you to take her to bed but then she runs off, crazy woman." She just drove off in her car she's definitely gone Rob." Christina said sitting on the settee. "She doesn't know what she's missed."

Christina and I continued talking for an hour. "She's back Rob". Christina kissed me on the lips and vanished. There was a quiet knock on the door "Come in Fiona?" She opened the door. "How did you know it was me?" She entered carrying a little bag. She changed from her jeans into a pink suit. "I hope you haven't got a gun in that bag". "No, it's my overnight" she didn't finish the sentence she sat by the fire. I made another coffee. "So you'd like to stay the night; which bedroom do you want?" She moved over onto the settee by me. She kissed me tenderly on the lips and neck. "Which one do you think" "Are you sure you want to do this?" She whispered in my ear "Yes, I'm very sure." I picked her up in my arms and carried her into my bedroom. "I better show you this first Rob before you sleep with me." She removed her jacket and blouse and she turned her back to me. There were scars across her back where she'd been beaten with a stick by her father as a child. Now I was feeling guilty I should have picked up her concerns long ago. She turned around to face me. She was about to explain and I put my finger to her lips. "You don't have to say anything. You are beautiful just the way you are." She smiled relieved. "I can get that fixed for you. I have contacts you would never dream of." She cried. "It would cost thousands Rob, plastic surgery. I couldn't ask you or accept you paying for that." "It won't cost a penny and stop asking so many silly bloody questions will you, woman, are you sure you want to sleep with me?" "Oh God yes." I could see the spirits circling overhead looking at Fiona's back. She climbed into bed and pulled the blankets up to her neck. I quickly undressed and joined her. I could still see the spirits circling, but she obviously could not, they felt my pain at seeing Fiona's back. I asked them to fix Fiona's back if they could without endangering themselves. I held her in my arms caressed her tenderly and finally we made love. This had never been my real intention but it happened all the same. She kissed me tenderly and enjoyed every moment of the experience. We awoke at 7:30 AM. She showered and dressed quickly. "I'll be late for work, oh, darn it." She kissed me on the lips, smiled sweetly and left. Jenny appeared. "The sisters have done as you requested. Fiona's back will repair itself over the next seven days. I kissed Jenny tenderly on the lips. "Thank you" "The sisters asked that you make Spring Summer and Autumn pregnant before the end of the year as payment." "Oh, I have to pay for everything now. Perhaps I should start with you?" "No Chosen One you may take me to bed but I don't want to be pregnant again." I kissed her passionately on the lips. "What will you do when I move to the realm you will be the first woman I search for." She smiled. "When you have a 1000 women to choose from I will be insignificant." She snapped her fingers and disappeared before I could say another word. I drove to Cranbury farm and made love to the three girls within an hour. I had fulfilled my obligation to the spirits. Susan looked on very disappointed. "I wish to be released and made pregnant so I can return to the realm, like my sisters". "Do you really mean that Susan, you're unhappy staying with the Chosen One?" She thought for a moment. Jenny came from around the corner. Susan ran into an empty stable. Jenny ignored me altogether and went straight into the stable. Somebody's ears were about to be burnt I decided. Jenny beckoned me in from the doorway. "She dishonours you Chosen One do you want me to send to the dark place?" Susan was on her knees crying and begging for forgiveness. Jenny continued. "She was given to you by the sisters Chosen One and if she doesn't please you, you may dispose of her or I will for you." Jenny reminded me of my ex-wife cold and calculated when she needed to be. Jenny then glared at me. "I am nothing like your ex-wife Chosen One please don't compare me it's distasteful." "I will keep Susan." Jenny snapped her fingers and disappeared. Susan hugged me, crying on my shoulder. I embraced her and reassured her she was safe.

Chapter 10
Sam Coming Home

Katie had gone to London airport to collect Sam I waited patiently in the house for her return. Sam ran over and jumped onto my lap kissing me frantically. "I've missed you Rob. I've really missed you." Christina appeared. Katie sat on the settee quiet, fearing the worst. Christina said firmly. "Well daughter you've had time to rest and consider what you want to do." "I'm staying with my husband and everyone who loves me in this house." Caroline came running in and stopped in her tracks when she saw Christina then quietly moved and sat down on the settee. Christina looked at Katie and Caroline "You have served the Chosen One well continue to do so." Without another word being spoken Christina vanished. Caroline ran over and hugged Sam saying she was glad she was safe and home. I picked Sam up in my arms and carried her upstairs. I'd missed her loving tender touch. I snapped my fingers and we were naked, we slid into bed making love in our own special way.

The rest of the month was uneventful, which was a pleasant change from recent events. Sam seemed content with everything. The three stable girls became pregnant and were transported back to the realm. Three more were sent as replacements we'd almost got a conveyor belt system in place. I drove over to Cranbury farm. Sam greeted me with a loving kiss and Susan introduced me to the new stable girls almost identical to Susan herself in stature and looks. How the sisters always had beautiful features is beyond my comprehension, it must be just something they put in the water for want of a better explanation. They each held their handout for me to shake. "My name is Geraldine." "I'm Donna." "I'm Josephine, you honour us Chosen One to be allowed in your presence." Susan quickly reminded them to call me Rob in public and not to bow. The girls scurried off to do their chores. Sam looked at me. "Just remember, I'm your wife Rob occasionally." She said with a heavy sigh. Susan brought out Snowdrop and Freddie our two favourite horses. We both mounted and trotted off out the yard. I reached across to hold Sam's hand. I could hear the thoughts of wondering how long it would be before I was sleeping with the new girls. Would one of them finally tempt me into leaving her. I pulled on the reins and Snowdrop stopped. Sam turned round and came back alongside me. "What's wrong Rob?" "You know what's wrong." I said dismounting and helping her off Freddie. I held Sam around the waist staring in to her beautiful hazel eyes. "I am not now or ever, leaving you for another woman, please stop thinking it you are driving me crazy with worry." Sam embraced me. "I forget you can read my mind. I just feel so insecure I don't know why." I lifted her up in my arms and helped her onto Freddie. I mounted Snowdrop and we continued. Winter was here again and there was a chill in the air. We finished our ride and Susan took the horses from us. We jumped in our own Range Rover and returned to Redbrick farm. I could see Fiona's car as I parked up. Sam parked behind me. Fiona came from the stables running to greet Sam and I "Excuse me for doing this Sam." Fiona flung her arms around my neck and kissed me passionately on the lips. Sam was surprised by Fiona's reaction. "What's all this about?" I asked. "You know Rob, my back the scarring it's all gone". Sam looked puzzled "Come in the house Fiona and explain everything to me I've missed something somewhere" Sam invited. We all went into the living room. Sam sat by Fiona on the settee. Katie came in to join us. "Please explain, I'd like to know what my husband's been up to while I was away Fiona." Sam voiced. Now the shit would hit the fan. Fiona looked to me, realising in all the excitement may have said too much in front of Sam. Fiona played with her fingers nervously. Sam spoke up. "You've obviously fucked my husband; you might as well tell us the rest Fiona." Katie placed her arm around Fiona "Don't be frightened, no one will hurt you here." I thought very kind of Katie trying to defuse the situation, which could be an unexploded bomb waiting to go off. "Well. Fiona?" The tears streamed down Fiona's cheeks; Katie dabbed Fiona's cheeks with her handkerchief. "I did sleep with your husband it was entirely my fault. He didn't encourage me in any way I just wanted to be with him. I've only ever had one boyfriend and once he'd seen my back he left me" Sam interrupted. "Okay, we've established you've been to bed with my husband. Where did your back fit into all this?" "I showed Rob my back my father had beaten me with a stick and scarred my spine and flesh. He was a religious fanatic and thought I needed punishing all the time. Rob said he'd fix it for me and I didn't need to sleep with him, but I just couldn't stop myself." Fiona burst into tears. Sam embraced Fiona crying herself "Oh my God what a horrible story" Sam remarked. "Please forgive him Sam. It's my fault and to make matters worse, I'm pregnant I'm having an abortion because I've got nowhere to live and support a child, I do want to keep it." The tears flowed from Fiona. Sam and Katie had joined in. Katie looked across to me with tear filled eyes. "Help her Rob you can't let her get rid of the child after all it's your child." Sam sat on my lap, drying her eyes and placing her arm around my shoulder. "I can believe you wanted to sleep with my husband, the next problem is what we do." Christina walked into the room. Sam looked horrified thinking she was in trouble. Sam introduced her mother to Fiona. "This is my mother Christina." Christina come properly dressed not in a white robe. They shook hands and Christina sat beside Fiona, placing her arm around her shoulder. "Now my dear, this is a minor problem don't upset yourself." We all watched intently Christine was being caring and gentle. I could feel Sam gripping my shoulder. Christina held both Fiona's hands. I could see Fiona's hands glowing slightly white as the power travelled up her arms and into her body. The spirits entered the room. Fiona had her eyes shut. The spirits surrounded Fiona and stayed there for a few minutes then vanished. Fiona opened her eyes. "I'm honoured to carry the Chosen Ones child. This will be our secret and that of the spirits who save my soul and life." We all just stared in astonishment. Christina came over and held Sam's hand assisting her to her feet. Christina embraced Sam and kissed her on the cheek, something she hadn't done for a long time. "Well done my daughter you are learning. Fiona will live with you Sam here where it is safe from the outside world. Don't worry about using magic in front of her. She will think it's quite normal and will say nothing to anyone she is now one of us." Christina bent down and passionately kissed me on the lips saying. "You honour the covenant by bringing in a new member to our fold, you will be rewarded". She snapped her fingers and vanished. Sam finally felt proud of herself and her mother had approved, which meant more to her than she realised. Katie smiled. "We have someone new in the family and pregnant." Katie kissed Fiona on the cheek and gave her another hug. Fiona timidly said. "You will have to show me what I must do. I don't want to cause you any trouble." She came over and knelt in front of me holding my hand. "I knew you were special from the moment you helped me out of that wreck. I knew I was going to live the minute you held me." I eased her onto my lap. Sam looked on smiling. Katie went upstairs to prepare a bedroom for Fiona. She had already quit the police force because of her condition and she didn't like the job anyway. "What can I do Chosen One?" She asked nervously. "You can help Caroline with the horses. You like working with the horses." "Yes please. I would enjoy doing that until I'm too fat and can't move." she smiled. Fiona rose to her feet and embraced Sam. "Am I allowed to sleep with Rob again?" "Of course, he is now your husband too but nothing too enthusiastic to damage the baby." Thank you Sam thank you all for your kindness. Caroline came in from the stables Fiona embraced her "My sister."

Caroline looked over Fiona's shoulder to Sam. Sam smiled. "She is now one of us in more ways than one." I grabbed Sam's hand pulling her down onto my lap and kissed her passionately. "I love you Sam" I whispered in her ear. Katie came from upstairs grabbing Fiona taking her to her new bedroom. Sam and I explained everything to Caroline and Caroline was very pleased with the situation. She would have someone who could help her with the horses and someone she liked talking to. Katie took Fiona in her Range Rover to fetch the rest of her belongings from her digs. Katie helped Fiona upstairs with her few belongings. It was the night of the full moon. Christina requested I take Fiona with me this evening. We drove to the cabin and entered. We seated ourselves on the settee. I snapped my fingers and our favourite drinks appeared Fiona was very nervous and held me close. The spirits appeared this time Fiona could see them swirling around us both. They vanished and Jenny appeared. "This is Jenny, our favourite nanny she will take care of you and the child." Fiona looked very nervous. Jenny smiled at my comment and encouraged Fiona to stand. Jenny gently placed her hand against Fiona's stomach. "Wonderful it's a girl." Jenny snapped her fingers and Fiona was naked Fiona screamed trying to cover her breasts with her hands. "Don't be alarmed no one is going to hurt you. I just want to check the scarring has gone from your back that's good." Jenny commented. Jenny then snapped her fingers and Fiona was fully dressed again. Fiona looked about herself astonished at what had taken place. Jenny then kissed me and disappeared. Fiona just sat there with her mouth open, trying to absorb what had taken place. I kissed her gently on the cheek and held her hand. "Would you like something to eat Fiona?" She nodded slowly still not speaking. I snapped my fingers and I could smell the food in the kitchen. I guided Fiona to the kitchen and seated her at the table. Fiona snapped her fingers. I read her thoughts. "Can we all do that?" I smiled "No is the short answer Fiona. Not until you enter the realm." She was only 21 and it was a lot for her to take in. Although her mind told me she was very happy to be wanted and loved, something she hadn't experienced all her life until now. She told me she was frightened of her father finding her when he was released from prison, which would be next week. I assured her no harm would come to her now, she was with me. She started stacking the plates and cutlery ready to wash. I snapped my fingers and the dishes vanished. She looked around surprised. "Where's it gone Rob? I was going to wash up." I picked her up in my arms and seated myself on the settee with her on my lap, she commented. "You smell just like freshly baked biscuits and I want to eat you." She smiled. "Where is your mother Fiona?" "She left long ago my father used to beat her too she wanted to take me with her, but was frightened he would kill her if she did. She did complain to the police several times, but they didn't do anything and that's why I became a policewoman hoping to make things better for other women." All her intentions were good and I was determined she would not have a miserable life from this point on. "Would you like your own room here Fiona? Or would you want to sleep with me tonight?" "I thought I was one of your wives. I want to sleep with you and I want you to love me like you did the first time we met." She looked at me rather hurt. "Don't you want me to sleep with you Rob?" "Yes of course I do you silly thing." I picked her up in my arms and carried her into the bedroom. I snapped my fingers as I placed her on the bed and we were both naked. She held me passionately and we enjoyed each other until the early hours and returned to Redbrick farm. Caroline came in and said "Horses," "I'll just get changed, sorry." I snapped my fingers and Fiona was changed. She smiled and ran out of the door to join Caroline. Caroline glanced back to me and smiled.

Chapter 11
Revenge is Best Served Cold

I drove to Cranbury farm and alerted Susan to Fiona's father and if he turned up to notify me. Sam came to me. I explained the same thing to her. "Can't you stop him coming Rob? Couldn't he meet with an unfortunate accident after what he's done to Fiona?" I was surprised at Sam's response. I placed my arm around her waist and kissed her on the cheek. "Yes, I could but should I?" Susan approached us. "I hear your thoughts I agree with Sam. He doesn't deserve to be on this earth and you will have full support of the sisters in whatever action you decide to take Chosen One." Sam kissed Susan on the cheek. "Has anyone considered he may have changed his way's?" Sam smacked my backside with her crop hard "How would you like to be beaten every day by me? it's inhumane." Susan laughed watching me rub my backside. "That hurt Sam." I protested. "Well, imagine how Fiona felt every day then perhaps you'll do something, be a man." Susan commented quickly. "You shouldn't have said that Sam." I threw Sam over my shoulder. She kept hitting me with her crop "Put me down Rob please I'm sorry." I threw her straight in the water trough at the end of the yard. It was freezing cold with ice forming on the top. She screamed. "It's bloody freezing you sod." Susan and the other stable girls were screaming in laughter. I held Sam's hand and helped her out of the trough. I snapped my fingers and she was dry, she burst out laughing. "That serves me right". Sam noticed a wet patch on the back of my leg. She put her hand to her mouth. "Oh God, I'm sorry Rob, did I hit you that hard?" Susan came running over "Come into the feed shed Rob I'll have a look." Sam, Susan and myself went in. I released my trousers. A large gash was on the back of my leg. Susan glowed white and placed her hand over the wound and it was healed and the pain vanished. I pulled my trousers up and kissed Susan "Thank you." Sam looked worried. "I didn't think I hit you that hard Rob" she said embracing me. My phone rang. It was Caroline "Rob come quick Fiona's father is here, he's got her by the hair slapping her face." I snapped my fingers and I was there. I snapped my fingers he curled up in a ball in extreme agony on the floor. Caroline grabbed Fiona and took her outside. I snapped my fingers again and he was tied to the beams by his hands. I thought of a whip and lashed his back until it was red raw. He "screamed" in agony. Fiona and Caroline re-entered the building Caroline put her hand to her mouth in shock. Fiona looked up "You bastard, I hope you die." I snapped my fingers and he vanished. "He's gone forever now Fiona. He will never touch you again." She embraced me. Sam came into the yard with her Range Rover Susan appeared knowing what I'd done. "You honour all women Rob by your actions." Susan held Fiona's face and removed the pain. Jenny appeared and placed her hand on Fiona's stomach. "The child is safe and unhurt." She snapped her fingers and vanished. Sam took Fiona into the house and Susan disappeared. Caroline held me. "I thought he was going to kill her Rob." "Where has he gone?" "To the dark place where there is no return, no life just emptiness." "Are you okay Caroline, did I frighten you again?" I kissed her tenderly on the lips, she replied. "You always frighten me when you're angry but I do know you love me and that's the most important thing." I went into the house to check on Fiona. Sam had taken a liking to Fiona and I didn't know really why. As long as everyone was happy so was I. Sam was sat on the settee talking to Fiona I seated in my usual armchair snapping my fingers and everyone had a drink. Katie came over and sat on my lap hugging me. "Rob, Nicky wants to go on a school trip to France. What do you think, can we trust her?" I sighed "I don't know; I don't trust any of my daughters 100%. I should be able to monitor her movements and see what she gets up to and I'm sure the sisters would help us. I'd let her go." Christina appeared this time in a white robe she looked at Fiona and Sam and Katie sitting on my lap, her smile broadened. "I feel the love in this room and the harmony I have longed for this to take place. And finally, you are making progress all of you. Come to me my daughter." Sam moved towards her mother nervously. Christina embraced her and kissed her on each cheek. "I love you daughter." Tears of joy filled Sam's eyes. Christina snapped her fingers and vanished. Sam re-seated herself by Fiona. "Rob my love, could you find Fiona's mother for her so she knows she is safe?" Sam asked softly. Jenny appeared. "Let me help you Chosen One". Jenny waved her hand in a small circle and we could see Fiona's mother sitting in a small dirty bedsit on the outskirts of London. Mould was on the walls we could see her mother counting her money on a grubby kitchen table. She emptied her purse on the table a knock at the door. She opened and there was a man standing there demanding the rent. She gave him all the money she had, the tears running down her face. I couldn't imagine so much hardship, Fiona burst into tears. Katie moved to support Fiona, Jenny sat on my lap. We continued watching her mother remove her blouse, displaying the scarring on her spine.

Everyone gasped, putting their hands to their mouth in shock. It wasn't just Fiona that suffered her mother too. Jenny snapped her fingers and the vision went. "Can the sisters help?" "Already being attended to Chosen One, watch." We saw Christina entering the room embracing Fiona's mother. Christina turned white as she healed her pain suddenly Christina appeared accompanied by Fiona's mother beautifully dressed in white satin. Fiona ran to her mother they embraced. Jenny snapped her fingers and disappeared. I reached for Christina's hand and eased her down onto my lap and kissed her passionately. "You do have love in you Christina." She smiled. "You have honoured us again Chosen One by bringing another member to the covenant, you will be rewarded by the sisters. I'm taking Fiona's mother with me to a little place we have in the country where she will be fed properly and treated with the respect she deserves. Then when she is well enough we will see." Christina explained everything to Fiona and snapped her fingers and they were gone. Fiona flung her arms around me. "You are so wonderful Rob, where have you been all my life?" she cried. In reality it was nothing to do with me. It was down to the sisters and the power they possessed to make things right.

Katie drove her daughter to catch the coach for the French trip. We all had some reservations after our last episode with Nicky although since Jenny had been involved, Nicky seemed to have calmed down and showed no signs of being really interested in boys. Things can change and very often without warning. Katie returned and entered the living room, sighing. "I hope I've done the right thing Rob by letting her go on that trip." "We'll find out soon enough Katie love." I drove to Cranbury farm and Susan greeted me with a kiss. We were now in January although there was no snow on the ground it was still cold. I could see Sam's Range Rover but couldn't find her. I searched with my mind and she was in the house which was no longer occupied. She was watching something on the television. I snapped my fingers and appeared behind the settee. Sam was watching a video of her and her old girlfriend naked playing with each other along with a few friends. Sam had lifted her jumper up and released her bra so she could play with her breasts. She'd also pulled her riding britches down and was playing with herself while she watched the video, she hadn't realised I was behind her. I shouted. "Sam, what are you doing?" Susan appeared alongside me. Sam Screamed and turned the television off, her face went white as she tidied herself. I started to glow white. Susan held my arm "Calm down Rob, calm down, it's not that serious." Sam didn't speak she just sat there trembling. She knew this could be the end of the road for her marriage and life, as she knew it. "What were you watching Sam?" Although I already knew, "Nothing just an old video of friends" How long are you going to lie to me Sam?" "I'm not lying". She cried. "I was just watching an old friend. You bloody killed her she'd done nothing to you." "You miss being a lesbian don't you Sam?" "No not since I met you, it's just old memories. I was going to burn the cassette anyway. I just wanted to look one last time and say goodbye." "How many more pornographic videos have you got?" "It not pornographic, we were lovers." I walked out; she had broken my heart again and my trust, although I was no angel myself, my love for her had never changed. I jumped in my Range Rover and drove and drove I know I could never escape. The sisters were monitoring everything I thought, I finally stop driving when I reached Inverness, Scotland. I pulled into a hotel booked myself a room and went to bed. I was surprised I hadn't been hassled by one of the sisters. Perhaps they knew I needed my space to calm down and make a rational decision. After breakfast I carried on driving and finally parked up at Fort George, standing on the battlements staring out to sea for an answer that doesn't exist out there. The air was cold coming in off the sea. I carried on driving to a place called Tain and sought accommodation on an old campsite. They had plenty of spare accommodation at this time of year I booked myself in for a week. Drove back into Tain itself and purchased new clothing.

I returned to find Jenny in my chalet. She was sat quite poised as she always did on a chair with arms folded and just looked at me. "Well say something Jenny, I'm sure you're going to" I said coolly. "What is there to say Rob? you left, you could have come to the realm. There is a place waiting for you. Stop looking at me like I'm your ex bloody wife. I don't like it." She protested. "Jenny, you swore" Which made me laugh. "I suppose you don't care Nicky's in France pole dancing naked for a dare, drugged up to the eyeballs with men mauling her" I laughed "That's a load of bullshit." Jenny waved her hand and a picture formed. It was Nicky and she was doing what Jenny had said. I snapped my fingers and within seconds I was in the nightclub.

I grabbed Nicky's hand pulling her away from the pole snapped my fingers and dropped her off inside the living room at Redbrick farm. Just as she was still naked. I snapped my fingers and vanished again back to Tain now my secret was really out Nicky would realise what had happened. Unless she was so high on drugs she wouldn't remember. Jenny had gone and I had hundreds of missed calls from Sam on my mobile I could hear Jenny talking to the family explaining the reason why I brought Nicky back home. Katie was horrified and so was the rest of the family. They asked how I was and when I was coming home. Jenny told them never. Sam started crying. I heard Jenny tell her "How many chances do you need Sam before Rob gives up on you and the rest of us? You would be dead now if your mother had her way, but she will not go against Rob's wishes. That's the only thing that is keeping you alive." I could see through Jenny's eyes Nicky was on the floor unconscious. Jenny administered some medicine and snapped her fingers and Nicky was fully clothed again.

I could hear Katie on the phone to the headmaster ripping his ears off and told him we were going to sue the school for gross negligence. Thank God she had the sense not to mention how we got her back home so quickly. Jenny reappeared in my room. "See you do care Chosen One. I like the way you set the fire alarms off and emptied the place." "Can you not take Nicky to the realm and keep her until she grows up and finally get some brains?" "No, we couldn't risk the contamination. She won't be allowed in the realm anyway not with her behaviour. Since I last treated her she's been to bed with two teachers to get the right grades. So, she is no longer a virgin" "Does Katie know?" "No, we haven't told her I would have thought you'd have realised what was going on Chosen One." I sighed "I'm not the brightest star in the sky you probably realise that by now." "You may not be Chosen One but you are the most kind and loving person we've found and that's all we are interested in." I phoned Katie and conveyed the information relating to the two teachers. She said she would take action and she hoped I would feel I could return home soon. I was missed by everyone. I lay on my bed looking at the ceiling, what happened

Charmed Log Cabin: Enchanted Life

could have been stopped by me if I'd only used the powers I possessed properly. I just seemed to be preoccupied with trivial matters and feeling sorry for myself. Jenny moved and sat on the side of my bed stroking my forehead and I finally fell asleep.

When I awoke the next morning Jenny had gone. I packed my things and headed for home. It took nearly all day to get back home. Katie greeted me at the door with a big hug. Everyone else was out. Katie sat on my lap and explained that the headmaster was taking action against the two teachers. The problem is, Nicky is nearly 18 and if she consented it would be her own fault. I explained to Katie that Nicky wouldn't be allowed in the realm. "Where's Sam?" "She's been spending a lot of time at the cabin. In fact, she sleeps there most nights in your bed. I can't get over what she did again Rob. She's even lost interest in the horses. Susan and Caroline are running the show." "I'll go, see what she's doing." "Don't run after her Rob she doesn't deserve you." "No, I want to get this sorted once and for all." "Rob when will you get it through your thick head she won't change?" "Everyone deserves a second chance." "If you had married me this wouldn't have happened." I kissed her on the lips and left.

Sam's Range Rover was parked outside the cabin. I saw her look out of the window and I went in, snapped my fingers for a glass of Bacardi and Coke and sat in my old armchair. She was sitting on the settee reading a magazine. "Well Sam, what do you want to do?" "Do about what?" I started to glow white. Christina appeared and intervened. "Chosen One stop it, she's provoking you she wants to die, she can't stand the guilt." I wondered why I hadn't picked that up. Christina read my thoughts. "It's because you love her and your confused." Sam jumped to her feet and tried to strike her mother "Let him kill me. It's what I deserve." Christina grabbed Sam's wrists and she was powerless; she flopped back down onto the settee finally bursting into tears. Christina shook her head slowly. "How can you possibly want this woman Chosen One after all that she's done to you? I could find 1000 women better than her" "You don't get it Christina it's called loyalty to the one you love." Sam looked across to me with her bloodshot eyes. "I can't ask you to forgive me Rob you've done it so many times." "You'll get there Sam. I haven't forgotten when you pulled me from the depths of despair all those years ago. You were the love of my life then, as you are today." "How much more pain can your heart take Rob before you are destroyed?" Christina asked. The room filled with spirits and they all engulfed Sam. I could see by the expression on her face that she was not enjoying the experience, but I knew I was powerless to intervene. They vanished. Sam opened her handbag and removed three videos and through them into the log burner. She grabbed my hand "Take me home husband". We jumped in my Range Rover and headed back for Redbrick farm. The spirits had definitely done something but what and for how long would it last, only time would tell I supposed. She walked in the house as if nothing had happened. Everyone stared at her and she took no notice. I seated myself in my armchair and she sat on my lap. We told her what had happened to Nicky and she was unconcerned; her only comment was. "Oh well we'll sort it out one way or another." Everyone just looked at Sam. Fiona was starting to show she was pregnant. Sam then spoke up. "I am the new Sam the old one has gone." I stood up becoming alarmed. Sam reached up and held my hand. "Don't be alarmed my love I'm still Sam just slightly reprogrammed, so I'm no longer interested in women or men, just you" "Nothing else Sam?" Jenny appeared. "She is telling the truth Rob. The spirits have blocked part of her brain pattern. She will give you no further trouble we hope." I didn't like the sound of that and neither did anyone else. We would just have to see what differences there were if any. Fiona excused herself and said she was tired and going to bed, just before she left, Jenny held her tummy "Wonderful, everything is quite normal." She snapped her fingers and vanished. Sam was not making conversation with anyone which was not normal. I feared they'd turned her into a bloody robot. I asked Katie. "Where is Nicky?" "In her bedroom Rob" "She's not Katie." Katie ran upstairs and returned quickly out of breath. "She's gone, find her please." There was no reaction from Sam whatsoever other than a comment. "I wouldn't worry she's probably getting fucked somewhere, she'll come home when she's hungry." My mind was so preoccupied with Sam's condition that I was struggling to pick up any thoughts from Nicky. We went back up into her bedroom to see if there was any information we could use. The sisters had disowned her and didn't really care what happened to her, so we were on our own. Katie looked under her bed retrieving two DVDs, she played the first one. It was showing Nicky naked with a teacher on a desk having sex. She put the other one in it was a different teacher, doing the same thing. Katie started to cry. "Just like my mother all over again." We went downstairs Sam was still sitting in my armchair unconcerned. Caroline had already gone outside looking into each stable that was empty, and we caught up with her. I told everyone to be very quiet round the back of one building there was a van that didn't belong to us. I sneaked up and open the back doors. There was Nicky naked with two men. She screamed "I'm nearly 18, fuck off and leave us alone." I grabbed her leg and slid her out the back of the van until she dropped onto the floor. Katie slapped her face several times and started walking her back to the house. The two men dressed quickly and came at me with an iron bar. I hit the one so hard with my fist it broke his jaw and the other I twisted the iron bar round his neck. I told them to get off my property and if they were ever caught here again they wouldn't live to see the next day. When I returned to the house Sam was still sitting in the armchair totally unconcerned. Katie was upstairs with Nicky. Caroline sat on the settee and I sat beside her. "That isn't Sam Rob" she said quietly. Christina appeared. She walked over to Sam and made her drink from a small bottle. Sam shook her head. "What's going on, did I miss something?" Christina put her arm on my shoulder, "I apologise Chosen One, we went a little too far trying to resolve your problem, she'll be okay now but I still think you should let me replace her." "While you're here Christina what can we do with Nicky?" "We could do the same as we've done to Sam although I don't see the point, the child is a lost cause. We treated her once before but only with a mild dose we would have to increase the dosage and you'd have to accept the risks involved." Katie came downstairs crying. Christina explained what she could do and what the consequences could be. "So you're saying Christina, we have three choices, we leave her as she is and she'll become a prostitute. You treat her and if you fail she'll become a zombie and if it works things will be fine?" Sam spoke up. "Go for the treatment

Katie otherwise you'll spend the rest of your life chasing her and when she's 18 there's no stopping her". We heard someone coming downstairs it was Nicky naked "Dad why are you hanging about with these old bags? Why don't you find something fresh like me?" Christina stretched out her hand and Nicky dropped to the floor asleep. Jenny appeared within seconds carrying a small bottle, which she administered to Nicky carrying her back upstairs to her bedroom. Christina commented. "That girl is possessed she's either on drugs or something, but she should be a different child in the morning I promise you." Christina my daughter, came downstairs. The two Christina's hugged each other "My grandmother at long last I meet you." "Dad, please let me go to the realm to live I don't like this world, mother please." Sam and I looked at each other we both know she'd be safe with her grandmother. I walked over to Sam she stood up and held me "What do you think Rob? Would she be happy?" "She'd definitely be happier Sam." Sam went to her mother, "Could we see her sometimes if you took her?" "Of course daughter, providing you behave yourself and do as the Chosen One tells you. I will personally transport you myself at least twice a year or I can send her back for a week to live with you. Okay then were in agreement." The spirits engulfed my daughter and she disappeared. Christina embraced Sam and me and then vanished. Katie was crying on the settee so was Caroline and Sam. As for me I flopped in my armchair thinking my world as just ended.

Chapter 12
Coming to Terms with the New Situation

We awoke the next morning realising Christina was no longer with us. There was a void inside us all. Sam had asked me to go to the realm and check on Christina and make sure she really was happy living there. I went downstairs. Katie greeted me with a kiss. "How is Nicky this morning?" "She hasn't come down Rob. I thought it would be best to leave her to sleep. What do you think?" "I think we'll both check on her just in case something is wrong." We went upstairs and knocked on her door; there was no answer. We knocked again still no answer, Katie open the door Nicky was sat on the side of the bed still not dressed. She looked to her mother and then me stood up kissed Katie on the cheek and me, then sat back down on the bed. Katie voiced "Don't you think you should dress Nicky?" Nicky smiled "In a minute mother." She said quietly. We both returned downstairs whatever tonic Jenny had poured down Nicky's throat had certainly calmed her down beyond belief. I just hope she would liven up just a little bit but we did know the consequences of our actions and what the outcome could be. Katie and I sat in the living room. Fiona stayed in bed she wasn't feeling very well. Sam had taken the children to school and was going round to the college to explain that Christina would no longer be attending. Susan appeared and kissed me on the cheek. "Chosen One, it's the full moon tonight, bring Sam, Caroline and Katie with you." She snapped her fingers and disappeared. "Oh bloody hell, that's all I need, more trouble." Katie remarked. "I'm going to the realm Katie to check on my daughter."

I snapped my fingers and I was in the realm. I walked into the cabin and much to my surprise my daughter was there in a long white robe, she snapped her fingers and my favourite drink appeared on the table. She greeted me with a big hug and a kiss on the cheek. "It's absolutely wonderful here dad. They let me live in your home and I'm to keep it ready for you to arrive anytime and I get to ride Snowdrop." Christina entered; she embraced us both. "Go child, I wish to talk to your father." My daughter went out of the door smiled and waved and I heard Snowdrop neigh. I looked through the window and saw her ride away. Christina placed her hand on my shoulder. You have raised a wonderful daughter Rob she is really pure hearted. I sat down on the settee and Christina joined me, holding my hand. "You are still very troubled Chosen One; you are carrying the world's problems on your shoulders. You have suffered so much unhappiness it will soon be time for you to come to the realm." I sighed "How much longer have I got?" "Just a few more years so get your affairs in order we will renew your bodies for the last time, because people were starting realise that you are not normal and your good looks are more than just good luck. Sam's father will die tomorrow and Nicole the day after it is the way of the world Rob. We cannot keep them going any longer." "When do the others join me?" "I cannot give you any details but you will all come together, you must not speak of this to any member of your family, the time and hour you will not know until it has happened." "Blimey, that sounds depressing." She kissed me tenderly on the lips and vanished.

I snapped my fingers and returned to Redbrick farm. I guessed it wouldn't be before Fiona gave birth because they could not transport her in that condition, so we definitely had a few more months left. I couldn't even tell Sam her father was going to die or her stepmother. Katie helped Nicky downstairs she wasn't very steady on her feet at all and we finally managed to get her to eat some breakfast. As the day went on she did improve and started to be more human. I drove to Cranbury farm, found Sam brushing her horse and kissed her on the cheek. "Hello you." I hadn't heard that saying for a long time. We all went to the cabin as requested in the evening I provided drinks for everyone and we sat and waited. The spirits arrived and went round each one of us repairing tissue damage and revitalising us all. Once the spirits had finished they vanished. Fiona was in great discomfort she hadn't long to go and I knew what was coming in the morning; more bad news. Jenny appeared and inspected the workmanship as if we were models and decided everything was good enough. She kissed each one of us on the cheek and then vanished. We didn't stay the night; we drove home to Redbrick farm. Fiona went straight to bed. Katie, Caroline and Sam sat on the settee. I made us all another drink with the old click of the fingers. I worried about what would happen to Nicky once we were gone. I decided to set up a trust fund so she couldn't squander the money. I would also contact the old firm of solicitors that Sam's father owned to run the business until Stephen was old enough to manage it himself. He was nearly 16 so it wouldn't be many more years. He was very well educated apart from him trying to go to bed with every six grade girl at school. He was an okay lad. I excused myself and went into my private room turned on the computer and dictated a letter to the solicitors instructing them what I wanted done in the event we should die, I emailed the letter that night. I returned to the girls sitting on the settee. There was a strange atmosphere in the air; everyone knew something was going on, but didn't know what and I was happy to leave it like that for the time being. Katie asked "Can we all sleep together tonight Rob I don't want to be on my own?" Sam answered "Yes I feel the same way too." We finally went to bed. Early the next morning the phone was ringing, informing Sam that her father had died. I held her hand and transported her to Switzerland. We made arrangements for her father's body to be flown back and buried in the local churchyard. I also made provisions for Nicole to be buried in the same grave. Sam decided the house in Switzerland should stay as a holiday home and not be sold, which I thought was a good idea. It will be a base for the spirits and also Stephen. We stayed overnight, trying to console Nicole but by morning she had passed away too, just as Christina had said. I arranged for both bodies to be flown back together. Sam's father had left a letter for her telling her to contact his firm of solicitors they would handle everything. I held Sam's hand and we were back at Redbrick farm within a flash.

Fiona had gone to hospital while we were away, awaiting birth of her daughter. I knew the clock was finally counting down and it wouldn't be long before we were taken. The local undertakers arranged everything and the following week we laid Rupert and Nicole to rest. We returned home after the ceremony. Fiona had given birth to an eight-pound girl, which she named Carol. She returned home a week later; everybody was doting over the new arrival, only I knew that any time now we would be taken. I just didn't know how Nicky had regained her senses; whatever the sisters gave her had obviously worked. She was more level headed and more interested in the stables. In fact, there was no part of the business she wasn't interested in. I actually saw one of our customers trying to chat her up and she told him to piss off, which rather made me smile. Everything was ticking along nicely; everybody was getting along. Sam and I would ride most days around Cranbury farm on our favourite horses. She remarked one day "I don't know how old I am Rob, do you?" "I haven't got a clue Sam but you don't look a day over 26". She smiled "You'd bloody lie anyway Rob." We returned to the stables and left the horses with Susan. We drove back to Redbrick farm. We walked into the house to find Katie dead with Julian and Caroline with Margaret. I ran upstairs and went into Fiona's bedroom she and the baby had both been shot dead. The place had been ransacked. I heard Sam scream and more gunfire. I ran downstairs and that's the last thing I remember.

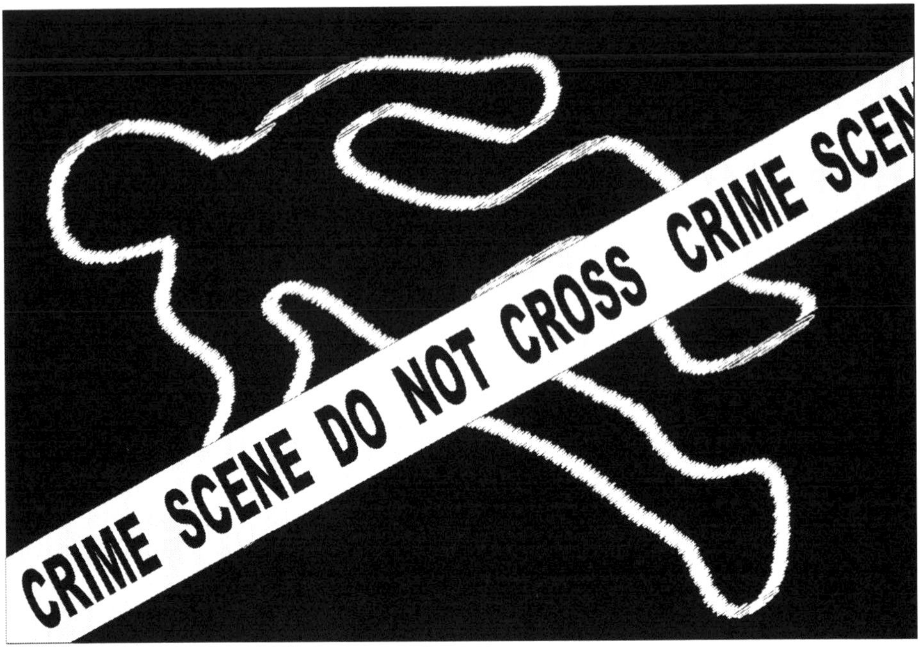
CRIME SCENE DO NOT CROSS CRIME SCEN

Chapter 13
The New Beginning

I materialised in the realm, remembering the last thing I heard was Sam screaming. I ran into the new log cabin to find. Katie in there Caroline, Margaret and Fiona with Carol and Sam. We all looked at each other. We all had beautiful bodies, Christina my daughter came in through the door. "Welcome to your new home everyone." She kissed everyone on the cheek and vanished. Sam's mother entered. "Don't look so sad, you're here safe and well, you will never suffer an illness, you'll never die, you have your whole life to look forward to." No one smiled or looked the slightest bit impressed with the situation. Katie looked around. "Where's Julian?" "You know why we couldn't bring him Katie." Christina said softly. Katie burst into tears she'd lost both her sons and almost her daughter. Christina held her head until the pain subsided "Remember you only have to snap your fingers if you need anything once you settle down and become accustomed to things. You'll be able to travel anywhere in the world you want as long as you seek permission from me first." Sam and I kissed each other it felt just as if it was like any other kiss, nothing had changed. Fiona sat down and started to breastfeed her daughter. Caroline held Margaret very close; she looked to me for guidance. "Can we all sleep together?" Christina smiled "Nothing has changed child just a different place and a different time. Come with me Chosen One, the sisters wish to see you. They have waited a long time". We walked out of the cabin through the forest into a clearing. I could hear Sam's thoughts as she spoke to the others. "This could be good if we work on it." The others agreed. "It's better than being dead." Caroline remarked. I'd longed to come here and now I was finally here. I wasn't so sure, but it was better than being dead like Sam had mentioned. I sat on the grass in the clearing. I didn't like the idea of wearing a white robe. Christina heard my thoughts and she snapped her fingers and I was back in my jeans and T-shirt which made me smile. Susan appeared. I asked "How are the farms?" "Everything is perfect Chosen One. Stephen has really grown up and so has Nicky. The solicitors are running everything perfectly for them. It's a whole earth year since you died." "It only seems like yesterday." "Time moves slower here" Christina advised "The sisters and I will be leaving the stables shortly to return to the realm we've done everything we can." I kissed Susan and thanked her for all she'd done. She sat beside me on the grass. Christina called out "Sister's." The open field filled with white robes. "Walk among them Chosen One and see all beauty before you". I started walking each sister was smiling and was of equal beauty to anything I'd seen. They all touched me as I passed; I noticed Jasmine and she smiled. I kissed her on the lips and Vicky. I also kissed each girl I'd slept with as I walked past. I held Christina's hand and Susan's. She had been a rock to talk to for many years. I asked. "Where is Jenny I haven't seen her". "Here Chosen One." I kissed her very passionately on the lips. "I feel your love Chosen One, for me." Finally, we reached what appeared to be an endless field of white robes. Christina remarked "You still want to take me to bed after seeing all these beautiful women? You amaze me Chosen One."

Christina snapped her fingers and we were back at the new cabin, we went inside. Sam and Katie were reorganising things; they each found the bedroom they liked. Christina spoke "Daughter come to me. I have a surprise for you." Sam approached cautiously. Christina kissed her on the forehead. "Now you are here you can bear children again but only with permission." Sam's face lit up like a torch. "I thought I was damaged goods mother." "In your old life you were my daughter. The spirits have checked and can find no trace of a defect now you are here." Sam jumped into my arms wrapping her legs around me shouting. "Take me to bed husband." Christina continued "That includes you Katie as well." Katie's smile returned. Christina called out "Caroline come to me." She came from her daughter's bedroom looking very sad. "I know what's bothering you Caroline, look:" Christina made a circle with her hand so Caroline could see her son he was with Nicky. They were both riding horses around Cranbury farm. Caroline smiled. "Thank you Christina." "You too can carry a child when we give you permission." Caroline hugged Christina "Thank you for showing me my son and for giving me the chance to have another child." Christina snapped her fingers and disappeared. Sam was so excited about the thought of bearing another child it was unbelievable. I hadn't seen her smile so much for many a year. I just hoped her smile would remain for as long as we existed. Sam snapped her fingers and she was in a very short miniskirt and see-through blouse with no bra "What do you think husband?" she smiled. Caroline did the same and so did Katie. Sam remarked "I hope the bed is strong enough tonight for all of us." Fiona was in her bedroom with the new baby, so she definitely wouldn't be interested in their planned event. Sam snapped her fingers and I was naked. "Look at this girls:" I couldn't stop myself from having an erection. Every time I snapped my fingers and re-dressed. Sam would undress me again until I gave up. "Come on you lot play fair" Sam escorted me into the bedroom she'd chosen for us; it was massive and so was the bed. You can sleep six at least. They snapped their fingers and they were naked. I lay on my back in the bed and they all took their pleasure one at a time. It was the early hour's morning before they'd finished with me. I felt a wreck, but enjoyed every minute of it and so did they. We all showered and dressed. Christina appeared. "It's barely daybreak come Chosen One you have work to do. Don't worry he will be back later." Christina grabbed my hand and snapped her fingers. We appeared in another building another log cabin called Treetop, somewhere in this vast space of time. "Out of all you saw yesterday Chosen One who would you like to sleep with?" She read my thoughts immediately, "Excluding me" She smiled. I want you, I am the Chosen One". I snapped my fingers and her clothes fell away. She snapped hers and they were replaced. "You may only have me after you have served somebody else. I will be your final prize today". It soon became apparent I was just here to father children, to increase the covenant membership. "I'll have Susan she has been very patient and kind to me." Susan was there in a second. She snapped her fingers and her clothes fell away. "How I've long for this moment Chosen One." She lay on the bed and we made love. Christina was watching which was rather off putting; she was making sure I did a proper job. Susan kissed me passionately "You have blessed me Chosen One."

I snapped my fingers and a coffee was made. I sat quietly drinking, looking out of the window over the tops of the trees, so I knew we must have been very high up probably on one of the mountains. Christina snapped her fingers and her clothes fell away. "Now you may take me Chosen One." I spent the next three hours in bed with Christina, driving each other wild with passion. We showered and dressed. "This is what you must do Chosen One take four sisters before each full moon and bring them here. To select a sister just wave your hand in a circle and make your choice." "Any sister I choose?" "Yes any sister." Christina snapped her fingers and vanished. I snapped mine and thought of the lake I'd seen on a previous visit. I appeared on the shoreline. I could see a sister sitting on a rock with her back to me, staring out onto the mirrored surface. I walked over and she turned to face me. This young woman was from Austria, with a beautiful complexion. She stood up. "I'm honoured Chosen One to be in your presence." "Why are you here all alone?" "Just enjoying peace and tranquillity gathering my thoughts remembering loved ones." "Have you been here long then?" "No only a few months, although it may be years, it's impossible to tell here." I invited her to walk with me along the shoreline. She explained her family had all been murdered including herself and was selected by one founding sister to live here. "I hear your thoughts Chosen One. And yes I am a virgin." I apologised immediately. "I'm sorry, I've never seen anybody like you before, not as attractive as you anyway." She blushed and looked to the ground as we continued walking she'd kick the occasional stick out the way of her path. "You already know my name is Claudette I know you are the Chosen One." "You can call me Rob, I don't mind." She smiled. "You are all that they say you are, kind and loving. I can feel your warmth inside me." I gently held her hand. She glimpsed to me with her beautiful eyes and then looked straight ahead as if that was her destination. "You had better go Chosen One. I am here most days if you wish to see me again." I was trying to read her thoughts. The most I'd managed to achieve was her name the rest of the information came from her mouth. I kissed her on the cheek and snapped my fingers and I was back at the cabin with the rest of my family.

They all greeted me. "Where have you been all day?" Sam asked. "Oh, just sleeping with women. You know what a terrible job it is." I joked. They all burst out laughing. Katie came across and kissed me on the lips so did Fiona and of course Caroline. Christina appeared. "I've been reading your thoughts Rob you actually met Claudette. None of us have met Claudette, she talks to us but she never transforms into human form for us. She is one of the founding members of the sisterhood. I hope you weren't rude to her Rob?" The girls stared on in amazement listening to the conversation "Well I was a bit but not on purpose. I couldn't read her thoughts but she was reading mine okay." Christina put her hand to her mouth. "You didn't, fancy thinking that Rob, of course she is a virgin. You actually held her hand you are so honoured and privileged?" I shrugged my shoulders. "I just treated her like any other sister, I did know who she was." Christina snapped her fingers and vanished without saying another word. Caroline voiced "Look Rob what I can do." She moved her hand in a circle and she could see Stephen. "This is wonderful Rob; It's like being home from home." Jenny appeared. "You and Carol come with me. I'm taking you to where all young mothers are to stay for a while, I will also take Margaret." Caroline looked horrified at the suggestion. "Why must you take my daughter?" "She has to learn our ways and be taught to use magic properly and responsibly, you can always see her by just circling your hand as you do to see Stephen." I cuddled Caroline. "She'll be alright love; Jenny wouldn't harm her nor would anyone else here." Caroline kissed Margaret and watched her go out of the door with Fiona and Carol following. She flopped down on the settee crying. Jenny placed her hands either side of Caroline's head to ease the pain, although she wasn't losing Margaret, it felt like it all the same. Jenny snapped her fingers and vanished.

Early the next morning I heard two horses approaching. I looked out of the window just as my daughter Christina ran through the door. She flung her arms around me and kissed me on the cheek. "Come on dad, let's go for a ride." She embraced her mother, grabbed my hand pulling me out of the door. Snowdrop placed his head on my shoulder as usual and I patted his neck. Christina mounted the other horse. I mounted Snowdrop, we rode along side-by-side through the forest "You happy here dad? I am" "Can't you read my thoughts?" "No I'm not permitted because you are my father. It would be a dishonour to do so." We rode on gently until we reached the lake. "We've never spent this much time together dad, before you came to the realm." My daughter was so full of life and contentment. I looked down the shoreline and I could see a white robe; I started to ride towards her. "Don't dad that may be Claudette, we must not approach, it is forbidden we are not worthy to be in her presence." "I am the Chosen One daughter you stay here if you're afraid." I rode on alone Claudette smiled and looked up to me on Snowdrop. I dismounted. "I see you have been told who I am and you are not afraid, although you have been told not to approach?" "I'm not afraid I'm already dead." Claudette smiled. She looked back to Christina my daughter and waved her hand beckoning her to come. Christina joined us very cautiously. She dismounted and went on hands and knees and bowed her head, not daring to look up. "I am sorry; my father doesn't understand, please forgive him. Don't punish him. I'm not worthy to look upon you." "Come child, sit beside me." Claudette said calmly, holding Christina's hand and easing her up from her knees. Christina sat beside her nervously on a large rock. Claudette placed her hand around Christina shoulder. "You have a wonderful daughter she will become a great leader among the sisters in time, her heart is pure and strong and only betrays love." Claudette then kissed Christina on the cheek. Christina voiced "I will never wash again." Claudette laughed. "I think your father would have something to say about that if you didn't. Be careful Chosen One I can hear your thoughts. I will allow you to kiss me, but that is all." Claudette rose to her feet. I held her in my arms; her eyes were studying my expression and I passionately kissed her on the lips. I felt her arms pull me closer. She pushed away. "That is enough Chosen One for now. Now leave me please. I have much to think about." Without hesitation, Christina mounted her horse and so did I. Claudette looked up to me and smiled. We rode away. "Dad, you realise you've just kissed Claudette and I have been kissed on the cheek by her." I smiled. "I think she is someone very special and powerful."

Jenny appeared as we entered the forest. She snapped her fingers and we were dismounted standing in front of her like naughty children. My daughter bowed her head in respect. Jenny folded her arms and started telling us both off for disturbing Claudette, suddenly a voice out of thin air said "Leave them alone Jenny or I will punish you." Jenny snapped her fingers immediately and vanished. My daughter embraced me. "I thought we were really in trouble then dad, I wonder who's voice it was?" "It was Claudette, I told you love, she's not one to be crossed." We mounted our horses again and rode on back to my new home. Christina took Snowdrop from me kissed me on the cheek. "I love you dad, I'll see you soon." She rode off. I snapped my fingers and I was transported back to Treetop, for as far as the eye could see was just the tops of trees. I made myself a coffee and sat there drinking, thinking about Claudette she absolutely intrigued me. You felt really special when she held you and to kiss her was a sensation I cannot put into words. Christina appeared. "You've done it again Chosen One, are there no rules you respect? Claudette listens to everyone's voice. Thousands of thoughts go through her mind every second correcting anyone's mistake and you go and kiss her and your daughter" Claudette's voice could be heard. "You dare to presume what I want and what I think Christina?" Christina went immediately on her knees and bowed her head. "I'm only trying to protect you from being disturbed." "I will choose who sees me and who does not. I do not need your help in making that decision. Do you understand me Christina?" "Yes it will not happen again please forgive my stupidity." Christina stood up I encouraged her to sit by me and I held her hand. "Wipe those thoughts from your mind Rob. Claudette will be offended. She has no time to carry a child and care for it." I unbuttoned Christina's blouse. She held my hand as I released her bra "You want to make me pregnant, make love to me. Yes, but choose another to carry your child." "You told me I could take anyone and I take you to bear another child." "No, I will not permit." Claudette's voice could be heard again. "You would lie to the Chosen One. This is the second time I have had to correct you today. I will not correct you a third time; do has he requests." I kissed her breasts tenderly and neck until she was aroused and could no longer resist; I penetrated her and spent the next two hours making love to her time and time again. She cried out "Take me, love me. I want you inside me." We showered and dressed. We sat on the settee together continuing to kiss and cuddle. I snapped my fingers and she was naked again. I carried her into the bed and made love to her all over again. She clung to my neck as if she was falling off a cliff of ecstasy. I would make sure she never forgot me. We finally showered and dressed and sat drinking coffee looking out of the window over the mist covered trees tops.

She placed her arm around my waist kissing my neck. "What will you call this daughter Chosen One?" I would like to call her Mist because she was conceived above the trees in the mist." That is a beautiful name Chosen One. Christina kissed me on the cheek and snapped her fingers, she was gone.

Chapter 14
Trying to Understand Claudette

I snapped my fingers and appeared on the shoreline where I'd last seen Claudette sure enough she was still sat there. I walked over. "You have many questions Chosen One?" I sat beside her on the rock wondering if I dare put my arm around her waist. "You may" she smiled. I nervously placed my arm around her waist and pulled her gently close to me and gently kissed her on the cheek. She did not flinch. "Can you explain to me how things work here?" "It would take two lifetimes to explain everything. The realm was established for any woman who qualified can enter who has a kind heart and only wishes to perform good deeds to their fellow women. Although I know we have the power to take life we do not do it easily or without consultation to justify the act. I know you have disposed of several people which I approved of and understood your reasoning." She said, holding my free hand. "Chosen One please stop undressing me with your thoughts." "I apologise Claudette you are so warm and inviting." "It is only because I say no that you want me more. I am just a conquest to you that's unfair." "Perhaps it is you that wants me?" "Choose your words carefully Chosen One." Claudette warned. "So free speech is not allowed in the realm. Everyone has to kiss your arse to live. I don't want to be here then thanks." I walked off not looking back. Yes, I probably did want to take her to bed but I was just trying to be nice and understand the realm and how it operated. Claudette appeared in front of me, searching my expression. "Perhaps I misjudged you." she said placing her hands on my head. "Yes, you do want to take me to bed but you also want to love and understand the realm." She snapped her fingers and vanished without speaking another word. I slowly walk through the forest heading for home, halfway back I decided I would camp out to be alone and think things through. I snapped my fingers and a large tent appeared. I entered and made myself a Bacardi and Coke. I snapped my fingers again and all the furnishings were present. I seated myself in the doorway looking up through the trees, seeing stars become brighter as nightfall fell. There were no hooting owls, no strange noises. I was neither hot nor cold. I waved my hand in a circle to see the old cabin by Cranbury farm a place I had fond memories of. I then saw Nicky and Stephen enter the cabin, they sat on the settee drinking wine and laughing, watching the television. I wondered why they had come to the cabin. It soon became apparent. Stephen pulled a pack of playing cards from his pocket. I could hear plainly what they were saying he said "Let's play strip poker, I dare you Nicky or are you too scared you might lose." He smiled. She took another sip from her glass of wine. "I'm not scared. I won't lose deal the cards." I could see the cards were marked. Stephen wasn't playing fair. It's a trick he used to use in school when trying to seduce the girls there. I was starting to become angry and disgusted. Whatever possessed him after all they were related. I was the father of them both if it had been any other girl I wouldn't have cared. I continued to watch after four hands had been played. Stephen had only lost his T-shirt. Nicky was down to her bra and pants. I wondered how I could bring this to a stop before it went any further. They played another hand and Nicky had to remove her bra. She didn't seem to be bothered in the slightest, one more hand and she'd lose her pants. She now had nothing on Stephen then said. "One more hand for a fuck." Go on then." She said smiling. He won the hand they went into my bedroom and she lay on the bed. I snapped my fingers and thought of the old cabin I was there running into my old bedroom. "What the bloody hell do you think you two are doing, you disgusting bastard." I shouted. Nicky immediately covered herself and ran into the front room screaming. Stephen just stared in disbelief at seeing me. He then ran into the front room and they both left the cabin.

I snapped my fingers and I returned to my tent in the realm. I'd stopped them on this occasion, but I was sure it would happen again in the future unless I had frightened them so much they dare not try again. I made myself another Bacardi and Coke. I finally calmed down and enjoyed looking at the stars and realising I could travel beyond the realm. Although I didn't have permission, that's nothing new for me. I was always pushing my luck. Jenny approached from out of the darkness shaking her head. "What will we ever do with you Chosen One, is there not one rule you will obey in the realm?" Claudette's voice could be heard. "Jenny why are you disciplining the Chosen One for doing what is only right?" Jenny fell to her knees and bowed her head. "He did not have permission to leave the realm." "Is that the real reason Jenny would you lie to me?" "No. Claudette, I apologise, please forgive my sin." "Tell the Chosen One why you have really come to see him." Jenny mumbled something that no one could hear. "Do you really want to annoy me Jenny? Speak clearly so I may hear and also the Chosen One." "I love him and I want him to take me to his bed." "Rise to your feet Jenny and face the Chosen One. she has lied to you Chosen One. What will be her punishment?" "I cannot punish someone for loving me. I will take her to bed where she may please me." "So be it Chosen One." I snapped my fingers and Jenny's clothes fell away. She sat on my lap kissing me desperately. As the sun rose Jenny had already gone. I snapped my fingers and my favourite bacon, and egg on fried bread appeared on a plate, not the healthiest of breakfasts, but what the heck I was already dead. It couldn't get any worse. I wondered whether I should tell Caroline and Katie what happened last night, then decided I should; they could watch them too and between us all, we may be able to avert a total disaster. I hadn't long finished eating before Caroline and Katie appeared outside my tent. "What are you doing here Rob? Why didn't you come home?" I made them both a coffee and explained what happened last night. They were both horrified and agreed they would watch Stephen and Nicky. I asked. "Where is Sam?" "She's gone riding with Christina. We decided to go for a walk and see if we could find a man that would make love to us, because were being neglected." She joked, snapping her fingers, allowing her clothes to fall away. Caroline did likewise. I went to my bed and rolled on my back. "Help yourself girls." They took it in turns time and time again until they wore their selves out. They both lay beside me. "Oh god Rob you're good" Katie remarked kissing me on the lips. Caroline remarked. "Don't make me pregnant please, I want to keep doing that day after day." They snapped their fingers and they were dressed. I walked back to the cabin with them holding hands. Sam was riding towards us with our daughter; she pulled up. "I can tell what you lot have been doing." She laughed. Caroline and Katie stuck their tongues out. Caroline commented. "He was absolutely brilliant." Sam remarked riding off "Isn't he always?" We continued walking back to the cabin.

We all sat on the edge of the porch and Sam joined us. Katie voiced. "It's my fault Nicky's a tart, I was like that at her age. I couldn't keep my clothes on for five minutes. I don't know what we can do to improve the situation" Caroline commented. I'd like to beat the crap out of my son the dirty bastard." Sam commented. "I don't think there is much we can do, they are both of age, although it's immoral what they're doing, I don't think it's illegal we'll just have to let them get on with it and hope Nicky doesn't get pregnant." Katie responded quickly. "Just because you have a goody two shoes daughter." "That's enough you two." "Sorry Sam, I didn't mean anything I'm just upset" Katie said. Katie waved her hand in a little circle and we could see them sat at Redbrick farm in the living room. Nicky was on the settee and Stephen was in my old chair masturbating his self while Nicky watched. They had a television screen fitted above the fireplace. We listened to the conversation between the two "Shall we play this old DVD I found of my mother?" Katie looked horrified "Where the bloody hell did they find that I thought I'd destroyed everything?" We watched Nicky slot the DVD into the player as she bent down, you could see she was wearing no knickers. Everyone put their hands to their mouth in shock. Stephen commented. "Don't you wear knickers, would you like to come and sit on this?" "You shouldn't be looking and it's not big enough for me" Nicky smiled, returning to the settee putting one hand between her legs. She pressed the remote control and sure enough there was Katie playing with other women totally naked and then much to my own horror Katie on top of me. Stephen commented. "I bet she's a good fuck I bet he's enjoying that. She'll lay on her back for anyone that old slag" "That's my mother you're talking about. Don't be so rude I don't have many pictures at least she looks alive when watching her." Katie was in tears, in fact we all were. Sam remarked. "It's a pity Rob can't go over there frighten the bloody life out of those two like he did in the cabin, make them think they're being watched all the time." Katie kissed Sam on the cheek. "That's a bloody brilliant idea, frighten them Rob." Caroline agreed. "And while you're there give him a good kicking, especially in the balls that will slow down the little pervert." "I will have to ask permission this time, I can't keep breaking the rules." We heard a voice. "You have permission Chosen One use your powers wisely" "Who the bloody hell was that?" Katie asked; everyone looked around. "That was Claudette". "She speaks to you Rob?" Sam asked. "Yes, we have some very interesting conversations about the realm." Everyone stared at me then focused back to what was going on at Redbrick farm. "Look." Katie said. "The little bitch is teasing him she's undone her blouse". We heard the doorbell ring. I concentrated and melted the DVD in the player it was now useless. Nicky tried to retrieve it but couldn't. Stephen answered the door, in walked two young girls one sat by Nicky and the other sat on Stephen's lap in my chair. We sort of breathed a sigh of relief for a moment. Nicky started fondling the girl while Stephen removed his penis and the other girls sat on it while he unbuttoned her blouse, displaying her large breasts. None of this is what we wanted to see. Katie was heartbroken so was Caroline "Please do something Rob if you can." They were both my son and daughter. What was I going to do? I had no idea. I personally thought whatever I did wouldn't change the situation. I'd already had one attempt at frightening the life out of them and that had lasted five minutes. Sam held my arm. "Rob love, please try for Caroline and Katie's sake." I kissed the three of them on the cheek and said. "I'll do what I can and you watch from here."

I snapped my fingers and I was stood outside Redbrick farm. I let myself in quietly through the front door. I peered into the lounge Stephen was making love on the floor to a naked girl. Nicky was lay on the settee playing around with the other girl "Excuse me children." I was dressed in pure white suit just to make it more effective. They quickly tried to dress. I snapped my fingers and their clothes all vanished so they were all standing there in the nude, they tried to run. I snapped my fingers and they were frozen to the spot. I was starting to enjoy myself this would be a lesson none of them would forget in a hurry. "You're dead dad, you can't be here." Nicky cried out. "Well if I'm dead what am I doing here daughter and son?" Stephen hadn't spoken he just stared in horror "Aren't you going to introduce me to your friends, don't bother I already know their names. Victoria, nice body for a 14-year-old, I wonder what your mother will say about this." I snapped my fingers and a camera appeared in my hand I took several photos everyone had started to cry "And your name is, oh yes Jane and you are only 13, nice body." I smiled. "Stop it dad, you're embarrassing me." Nicky complained "We can do what we like were old enough." "What about these two though? that reminds me, a message from your mother Stephen." I waved my hand in the air and he was smacked across the face hard and then I kicked him in the balls he fell on the floor in agony. "That should slow you down for a while son." Nicky saw me look to her. "Now what was it your mother told me to do to you, oh yes I remember." With the movement of my hand she was slapped hard across the face. I then held her in mid-air and pounded her backside until she screamed for mercy. I looked at the two girls. I snapped my fingers and they were dressed they stared in horror. "Go now and never return". The two girls ran like the wind. Stephen was still on the floor in extreme agony. I snapped my fingers Stephen and Nicky were dressed. I lifted them in the air using the power of thought and sat them on the settee side-by-side. "You are a disgrace you two, I left you everything and this is how you repay me and your mother's. If I ever have to come here again I will kill you both. Do you get the message?" They both nodded then Nicky voiced. "I'll get an exorcist in then you'll be fucked, you won't be able to touch us." "You don't learn daughter." I produced a large cross in my hand she watched me hold it to my forehead and it didn't burn me. I snapped my fingers and held the Bible. "If God was so angry I'd be dead by now daughter. Just remember, we are watching you, night and day. You have nowhere to hide wherever you are in the world I can find you in seconds. Do you understand Nicky?" I slapped them both across the face again with the movement of my hand "If I ever see you two improperly dressed again you know the consequences and remember your mother's are watching too and they will decide your punishment as they have tonight." I looked at the hexagram on Stephen's hand. I snapped my fingers and it vanished, he didn't deserve to have any protection my hopes for him had long gone out of the window. I snapped my fingers and I was back in the realm inside the cabin. Sam remarked. "Shush, Rob look at this. Katie's been watching everything that had happened at Redbrick farm along with the others." Nicky voiced trembling. "Oh fuck, what we going to do Stephen" Stephen had moved to my old chair in terrible agony. "I'll tell you one thing Nicky, I'm not coming near you and I don't think I'll ever have sex again the way I feel. If they can see us all the time we've had it and I definitely don't want to die. Dad meant it you know what he's like." Katie jumped into my arms. "Thanks Rob that was a brilliant job they were almost shitting themselves." Caroline was just silent sitting on the settee. I lowered Katie to the floor and went over and sat by Caroline and placed my arm around her shoulder. I could hear her thoughts she was frightened it wouldn't work, although she was pleased with the immediate outcome. "Don't worry Caroline I only threatened to kill them." "Yes, but you removed his hexagram protection." "If he changes his ways Caroline I'm sure the sisters will replace it but if he doesn't love, he's no good to any of us here." She smiled and hugged me. "Thank you for trying Rob." We heard a voice "See me tomorrow Chosen One." Sam enquired "Was that Claudette." "Yes, I'm probably in trouble". We all retired to bed.

Chapter 15
Finding a Replacement for Stephen

I strolled to the shoreline and there was Claudette sitting in her usual place on the rock; looking out across the lake. I stood before her. She patted the rock indicating for me to sit, I did as she requested. She held my hand. "I watched your performance last night Chosen One and I was extremely impressed with the decisions you made including removing Stephen's hexagram. He is not good enough to be considered for any position relating to the covenant." "Thank you, I thought I was in trouble." "Your heart is pure; whatever decision you made was solely for the benefit of us and we could see that plainly in spite of Stephen being your son. You still removed his protection you honour us with your sacrifice." She slapped my leg. "You may kiss me, but you are not taking me to bed. Remove those thoughts from your mind." She moved around to face me and we kissed passionately for several minutes. "That's enough, go away and yes they are 38D." She smiled. I smiled back and snapped my fingers till I was in the middle of the forest walking along the track. I snapped my fingers and I was in Treetop cabin. I sat there quietly drinking my favourite tipple. I snapped my fingers and a television appeared on the wall. I thought I would see what was going on at Cranbury farm the picture was very clear and crisp. I listened to people talking and riding the horses around our arena. I was starting to miss the old place then suddenly became very bored. There was nothing to mend nothing to do other than have sex, which is okay in moderation, but like anything else you can soon become bored. I snapped my fingers again until I was by the lake. Claudette appeared beside me she held my hand and eased me down to sit on a log "We must find a replacement for Stephen and there are only two women in the whole realm that are good enough to carry a male child, that is myself and your daughter". I looked at her alarmed. "Surely you do not expect me to sleep with my own daughter that would be absolutely disgusting" "Claudette looked into my eyes. "I cannot become pregnant Chosen One. I am here to control the realm; without me chaos could destroy us all." "I will not sleep with my daughter under any circumstances you may kill me if you wish." "We knew that would be your response and rightly so, however, if there is no alternative you will have to. We are presently searching the world to find a suitable woman and you will have to impregnate her." "That I will agree to it's a better alternative than the other, although I would not mind making you pregnant" I smiled. She kissed me tenderly on the lips. "I can read your mind like a book your feelings for me are so strong it invigorates me. Yes, I could remove my robes and let you take me and my heart is aching to do so." I wrapped her in my arms. "Let me fill you full of love I have longed to hold you since the first day I saw you." "Not yet Chosen One, the time is not right. One day I will let you make love to me, but not at this moment, you may kiss me, you may hold me, but do not try to go any further." I kissed her on the forehead and on the lips. "I hear your daughter approaching with two horses." I could hear absolutely nothing. Sure enough, she turned up a few minutes later, dismounted and kissed Claudette on the cheek. "Has he agreed Claudette?" "No child, his love for you is too great and his decision is very understandable. You must not be cross with him. He is your father and our Chosen One but you can encourage him" I looked at them both very confused wondering what they were talking about. "Let me talk to him Claudette. I'm sure I can change his mind if he really loves me as his daughter" "May I enquire what you two are conjuring between yourselves?" I was trying to read my daughter's thoughts but they had been blocked. I could receive no information. I just hoped it wasn't anything to do with what we were discussing earlier and I knew Sam would definitely never agree to it in a million years. "Go with your daughter Chosen One, that is my wish." I mounted Snowdrop, Christina mounted the other horse and we trotted off side-by-side. We rode into the forest. My daughter dismounted. "Let's walk dad and talk." I dismounted and walked in front of Snowdrop holding his reins "Would you say I'm attractive dad?" "You are like your mother beautiful. Why ask? You have the same hair as your mother the same skin complexion and obviously the same figure." Christina smiled. "What are you getting at daughter?" "Oh nothing." I looked towards a disturbance in the forest. When I looked back to Christina her white robe had vanished and been replaced by a pink skirt, pink blouse. I did not respond or pass a comment. I could feel where this was heading and it was not going to happen no matter what she did. We continued walking she looked to me. She was now wearing cosmetics and looked very grown-up "Dad you remember when I was abducted by those four men in the van and they dragged me into that building and tied me up against the wall. Did you look at my body when I was naked? Did you think I was beautiful?" "I didn't have time I was too busy trying to rescue you." I tried not to smile. "Yes, you did. You saw them touching me I can see it on your face. Did you know before you came in they were kissing me all over? It was quite a nice sensation". She smiled. "Well they won't be kissing anybody else, I fried them." "It's quite warm today don't you think?" "It's okay for me." She was being very subtle the way she was trying to arouse me but whatever she did wasn't going to work. There was another distracting noise in the bushes I looked across the track which I thought was odd as there were never any strange noise's here. I looked back to my daughter in the seconds I'd looked away she had unbuttoned her blouse, allowing her breasts to be seen. I ignored it and carried on walking I paused and turned to face Christina. "What is your game Christina this is so unlike you, cover your breasts." "Why, aren't they perfect and large?" "You still haven't answered my question what do you want?" She sighed. "I want you to make me pregnant, so does Claudette, it is her wish and you must." "Bullshit! I've already told her I won't sleep with you. You're my bloody daughter for Christ sake, what's the matter with you? I'll tell you what Christina; I'll sleep with you if you can get your mother's permission and she tells me herself; no better still, include Katie and Caroline in that decision." Christina buttoned her blouse and jumped on her horse and rode off towards home. I knew for sure Sam would definitely say no and with the backing of the other two. There was no way I could lose. I mounted Snowdrop and gently rode home there was no rush I didn't want to be involved in a blazing row, I thought how clever I'd been. My daughter's horse was gone from outside the cabin by the time I'd arrived. I went inside feeling very pleased with myself. Sam, Katie and Caroline were all sitting on the settee; they almost look like a firing squad. I sat in my armchair and snapped my fingers for a drink of Bacardi. The three of them glared at me as if I done something wrong. Sam spoke first. "Our daughters just been to see me Rob, she tells me you refused to sleep with her." "What did you expect Sam would you really want me to sleep with our daughter?" "Only for a very good reason Rob." You two feel the same, especially you Katie after you sent me back to stop Stephen fucking your daughter?" "Well that's slightly different." "And you Caroline, what is your view on the subject?" This was not going how I'd planned and I didn't know why; I would have preferred Sam to have hit me over the head with a shovel, when I walked in the door for just looking at our daughter's breasts. "I do agree with you Rob but sometimes there are extenuating circumstances you have to bend the rules for the good of all." I just couldn't believe my ears. What could Christina have said to make them so indecisive and make the wrong decision. I snapped my fingers and I was back in my old log cabin. Whether I got into trouble or not, I didn't care, I definitely wasn't stopping there to be manipulated. I made myself a drink and sat watching television suddenly Jenny appeared. I thought oh shit, she seated herself beside me. "You're at it again Chosen One, breaking the rules." "What are you going to do, drag me back screaming?" "No, we are still searching for an alternative solution." "I don't know why Claudette won't let me rip her knickers off." "I believe she's explained the reason why and be careful Chosen One she can hear everything we say and think." "Well then, if she is such a great leader, why doesn't she carry the child herself and run the realm?" Jenny placed her hand over my mouth "You're going too far Chosen One." I was about to speak again and Jenny planted a kiss on me so I couldn't talk. She held me so tight I nearly stopped breathing. She pulled away and put her hand back over my mouth. We heard Claudette's voice "You challenge me Chosen One; you are brave and very foolish. I will hold a meeting with the sisters and decide your fate you will stay there until a decision has been made. I have removed your ability to travel." "Now you have really upset Claudette Chosen One." "She must have bribed Sam and the others to agree to me sleeping with our daughter." I read Jenny's thoughts revealing Sam, Katie and Caroline would be allowed to have one child each so that's why they were giving in so easily. I knew it was something they all wanted desperately I thought honesty was part of the covenant, but only when it suited them. Why didn't Sam and the others admit they been offered children if I agreed. Jenny knew I'd picked up her thoughts. "It was a means to an end Chosen One, I'm sorry for the deception. Under normal circumstances that would never be allowed. Claudette would have banished anyone to the dark place for even having a thought like that." I held Jenny's hand and kissed her tenderly on the lips. "I do love you Jenny." "I know Chosen One and I you." Jenny waved her hand in a little circle "Look what Nicky is doing, she's hired a priest to remove all the ghosts from Redbrick farm." Jenny laughed. "That will not make any difference." "I can hear a big row in the realm. The sisters are all upset with Claudette for her attempting to deceive you. They feel it is wrong and against their principles. Sam is there and the other two. The sisters are throwing electric shocks at them. Sam and the others are running home. I've never seen the sisters this upset." Jenny kissed me once more. "It's moments like this when I'm alone with you that make me wish I was your first wife. I would have stayed loyal and enjoyed every second of you with me." "You're so much like her Jenny even in bed; that's why I thought you were her originally. I'm taking you to bed Jenny" "No, please don't Chosen One, Claudette will punish me." "Oh, I didn't realise she'd do that to you, she's a mean old bitch." Suddenly I was filled with pain and rolling about on the floor in agony. Claudette had heard what I'd said and now she was going to make me pay for the comment. Blood started to pour from my nose. Jenny stared on in horror daring not to touch me for fear of reprisal. After 10 minutes, Claudette stopped and Jenny helped me back onto the settee. She mirrored my face with her hand and the blood disappeared. She held me close trying to take away some of the pain. I felt like I'd been run over by a 10-ton truck. "Your powers have been restored Chosen One, I can feel them in your body and I've been summoned by Claudette." She kissed me tenderly on the lips. "Remember Chosen One I will always love you with all my heart whatever happens." She snapped her fingers and disappeared. I made myself another drink, feeling like crap. I was in no rush to return to the realm. My daughter Christina appeared. She could see the blood on my shirt she looked quite alarmed. "What happened dad, was it punishment from Claudette?" I nodded. She was wearing her pink skirt still and blouse which I thought was odd as nearly all the sisters wore the white robe. Why she had travelled in this attire I did know. "Do you mind if I sit by you, dad?" "No, of course not, you silly girl." She sat beside me. "I suppose you knew I bribed mom and the others." "I do, and I'm surprised you would do that." She held my arm and lent her head against my shoulder. "I'm sorry." I noticed the buttons on her blouse were undoing themselves one at a time until her breasts were on full view. Surely she was not going to try again to seduce me. I was struggling to stop looking at her breasts and she knew it by the smile on her face. "Claudette has arranged a surprise for you." "What is it?" "I don't know." I notice Christina's skirt had become a lot shorter I could see her white knickers. Suddenly the door opened and in walked Nicky as casual as you like "So you are real and you, sis, you're not ghosts?" "I'm real at the moment Nicky". She sat herself beside me "Magic me a drink then a double scotch or have I got to fetch one from the kitchen myself?" Christina snapped her fingers and there was a double scotch on the table. "Thanks sis" I was wondering what the whole point of the exercise was and what would be achieved. "I've still got the bruise on my arse from where you hit me dad" "Serves you right girl." "What is your problem old man? I'm over 18, I can fuck who I like" She was wearing a similar outfit to Christina. She opened her blouse fully exposing everything and pulled her miniskirt right-up. "Top me up again, sis" Christina filled her glass full of scotch she was certainly not helping matters and were both rubbing my leg slowly with their hands. My blood was starting to boil. I wasn't going to tolerate much more of this but I wanted to know why Nicky was here? Nicky knocked her drink back and stood up and walked to the other side of the room. Christina didn't move, she watched "This is how you do it sis" She slowly started removing her clothes until she was standing naked she was the splitting image of Katie virtually in every detail. "Mom said you've got a big dick let's see it old man, stick it up this. She told me before she died, come fuck this if you're a man." She continued playing with herself. Christina stood up and joined her removing all her clothes. They started kissing each other. I was about to snap my fingers. "Don't do that dad." Christina voiced. "Claudette said if you don't make love to me she's returning me to Redbrick farm as punishment for my failure. You will condemn me father, is that what you really want?" Now, I didn't know what to do for the best. Claudette spoke. "She is telling the truth Chosen One do not disobey me". I snapped my fingers trying to return to the realm but nothing happened. Jenny told me my powers have been restored, but obviously taken away again. I felt sick to my stomach how the hell can I get out of this situation. Nicky and Christina seated themselves beside me each rubbing one of my legs. I wanted to clobber them both but it would achieve absolutely nothing now. Claudette spoke again "Take Nicky first those are my instructions do not disobey me." I didn't move; I felt pain again, curling me up into a ball on the floor. The girls watched on showing no emotion for my predicament the blood poured from my nose and mouth. Christina finally cried out "Claudette stop it you're killing him." Nicky ran to the kitchen bringing a roll of kitchen towel mopping the blood from my face and off the floor. I must have lost nearly a pint. They help me back onto the settee.

Chapter 16
The Recovery

The next thing I remember is waking up in the realm in my own bed with Jenny mopping my brow. "It's over Chosen One you are safe." "What's happened to Christina and Nicky?" I asked. "Christina is here safe and well and Nicky was transported home and her mind wiped so she would not remember the event." I eased Jenny's head down till I could kiss her tenderly. "I love you Jenny." "I know Chosen One; you should never have been tortured that's not what the realm is about." "Be careful what you say Jenny Claudette may hear you." "It doesn't matter now Chosen One; she has disgraced herself. All the sisters are up in arms over your treatment they all love you so much like I do." Do you wish to see Sam and the others or shall I banish them to the dark place and remove any chance of deceit in your life again." "No Jenny we must show compassion and understanding, you were desperate yourself for a child once if you remember." She smiled and nodded. "How long have I been in bed Jenny"? "Nearly a week Chosen One, Claudette really messed your insides up when she tortured you. We didn't think you would survive." I sat up in bed and Sam appeared around the door. "Can I come in Rob please?" I nodded. She knelt down by the side of my bed holding both my hands. "We all saw what she did to you and you still refused to take our daughter to bed or Nicky, you are so brave." Katie and Caroline peered around the door. "Can we come in also, Rob?" They asked quietly. They all sat by the side of my bed. Jenny left. Katie's eyes were filled with tears. "We never meant that to happen to you Rob. You must believe us we did know she was going to torture you and you didn't sleep with our daughters either. How you withstood the pain I'll never know." I joked. "She's got your tits." Everyone laughed. "There's not an evil bone in your body Rob and we treat you like dirt." Caroline said drying her eyes. "There's someone else here that wants to see you Rob if you'll let her." "Of course" Christina entered throwing herself on top of me. "Oh dad, I thought you were going to die. I'm so sorry dad I'm not a tramp really I was just doing as I was ordered." "I understand love please get off me before you break the rest of my ribs." "Sorry." She stood up and kissed me on the cheek commenting. "I do have great boobs don't I." She smiled and left the room. I shook my head at her comment. If only I wasn't her father, things would have been very different. Jenny appeared. "Chosen One would you come to the field the sisters wish to speak to you." I rose from my bed, snapped my fingers and I was dressed. I walked through the beautiful forest to the clearing. Jenny held my arm; a woman in a white robe appeared. She kissed me on the cheek. "My name is Simone Chosen One, you have seen me before among the crowd, although I do not suspect you may remember me." I shrugged my shoulders. "I'm sorry I don't wish to be rude but I don't remember much of anything at the moment." "It is understandable Chosen One, Claudette damaged you terribly. And you honour us by staying true to the path of the sisters even under sentence of death." Simone clapped her hands and the field filled with sisters. Simone called out. "Even now, after all that we have done to him. Do you feel his love?" "We do". They called back. "From this point on the Chosen One is not obligated to take four sisters per month. He may choose how many of us he wishes to sleep with and give us a child. Furthermore, he may travel without question anywhere he wishes. He has proven his love time and time again. He will not harm any of us or the realm. Any woman who refuses to bear his child will be sent to the dark place immediately. No one is excluded from his approach. No one, do you hear me sisters, do you agree?" "We agree." The sisters all vanished as quickly as they had come. Simone turned to face me. She placed her hands on my forehead. "I'm over 8000 years old Chosen One; I'm one of the founding members of the sisterhood. I'm ashamed of what we allowed to happen to you by one member." she glowed white. I could feel the pain from my body vanishing. She released her grip. I kissed her on the lips she was rather surprised and smiled. She snapped her fingers and vanished.

Jenny and I walked back to the cabin. I sat down on the settee beside Katie and Jenny vanished. Katie placed her arm around my shoulders and kissed me gently on the cheek, she waved her hand in a little circle. "Look Rob, there was a big poster in the lounge at Redbrick farm. It read. "Dad, please come and see me I want to talk to you, I love you and mom" "I know it's a lot to ask Rob, but would you go and see our daughter again and make things right with her. She needs all the help we can give her." Katie professed. I waved my hand in a circle showing the inside of Redbrick farm. We searched the house trying to find Nicky and finally we found her in a dark cupboard with a bottle of scotch she was crying. I snapped my fingers and I was at Redbrick farm in the lounge I went upstairs to Nicky's bedroom. I could hear her sobbing behind the wardrobe doors. I opened them, seeing she had consumed over half a bottle of scotch; she looked in a right state. "Dad, you came to see me." She slurred struggling to her feet. How long she'd been in the cupboard I don't know but she was in a right mess. I guided her to the side of the bed and seated her, placed my arm around her shoulder. "Why are you like this Nicky? You have your whole life to look forward to. You are like your mother, very attractive. There are hundreds of suitable men out there for you to find and make a good life for yourself." "I don't understand myself, dad." She went over to the wardrobe and removed the blouse and skirt. She stripped in front of me and replaced her garments still leaving her blouse fully unbuttoned "Don't forget to do your blouse up love". She ignored my comment "Is mom okay dad, is she happy? Would you bring mom some time to see me?" "You behave yourself and show me you are really trying to improve your life. I can see everything you do from where I am and so can your mother. You're really upsetting her." I felt so sorry for her with a mixed up mind. I risked the wrath of the realm and snapped my fingers and Katie appeared in her white robe, I was in my white suit I rather liked wearing it there's vanity for you. Nicky "screamed" jumping to her feet embracing her mother. Katie eased her away and buttoned up her daughter's blouse "You shouldn't go around like that Nicky you don't want to be labelled a tart like I was." "Can't I come and live with you, mom? please I'll do everything you say I will change please." I left them to talk. I knew Nicky would never be allowed in the realm. She was too unpredictable and carried too many sins, but I would have to ask all the same. Simone appeared in the lounge. I thought now I'm in for it. She reached for my hand "Take me to your daughter Chosen One. I have more power than most sisters. I may be able to help her." I led Simone upstairs. Katie stared as Simone entered the room and so did Nicky. "You're not going to kill me?" Nicky said quickly. "No child I'm here to help you become what you want to be." Katie moved away. Simone placed her hands either side of Nicky's face. She glowed brilliant white for several minutes then released. "Nicky do you understand, Nicky?". Simone asked. "Yes I understand I will do as I'm told thank you." Katie and I looked at each other wondering what had gone on. Simone was another sister whose mind you could not read because of who she was." Chosen One. "If Nicky feels threatened or upset or needs guidance. I have told her you will come and see her with Katie, providing I see her trying to improve over the next years. I may let her live in the realm. I will talk to the other sisters, but it's down to her, herself, to make the effort first." Nicky embraced Simone. Simone smiled, stroking Nicky's head. We all kissed Nicky on the cheek and said goodbye and we were back in the realm. We both hugged Simone for her kindness to Nicky.

Simone commented. "It's up to her now Chosen One, to make the effort; I will be watching." Simone snapped her fingers and vanished. Katie and I made ourselves our favourite drink and sat on the settee holding each other. The outcome was far more than we'd ever hope for. Fiona entered the cabin looking more beautiful than she'd ever done before. She sat beside us on the settee. I asked. "Where's Carol?" "Being looked after by Jenny and the sisters like all the other children. I've missed you Rob. I've missed you all" "It's good to have you back Fiona." She leaned across and kissed me on the lips tenderly. I could read her thoughts she was desperate to get me in bed it had been a long time since we'd had sex together. I grabbed her hand and took her into her bedroom and obliged. We both showered and dressed. "Now I feel wonderful." I told them I was going for a walk; I needed time to think. What I really wanted to do was talk to Claudette. I snapped my fingers and I was on the shoreline of the lake, Claudette was sitting on her rock. I approached and stood directly in front of her. She looked up. "I see you want answers and wonder why I didn't kill you for disobeying me." She patted the rock encouraging me to sit down. "I thought I was doing the right thing for the realm but in hindsight it wasn't. We really don't need another male on the outside you have proven your loyalty and the sisters trust you completely, as I do now." She shook her head from side to side in disbelief. "Still you want to take me to bed." She smiled continuing. "You certainly are a strange one, no matter what we do to you, you still love us all." My daughter came riding along on her horse and stopped. "You summoned me Claudette." "Yes, daughter of the Chosen One." Claudette rose to her feet. She snapped her fingers and we were in the treetop cabin. Claudette had made herself look identical to Christina my daughter. She dressed the pair of them in mini-skirts and blouses I couldn't tell them apart. I seated myself on the settee looking at them both. "What game is this Claudette?" They both spoke in harmony. "The sisters have ordered that you may sleep with anyone you choose and they cannot refuse you. Choose which one of us is Claudette or sleep with us both to make sure." It was obvious she didn't like losing and I had dented her pride considerably. Now, she was going to make me pay for it. They both started unbuttoning their blouse until their breasts were on display there was no difference in my opinion. Simone appeared and snapped her fingers and Claudette was revealed. Christina quickly buttoned her blouse shaking her head, wondering what was going on she was under some type of spell. Simone snapped her fingers and Christina vanished. "You shame us all Claudette, the sisters have ruled." She snapped her fingers again and Claudette was gone. Simone got on her knees before me and bowed her head. "I apologise Chosen One for all the sisters, please forgive us we did not know what she was planning." "What have you done with her"? I asked easing Simone to her feet and guiding her to sit by me. "She's gone to the dark place where there is no return we cannot have someone like that in the realm. Something has twisted her mind and she is unsafe to be left alone with the power she possessed. I kiss Simone passionately on the lips. She embraced me "You want to take me to bed?" "Yes Simone you have shown me kindness and Nicky, you been fair and understanding, you will make a good mother." Her smile broadened as I carried her into the bedroom. We made love several times showered and dressed and returned to the settee. I snapped my fingers and coffee appeared. "You are all that they say you are Chosen One, every woman that has slept with you in the realm sings of your love and tenderness. You taking me to your bed I had never dreamt of happening." "You are a beautiful woman and caring that attracts me most of all. I could feel your love for me unlike so many others." "What will you call our daughter Chosen One?" I would like to call her Heather" "That is a sweet name Chosen One and she was made by two people that will love her forever." Simone kissed me on the cheek and snapped her fingers and vanished. I thought of Sam and snapped my fingers and she appeared. She embraced me. "Why did you bring made love?" I guided her to look over the treetops with my arm around her waist. I kissed her passionately and told her she was my first love and would be my last.

What happens next is another story.
Written by
Robert S Baker

Made in the USA
Charleston, SC
22 February 2016